Entangled Galaxy Books

Enemy Immortal (2019)

Umlac's Legacy (September, 2020)

ENEMY IMMORTAL

First Contact

JIM MEEKS-JOHNSON

Acknowledgments

I am grateful to innumerable people who helped form this book. Some, like David Brin, Nancy Kress, Jack McDevitt, and Walter Jon Williams are well-known science fiction writers. Others, including Marcia Kelly, James M. Thompson, Stephanie A. Cain, Madeleine Dimond, Laura VanArendonk Baugh, Garrett Hutson, Stephanie Ferguson, Peggy Larkin, Joy Basham, Rob Dearsley, Barbara E Hill, Trina Phillips, Kelly Horn, and my family are my heroes for reviewing all or most of the book. The cover is by the talented Levierree.

DEDICATION

To Sally

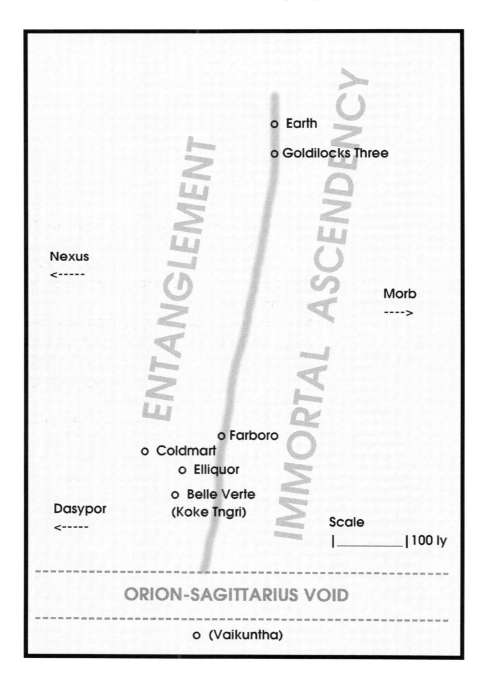

1

Immortal

Umlac oozed his glistening black, ten-ton body through a slime-lubricated tube deep in the bedrock of planet Morb. He'd dug this passageway fifty thousand years ago while mining neodymium to improve the magnetic solenoids in his cyborg body.

His flesh—the part of his body that was protoplasmic—craved nutrients. Happily, a ship from the Entanglement had strayed into his territory. Its crew waited for him at the bottom of his feeding pit, and the thought of terrorizing his prey before ingesting them titillated his feeding organs.

A gray blob obstructed part of the tunnel ahead—a Hydra feasting on a food-thrall who had exceeded its useful time as a slave. This wouldn't do. Eating was no excuse for an underling to get in his way. Hydras weren't particularly tasty, but Umlac disdained incompetence. Better to make an incompetent vassal useful as food. Umlac charged the hapless Hydra and chewed it to bits, ingesting only enough to prove his point. Scavengers would devour the rest of the carcass.

At the feeding pit, Umlac draped his glistening body over the edge, posing for a moment as a magnificent black curtain of death so his lunch would know his glory and fear his power. Cameras recorded his every move. Playing recordings of a good feeding session heightened the level of fear and obedience in future food-thralls of the same species.

He'd long ago incorporated an Entanglement translator into the electronic portion of his cyborg body. "I am Umlac. Come to me," he thundered at the captured crew.

None of the fur-balls cowering in the far corner came forth. This was wrong. Lesser creatures should fear and obey greater creatures. That basic principle ordered all the Immortal Ascendency.

"A Shoggart must always be obeyed." Umlac extruded a crossbow through his flexible outer membrane. He'd manufactured the simple device with one of his internal fabricator units, so his prey would see and understand their impending death. He launched a barbed bolt into one of the puny creatures' appendages.

The hairy creature had four permanent limbs and a sensor-laden "head" jutting upward—a Wolferlop of some kind. Umlac jerked the cord to set the bolt and reeled the line in slowly, so his lunch experienced loss of control and had time to fear Umlac's glory.

The Wolferlop yowled and fought to escape. When it proved no match for the cord, it stretched an arm out toward the other weaklings in the corner. "Sing my story to home nest. Tell them I love them all."

"We will," said a pitiful chorus from the corner.

"They lie," Umlac boomed out. "None of them will tell your story. None of them will leave this pit."

Umlac ate the Wolferlop's fingers and toes one at a time, savoring his dominance over the creature as much as its buttery taste. The rest of the creature's body followed bit by bit until only the brain remained. Umlac assimilated the Wolferlop's brain and examined its memories for any significant or unique events. He found a few access codes he would pass on to his spy network in the Entanglement, but nothing exceptional. He filed the Wolferlop's memories in a small DNA capsule along with the others in his library pouch.

He singled out another Wolferlop. "Come to me. It all ends the same. With more or less suffering."

The Wolferlop came, and Umlac devoured it in one gulp. This was the lesson in the recording; even in death, obedience was best.

After feeding, he gave the recording of the feeding session to a Hydra to show future captives and went to his secure communication room to answer some calls from underlings and spies. There was no avoiding the bureaucracy of ruling fifty-two civilized planets and adjoining territories.

A Hydra fleetmaster on the border with the Entanglement reported. "Most Worshipful Lord Umlac, the Xandor invasion was a complete success. We destroyed the interstellar comm-link before Xandor's inhabitants alerted anyone else in the Entanglement. Then we crushed their pitiful defenses."

"What about casualties?"

"Most Worshipful Lord, I'm pleased to report we had no casualties."

"And the enemy?"

"All of their fighters died, along with eighty-two disrespect-ful civilians."

"Fool! I can't use dead civilians. I need a fresh supply of food-thralls for my vassals and their slaves."

"Most Worshipful Lord Umlac, forgive this humble fleet-master. I put the bulk of the colony's population in corrals. Eight thousand new thralls are ready for work assignments."

"In that case, as a reward, each slave in your fleet may take one captive as a food-thrall. Each Hydra vassal may have six captives, except you. Put the rest of the captives to work under my protection digging tunnels for a proper Immortal city from which to rule the planet."

Umlac disconnected the fleetmaster and took a call from his chief administrator on Morb. "Most Glorious Lord," the Hydra began. "I have the best possible news. Deus Telekil has been interviewing your vassals about your conquest of Omuz and Xandor. He is considering promoting you to Vice Deus!"

Umlac's internal organs twisted in fear. Deus Telekil would never take a Vice Deus. It would threaten his dominance. No, Deus Telekil, overlord of the Immortal Ascendency, was sending him a message. Umlac would have to fission soon—divide his body and divide his holdings—or else face a takeover by the one being more powerful than a Shoggart.

"Send the full details by encrypted data capsule." He broke the connection.

He wasn't ready to fission yet. He wanted to leave his core of forty worlds intact for his heaviest offspring, and he was nowhere close to forty comparable worlds in the rest of his empire for the fifty-fifty split required by law. Where could he find so many planets in short order?

Deus Telekil planned to invade the Entanglement, using his vassals, Umlac and other Shoggarts. Umlac had counted on that invasion to increase the size of his vassaldom before he fissioned.

He called one of his spymasters—a young Hydra on a distant planet who'd proved both competent and loyal—fearing that Deus Telekil monitored his usual operatives.

"I wish to honor you with a most delicate task, but if you fail, I will have to sacrifice you like a food-thrall."

"Most Brilliant Lord, I will uphold your honor with every drop of my mass."

"Deus Telekil is planning to invade the Entanglement. My brother Shoggarts know of this, but not the timeline. I want you to craft a message for each of my closest seven brothers and me as well—a message that appears to be from Telekil to say the invasion starts one month from today. Tell us not to reply to the message. Say the timeline must never be mentioned in normal channels of communication."

"My Most Brilliant Lord, it shall be done as you command."

"Remember, Deus Telekil won't give reasons, just orders."

"Of course. As I would to my slaves."

Umlac chafed at the comparison of him to a slave before Deus Telekil, but he couldn't disagree. The Hydra demonstrated the right idea for the messages.

Umlac disconnected and called his fleetmaster on another border planet slated for conquest. "Why haven't you called to report?"

"Most Glorious Lord Umlac, I am happy to report that our fleet is on course and in tip-top shape."

"What's the bad news?" Umlac asked. A fleetmaster wouldn't begin an overdue call with trivially good news unless that was the best he had to offer.

"Most Glorious Lord Umlac, an Entanglement ship has arrived at the target planet, and it's aware of our incoming fleet."

So much for another easy coup like on Xandor. This invasion would be messier. "How did you let that happen?"

"Most Glorious Lord Umlac, we avoided the standard detectors used by the Entanglement, but the inhabitants of the target system deployed non-standard instruments."

"How can that be? The natives only have pre-Quillip technology."

"Their inner planets are at war with their outer planets. They aimed sensitive instruments intended for each other at us. I have already executed the incompetent sciencemaster— the one forced on us by your brother Dismax."

"One more screw-up like this and I will dine on your carcass."

Umlac disconnected, mollified by the thought that Deus Telekil would most likely blame Dismax for the oversight. Besides, a month from now he would be invading the Entanglement, and it wouldn't matter if they knew he was invading Earth.

2

Soft Invasion

*D*amn, *noisy crowd.* Jade Mahelona cursed silently at the knot of protesters gathered in front of the clinic in Deep Indianapolis.

Corporal Loganal Mulcraft mumbled as he stood next to her. "I don't know if I can stand another day of this crap, let alone a whole freakin' week. I didn't sign up to be a target in a police line."

Jade gave him a sour look. "I know. You're an interplanetary communications specialist. Well, cry me a river. I'm an electronic weapons specialist, and I'm supposed to be piloting spacecraft in the asteroids. But when your ship is in dry dock, it's time for cross training. So, buck up, soldier."

Loganal's brainsong screamed with resentment of her. She couldn't tell if he disliked that she was his temporary commander and she was Hawaiian, or was female, or was a Lieutenant in the Solar Defense Force instead of the Marines. Or if he was jealous of her unique ability to sense electric fields, or... Who knew? She could only sense general emotions, not thoughts.

Jade ignored Loganal and let the noise and confusion of the crowded tunnel-street flow through her body. Her legs itched from the hum of electric powerlines under the street, and her chest prickled with bursts of static from electric cars driving by. Microwaves reflected off metallic surfaces of storefronts, cars, and police gear, giving the tunnel-street a ghostly shimmer.

Jade concentrated on the tingling in her scalp. The electric field from the brain of the nearest protester resonated in her head with the pastoral melody of a daydream. She turned to point her head at the protester next to him, and her scalp resonated with forlorn notes of worry. The electric fields from the primitive parts of all human brains broadcast the same melodies for the same emotions, and she knew them well.

She scowled at the crowd. They should be angrier. A man near her in a worn jumpsuit waved a sign saying *Ban Alien Medicine on Earth.* The crowd chanted *No Alien Clinics*--but they remained calm. Radical Separatists hated the aliens and wanted them out, but the protester's brainsongs lacked the bagpipe drone of anger.

She glanced left at the pink-white face and curly blond hair of Marine Corporal Loganal Mulcraft. "I expected Radical Separatists to be angrier."

"These are just folks who got nothing better to do," Loganal replied. "A lot of them are wearing second-hand clothes that don't fit. They got no money. They got no job."

"Yeah." Jade stared at the crowd. He was right about that. She gave a wry grin at the example of what leadership training said about diversity being an asset on a team.

Unlike Loganal, she didn't resent being here. She wanted to learn, and she wasn't about to let her rival, Lieutenant Keolo Davis, get ahead of her in electives. But crowds gave her headaches.

Keep the aliens safe. That was her mission today. Not that she had seen any aliens—ever in her life.

Protect the aliens' property. That was her secondary objective. Replacing alien medical equipment could be expensive. The Entanglement could fabricate most replacement items in Earth orbit, but the aliens had to import quantum-entangled devices and some special materials from another star. Interstellar teleportation was unbelievably costly.

Facilitate crowd safety. Humans came third. Making a good impression on the aliens was paramount.

A taxi dropped off an elderly gentleman at the police line near the door. The closest officer checked his credentials and waved him through.

"That guy's got money," Loganal said. "Tailored jacket. Hand-shined shoes—bet he didn't shine 'em himself."

"Insurance doesn't cover unapproved alien medical procedures," Jade said, "And they have ridiculously high prices, not to mention strange conditions, like not eating mammals or reptiles."

"Why shouldn't the Entanglement ask for whatever they want if they have better doctors?"

Jade glanced at Loganal's pasty European face. "You wouldn't understand."

It wasn't the medicine she objected to; it was the alien culture, insinuating itself on Earth ever since the first radio contact a hundred years ago and pouring into popular culture after the Quillip ship arrived a few months ago. Too many kids saw everything from the Entanglement as wonderful, and everything human as out-of-date.

It was Jade's grandmother reciting the ancient stories of beautiful Laka and fiery Pele—telling her how distorted the popular image of Hawaiian customs became after nineteenth-century *haole* tourists invaded and invented the luau so they could party. It was the fallacy that superior technology implied superior societal values. She didn't want to lose the Hawaiian Preservation on Maui where she could listen to the old stories or study hula dance and outrigger building. Where she could surf or soak in the sun on the beach while the waves serenaded her—just like her ancestors. Best of all, the electrical noise of the city was so distant she could feel the faint crackle of fish swimming in the reef. She wanted Hawaii everywhere.

She shifted her weight uncomfortably, not used to so much

standing in one place. "It doesn't matter what price the Entanglement demands," she said, "we have to pay it. The fleet from the Immortal Ascendency arrives next year, and they will enslave and *eat* humans."

"That's what the Entanglement says, but—"

Jade lost the rest of Loganal's comment as a blaze of hate-filled anger from someone in the crowd of protesters burned through her body; a shrill howling brainsong demanded her attention. And then it was gone, lost in the electrical noise around her.

Jade took a step forward, seeking the source of the hate.

Loganal had fallen silent, but now he said, "You'll get in trouble if something happens and you're out of the police line."

She took a second step forward to get away from Loganal, turning her head side to side, trying to tune in on the squealing anger. It had been so clear for a moment, contrasted against the bland crowdsong.

"It's a sham," Jade said. "These people don't care if the aliens establish an Entanglement medical clinic here or not."

If the crowd wasn't here because of the clinic, why were they here? Before she made sense of it, loud excitement, not anger, swept through the crowdsong. A silver-domed car eased to a stop right in front of her, and an Entanglement healer stepped out.

The Wolferlop-M healer was shorter than Jade, with a yeti-like appearance, and Jade's electrosense could tell she was female. She wore a gray and red kilt and a translator belt from which dangled alien tools and mysterious pouches.

Like all Entanglement species, she was highly specialized. The hairs in the fluffy white fur covering her body could bristle into needles full of medicines from special glands in her skin. Her nose could detect diseased tissue; her sensitive fingers aided in probing injuries. Her brainsong pulsed unlike that of any human—a series of waves, slapping to a crescendo, then retreating and coming again.

The healer's big brown eyes focused on Jade. "May evolution favor you. My name is Tshimmed."

Oh crap! The alien thinks I'm out front to greet her.

Jade signaled the police line to guard her flanks, satisfied that the car behind the healer would protect her from the crowd in that direction.

"And your descendants forever," she said. "I am Lieutenant Jade Mahelona." Traditional greeting completed. Now what?

The healer's eyes wandered over the crowd pressing towards them, the police blocking the way. "So many patients. Yet I don't smell any ailments human medicine couldn't cure."

"They're not patients," Jade said. "They're protesters."

The healer continued staring at the people. "A strange custom. Humans who don't like something travel to see the thing they dislike. What are they protesting?"

Jade squirmed and looked around. No one was coming to her aid. "Your clinic," she said. "Alien medicine on Earth."

"Why would anyone object to healing the terminally ill?"

Jade frowned. Was the healer that naïve? "The problem isn't that you cure disease. They resent your demand for humans to join a Guild and elevate the needs of that Guild above the natural evolution of humanity."

"It's a joy to be the best you can. It's a joy to help others. The Guild system encourages these." Tshimmed turned her full gaze at Jade. "Change can be hard, but once you come to know the joy of filling a niche in the Entanglement, you will find it worthwhile."

The joy of filling a niche in the Entanglement sounded a lot like the joy of doing laundry for *haole* tourists. Once the Entanglement assimilated Earth, they would all be serving foreigners. But before Jade could say anything more, Loganal said, "Perhaps we can escort you safely inside where your patients are waiting."

The healer drew her gaze to Loganal, her brainsong suddenly a foghorn, signaling a change in the alien's emotions. "Escort? Has Earth joined the Police Guild?"

"Change is hard," Jade said. "Earth has its own police force. We have doctors, lawyers, scientists, and engineers, too."

The healer ran her fingers through the hair on her arms, and her brainsong returned to even pulses. "Yes, of course, my apologies. It doesn't come naturally for me to rely on anyone other than the Police Guild for protection, but I'll have to get used to it. The ambassador says humans are good at many things. You should be able to find a Guild that will accept you without too much genetic optimization. Soon Earth will be able to afford Guild police."

Jade scowled. "It's not that simple. People don't all want the same thing."

"Wolferlops did not all want the same thing either," Tshimmed said. "That's why we diverged into Wolferlop-M for medical doctors, Wolferlop-P for pilots, and so forth. But such divergence is the exception. Most likely your species will choose to perform a single function for the Entanglement."

Jade shook her head to clear it. *Not my problem.* "Let's get moving. No doubt your patients are anxious for your arrival."

Jade and Loganal walked the healer behind the police line toward the clinic doors. The crowd surged forward and pushed a young woman carrying a sign reading *Human bodies, human doctors* through the line. Jade felt shrill flutters run across her body from the protester's brainsong pouring out alarm and confusion as the woman stumbled toward Tshimmed.

Jade leaped between the protester and the healer, shouldering the woman to one side. She grabbed the woman's arm and swung her back to the crowd side of the police line.

Up close, additional themes in the woman's brainsong became discernable. She was protesting for money! Why would someone hire protesters when legitimate Radical Separatists would gladly come out for free?

Jade felt the hateful anger again, stronger than before, coming closer.

She looked for people shoving their way forward and found

the anger's source—a scowling middle-aged woman in an oversized coat, carrying a sign that said *ETs go home.* A tingle of danger ran like spider legs down her spine. The woman wasn't just angry; she was murderous.

"Protect the healer," Jade shouted to Loganal and the other police as she started forward.

She pushed through several protesters to confront the angry woman. Jade's electrosense told the rest of the story. Reflected microwaves from nearby data lines gave a glistening picture of metal wires and hardware under the woman's coat, as well as a thick girdle of dark material Jade assumed to be explosives. A donut of shrapnel—nails, wires, and ball bearings—circled it all. A trigger covered the bomber's heart, with two wires running to a primer over her abdomen.

Jade's stomach turned as the full cynicism behind the terrorist plan hit her. Someone had hired people to protest so no Radical Separatists other than this bomber would get hurt when she blew herself up. On the other hand, several police officers and MP trainees were nearby. Worse, the healer and Loganal were still outside.

"Bomb!" Jade yelled and surged forward.

The woman was quick to sidestep, with the reflexes of a trained professional. But her heavy load of munitions slowed her movements. Jade grabbed the woman's coat with one hand, and the woman spun around, dropping her sign and throwing a punch at Jade's face.

Jade ducked and reached under the woman's coat with both hands. She grabbed the wires running into the explosives and yanked.

The woman struck the trigger over her heart. The buzz of electric current surged through the wires.

No explosion. Jade had pulled the leads out in time to keep them from detonating the explosives.

The woman's brainsong howled in frustration. She had a strong will to live, odd in a suicide bomber.

The woman grabbed the sign off the ground and swung.

Jade's arms were still tangled up in the coat, and she was unable to block. She twisted to the side, and the pole of the woman's sign glanced off her forehead.

The woman swung again, and the pole smacked Jade dead on.

Jade lost her grip as everything faded to darkness.

3

Healers from worlds apart

J ade awoke, well rested, although she couldn't have been out long. She opened her eyes and saw a circle of police boots. She was on the sidewalk where she had fallen; the protesters were gone; some police were leaving. Tshimmed knelt beside her, and Loganal stood at ease.

Jade sat up and hissed at Loganal, "I said get Tshimmed inside."

"Well," Loganal drawled, "she refused to leave you, and she wouldn't let us move you until she mended you."

Jade's hand shot up to her forehead where the blows had struck. A bright blue, cloth-like patch fell off in her hand. The underside was moist and smelled of cinnamon and nutmeg.

She handed the patch to the Wolferlop-M. The *ETs go home* sign lay at her feet, still attached to a bloody stick. Jade rubbed the spot where the blow had struck. No pain. No blood. No scab. Just soft, smooth skin.

"Thank you," she said to Tshimmed.

"I am merely repaying you. You may have saved my life."

The bomb. The hate-filled woman. "*May* have saved your life?" Jade echoed. She glared at Loganal. "Didn't you catch the bomber?"

"The suspect got away," Loganal replied. "I didn't see a

bomb. Nobody saw a bomb under the coat but you."

Damn, worthless Loganal.

She stood, offered Tshimmed her hand, and pulled the healer up. Together they started down the sidewalk toward the clinic door.

The police dispatcher called on Jade's communication implant. "Lieutenant Mahelona. Where are you? You should be at the station filling out an incident report."

"I just came to," she subvocalized. "I'm still at the clinic."

"Then I'll arrange for a physical, too. Get over here. Out."

The healer's arm was warm and furry, like a kitten. Tshimmed wiggled her fingers where they touched Jade's arm. "You have an unusual biology. Primarily proteinic, but with nanomechanical components like a Dasypod. Is that what caused you to sense a bomb?"

"Yes," Jade smiled, impressed by the alien healer's insight. "Nanomechanical mitochondria. They act like little electrical antennas, making my body sensitive to vibrations in the electric field. It's like I hear electric vibrations in the sonic range and see electrical vibrations in the microwave range."

"An interesting ability. Is it helpful in your line of work as a police officer?"

Jade chuckled. "Yes and no. I mean, no, I'm not a police officer. I'm an SDF soldier with a specialty in electronic space weapons. But yes, my electrosense is helpful in my line of work. It gives me an edge in combat and an inside view of electronics. However, sensing electric fields is only a side effect. My mitochondria extract energy from the electric fields passing through me. I don't need as many food calories as the average person."

The healer looked at Jade and made sniffing sounds. Remembering her smell? Then her translator belt said, "What a marvelous story. Are there other humans with your abilities?"

Maybe the sniffing sound was Tshimmed's native language.

"No," Jade said, "It required a very complicated modification of my DNA to get the proteins and nanomechanical particles in my body to work together. My mother only did it one time."

"Your mother is a talented woman. What else did she do?"

"Nothing," Jade said, feeling small. She rarely talked about her past, but something about the healer's unhurried openness made Jade want to respond in kind. "Word of her project got out, and a mob who thought she was creating a monster killed her."

"But she wasn't creating a monster?" the healer asked gently.

Jade stopped at the clinic door. "Only me. I'm her only creation."

She glanced back at the police milling about, wishing she fit in. But her differences made it so hard. One of the police was a hulking, genetically modified super soldier, talking and laughing with the others. Even he was more accepted than she was.

"Your mother would be proud of you," Tshimmed's soft voice purred beside her.

How could the healer know that? Jade wanted to believe it, but she wasn't a brilliant scientist like her mother. "I've done nothing to deserve it."

"You've become a caring, competent woman," the Tshimmed said. "Isn't that what your mother would want? Isn't that what you would want for your daughter? To be *her* best?"

To be her best. That was all Jade could be—all anyone could be. She'd taken after her father, not her mother. She aspired to become an admiral like him. Make space safer. Beat down the pirates. Protect the innocent. And after all, her mother had loved her father.

A small burden fell from Jade's shoulders. "Yes, when you put it that way. Thank you."

Tshimmed patted Jade's arm. "It's been a pleasure meeting you. I'm sure you will find your place."

Jade wasn't sure, yet, but at least she was sure finding respect and love was a possibility.

"You're a shrink, too. Aren't you?" Jade burst out.

"There are many kinds of healing." Tshimmed stepped into the clinic. "Thank you for your story. I will tell of you at home-nest storytelling. And good luck in your search for a Guild. Humans won't make good healers or good police—that woman knocked you out too easily—but I'm sure you'll find a Guild soon."

The door closed. Jade stared after Tshimmed, stung by the reminder that humanity had to join an Entanglement Guild, or else. She turned away and straightened her shoulders. If the Entanglement was cultural death, the Immortal Ascendency fleet that Earth telescopes tracked was utter annihilation.

At least she could go back to hunting pirates in the asteroids in a couple of weeks. Finding an Entanglement Guild for Earth was someone else's problem.

❊ ❊ ❊

Jade stepped into the mundane world of a metropolitan police station lobby. The Wolferlop-M healer had seemed genuinely curious about her and interested in her stories. Perhaps her stories would promulgate human values—or human foibles. The Wolferlop-M said "not the Healer Guild and not the Police Guild" for humans. What would the healer say to her nest mates?

Doctors were rare on Earth—machines handled most medical problems. The Entanglement hadn't automated routine tasks to the extent humans had. Rather, they used beings who liked those routine tasks, which gave everyone something to do. Jade shook her head. How unlike humans, who were developing an ever-growing class displaced by automation.

The dispatcher scowled at her from behind his desk and held out a tablet. "You'll need to find a desk and fill out this incident report. But first, go to the infirmary. Have the report back by 1500, so I can review it and send it on."

The infirmary smelled of disinfectant and lemon scent to cover the disinfectant. The medscan machine was powered up and ready.

The medtech couldn't be any older than she was. He hurried Jade into a chair, and as he stuck sensor patches onto her arms, legs, torso, and head, his brain moved close to her. She listened uncomfortably to his brainsong growling in a loop of some unknown thought—a strategy people often used when they were afraid that she would read their minds. He must have read her medical record—too bad it had to describe her electrosense and how it could work as a lie detector. But the looping thought in his cortex did little to mask his emotions in the lower portion of his brain. His midbrain's relentless moan of guilt and lust suggested he was cheating on his wife or girlfriend. A whiff of sex on his body reinforced the idea.

To distract herself, Jade focused her attention on the electronics in the room, which operated at much higher frequencies than the human brain, placing the medtech in the background. The medscan glowed like a giant jellyfish— a transparent shell covering a medley of colored strings and shapes. Wire tentacles dangled from it, bright with gold-blue electric vibrations, the hallmark of a standard six-strand universal interface. The unit's commlink radiated bright violet as it exchanged data with Central Records. The motherboard shined deep mulberry, and the local memory card had the reddish tinge characteristic of ten-year-old chips.

The electrical pulses from the machine played through a rainbow of colors as it scanned her up and down the frequency scales of various sensors. The scan repeated, taking an unusually long time. The med tech cursed, powered off the medscan, and left the room.

A minute later, he came back with a portable unit. That couldn't be good. But at least he was taking his job seriously and double-checking whatever problem he'd encountered using the first machine.

As he reran Jade's physical, his brainsong chirped and

hooted with puzzlement and suspicion. Finally, he unhooked her.

"It's crazy, but the machines agree. Your electrolyte balance is perfect. Your hemoglobin is up. Your heart rate and blood pressure are down. You're healthier than you have any right to be."

Jade felt violated. Evidently, the healer's patch had done more to her than fix bruises. While it was great to hear she was in tip-top health, the Entanglement healer had done who-knew-what to her body without asking her permission or giving an explanation. In her kind service to Jade, the healer acted as if Jade had no rights even over her own body. This was the high-handed intervention she feared would happen at a cultural level, too—"fixing" humanity's problems without asking what humanity wanted.

She wandered to a cubicle in the police desk room, distracted by trying to determine what the Wolferlop-M healing patch had done to her. She tried to decide if any part of her felt different, but the mere act of paying careful attention to any part of her body made that part feel strange.

The buzz of a priority military call interrupted on her communication implant. A voice rich in authority said, "Lieutenant Jade Mahelona, acknowledge."

"Here, sir!"

"Admiral Vincent Hammer at North American Headquarters orders you to report to him immediately for a special assignment. Acknowledge."

For a moment, Jade was too stunned to reply. Admiral Hammer? The top admiral in Solar Defense Force? Why would he want to speak with her?

"What kind of special assignment?" she blurted out.

"I don't know." The voice from HQ sounded impatient. "Just acknowledge that you'll be here ASAP."

"Acknowledged," Jade replied, chastened.

The command channel went silent.

She stared at her blank police incident report forms, then smiled. The admiral's aide had said immediately. She'd never get a better excuse for skipping paperwork.

At the exit to the police station, she grinned at the dispatch sergeant. "Sign me out, please."

Jade expected the dispatcher to object to her leaving, but instead, he nodded. "Good luck. I see you have a new top-priority assignment."

Jade perked up. "You do? What does it say my new assignment is?"

The dispatcher poked at the screen on his desk a few times, then cursed. "It says I have no need to know."

4

The Hammer

A bevy of rear admirals in the waiting room gave Jade quizzical looks when she arrived to see Admiral Hammer. Their brainsongs pounded in rhythm to their heartbeats, a sure sign of stress at seeing the big boss.

The Artificial Intelligence that served as the admiral's assistant, AI Commander Genie Wirth, signaled Jade into the admiral's office ahead of the assembled brass. Their silent hoots of outrage struck Jade's back with almost physical pressure—adding to her nervousness at seeing The Hammer.

Inside the office, waves of electric signals pummeled Jade's body like a high-pressure shower. Electronics were everywhere. The room wasn't an office; it was a war room. The wall to her right displayed Earth's ground defenses: missile silos, hardened bases, and ships on the ground. The wall on her left glowed with a cross-section of near-Earth space: communication satellites in low orbit, then concentric circles of zero-gravity manufacturing facilities, residential and entertainment properties, defense platforms, the Entanglement's Quillip ship, GPS satellites, and captured-asteroid mining operations.

Electric pulses from the wall behind her told her it displayed the entire solar system, but without turning around to look, she was unable to see much detail.

Admiral Hammer sat front and center at the far end of the room, behind an imposing black desk emblazoned with the Solar Defense Force logo: a pale blue dot centered in a solar corona. He furrowed his leathery brow along well-worn grooves under a graying buzz cut. He was studying a report on his desktop—likely her personnel file, Jade realized with a sinking feeling in her stomach.

The admiral's steel-gray eyes rose to meet hers.

She saluted. "Lieutenant Jade Mahelona, Electronic Weapons Specialist, reporting as ordered, sir."

He returned her salute. "At ease, Lieutenant." He motioned to a semicircle of leather armchairs in front of his desk. "Have a seat."

Hammer's eyes followed her. It was impossible to separate his brainsong from the electrical noise in the room, but she had no doubt he was sizing her up.

"First," he said, "congratulations on apprehending Leo Greko and his pirate crew. It wasn't your fault some ass at Brussels, Mars, let him escape."

"Thank you, sir. It was rather disappointing that he got away again. I recommend bringing him to Earth next time I catch him."

The admiral's gaze never wavered. "So noted. Secondly, the Ambassador from the Entanglement asked me to extend his/her thanks for stopping the suicide bomb suspect today. It's a shame the bomber presented such an unstable example of humanity to the Entanglement, but your actions may yet get us into the Police Guild."

Jade frowned. "Thank you, sir, but Tshimmed made it clear she was disappointed in my performance as a police officer."

"Who's Tshimmed?"

"The Wolferlop-M healer at the clinic. I talked to her a little. She said I was knocked out too easily to be in the Police Guild."

"Interesting." The Admiral tapped his fingertips together. "Apparently, there's plenty of room for differing opinions within the Entanglement. Maybe that's why they need a Supreme Council—an ultimate decider."

He took a breath and continued in a slightly more collegial tone. "However, I asked you here about a different matter, one so vital to the future of humanity that it will require you to leave the *Falcon* and report directly to me. Forget about the clinic incident. Central Security will handle it. I need you to focus completely on your new assignment."

Jade tried not to let her excitement and confusion show. What was he talking about?

"The Ambassador wants you to join an interstellar rescue mission to a lost Entanglement colony. This is Earth's best chance yet to prove our worth and get into an Entanglement Guild."

Jade caught her breath. Only ten other humans had traveled into the Entanglement—a few Entanglement-sponsored scientists and a troupe of dancers—no soldiers. It was an amazing opportunity. She tingled with excitement all over and felt her skin grow warm.

"Interstellar rescue?" Her voice squeaked. "Through the Quillip gateway?"

The admiral nodded. "The Ambassador also invited Professor Conrad Singleton, who is Earth's leading linguist and cultural xenologist. We can understand the Entanglement picking Singleton, but we're having a devil of a time figuring out why they asked for you. Not that you're incompetent—your scores are top-notch both in combat and in electronics—but you have no search and rescue experience. You don't have much experience at all."

"My electrosense?"

"Probably, but we can't figure out why it is relevant to a frontier rescue mission."

Jade cleared her throat. "I wonder if they realize it will give me more insight into their technology than most others would have." She fidgeted with her fingers. "You said they wanted a linguist. Does that mean this will involve contact with a new alien species?"

"Your guess is as good as mine. Let me tell you what I do know before we speculate on what we don't know. I have another meeting in ten minutes."

Jade pursed her lips and nodded, hungry for information.

Hammer glanced at something on his desk. "The colony is on a planet called Belle Verte—location unknown. The Supreme Council itself is organizing the rescue mission on behalf of the sponsoring species—sponsoring species unknown. The mission leader is a Dasypod named Ironsides. And there is a fourth team member—an Obnot named Quist Quillipson."

The admiral stopped. Jade was eager for more. "Yes, sir. What else?"

"Nothing." Admiral Hammer seemed to have a sour taste in his mouth. "You'll get the details of the mission *en route*. Once you leave the solar system, you will not communicate further with Earth until you return. The ambassador said events at the colony might generate unwanted interest from third parties. Presumably, he/she meant they wanted to keep the Immortal Ascendency out of this."

"That's all?" The Entanglement must be very serious about not giving out clues on the location of Belle Verte. "The lost colony could be anywhere in or near Entanglement space."

The admiral nodded. "I tried to get more details on the mission, but the Entanglement didn't budge. This rescue must be important to them if the Supreme Council is involved. Earth must take a chance and go along—send you and Singleton into the unknown."

Jade thought the composition of the team might be a clue. A Dasypod made sense—they were the backbone of the Police Guild. But an Obnot? One of the legendary scientific geniuses behind the technology of the Entanglement? Jade frowned a little. Usually, Obnots stayed behind closed doors in their ivory towers.

"A linguist, a technologist, and two military types," she said. "That suggests a need to communicate with someone, unexplained scientific phenomena, and plenty of danger. Perhaps an encounter with an advanced civilization that didn't go well?"

Admiral Hammer may have cracked a tiny smile. "Good observation. My analysts say the same thing, but with more words and a lot more hedging. They also say such a small expedition is unusual for the Entanglement. No biologist. No diplomat. No healer. You will act as the pilot and driver at Belle Verte. They didn't give an explanation for the small team."

The Hammer's look hardened. "You will go directly from here to the Earth Quillip ship, where you will teleport from Earth to Goldilocks Three as soon as possible, along with Professor Singleton and Quist Quillipson, who has been doing some research here on Earth. You will rendezvous with Commander Ironsides at Goldilocks Three. Your assignment is top secret, and you may not discuss it with anyone. Period."

Jade suppressed a wry grin. Too bad she couldn't tell Keolo —Lieutenant Keolo Davis, the lead vocalist and songwriter in the Misfit Platoon, the band Jade danced with. Keolo also commanded a three-person scout on the pirate hunter *Falcon*. He and Jade had an intense rivalry, and there was no way he'd match this assignment.

The admiral lowered his voice, and Jade leaned closer. "Moving on. The reason I'm seeing you in person is to convey additional orders for your ears only. The Immortals aren't the only ones hungry for intel on the Entanglement. As a second objective, I'm ordering you to bring back everything you can about Entanglement science, technology, military deployment, and industries. Everything you can collect. Discreetly, of course."

"Are you looking for anything in particular?"

"No. Bring everything. It will be useful to someone. But for me personally, I can't figure out why the Immortals bother to honor their treaty with the Entanglement. If the Immortal Ascendency is as greedy and ruthless as they seem, they should have overrun the Entanglement long ago. I want to know why they haven't—especially if it's a secret weapon Earth can copy."

Admiral Hammer pulled a satchel out of a drawer and slid it over his desk to Jade. "I want you to use your two-kilo personal baggage allowance for some undocumented spy gear. Most of this tech is top-secret. You'll have to return everything when you get back."

Jade leaned over the admiral's desk for the satchel. At this range, Hammer's brainsong was loud and clear. Chords of ruthless determination dominated counter movements of fear and compassion. No traces of deceit. The Entanglement, not the admiral, was withholding information about her mission.

Not that Jade had ever thought otherwise. Then it occurred to her that the admiral must know she could read his brainsong. He'd deliberately given her a peek. Her respect for him ticked up a notch.

As Jade sat back down, something on the admiral's desktop interrupted him, so Jade peeked into the satchel. Black and white labels marked everything: spycams, an infochip marked "security monitoring genie," an encryption/decryption toolkit, a chip labeled "Instructions. Read and destroy," nasal air purifiers, and a med kit. She started to push aside the top layer to see what was underneath when the admiral cleared his throat. She zipped the satchel shut and looked up.

The Hammer leaned forward in his chair. "Try to get library access beyond Earth standard and download as much as you can into the blank infochips. Deploy the security-monitoring genie and the micro cameras on Belle Verte. Bring back whatever the genie tells you to."

He glanced at his desk. "I have another appointment now. I'll expect a personal debriefing when you get back. I'm counting on you to impress the Entanglement with your skills and get us into the Police Guild. Get us Entanglement protection and get us Entanglement technology."

5

Forbidden Zone

U mlac saw no evidence his brothers were preparing to invade the Entanglement, which was good in a way —Deus Telekil wouldn't notice either—but left him unsure if they had embraced his new timeline. His spymaster had said he'd fabricated the fake messages from Telekil, but then the spymaster lost a duel to the death, cutting off any follow-up information. Time was running out. His annual pilgrimage to worship Deus Telekil was in two months.

Meanwhile, he had to keep up with business as usual.

"Most Exalted Lord," said his spymaster on the planet Nexus, "I have news of an unusual event for you. My agent has reported a secret meeting of the Supreme Council of the Entanglement to discuss the sudden mass disappearance of all citizens of a new Entanglement colony on the planet Belle Verte. Communications remain intact, but no one answers the calls. Periodic reports are due, but no one sends them. The Supreme Council is bewildered and is sending a team to investigate."

Umlac's body tingled with interest. Years ago, he'd seen a similar inexplicable disappearance. He was commanding a wing in the invasion fleet at the Entanglement stronghold of Aniscore. He left the bridge for a short time to strike the fear of failure into the fighter pilots he was about to send into battle. When he returned, the bridge was empty—nobody was running the ship.

A replay of the bridge monitors showed that his command team had suddenly vanished. He had no contingency plan to fight such a power, so he abandoned ship—just as missiles from the Entanglement fleet slammed into the brain-dead Immortal fleet.

"Give me the coordinates for Belle Verte."

"Most Exalted Lord, I don't know them. The colony's owners are very secretive."

As well they might be. "Perhaps they suspect you are spying on them."

"Oh, no, Most Worshipful Lord. I have taken every precaution."

Umlac's body continued to tingle. If he could make his enemies disappear, he could defy Deus Telekil and retain his entire vassaldom. Better, he could defeat Deus Telekil in a full-contact duel. He would become Supreme Deus of the Immortal Ascendency himself. He could live without fear of a master.

"What race is sponsoring the colony on Belle Verte?" Umlac demanded. That would narrow his search area.

"Most Exalted Lord, I don't know. They speak only through an Arafaxian lawyer."

Umlac's frustration at the lack of details was building, sending ripples along the surface of his taut outer membrane. "What *did* the Council say?"

"They reviewed the contracts for the rescue team to the missing colony, approving contracts for the services of a Dasypod, an Obnot, and two humans. They also approved the use of Dismax's Quillip link from Goldilocks Three to Farboro."

Interesting. Belle Verte must be in the Farboro sector. And the Council must be in a great hurry to risk taking the shortcut through his brother Dismax's Quillip link. They should have selected a team from nearer to the colony. They must want humans on the team badly.

Humans were a new species he'd never tasted, never assimilated into his memories. He would have to remedy that. He dismissed his Nexus spymaster and summoned another spymaster to arrange for the capture of the humans on the rescue team.

But Umlac knew that when he stopped the rescue team with humans on it, the Entanglement would just send another. He couldn't risk letting the Entanglement get to Belle Verte before he did, lest they gain control of the power there. It was time for extreme measures. He called for a meeting with his seven closest brothers. He already had a plan to get to Belle Verte first.

* * *

Umlac met his seven brothers on the remote, airless planet Luciflorigum. None of his brothers would meet him on Morb. Meeting his brother Shoggarts in person was risky, but Deus Telekil could probably tap their communication links, and Umlac dared not involve his lord just yet.

The Shoggart brothers were all direct descendants of the same great-grandparent, with identical memories up to twenty-seven hundred years ago, or less—his twin brother Winzar's memories only differed from Umlac's by nine hundred years.

The brothers were all as devious, untrustworthy, and powerful as Umlac. They were all vassals of Deus Telekil. Umlac counted on the fact that the last time he had demanded a meeting, the surviving brothers had profited handsomely. Greed and the fear of being labeled a coward ensured they all came.

Umlac thinned his tough outer skin and pushed out the steel mouth of a cannon barrel. None of his brothers showed any alarm as he fired a cannonball into his nearest brother. The amorphous body of his brother absorbed the projectile, and then his brother shot Umlac with a similar cannon.

Umlac repeated the ritual with each brother in turn, and his brothers with one another. Then, after completing the traditional greeting, which his kind had evolved to identify and eliminate weaklings, he extruded an antenna and transmitted. "You have traveled far and risked exposure to unfriendly forces to be here. I owe you all one medium favor."

The rowdy settlement of favors continued for several rounds. Cutbloc demanded a large favor since he had to postpone the conquest of a new vassal planet to be here. Winzar and Dismax hadn't spoken for several cycles and had several personal favors to settle with each other.

Eventually, Umlac resumed the meeting. "I brought you all here to double the number of your vassal planets."

His brothers stopped haggling. He had their attention.

"Each of you has a Quillip ship in a star system that is also on the Entanglement teleportation network. We'll use your Quillip ships to launch an eight-pronged invasion. The Entanglement will crumble like sandstone before a glacier, and we'll divide their fat planets among ourselves."

One of the brothers threw a boulder at Umlac. "Eight-pronged invasion? Have you grown weak? Why not conquer them yourself?"

Another brother grumbled, "What of the Treaty of Aniscore? Deus Telekil himself agreed to the Treaty of Aniscore."

It frustrated Umlac that he couldn't just dominate the lot of them and take their empires for his own, but to the circle of Shoggarts, he said, "Deus Telekil has ordered me to invade the entanglement in a little under two months. Did you not receive a similar order?"

"My orders from our Most Worshipful Lord are none of your business."

Umlac shot a volley of explosive shells at his brother in disapproval. The brother shuddered a little but absorbed them without further comment.

"As to Deus Telekil," Umlac continued, "we all know he doesn't plan to honor the treaty of Ansicore much longer. If we wait for him to organize the invasion, he'll likely assign much of the invasion to our cousins from the outer rim. Our gain will be less. In the end, he shouldn't care—our gain is his gain."

Dismax objected. "You must have gone stupid to plan an invasion of the Entanglement. They lie inside the Forbidden Zone. None of our cousins who ventured there returned."

Umlac wagered the sudden disappearances on Belle Verte were due to the same mechanism as that behind the Forbidden Zone. He needed to steer the conversation in a different direction. He pushed out the barrel of a laser cannon and fired with all the power his cold fusion organ could generate. "Coward! The Entanglement thrives in this so-called Forbidden Zone. Clearly, it's not forbidden anymore. You should fear crossing *me*, not some ancient space myth."

Dismax excreted liquid coolant, which billowed into white steam where the laser struck. "Shipmaster Harlex disappeared in the Forbidden Zone only eighty years ago. Umlac, you are too rash and greedy. You give no more thought to danger than an Ambo at a feeding trough."

The comparison to a lowly thrall like an Ambo caused Umlac's pseudopods to contract in anger. He hadn't survived dozens of millennia by being rash—nor by allowing himself to be the object of insults. "And you are a coward, Dismax. Afraid of Merkasaurs and Dasypods. Give me your Quillip ship, and I'll invade for you."

Dismax shot back with his own laser. "I'll take my share of the Entanglement, but from the frontier—planets like Goldilocks Three and Earth. You are foolish to attempt the conquest of Nexus, but that's your problem, not mine. When do we attack?"

Umlac's nucleus tingled pleasantly. He was getting his way, as it should be. "As soon as we return to our home planets."

6

Annihilated

T
wo hours after leaving Admiral Hammer, Jade wedged herself between Professor Conrad Singleton and Quist Quillipson the Obnot in a life-support capsule in the dark, zero-gee vacuum of a Quillip chamber. She was at the heart of the alien mothership, waiting in the underworld for the dark god Kanaloa. In a few seconds, a large relativistic mass would strike her at nearly the speed of light.

Quist's metallic exoskeleton pressed against her stomach —warm to the touch and glowing with alien activity across the electromagnetic spectrum. Quist stopped broadcasting a microwave data stream and folded his last remaining antenna into his cocoon-like body. His brainsong leaked out through numerous nonmetallic fixtures, sounding like a brass band in concert. So far, his only communication with Jade had been to say that he wished to devote his full attention to his local research while he still could.

Conrad's hairy chest pressed against the smooth skin of her back. He was shorter than Jade, but with an oversized head covered in short black hair, which gave him a boyish appearance. Every ounce of mass teleported was more precious than gold. Jade and Conrad wore only underwear as a token of modesty. They'd get new clothes at their destination.

Conrad had rushed in as the capsule was loading, like the proverbial absent-minded professor. Now his brainsong reverberated in Jade's so-close body. A loud twang from his amygdala was the usual tune for a man nestled against a lithe, young woman wearing practically nothing. His midbrain twittered with excitement and nervousness. His cortex hummed with curiosity and wonder.

All of this was normal, but layered on top of his brain was a genetically engineered ubercortex, which jangled like a wind chime near the front and whistled like an empty beer bottle in the rear.

"Do you think this annihilation will work on humans?" Conrad asked. Shrill notes of anxiety were growing louder. His heart rate was up. "Ten people have undergone the process, and none have returned—a disturbing pattern."

"You mean the annihilation of our current bodies by the Quillip teleport engine?" Jade asked. "The Entanglement does this all the time. You can't blame the people who left Earth if they are in no hurry to return."

"That pattern fits, but alternatives are possible, too."

"*Dissonance*," Quist replied. "Annihilation is an essential part of the Quillip process."

Jade was glad Quist had finally spoken, now that he'd lost his data link to Earth. She wanted to keep him talking. "Can you explain the Quillip process?"

"Yes."

Jade waited a few seconds. Was Quist thinking, or had he taken her question completely literally? "Please explain the Quillip process to us."

Quist began spouting mathematical equations. Jade quickly switched on her recorder for the benefit of scientists back on Earth.

Unfortunately, Conrad interrupted, "Can you explain in simple words? I understand a lot of languages, but mathematics isn't one of them."

"*Dissonance*. The oversimplification from the nonmathematical expression of mathematical equations creates a lack of precision. However, if you wish, I will attempt the conversion."

Jade wanted the equations, but Conrad said, "Yes, please use simple words."

"Very well," Quist replied. "The Quillip engine accelerates a quantum-entangled mass a little larger than the mass of our capsule to 99.99999% of the speed of light. At that speed, it will imprint every atom of the capsule before the shock wave of destruction has time to cross it. You are correct that this will annihilate our bodies, but a twin quantum-entangled mass at another star instantaneously mirrors the imprint. The twin collides with a fourth mass consisting of coherent matter waves. The imprint process reverses and reconstitutes every atom of our bodies. The Quillip process is much like the imaginary human concept of teleporting an object."

"Then what becomes of our bodies left behind at Earth?" Conrad asked.

"Obviously, the high speed collision releases significant energy. Our old bodies are heated into a gaseous state and flushed out the exhaust tube."

Conrad's brainsong vacillated between wonder and worry. "Such power and precision are way beyond human engineering. It's hard to imagine how it's possible."

"You will see for yourself in five seconds."

To Conrad's credit, he simply started a countdown. "Five, four, three."

Jade's heart beat faster. She held her breath and stared into the darkness in front of her. She knew the general theory behind Quillip teleportation, but the darkness of the chamber and Conrad's weird theories about previous travelers reminded her of the danger in the reality of it.

"Two, one, teleport," Conrad finished.

The chamber lit up with a bright white flash—leaked radiation from their explosive collision.

Conrad paused for a beat, then said, "We made it!"

Subtle changes in the Quillip chamber—the color of electric energy in the data grid, the shape of the airlock door —confirmed their arrival. They were twenty-four light-years from Earth in a ship orbiting Goldilocks Three—so named because it was the third planet Earth astronomers had cataloged in the Goldilocks zone—not too hot, not too cold—for life to exist.

Jade's stream of consciousness appeared to continue uninterrupted. Conrad's countdown echoed in her mind. His brainsong remained unchanged, except that relief gradually replaced worry.

A tentacled space suit covering a Dekapus from the Maintenance Guild sailed out and hooked a cable onto their capsule. The cable pulled them into the airlock.

Jade cycled through with Quist and Conrad. The dank smell and chilly air in the antechamber gave Jade goosebumps. The gray dirt walls, floor, and ceiling gave the impression of an underground cavern. Dim orange globes lit the room like a Halloween haunted house. The weightlessness at the center of the alien ship gave every movement a ghostly, floating quality.

"Interesting." Conrad's ubercortex pinged as he scraped at the dirt covering a nearby wall. "I hadn't realized it until now, but the steel and plastic corridors of the Quillip ship at Earth must be a courtesy to humanity because that's how we build things. The Quadricorns who are native to Goldilocks Three evolved in underground burrows, so of course, they'd prefer a mud-covered decor."

Quist's metallic exoskeleton began transforming from a compact oval shell to a creature with six legs. Antennae sprouted across his back, and wings unfolded from his sides. His forward sensor clusters extended to give him an inscrutable face. He reminded Jade of the dragon her uncle used for the logo on his dojo.

Quist twisted his wings at various angles. The electrical activity in them mirrored their environment—the wings were giant compound eyes.

Shivering, Jade spied a universal fabricator on the far side of the room. She leaped through the zero gravity to land next to the fab unit. It had already spit out a Solar Defense Uniform in her size, which she eagerly donned. Then she grabbed one of the universal translator belts from a rack.

A belt was the standard shape for an Entanglement translator, a shape which most species could wear, and which was large enough to contain a small jetpack to help navigate in the zero-gravity parts of the ship. The belt translated to and from any language in the Entanglement, including those based on sound, color patterns, touch, smell, and radio. Conrad's biggest claim to fame was that he had led the team that taught the belt Earth languages.

She fastened the belt around her waist and accessed a local news channel to verify that the belt linked her implant to the Entanglement network. The headlines were all about some local Goldilocks Three festival, so she skipped reading the details. Instead, she asked the fabricator to make her a dart popper and a balanced long knife, suitable for throwing or close fighting.

It made the knife, then said, "Only the Police Guild may carry power weapons on this ship."

She sighed. It had been worth a try. A dart popper was her weapon of choice. It fired tiny rocket-propelled darts, and she could select the payload and the targeting method with a thumbwheel.

But the fab had made the knife.

"Can you make a *katana* for me?"

"This unit is unable to fabricate swords longer than 51 centimeters."

Unable to fabricate a long sword, not *unauthorized.* "Okay, make a 51-centimeter *wakizashi*."

"Fabrication will require 110 seconds and cost an additional 12 nano-credits. Do you approve?"

"Yes." Jade didn't expect to need a sword on an Entanglement ship, but she wanted to prove the new limits of her fabrication authorization. Entanglement fabricators on Earth were limited to making food for humans.

"We must go," Quist said. "Commander Ironsides will meet us in 17.8 minutes. It would be most efficient if we were already in the conference room when he arrives."

The fabricator completed Jade's sword, and she buckled it on. Conrad was still poking around in the dirt wearing only his boxers and shaking like a leaf in a breeze. Jade grabbed a khaki jumpsuit next to the fab unit and took it to him. He pointed at the hole he'd scraped in the wall. "Look! You can see little tunnels where insectoid organisms live. I saw one that looked like a giant stag beetle, except it was red."

Jade mumbled something polite and handed Conrad his jumpsuit. He pointed to her sword. "Blades and stun guns allowed, of course, but not laser or projectile weapons."

She'd reached the same conclusion, using trial and error and deductive logic, although she hadn't tried stun guns. "What makes you say that?"

"It's part of the paternal police pattern—the best fit for Dasypods."

Conrad pulled his jumpsuit on, and they followed Quist down a dirt-encrusted tunnel. They soon came to several granite-surfaced doors, one of which opened automatically for them.

Jade gasped. "It's a room-tram, identical to the ones on Earth's Quillip ship. Surprising, given the way they decorated the hallways."

Conrad chuckled. "Room-trams are considered personal space. No doubt a Quadricorn on Earth would get a dirt-lined room-tram."

A furry orange octopus-like creature the size of a cat skittered into the tram just before the doors closed. Quist identified it as a fuzzling—a pet common among the Dekapus who formed the core of the Maintenance Guild. The fuzzling hid under a chair in the corner.

"Come on out little fella." Jade reached slowly under the chair and gentled the creature the way she'd learned to treat kittens at Grandma Norton's house when she was little.

"He likes you," Conrad said as Jade pulled the fuzzling out and cuddled it in her arms.

"This fuzzling belongs to Affendrop," Quist said. "He'll meet us near the conference room to retrieve his pet."

Jade's jaw dropped. "How do you know its owner?"

"Even fuzzlings have unique biometrics, and databases in the Entanglement are faster to search than those on Earth."

Jade was a little surprised Quist had answered at such length. If he was in a talkative mood, maybe she could find out more. "May I ask what you were doing on Earth?"

"Yes," Quist replied.

She tried again. "What *were* you doing on Earth?"

"I wasn't on Earth. I was on the Quillip station orbiting Earth."

"Okay, and what were you doing there?"

"I was analyzing the structure of Earth's infonet and cataloging its vermin."

"What vermin?" Jade couldn't help but think of rats getting into garbage cans at her grandmother's house.

"The viruses, worms, demons, and genies used by humans to corrupt their sources of information—a uniquely human perversion and the topic of my qualifying thesis at Obnot University."

Jade shook her head. "I hadn't realized we were unique in that way. What's your conclusion?"

"In an application of natural selection to a non-biological system, the competitive environment of Earth's infonet has led humans to develop many new and interesting encryption algorithms and hacking methods."

Jade cocked her head, unsure if she'd heard correctly. Obnots were the quintessential science and engineering species. How could they find anything on Earth new and interesting? "How did you manage to get conscripted for this mission?"

"I was not conscripted. My infonet research is complete, and my participation in this mission is voluntary. While I was on Earth, I became interested in how human teamwork differs from Entanglement teamwork. This team is a perfect opportunity to study those differences."

The tram doors opened, and they walked into another dirt-lined hallway. Jade's full weight had returned, so they must be near the ship's hull. The dirt here was drier and more porous than in the anteroom, and she could sense the rudimentary nervous systems of numerous little creatures moving about in it. The fuzzling in her arms pinged and twitched when one of them peeked briefly out of its burrow.

Quist stopped a few paces from a cross tunnel. "Wait."

The air took on the ripe odor of a pigsty. Squishy, slurpy sounds whispered down the tunnel. A meter-tall blob of translucent gray jelly quivered into the tunnel in front of them.

Jade slid into a combat stance, resting one hand on the hilt of her sword and holding the fuzzling tight to her chest with the other. "What's an Immortal doing here?" she whispered to Quist.

"The Immortals have a Quillip ship in the Goldilocks Three system, too," Quist replied. "They have a diplomatic office aboard this ship, and sometimes Ambos travel through the ship on errands."

The creature hesitated as if assessing the trio and then humped its way across the passage and disappeared. A second Ambo peeked around the corner and humped across the tunnel, then a third crossed, pushing a metal barrel.

"Why so many? What are they doing?" Jade whispered.

Quist replied, "Obviously, an Ambo police squad is taking

away a berserk Ambo in that container."

Ambo Three flicked the barrel along as easily as if it were empty. "Ambos must be very strong," Jade said, "but what's a berserk Ambo?"

"Explaining the obvious is inefficient," Quist said, "but you are on my team, and I'll do as you ask. Ambos sometimes lose control and eat everything they can. The Ambo police come and take them back to the Immortal ship, so they don't cause any serious damage."

"Damage from eating?" Jade asked. "What do they eat?"

"Citizens, obviously. Ambos prefer live food. Berserk Ambos prefer citizens."

So the stories about Immortals eating people were true. She stroked the fuzzling with her fingers. Pets could be so comforting.

Just then, the fuzzling jumped out of her arms and chased after a shrew-like creature. The shrew followed Ambo Three into the cross tunnel, and the fuzzling followed the shrew.

"Come back!" she shouted after the fuzzling.

"It is unlikely to return," Quist said. "Even sane Ambos eat pets."

Jade's nostrils flared, and she breathed in deeply, letting the horrible odor fuel her adrenaline. She ran into the side tunnel after the fuzzling. "Come back. Stay away from the Ambos."

She caught the wayward pet where it had stopped to poke a tentacle into a little burrow in the dirt. She gave it a gentle hug. "Naughty kitty. You don't need to eat that badly. Let's get out of here."

She turned to go, but a fourth Ambo appeared in the tunnel behind her and blocked her way.

Ambo Three turned around and closed on Jade from the other side. "You are not a Dekapus. That's not your pet. You have no right to it."

"I'll return it to its rightful owner," Jade said, backing away.

"So you admit you're not its owner," Ambo Four said. "If you're not going to eat it, I claim the wild fuzzling as my own."

"I claim the fuzzling," Ambo Three squawked. "You just ate."

Ambo Four moved faster toward Jade. "It's mine."

Ambo Three accelerated. "My lunch."

She was trapped between two Immortals intent on eating the kitty in her arms. Maybe these Ambos were going berserk. Maybe they would try to eat her, too.

Desperate, she drew her sword and ran toward Ambo Four, veering toward its right, between it and the wall of the passageway.

The Ambo closed the gap on its right flank, but this widened the gap to its left. With a burst of speed, Jade cut left.

No good. A glistening, slimy pseudopod as thick as a leg popped out to block Jade's path.

All Jade could think of was getting past that Ambo. With a swipe of her sword, she hacked off the pseudopod, leaped over the writhing limb as it fell to the floor, and ran past the squealing Ambo.

She sprinted to her companions. Ambo Four followed with surprising speed, not severely hampered by the loss of a single pseudopod.

"Quist, do you have any weapons?" Jade stopped beside the Obnot and turned to face the Ambo.

"Weapons are not permitted," Quist replied. "However, I have a laser cutter and several other tools that Ambos find distasteful."

But Ambo Four stopped at the corner of the cross tunnel. He studied Jade, Quist, and perhaps Conrad cowering behind Quist, then said, "My master says I must go now. But I'll be back, Ambo Slasher, and I'll have you for lunch."

7

Meta Civilizations

When the squishy dragging sounds of the Ambo posse faded to a whisper, a human-sized spiderlike creature scurried down the hall to meet Jade.

The little fuzzling squeaked and ran to the newcomer. Jade's shoulders slumped as the pet abandoned her. This must be the Dekapus who owned it.

Her translator belt spoke with a new voice, high pitched and squeaky. "May evolution favor you. I'm Affondrop, and I owe you many thanks for Fluffpaw's safe return. He has been a very naughty pup."

"And your descendants forever," Jade replied. "He's an ornery one all right." She pointed to the cross tunnel. "He ran after some little animal and almost got eaten by a couple of Ambos."

Affondrop's body quivered. "Ambos? Nasty creatures. I'm surprised they let him go. They can be very unreasonable when it comes to pets."

Fluffpaws scuttled back to Jade and hugged her with warm little tentacles. Jade perked up and chuckled. "Well, I admit I had to use a bit of cold steel persuasion."

Affondrop stopped quivering and pointed a tentacle at Jade. "What does 'cold steel persuasion' mean?"

"It means I used a sword to slice an arm off one of the Ambos."

Affondrop wailed and shivered harder than ever. "I'm so sorry. If you're a target now, my negligence is to blame."

Jade tensed, recalling the Ambo's parting threat to return and eat her. "I wouldn't take its threats too seriously. You can smell them coming at a hundred meters."

"It's unwise to minimize the danger. Immortals take grudges very seriously and hold them forever."

Affondrop hurried away, and Jade turned to Quist, recalling that at least in theory Immortals could remember forever. "Will that Ambo really come back?"

"Unknown."

"Well if he does, I'll still have my *wakizashi*."

Conrad grinned. "*Ambo Slasher*—a great name! You have achieved a rank among the Immortals. They rate all intelligent creatures in a simple linear power hierarchy."

Quist started down the hallway. "Swords are infective against Ambos. So are small projectile and energy weapons."

Jade hurried to keep up with Quist. This sort of information wasn't available on Earth. "Surely, plunging a sword into an Ambo will stop it."

"Incorrect. Ambo vital organs are diffused throughout their body. A single blow seldom affects their health."

A tingle of dread crept up Jade's spine. "What *does* work against an Ambo?"

"A large explosion is the most effective defense. A flame-thrower can be effective too but takes longer. The best strategy is to avoid Ambos."

Jade grinned to cover the knot of fear growing in her belly. "As I said, their smell makes them easy to avoid."

* * *

The conference room was a dirt cavern like the Quillip

anteroom. A flat-topped boulder in the center served as a table, and dim orange lanterns provided light.

On another level, the grotto glittered with yellow and violet electrical activity, mostly from a room comm by the door and a holo display in the back. The holo showed a crowd of massive beasts, much like Triceratops, but with four horns and shovel-shaped tails. These must be Quadricorns, the local intelligent species.

The rough-hewn décor notwithstanding, artwork dotted the walls—art from Earth. Conrad flitted from one piece to another. "This bust of Nefertiti is from the Amarna Period about 1300 BC ... This vase is from Qin Dynasty ... I can't believe Botticelli's 'The Birth of Venus' is here. Surely these can't be the originals."

"Obviously they are originals," Quist said. "The purpose of their display is to showcase the wealth of the Earth Investment Consortium."

"But—"

A loud trumpeting sound drew everyone's attention to the hologram, where a ring of thirty Quadricorns passed a massive boulder around the circle.

"What are they doing?" Jade asked. Now that Quist was talking, she wanted to keep him going.

"Demonstrating their strength," Quist said.

"I can explain," Conrad said. "The Quadricorn's Guild is mining. We are seeing their annual mating games—a series of contests designed to showcase the attributes of a good miner and attract a prime mate."

"Not a Guild humanity will want to join," Jade observed. "But it's amazing how the Entanglement got such different species to work together."

Conrad moved closer to Jade. His brainsong rang with multiple themes at the same time—tweets of curiosity when he glanced around the room, lute songs of wonder when he studied the Quadricorn display, pings of new patterns forming, and twangs of physical attraction to her.

"The entanglement of species within the Entanglement, so to speak, is not amazing at all," Conrad said. "Their interdependence has existed for over fifty thousand years, during which time it has fine-tuned the genetic makeup of its constituents. The Entanglement started with five species that already had very different strengths—Merkasaurs, Obnots, Arafaxians, Venmars, and Dasypods—and enhanced their strengths: business, science, law, diplomacy, and keeping the peace. Then they gradually added other species. As the Elohoy said, *Diversity is unity*."

Jade raised an eyebrow. "Who are the Elohoy?"

"I can explain that too," Conrad said. Jade resisted rolling her eyes. He was showing off, but she needed to learn everything she could about the Entanglement. "The Elohoy lived in our part of the galaxy about two million years ago. Older civilizations like the Yarks remember them as evolving to godhood and transcending into another dimension. They are best known as the creators of the four forbidden planets, but they also left us the Four Laws of Self-Managed Evolution:

You become what you love.

Change is permanence.

Diversity is unity.

You are not God."

Jade frowned. "Doesn't the third law about diversity go against the Entanglement's extreme specialization for member species?"

Conrad shook his head. "It might if the Four Laws were limited to the micro-evolutionary level. However, on the galactic-empire level, diversity *among* interstellar civilizations is what counts, not diversity within any one species. Think of the species in the Entanglement as the organs in a body—liver, heart, whatever. These specialized organs couldn't survive on their own, but as part of a body, they can outcompete colony organisms like corals or pyrosomes. So too the Entanglement can outcompete any single-species civilization."

"Ha!" Jade said. "The Immortal Ascendency competes as an

interstellar empire, and it doesn't have guilds. Right, Quist?"

"Correct," Quist replied.

"Yes," Conrad said. "Another interesting metaculture. They use a horizontal division of labor rather than a vertical one."

"What?" Jade had to ask.

Conrad paused to watch the Quadircorns passing the boulder around, then turned back to Jade. "The Immortal Ascendency species are generalists, but with differing levels of power and control. The Ambos are the lowest, Hydras, or maybe something even bigger are at the top of the power pyramid. It's a little bit like a feudal society on Earth, but with the rulers capable of acting as farmers or knights or smithies when necessary."

"That sounds like a better fit for humanity," Jade said. "There is no way all of humanity will agree on which super-specialized guild to join."

Conrad looked shocked. "You can't seriously consider surrendering to the Immortal Ascendency. Humanity would be the lowest of the low—slaves to Ambos—and you've seen firsthand what Ambos are like."

"No, of course not," Jade admitted, "but I still have a hard time imagining you as a soldier or me as a linguist."

"That's where education comes in. It's not us, but our descendants who will specialize." Conrad tapped his chest. "I was raised by anthropologists. If you had been too, you'd likely find anthropology interesting—perhaps physical anthropology instead of linguistic analysis, but we would both enjoy furthering the understanding of other cultures."

Jade pursed her lips. "I'm not convinced. I love physical activity—a good workout—a good fight." She enjoyed the cerebral challenges of warfare as well—strategic engagement, tactical maneuvering—but wasn't going to mention that with Quist present.

Conrad continued, "The process of self-managed evolution is multi-faceted. Scientists induce genetic changes to enhance the necessary capabilities. Educators teach the desired skills, and somehow, the population is culled to ensure the survival of the fittest, as defined by the needs of the guild."

Culled? Jade doubted that would work as planned. Social programs always had unintended consequences.

The round-robin rock-toss ended, and Conrad examined the artwork more closely. "The Greek gods seem overrepresented. Hm. One of each ..." Conrad's ubercortex chimed with his recognition of a pattern. "It's the cultural identification pattern—the division of skills among the Greek gods is like the guild system. What do you think of that comparison, Quist?"

Jade glared at the paintings. No Maui, no Pele, no Laka. Another reminder of the unimportance of minor cultures in a dominant culture.

"Unproven," Quist replied. "And your idea doesn't account for major facts."

"Like what?" Conrad asked.

Quist moved closer to the far wall as if examining a painting there. "The Earth Quillip Consortium will sell these antiques back to Earth for a profit once you can afford it."

"Ah, the art speculator pattern," Conrad replied, "The Merkasaurs have indeed made the Entanglement into an efficient wealth-extraction system."

Jade's cheeks grew red. "Don't give the Merkasaurs all the credit. Earth didn't need to sell out so quickly. My mother had an alternative solution to the Great Malthusian Famine, but the Merkasaur deal to sell food fab and cold fusion technology caused the government to abandon the electric-powered mitochondria program after I was born."

"Incorrect," Quist said. "The government continued the program. They tried six hundred thirty-two additional test subjects, and no surviving scientist understood why you were the only one that worked."

"How do you know that? I never heard that before," Jade replied, stung by the words "surviving scientist."

While Jade blinked back tears, Quist answered her question

matter-of-factly. "Many of the research files are still classified, but I found hacker tools on the Infonet that allowed me to access the full medical records of you and the other test subjects."

Conrad's brainsong hummed discordant notes of anger and deception. "If you accessed my classified medical records, don't talk about it."

Jade felt uncomfortable not knowing what else Quist knew about her, but it was Conrad's reaction that interested her most. He wasn't angry about a breach of privacy. He was hiding something about his medical record.

The military march of Quist's brainsong wavered, then resumed a slightly slower cadence. "You're on my team, and I'll do as you say."

A new storm of electrical activity approached in the hallway outside—a powerful brainsong packed into a small space. The new song had an eerie, whining quality. Clicks and clacks around it probably came from other organs in an alien body.

Quist moved closer to the door, "Commander Ironsides has arrived."

Jade forgot about Conrad's medical records. She stood at attention to greet her new commander.

Ironsides rolled into the room like a giant tumbleweed. His tentacles were so numerous he looked like a briar patch— a suitable analogy for a mobile plant. Those tentacles served as arms, legs, and roots—"root-feet" was the proper term for them. At the center of the briar patch was a solid core, small but densely packed by the Dasypod's unique nanomechanical biology.

"May evolution favor—" Ironsides root-feet stiffened and quivered. Several high-pitched screaming sounds were probably his laser-eyes charging. His root-feet spread apart to clear the way for his laser-eyes to peer out into the room.

He focused his incredibly powerful laser-eyes on Jade. "You smell like a rancid drillsnake. Yet you stand frozen like a frightened forest-pig instead of attacking. Tell me why I shouldn't burn you full of holes."

Surely he didn't mean her? What was a drillsnake? What was a forest-pig? *What was he talking about?*

Sweating, she held out her open hands. "I'm human. Lieutenant Jade Mahelona, Electronic Weapons Specialist, reporting for duty, sir."

"Liar. The human by the wall smells like the ocean. You smell like a drillsnake. For the last time, what are you?"

Ironsides' eyes reached full charge. Jade's forehead itched with one of the things her electrosense dreaded most. The sting of a laser targeting dot.

8

Reflexion

Ironsides had arrived at Goldilocks Three a few hours earlier tired and hungry, craving a deep pile of nanotube-enriched dirt and plenty of bright sunlight. Eighteen hours was a long time for a plant to be mobile, even a sturdy mechanochemical plant like him.

His room-tram came with a pile of fresh dirt and three sunlamps. He set the sunlamps on maximum and sank his lower root-feet into the soil. His upper root-feet stretched toward the light, and he shuttered the laser eyes encircling his body.

Ecstatic paralysis spread through him as his awareness shifted from mobile mode to photosynthesis mode. Planting was a time of meditation, initiated with the invocation prescribed by the *Dasypodia*. "Thanks be to the Creator, who made me a plant that I may know deep meditation and fully perceive my purpose and my flaws. Glory be to the Creator, who made me mobile that I may act to fulfill my purpose and repair my flaws."

Dasypods had a unique right to believe in a Creator. Of course, they'd evolved through natural selection, but nanomechanical chemical assemblers were the building blocks of Dasypod metabolism. Unlike species build from naturally plentiful amino acids, no process of nature could have created the first life on Dasypor. Only the direct intervention of the Creator.

A stream of carbon nanotubes, seasoned with iron, titanium, tellurium, beryllium, and a dozen other trace elements, trickled up his root-feet. Sunlight warmed his body. The joy of planthood filled him with bliss.

As he savored the soil and sun, memories of the previous day began discoloring his clear bliss. The wisdom of the *Dasypodia* refracted through his actions, revealing imperfections in need of repair.

He recalled the previous morning on Nexus when he'd awakened from his last planting with an urgent need to call his oldest offspring, Spike. Comqubit telecom from Nexus to Dasypor was expensive, but he must make amends. "My son, I should have been more helpful when we talked yesterday."

"No, Dad, I thought about it, and I'm sorry for bothering you with my problems. It was childish, and I must not be childish if I am going to pass the culling."

It was good that Spike had reflected on their conversation. Nevertheless, Ironsides was the adult. "Dear Spike, although you are nearly full grown, you'll always be welcome to whatever advice I can provide. I am confident that when you face your drillsnake, you will prevail."

One of the hardest things about Dasypod parenthood was that after you devoted fifteen years to preparing your child for the culling, your child came back only half of the time. "Remain true to the teachings of the *Dasypodia,* and you will survive."

"I will."

They chatted a bit, and then Ironsides straightened his root-feet. "I have to go now. I'm meeting the Supreme Council for a new assignment."

"Wow! The Supreme Council. If you see any generals, tell them I'd make a terrific cadet aide."

"I will, for it is the truth. May you bring joy to the Creator."

"You, too."

Ironsides mulled over his exchange with Spike. Overall, his conversation had been satisfactory, but he'd ended it too abruptly. He would apologize the next time he talked to Spike.

He turned his attention to his audience with the Supreme Council. He'd expressed his tremendous gratitude when they named him ambassador to a new colony world. But he'd expressed too much concern when he found out that the colonists had all disappeared. He should have had more faith that the Council would provide him with adequate resources for the situation. Then again, he wasn't sure they had.

"In addition," said the Arafaxian representing the missing colony. "My sponsors will fund a team of three assistants for you."

This seemed like good news. Ironsides knew who he would pick.

"They have selected an Obnot and two humans as your assistants," the Arafaxian concluded.

Ironsides involuntarily curled the ends of his root-feet, then caught himself and forced them to straighten. "What is the human guild? I've never heard of humans."

Silver Streak, the Dasypod representative to the Council, twisted his root-feet in knots, "Humans are not members of the Entanglement. They have not petitioned the Council for guild membership. I've heard that certain neo-liberals on the Council are encouraging humans to apply for the police guild, which has always been the sole responsibly of Dasypods. We oppose human police, and we propose sending two more members of the Police Guild instead of the two unguilded humans."

"My sponsors insist on this point," the Arafaxian said. "Moreover, they have identified the specific humans they want."

Silver Streak jerked his body to align with the Merkasaur who headed the council. "Jakkar Ten, the Entanglement has relied on Dasypods for security since its beginning fifty thousand years ago. Would you please put an end to this nonsense?"

Jakkar Ten polished his claws. "As long as the sponsoring race pays all costs, they decide how to spend their money. The council's only real prerogative is naming our ambassador. It comes down to this: Ironsides, can you manage two human assistants?"

The sudden question flummoxed Ironsides. What were humans like? But practical considerations aside, any answer would disappoint someone.

It would be easier to make amends with Silver Streak than with Jakkar Ten. "Yes, I can handle two humans."

* * *

Ironsides remained transfixed in the timeless meditation of plants until he had taken his fill of nutrients and light. Eventually, his bliss faded, and thoughts of action tempted him into the mobile world.

When he awoke, he hurried to send his apologies to Silver Streak but was too late. A message from the Dasypod council member had queued for him at the communication kiosk. "Ironsides, I apologize for putting you in such a difficult position in front of the Supreme Council without adequate warning. Please allow me to make it up to you when you return to Nexus." Ironsides' mood soared. When he returned, he would ask Silver Streak for a cadet aide assignment for Spike.

He savored the silicate and carbonate odor of the dirt-lined tunnel as he rolled to meet his new team. Goldilocks Three Station wasn't Dasypor, but it smelled better than most other Entanglement ships to his keen root-feet olfactory organs.

He bounced a little as he cartwheeled down the corridors, but as he neared the Earth-artifact meeting cavern, a malodor of danger tainted the air. Reflexes honed by generations of duels with drillsnakes poured energy into the charge capacitors for his laser-eyes. His logical mind told him no drillsnake could have passed down this hallway recently, but in his hearts, he felt otherwise.

He entered the conference room and tried to make his greeting sound upbeat. "May evolution favor you."

An overpowering stench burned his sensitive root-feet as they swiped the air to get a direction for the odor. His power-gorged laser-eyes sought a target. "What is that stink?"

9

Think Outside the Ecliptic

Tis was absurd. Jade had no idea how close Ironsides might be to firing a laser bolt through her brain, but, surely, she didn't look anything like a drillsnake. Not that she knew what a drillsnake looked like.

But if drillsnakes were from the Dasypod home planet, they must have a nanomechanical biology. Ironsides had specified her odor, and there was one unique thing about Jade's chemical makeup.

"I have nanomechanical mitochondria—little organs in my cells," she said. "You probably smell those. They're an auxiliary energy source. Otherwise, I'm completely human."

Ironsides was silent for a few seconds and then turned off his laser dot. "Your file confirms your abnormal biology. Your odor sickens me, but the *Dasypodia* says 'If your commander tells you to cross a graymold swamp, pause your breathing tubes.' My orders are to work with you, but please move to the back corner, as far away from me as possible."

Ironsides shined a laser dot on the room comm. Jade heard subtle communication modulations in the laser beam and soon felt the soft breeze of increased ventilation. Her hands still trembled from adrenaline, but she stepped to the back corner.

Ironsides cartwheeled on the tips of his root-feet to the head of the stone table."We are meeting in this secure room under orders to keep our mission secret—"

"That's incorrect," Quist said.

"Obnot, it's improper to interrupt. I'm the commanding officer here."

"But your facts are incorrect," Quist said. "Hence your actions will be incorrect."

"You are the one who is incorrect. Our mission is top secret, by order of our sponsoring race and by order of the Supreme Council itself. You can't dispute that."

"I don't dispute our orders. However, this room isn't secure. You said it was."

Ironsides swiveled around, studying the room with his laser-eyes. "The Facilities Office assured me this was the most secure room on the ship."

"Irrelevant." Quist pointed an antenna at the room comm. "The input devices are tapped. Also, a sensor on the wall behind me is wired directly to the Immortal Ascendency Consulate."

Ironsides started toward the door. "Then we will go to another room."

Quist stayed where he was. "It would be more efficient to contact the Facilities Office via the room comm."

Ironsides stopped; his root-feet quivered. "Nonsense. You just said the room comm had been compromised."

"I said it was tapped, not dysfunctional."

Ironsides twisted and untwisted the tips of his root-feet. "We won't rely on any of its functions. The *Dasypodia* says, 'Do not enter a valley if you see just one snap-mole. Underground, there are a hundred you do not see.'" He started rolling toward the door again.

Jade had been studying the room with her electrosense. The metal bulkhead behind the dirt façade glinted with reflected microwaves. And, sure enough, on the wall behind Quist, a subtle fuchsia glow emanated from beneath a painting of a woman holding a wicked pike in one hand and petting a centaur with the other. Jade recalled Conrad scraping a hole in the dirt wall in the Quillip anteroom.

"There's another option," she said. "I can disable the bugs in this room. Then we won't have to move."

"Consonance," Quist said. "Disabling the bugs would be more efficient. Humans are correct to pride themselves on thinking outside the ecliptic."

Jade was pleased with Ironsides' metaphor of her ideas as satellites moving outside the usual plane of orbit.

"Not by my reckoning," Ironsides replied. "We don't know how long it will take the Maintenance Guild to get here to disable the bugs, but it's usually one to four hours."

"Jade said she could do it."

Ironsides' root-feet quivered. "She's not Maintenance Guild."

"Humans are unrated," Quist said. "Perhaps the Supreme Council sent two humans along to find out what they are good at. Perhaps their guild will be ship maintenance."

Ironsides' root-feet quivered harder. "It's no secret Dasypod leadership doesn't want humans in the Entanglement. They are too immature. They are too good at making trouble, and that's all we need to know. If you don't want to wait on the Maintenance Guild, disable the bugs yourself."

"The Science Guild doesn't fix things," Quist said. "We observe. We devise theories. Sometimes we build scientific instruments or engineering prototypes. However, Jade is not constrained by any guild, yet."

Ironsides held his root-feet stiff for a few seconds then relaxed and focused his laser-eyes on Jade. "We'll follow Quist's recommendation. Disable the bugs for him."

Jade's anger flared briefly. Disabling the bugs was her idea, not Quist's. She took a deep breath, then skirted along the wall to keep her distance from Ironsides while she rifled through her med kit to find a stick of wound putty. At the room comm, she pinched off a glob and mashed it into the sound pickup.

She plastered another wad over the video camera.

She turned and strode to the picture of the woman and centaur, pulling a steel knife out of her satchel.

"Stop!" Conrad jumped up. "That's an original Botticelli."

She ignored him and dug into the dirt wall under the painting, then severed the wire to a microphone. "How now, Quist?"

Quist rotated one of the antennas sprouting from his head around a couple of times. "The room is secure."

"Thank you, Quist. Obnot instrumentation has lived up to its reputation." Ironsides relaxed his root-feet and somehow made his translated voice sound even more formal. "Let's get back to business."

Jade frowned and stalked to her corner. She had solved the problem, but Ironsides was giving Quist all the credit. Apparently, he couldn't imagine her doing anything worthwhile. How like too many human bigots.

She took a deep breath to calm herself and concentrated on Ironsides' words.

"Two months ago, a scout ship from one of the Entanglement worlds arrived at the planet Belle Verte. The small scout contains a very limited supply of quantum-entangled matter for teleportation. The sponsoring race can only send forty couples to settle the new colony. They'll remain physically isolated from the rest of Entanglement for at least a century until a full-scale colony ship can arrive. The forty males went first, to prepare the way for their mates. There was no sign of trouble for several weeks, until two days ago, when all of the colonists disappeared."

Jade listened carefully. The size of the scout ship was new information, but that was about it. Ironsides still hadn't provided any clue about what happened at the lost colony or what the rescue team would be up against on Belle Verte.

Ironsides rolled back slightly. "The colonizing world contacted the Supreme Council, which agreed to sponsor our team. The details of the disappearance are top secret. We'll get them at the home planet of the sponsoring race."

"Who is the sponsoring race?" Jade asked.

"That information is classified."

"Where is Belle Verte?" Conrad asked.

"Its location is classified, too," Ironsides replied. "However, I can say that the next leg of our journey is to Farboro."

"Where's Farboro?" Jade asked.

Ironsides vibrated the tips of several root-feet in Jade's direction—apparently, a sign Jade had asked a stupid question.

Conrad said, "Farboro is a major trading hub five hundred light-years rimward at the outer edge of the Orion Arm."

Quist's brainsong seemed to skip a beat. "Farboro is eleven Quillip jumps from here. Assembling a team on Goldilocks Three instead of near Farboro is an unusually inefficient use of resources. Why all the expense? To send humans? Am I the only Obnot willing to go?"

"Now you are the one who is incorrect," Ironsides said. "Travel time and expense will be low. We'll use the Immortal Ascendency's network. We'll teleport directly from Goldilocks Three to Farboro—one jump."

Jade's heart rate shot up. Use the Immortal Ascendency network? Go into Ambo territory on purpose? That sounded crazy.

"The safety of the Immortal Ascendency route isn't proven," Quist said.

Jade nodded her head.

"We can't trust the Immortal Ascendency," Conrad said. "They may be behind the disappearance of the colony on Belle Verte. After all, if the planet is unoccupied, it'll be easier for them to claim it, in which case they won't want us there either."

Jade nodded her head in agreement again.

Ironsides wriggled his root-feet. "Don't worry. I have been appointed as ambassador from the Supreme Council to Belle Verte."

"Dissonance," Quist said. "You are not in the Diplomatic Guild."

"True, this is an honor rarely given to Dasypods, but Belle Verte is not yet ready for a member of the Ambassador Guild since there are no residents there. However, my title of Ambassador gives our team full diplomatic priority, rights, and immunity. The Immortal Ascendency won't harm us."

"The Immortals don't believe in rights," Conrad said. "They'll detain us if it's to their advantage."

"That's why I'm leading this expedition," Ironsides said. "I know the threads, as humans would say. Ever since Silver Bar the Great, of whom I'm a descendant, defeated the Immortal hordes at the battle of Aniscore, the Immortals have honored their treaty with us. They value their diplomatic immunity on our starships. They won't put that at risk by violating our diplomatic immunity on theirs."

Jade grimaced. The team's safety hinged upon the Treaty of Aniscore. Truthfully, it surprised her the Entanglement had defeated the Immortal Ascendency. However, details of the Battle of Ansicore weren't available on Earth. She made a note to ask the Goldilocks Three library about the battle if she got a chance.

Ironsides backed away from the table. "Before I end this meeting, I have one more announcement: The Supreme Council named Jade as second in command. As a result, I must speak with her in private. Quist and Conrad, you are free to tour the ship and use its facilities. Return here in fifty minutes. Don't be late."

Jade blinked at the unexpected news. What did the second in command do on an Entanglement team? Maybe this would turn out better than she feared.

Quist and Conrad left. Ironsides focused his laser-eyes on Jade. "I can't send you back because none of the other members of my team is remotely qualified to be second in command, and I can't ask for a replacement on our tight timetable."

Jade's newfound hope collapsed.

"Not that the Council would listen anyway," Ironsides continued. "The sponsor race irrationally likes humans, and they have the final say."

He shook his root-feet, and some of the shriller notes of his brainsong disappeared. Jade guessed he must be doing the equivalent of taking a deep breath.

Ironsides spoke briskly. "Regulations require either first or second in command to be unplanted, or in your case, awake, at all times. Therefore, we'll have complimentary rest cycles from now on. Your sleep period begins in seven hours, travel permitting, and my planting will occur shortly after you wake up."

"Yes, sir." At least he was taking her role as second in command seriously.

"When I'm planted, you'll refrain from making any major decisions and from making any decisions of any kind which are opposed to my wishes."

"Of course, sir." That was more or less standard operating procedure on Earth.

"Regulations also require me to share all command-only information and orders with you so you can be an informed leader in the unlikely event of my death and your survival."

Jade didn't know how to read the shift in Ironsides' brainsong, a staccato piping tune.

Ironsides' root-feet stiffened. "The sponsor race believes some new kind of technology, or possibly a heretofore unseen force of nature, took their colony. Therefore, they took the unusual step of sending an Obnot on a potentially dangerous mission and ordered us to secrecy."

Jade nodded. "That makes sense." She was beginning to like being in Ironsides' confidence.

The shrill notes returned to Ironsides' brainsong. "I don't like having humans on this expedition. You don't belong to a Guild, and I hope you never do. In the unlikely event I'm captured or killed, and you assume full command, you are ordered to abort the mission and leave Belle Verte at once."

Jade frowned. Whether to abandon the mission or not should depend on the circumstances at the time. And, besides, if for some reason she were to assume full command, her orders would be as valid as Ironsides', and she could countermand his.

"Is that order from the Supreme Council, sir?"

Ironsides' laser-eyes surged with power. "The Supreme Council ordered you to obey my orders, and that's my order." Ironsides rolled to the door. "Be here when I return in forty minutes. Meanwhile, I need to get your stink out of my breathing tubes."

Jade stared at the empty doorframe. She didn't have a problem with authority, but crazy authority? She didn't know how much more of Ironsides she could take. And "some new kind of technology" sounded dangerous. Especially, when Ironsides no doubt considered her the most expendable member of the team.

10

Berserk Ambo

Jade jogged to the closest library terminal with a holographic display and high speed download, located in Shuttle Dock F-13.

The shuttle dock staging area was the size of a tennis court, adequate only for small, private yachts. A heavy metal door slid shut behind her—an airtight bulkhead to contain a hull breach. A rack of universal spacesuits hung next to an airlock on the far side of the room. Beneath the spacesuits was a row of breathing tanks: green for oxygen, pink for methane, and blue for oxygenated water.

The library terminus in a shallow alcove to her right greeted Jade with the rumbles and moans of Quadricorn speech. Her translator belt interpreted. "How may I be of service?"

The library gave her unrestricted maps and schematics of the Quillip ship. For the first time, she saw not just general passenger areas, but every room of the passenger-teleportation sphere at one end of the dumbbell-shaped ship and details of the engine-antimatter-containment complex at the other. She downloaded the maps to an infochip. Admiral Hammer would be pleased.

"May I help you with another topic?" the library asked.

"Can you provide a summary of the Battle of Aniscore?"

"Certainly. An invasion force of 1917 Immortal Ascendency carriers and battlecruisers converged on the planet Aniscore, which was defended by 132 Dasypod destroyers and a dozen major fixed installations. The Immortals outnumbered and outgunned the Entanglement by an estimated ratio of twelve to one. Nevertheless, the Dasypods flew into the heart of the Immortal battle fleet, and the Immortal fleet crumbled and scattered."

"And a summary of the Treaty of Aniscore?" Jade asked.

"The immortals quickly agreed to an immediate ceasefire along their entire border with the Entanglement. They agreed not to expand into territory claimed by the Entanglement and *vice versa*, and they agreed to fair and safe diplomatic protocols."

Jade needed to know *how* the Immortals were defeated so humans could imitate it. "Why did the Immortal fleet crumble if it had a twelve to one advantage?"

"There are several theories on that matter," the library rumbled. "Dasypods claim superior tactics in one-on-one matches won the day. Obnots claim superior Entanglement technology led to the victory. Venmars claim competition between subgroups of Immortals caused them to implode. Merkasaurs claim that the Immortals must have lacked a clear chain of command."

From which Jade deduced the Entanglement had no idea why it won. "I'd like to see the details of the battle, ship by ship."

"That information is not available." So Jade had found the limits of her access after all.

"However," the library continued, "I can download them from Nexus for twenty-three milli-credits. Do you authorize payment?"

Oh. She had found the limits of her *free* access.

"Yes, please obtain the details of the Battle of Ansicore and download them to my infochip," Jade said. Who knew, maybe that information would prove useful on Belle Verte, so she would try to justify the expense that way if anyone asked.

"Request sent. Estimated time to completion of the download is five and a half minutes. May I help you with another topic?"

Jade recalled that Quist seemed to know more about Immortals than she'd been able to find out on Earth. "I'd like to hear your summary description of the Immortals."

The library replied, "The Immortals are the dominant species archetype outside Entanglement space. The reason for this is unknown, but Obnot University suspects the ratio of iron and carbon in the interstellar gasses plays a role in their phylogenesis. The name Immortal comes from their method of reproduction, which is akin to cell fission. The parent Immortal grows too large and divides itself in half, replicating its DNA when it does so. The DNA stores the complete memory of the parent, effectively making the mind of the parent Immortal."

Jade stopped the library. This summary was interesting but seemed to be more relevant to Conrad's xenobiology than her electronics.

"Show me the specifications for the sensors used by Dasypod police ships."

The library obliged, and she got lost in the details, trying to learn enough to be able to build a sensor cluster of her own when she returned to Earth. Eventually, she realized she was running out of time and downloaded the specs for future reference.

One minute left. Enough time for one last thing.

"I'd like to download the specs for Entanglement interplanetary ship engines."

The library rumbled. The translator belt said, "There are three main types of shuttle engines in operation. Which—?"

"Must eat! Must dominate!" The imperative shouted at her from her translator belt, drowning out the library's rumble. The door from the hallway burst open, and the quivering jelly blob of an Ambo filled the doorway.

Too late, her implant squawked, "Emergency alert! Emergency alert! Berserk Ambo in shuttle bay F-13. Evacuate shuttle bay immediately."

The Ambo pushed into the room, and the door snapped shut behind it. Its putrid odor hit Jade, and her stomach wrenched in revulsion

White noise jammed Jade's implant, apparently coming from the football-sized artifact the Ambo laid beside the door. The Ambo extended a long pole upward and covered the lens of the security camera with a black patch.

"It's just you and me, Ambo Slasher," the Ambo said. "You marked yourself as the benchmark *Homo sapiens*. A new species to dominate. A new species for Ambos to eat."

Jade drew her sword with one hand and her long knife with the other. "If you try to touch me with your slimy arms, I'll cut them off."

But Quist said a sword wouldn't stop the main body of an Immortal. He'd mentioned explosives and flamethrowers. The Ambo coalesced into a roughly spherical blob and extruded eight ten-centimeter, curved steel knives—like eagle talons on stubby arms—and began slithering across the room at her. "Ambo Slasher, meet Human Slasher."

She ran toward the left-hand side of the room, trying to outflank the Ambo, but it zigged to stay between her and the door, all the while moving closer to her.

The only other exit was the airlock. If she got in the airlock and kept the door closed long enough to put on a space suit, she could try a spacewalk to another shuttle dock. She'd have to get an oxygen tank. *Green for oxygen, pink for methane— That's it!*

"Must eat! Human smells sweet like blood and spicy like Dasypod. Squeeze out the juice. Chew the flesh. Crush the bones. Dominate humans. Master will be pleased."

Jade ran to the airlock. The Ambo was less than ten meters away when she grabbed a steel tank of methane. The cold metal bruised her fingers as she twisted open the stubborn valve and pointed the hissing stream of gas at the rapidly approaching Ambo. Cradling the tank in one arm, she used her other arm to toss her long steel knife at the rocky dirt floor in front of the Ambo, hoping for a spark.

Nothing happened.

"Human has no place to run." The Ambo was only five meters away. "No place to hide. I'll eat until I split in two. I'll devour your limbs, your heart, your ribs—all of you except your head. Save your head for Master."

Jade yanked a second tank off the rack and side-armed it at the creature.

The Ambo caught the heavy steel tank in one of its appendages without slowing its approach.

Jade's last steel object was her sword. Throw it or keep it? Take a wild gamble or hack off a few Ambo arms to postpone an inevitable death?

She tossed her sword.

The sword hit the tank the Ambo was holding with a loud ting and a shower of sparks. The methane in the air ignited in a roiling ball of blue fire, singeing Jade's hair and knocking her backward against the wall.

The flare subsided quickly, leaving Jade clutching the methane tank in her arm. The gas from the tank formed a long, blue jet of flame.

Jade centered the stream of fire on the Ambo.

The Ambo squealed and stopped, three meters away.

Then the creature said, "Retreat means slow death. Must obey Master," and it lurched forward again. "Food will cure all."

As the Ambo came closer, its outer skin sizzled and popped. The crisp membrane cracked open, and the Ambo's inner fluids oozed out, boiled, and congealed. The amount of punishment it absorbed was unbelievable. A person would have died long ago.

One meter to go. The smoldering horror moved closer.

"Must ... dominate."

Jade rallied, leaning forward to intensify the heat of her makeshift blowtorch on the Ambo, but staying—she hoped—out of its reach.

So close Jade could reach out and touch it without stretching, the Ambo stopped. The stench of its burning flesh turned her stomach, worse even than its fecal odor. Yet she didn't move to fresher air. Not until the methane flame finally sputtered out.

11

Creative Corruption

Bathing always refreshed Umlac. He absorbed deuterium from the heavy water bath until it saturated the protoplasm of his massive black body. The abundance of fuel for his cold fusion organ gave him a giddy feeling of omnipotence.

He caught up on his messages in his private communication hub. His informants reported vast corruption across his empire. This was good. Self-interest and maneuvering for power were signs of a healthy predator society. The important thing was that no vassal had amassed enough power to threaten his dominance.

He took an urgent call from Slitcut, his Hydra spymaster at Goldilocks Three. The rescue team with the two humans was passing through Dismax's ship about now. This call could be about the Belle Verte project.

"Most Worshipful Lord, you asked your humble servant to report anything unusual about the humans on Goldilocks Three. Dismax sent an Ambo to dominate them."

Umlac crushed a boulder in his pinchers. He hadn't expected Dismax to be so stupid as to risk breaking the Treaty of Aniscore before the invasion. He needed the rescue team to get to Farboro where he'd laid his trap for them.

Ripples of fear replaced Umlac's frustration. What if Dismax was also after the power on Belle Verte? "Did Dismax take the rest of the team captive?"

"Most Worshipful Lord, he didn't. And the human dominated the Ambo."

That was news! Humans looked so much like hairless Wolferlops, Umlac had assumed they would be as weak. Now he understood why Dismax wanted Earth as part of his dominion. If Dismax owned a species more powerful than Ambos and could breed them fast enough, he could create an army capable of tipping the balance of power among his cousin vice-regents. A lot of these little bipeds could be packed into a troop transport—and feeding them was likely to be less of a problem than feeding hundreds of Ambos.

"Where are the humans now?"

"Most Worshipful Lord, they are on the Entanglement ship awaiting transport to Dismax's ship."

Umlac was sure Dismax would try again to capture a human while they were in his territory. He needed a new plan. He brought forth the minds of several great warmasters from his library of ingested minds and discussed the options with them. Either he needed to grab a human before Dismax struck again, or he needed to keep Dismax from grabbing one until the rescue team made its way to his ambush. Given the distribution of his assets, the latter had the best chance of success.

He ordered Slitcut to protect the Entanglement team from Dismax on Goldilocks Three and contacted Deathkur, his spymaster on Farboro. "The female human from the Entanglement has dominated an Ambo. She is the benchmark now. Dominate her yourself, and then bring the rest of them to me for interrogation."

"Most Worshipful Lord, consider it done. But I'll have to kill the Dasypod, too. There is no good way to transport a living Dasypod."

"No, I want the Dasypod alive." He was the leader. He might be the only one who knew where Belle Verte was located. "An

EMP at two thousand Hertz will disable him." It was time to use this tidbit of information from his spy at the Entanglement Supreme Council.

"Most Wise Master, you know everything. I'll disable the Obnot and humans by adding halothane to their air and bring them to you."

Umlac was satisfied. Deathkur seemed competent, though of course, Umlac made contingency plans as always.

Umlac's bath had energized his electronic components but left his organic parts hungry. He tingled with excitement at the thought of becoming the first Shoggart to taste human flesh.

12

The Art of War

J ade ran out of the shuttle bay, leaving the rancid, smoldering body of the Ambo behind. She was late. She didn't want to be late.

She ran to the conference room and burst in. It was empty.

She contacted the local network. "Where is the rest of my team?"

"That information is classified."

"But they're *my* team."

"No public relay unit may access classified information."

She checked her messages. Nothing. Ironsides must be trying to embarrass her.

Back in the hallway, there were only two ways to go, and she'd come from one of them. She started jogging down the other. Soon she found her team packed in a room with an assortment of other aliens.

A Quadricorn dominated the right half of the room. Its scarred hide and pocked head bones marked it as a veteran of dangerous mining conditions. But all eyes were on the creature dominating the other half of the room, who looked like a velociraptor with a large dog's head and sharp black eyes. A Merkasaur—one of the powerful Merchant Guild. He wore glittering garlands of platinum, osmium, and palladium disks, an accounting of his wealth for all to see.

Ironsides and another Dasypod sat next to a pool of water. In the water was a mermaid-like creature, which Jade recognized as a xenoerotic Venmar. They used a flexible internal muscular structure to achieve limited shape-shifting ability —sufficient to become attractive and available to many species, including humans. The other half of the Venmar's long body emerged from the pool and morphed into the likeness of a wet, naked merman.

The shoulders of the Venmar's male half broadened to remind Jade of a Hawaiian warrior. The sexy mermaid half of the Venmar had a Hawaiian look, too. Then Jade got it. The Venmar was reading her emotions and those of Conrad. The book said they could do this by sensing small changes in expressions, pheromones or other physical cues, but Jade hadn't realized what this meant in practice. The female half of the Venmar had morphed into an idealization of her, Jade, based on unconscious signals from Conrad.

Before Jade had a chance to recover from that shock, Ironsides twitched the tips of his root-feet toward her and said, "The tardy arrival is Lieutenant Jade Mahelona, a semi-human from Earth."

Jade's instincts screamed at her to dodge the huge reptilian Merkasaur as he came at her with razor-sharp claws extended. His brainsong reverberated dully like a hollow tree trunk—utterly alien, giving her no idea what his intention was.

"May evolution favor you. I'm Kilwee Five, captain of this ship."

Jade shook his hand, carefully, to avoid the sharp points of his claws. "And your descendants forever."

She didn't know if she should be impressed Kilwee Five had taken the time to learn some human customs or if Merkasaurs normally shook hands. Another thing the manual hadn't mentioned was Kilwee Five's distinct pine odor. Maybe the alien instruction manuals weren't as complete as they pretended to be.

The captain pointed a claw at the Venmar and then at the other Dasypod. "The Venmar in the pool is Pannap, Ambassador from the Supreme Council, the Dasypod is Blue Steel, our Chief Security Officer, and the Quadricorn is Tuskandera, the local representative."

Pannap flexed the male half of his body, which was now a bit too beefy for Jade's taste. "I have an update on Ironsides' diplomatic immunity, but pleasure before business. Jade, would you care to join me while we talk? The waters of my pool are warm—a hot tub, you might say." Pannap's female half added, "And you too, Conrad—come and enjoy my waters." She even managed to produce a sultry female voice from the usually bland translator belts.

Jade looked at Pannap's male half again. He was slimmer and smoother. Her heart rate ticked up slightly.

She looked sidewise at Conrad. He was the expert on alien cultures. Let him handle this.

Conrad tensed a little. "Sorry, Pannap, but the human custom is business before pleasure—"

"I accept. Business, then pleasure." Before Conrad could make any further objection, the female half of Pannap continued. "Regarding business: The Immortal Ascendency has granted Ironsides temporary diplomatic status as Ambassador, but they say we must provide the location of Belle Verte for them to fully recognize him as ambassador to it."

Quist turned an antenna to towards Pannap. "Temporary diplomatic immunity can be revoked at any time. Perhaps we should reconsider traveling into the Immortal Ascendency."

"We are arguing that a defect in their databanks isn't our problem," Pannap said. "You should be safe long enough to get to Farboro."

"You are using your resources wisely," Kilwee Five said. "The direct Quillip link through the Immortal ship is faster and cheaper by a factor of eighteen than teleporting through multiple nodes to Nexus and then another multinode transfer from there to Farboro. I have often said the Entanglement should make greater use of this off-network connection."

Jade wasn't sure what her status was in this meeting, but she couldn't keep quiet. "I was attacked by an Ambo a few minutes ago. I don't believe going into Immortal territory will be safe at all."

Blue Steel said, "Yes, we had a report of the incident with Afondrop's fuzzling. It does complicate matters."

"I was referring to the Ambo that attacked me in Shuttle Bay F-13," Jade said.

"Oh," Blue Steel said. "You must have seen the berserk Ambo. The Ambo police should be here soon to take care of it."

Jade felt faint for a moment, recalling the stench, the fire, the sizzling flesh, the squealing Ambo, but her head cleared quickly. "They're too late. I killed it."

"Killed it?" Blue Steel curled and uncurled his root-feet. "Unlikely. Other than bigger Immortals, only a Dasypod has ever killed a berserk Ambo in unarmed combat."

Jade shook her head. "I don't know about that. The important thing is, I don't believe the Ambo was berserk. It kept saying it needed to dominate me to satisfy its master. I think someone sent it, which means they will try again."

Pannap splashed for attention. His male half smiled at her, then turned to address Kilwee Five. "I know it is customary to avoid commenting on a human's odor, but this is pertinent. Jade smells like Ambo slime and burnt Ambo flesh, so I believe she incinerated an Ambo. And by definition, berserk Ambos only want to eat, so a berserk Ambo should not have spoken of domination."

"Thank you, Pannap." Encouraged by Pannap's support, Jade continued, "Another thing has been bothering me, too. The Ambo police were pushing a barrel that supposedly contained a berserk Ambo. How do they normally subdue the berserk Ambo? Do they take it away dead or alive?"

Jade was surprised at how suddenly Blue Steel's root-feet stiffened. "We don't know. The Ambo police block our monitors during the capture, and they take the berserk Ambo out in a sealed barrel."

A tingle of fear crept up Jade's spine. She was going out on a limb, but human military history from Sun Tzu to the Martian assassination campaign backed her. "How do you know the Ambo is in the barrel at all? Isn't it possible the berserk Ambo stayed behind, say as a spy, running around the air ducts and back hallways of this ship?"

The brainsong medley in the room changed dramatically. Kilwee Five's brainsong hummed louder. Tuskandera, Pannap, and Conrad sang more active tunes. Ironsides and Blue Steel seemed to growl.

"Dissonance," Quist said. "You are introducing a radical theory to explain a few simple facts."

Conrad's ubercortex pinged. "No. Jade has identified a common military pattern. But the pattern is incomplete. Are there any other recent unexplained facts or odd events?"

Tuskandera the Quadricorn rumbled, and Jade's translator belt said, "We have had a big increase in missing pets over the last month, especially rock-puppies."

Jade thought of Fluffpaw, and her heart sank.

Kilwee Five brought his face level with Jade's, less than a meter away. She felt his hot breath on her cheeks, and the pine odor intensified. "The Immortal Ascendency has never broken the Treaty of Aniscore. Why would they jeopardize their status as a preferred trading partner with an elaborate ruse to smuggle Ambos onto my ship?"

Jade had played enough simulated war games that the answer seemed obvious. "The Immortals could be using the Treaty of Aniscore to infiltrate spies and agents into the Entanglement. It all fits into a pattern, as Conrad says. Diplomatic immunity would let them install bugs and enlist or intimidate corruptible Entanglement citizens. Fake berserk Ambos could be lurking about as local operatives. Once everything is in position—" A sharp crack rang out as she slapped her hands together. "—a surprise attack."

Blue Steel's root-feet writhed as if grappling with some unseen foe. "That's barbaric. The *Dasypodia* says 'Civilized beings are separated from ground creepers by following the laws of society rather than the laws of nature.' Where do you get such uncivilized ideas? Are humans no better than ground creepers?"

Jade put her hands on her hips and faced Blue Steel. "The question you need to ask is, are *Immortals* no better than ground creepers? The question you need ask is, have there been any other unusual trends or events recently? Accidents? Deaths? Odd happenings?"

Tuskandera said, "The police have had a lot of accidents."

Blue Steel's root-feet twisted themselves into knots. "Sadly, she is correct. In the last year, our police force had four injuries and one death. In the five preceding years, we had only one injury and no deaths, total. The morale of the police is very low right now."

Jade nodded. "The ancient general Sun Tzu says, *if your opponent is of high morale, depress him.*"

"Your ancient writings—are they all about war?" Pannap's hips swayed from side to side. *When had he developed hips?*

"No, I just favor those because I'm a soldier. So let's pursue how a soldier thinks a bit further. What if several Ambos appeared to go berserk at the same time? Would the Immortals send over several police shuttles all at once? Would that be enough to start an invasion?"

Kilwee Five curled and uncurled his tail with a thump. "It wouldn't work. Ten shuttles of Ambos wouldn't be a match for our fine Police Guild contingent.

Blue Steel's root-feet straightened at praise from the captain.

But Jade shook her head. "What if they didn't send Ambos in those shuttles. What are the biggest, baddest Immortals they could send?"

Blue Steel's root-feet twisted together again. "Hydras! I quiver to think of even one shuttle full of Hydras aboard our ship."

Jade mused. "And the Ambos running around the air ducts. What if they disable your communication or power systems during the attack?"

Kilwee Five aimed the tip of his tail at Blue Steel. "Chief Security Officer, are we prepared for a scenario like the one painted by this human?"

Blue Steel's root-feet stiffened a little. "Certainly not! My budget barely allows proper policing of a full-sized Quillip ship. It does not include fending off an invasion by Immortals."

Kilwee Five pointed his tail at Jade. "How would *you* prepare for such an invasion?"

Jade was sweating profusely. Stellar defense strategies were fun as a game, but this was real. "For starters, I'd try to catch one of the so-called berserk Ambos. See if you can extract the target date or attack signal from it. Ideally, you'd catch all the Ambos. When the Immortals attack, the Ambos won't provide the support they expect. Ambush their shuttles. Counterattack immediately."

Kilwee Five turned his big eyes to stare at Jade. "Counterattack sounds expensive. And what would be the point?"

Jade's jaw dropped a little at his naiveté. "Just because you've repulsed their first attack doesn't mean they'll stop. You need to take away their ability to launch future attacks."

Kilwee Five fidgeted with a palladium necklace and pointed his tail at Blue Steel. "What would a counterattack cost?"

Blue Steel's root-feet vibrated. "It would take a ten-fold increase in Police Guild forces. We'd need three Obnots to manage the fabrication of weapons, sixty Wolferlop-P from the Pilot Guild, thirty Dekapus from the Maintenance Guild, and another fifty miscellaneous support guilds. Altogether, I'd estimate a hundredfold increase in budget and a hundred days to prepare."

The captain released his necklace. "Corporate Headquarters would never authorize such a large budget increase."

Pannap splashed for attention. "Don't let this human rush us into war with the Immortals. The Treaty of Ansicore has been the law for hundreds of years, and it is unlikely that this will change in the next few days. You should increase funding to the Diplomatic Guild's efforts to improved verification methods, so that conspiracy theories such as this one can no longer find ground to grow in."

Jade opened her mouth to speak, but Ironsides interrupted. "Jade, be quiet. You've already contributed more than enough to the discussion. Let superior species attend to business. The Dasypodia contains fifty thousand years of experience—from long before Sun Tzu was born. It says *Diplomacy is preferred to military action.*"

"And much more cost-effective," Kilwee Five said. "Pannap, would you consult with your guild? I will support a five-percent budget increase for negotiating a more vigorous verification program."

Tuskandera looked at Jade, then at Kilwee Five. Jade thought she was about to weigh in with her concerns. After all, this was her home planet. But Quadricorns were by far the junior Entanglement species present. Tuskandera said nothing—another reminder of how little Jade wanted to encourage the assimilation of humanity into the Entanglement.

13

Immortal Slime

J ade waited at the back of the shuttle dock, as far away from Ironsides as the room allowed. Going into Immortal Ascendency territory scared her more than the prospect of annihilation by the Quillip engine had. If Ambos were at the bottom, what was at the top? If she met the Ambo she'd rescued the fuzzling from, would it attack her? She'd tried to take along a tank of methane, but Ironsides had insisted on nothing threatening. The sword and knives she carried didn't seem to count.

"Lieutenant Mahelona, you are rearguard until further notice." Ironsides' laser-eyes gazed at her from across the room. "Conrad, line up."

By the time Jade entered the shuttle, Quist had already attached his exoskeleton to cargo anchors in the floor of the bare metal shuttle. Ironsides and Conrad were buckling into bolted-down acceleration seats. One seat remained for her, next to the door.

The pilot, a Wolferlop-P with a black mane down her neck and an otherwise gray pelt, greeted them and sat in front where she had a good view out of a large window.

Recalling how the Wolferlop-M had enjoyed sharing stories, Jade leaned forward and said, "May evolution favor you. How long have you been piloting?"

"And your descendants forever. I have always piloted—as copilot for an adult from my first memories, and as an adult shuttle pilot for nine years. I qualified to pilot Quillip class ships five years ago."

"Wow. How does handling a shuttle compare to the big ships?"

"Flying big ships is automated and slow," the pilot said. "Small ships can be flown in manual mode and feel like an extension of my body, or rather my body as it should be."

"Do you have storytellings like Wolferlops?"

"Of course. Home nest storytelling is the highlight of every Wolferlop's week. Home nests are very close, and while the individual members come and go with birth and death, the nests are often thousands of years old."

Jade leaned forward with interest. "Where is your home nest? How big is it?"

"My home nest is on Goldilocks Three, and it has sixty-two members. Our main function is to provide pilot services to the planet, and we share many stories about local passengers and places, which greatly aids our efficiency as pilots. My home nest is part of the Frontier Clan which specializes in serving frontier planets like Earth and Goldilocks Three. Sadly, we are in a risky sub-niche. My cousins on Xandor have been cut off from the rest of the clan. I will miss their stories at the annual regional gatherings."

Jade frowned. "Surely communications will be restored soon. When is the next regional gathering?"

The ocean waves in the pilot's brainsong rushed in faster. "No, it's more than a simple communications problem. Multiple comm channels went down at the same time, as well as Quillip teleportation to Xandor. Only something massive and sudden, like a breach in the main antimatter containment chamber, could cause this."

Curious, Jade asked, "Has this ever happened before?"

"Omuz was cut off three years ago. Without faster-than-light communications, we won't know why for another three years."

The Wolferlop glanced back at Jade. "Tell me your story. My home nest knows very little about human home groups."

Jade tried to mimic the pilot's storytelling. "Home groups called families are very important to humans. We also have larger groups like your clans, which might be called ethnicities or cultures. My family is very small, just my uncle and me, with my grandmother sometimes. My family is part of the Hawaiian ethnicity, which has many unique stories and rituals."

"How often does your ethnicity meet?" the driver asked.

"There are too many Hawaiians to meet all at once. However, Earth has set aside preservations for many ethnicities. I usually vacation at the Hawaiian Preservation two or three weeks a year."

"This is so strange! You designed these preservations without the help of a Wolferlop-A? You tell amazing stories."

Jade laughed. "You can find better stories on the entertainment channels."

"No! Lies are not good stories," the pilot replied. "Only personal stories are of interest to the home nest. Only true stories."

"Well then," Jade said, "Wolferlops are my kind of people."

A rocky asteroid began to fill the cockpit window, and the pilot became too busy to talk. The Immortal's Quillip node was inside a hollowed-out space rock. As far as Jade could tell, all Immortal spaceships, big and small, were hollowed-out rocks.

The Immortal ship grew larger and larger. "Shouldn't we slow down?" Jade asked. "We're going too fast."

"Brace for impact," the pilot announced, flipping the ship around to hit tail first.

Jade felt a slight deceleration. Not nearly enough to slow for a smooth landing. "Slow down! We're going to crash."

The pilot ignored her and guided the shuttle to a smooth circular area on the surface of the asteroid ship. When it hit, the shuttle decelerated so rapidly it was painful, but the shuttle survived intact. The stars Jade had been watching through the cockpit window disappeared, replaced by a uniform red brick color.

"Wh-what was that?" Jade asked.

The shuttle landed gracefully on a lip of rock. The pilot idled the engines and said, "To answer your question. We penetrated a bubble airseal—a membrane that blocks air but passes heavy objects with sufficient momentum. The trick to piloting through a bubble airseal is to hit them with enough velocity to pass through, but not so much that you have difficulty stopping in time on the other side."

The pilot opened the shuttle's inner airlock doors and gestured toward them. "It has been a pleasure sharing stories with you, but please hurry. I don't want to be in this place any longer than I have to."

The air in the Immortal ship was supposed to be breathable, but the pilot insisted that all of Jade's team enter the airlock and close the inner door behind them before opening the outer door. The reason quickly became apparent. Jade gagged on the overpowering stench, something like rotten oranges mixed with the fecal smell of Ambos.

The coarse rock wall in front of her glistened with slime in the dim light of tomato-red globes that dotted the walls. Jade scooped some of the green speckled slime at her feet into a cup for a closer look. It squirmed, alive with nasty little creatures armed with stingers and pinchers.

She was glad she'd ordered bulletproof combat fatigues for her and Conrad and hoped it would be enough. She pulled gloves and facemasks for them from her backpack.

Conrad grabbed her arm to keep from falling. "These floors are nearly impossible to walk on. Observe the irregular ribs. The Immortals probably use those for traction under the slippery lubricant."

When Conrad didn't let go of her arm, Jade pulled out collapsible walking sticks with pointed ends for Conrad and herself.

"Come to me." A deep, loud voice boomed across the cavernous shuttle bay.

A gray pebble-skinned Immortal the size of a six-passenger car stood in front of one of the tunnels into the bay. It looked like an elephant with six trunks and no legs.

When nobody moved, it repeated, "Entanglement Weaklings, come to me."

Jade fought down an impulse to draw her useless *wakizashi*. "That has to be a Hydra. I expected nine heads."

Conrad's brainsong trumpeted with pride. "I came up with names for a lot of things in the Entanglement as part of building Earth's interface to the universal translator. Hydra is short for hydraulic, because of the organic hydraulic tubules permeating their bodies. These brutes can crush a boulder with their bare hands, so to speak."

The Hydra came closer. Jade could sense dark veins in the electric field running throughout the creature, presumably the hydraulics. Signals from its central nucleus were reminiscent of an Ambo but larger and louder. Bright yellow nerve channels distributed signals throughout the body.

"There's nothing amazing about crushing a rock," the Hydra said from a translator belt it wore around its head like a crown. "The amazing thing is that weaklings like you survive at all."

To prove its point, the Hydra picked up a rock the size of Jade and ground it into gravel.

"Call me Shardrock. I will see you safely through this ship. Stay close to me."

The Hydra edged toward Jade. "Ah, Ambo slayer. I have something for you." It extended a pseudopod tipped with a cone-shaped device pointed at her.

Jade drew her sword, ready to cut off the pseudopod.

Shardrock continued, "As a token of my good intentions, I give you this Ambo stunner. Use it the next time an Ambo bothers you. I don't want to lose any of my Ambo slaves to you."

"This is nonsense," Ironsides said. "I've never heard of an Ambo stunner."

"The Entanglement is ignorant of many things," Shardrock replied. "Allow me to demonstrate."

Shardrock whistled, and one of the Ambos in the distance hurried forward. "Most Powerful Master, what is your command."

"Stop there. Catch."

Shardrock tossed a skull-sized rock to the Ambo, who caught it easily.

"Shoot it, Ambo Slayer."

Jade was incredulous. Surely, this was a trick. Maybe to get her to hurt an Ambo so he could arrest her.

"I said, shoot it," the Hydra repeated.

"Ironsides, what should I do?" Jade asked. He was in command. Let him decide.

Ironsides curled and uncurled his root-feet. "I'm no Venmar or Merkasaur, who divines alien intentions. I follow orders and try to live by the Dasypodia, which says, *When planting yourself in a strange field, listen to those already planted there.* Jade, do as our host requests."

The stun gun had an awkward grip and was improperly balanced—too heavy in the front. Jade didn't trust Shardrock, but if he wanted to do her harm, he would have many other chances. There wasn't much percentage in denying this one.

"Conrad," she said, "I promised to return my satchel to Solar Defense Force. If something goes wrong, and you survive, and I don't, would you please return it for me?"

She pulled the trigger. A deep, resonant sound echoed off the walls of the shuttle bay. The vibration in her hands was so strong that coordinated movements were impossible. Shardrock tossed the Ambo another rock, which bounced off and clattered to the floor. The Ambo was frozen in place.

She released the trigger. She and her team recovered quickly, but the Ambo stayed in place as Shardrock bounced another rock off it.

Jade snapped a carabineer through the trigger guard and attached the stun gun to a belt loop. "This stunner is a keeper. Ready when you are."

"Efficient," Quist said. "And not a weapon regulated by the Treaty of Ansicore."

Shardrock made a growling sound which did not translate, then said, "Follow me," and disappeared into a tunnel.

Jade and the rest of the team followed. Just before the shuttle bay disappeared behind Jade, the Ambo shook itself and moved out of sight.

"About a minute," Jade said to Conrad.

"What?" Conrad shook his head and pointed. "Look at the wall lining. It's an enormously complicated ecosystem."

"The effect from the stun gun lasts about a minute," Jade said. "And don't mess with the wall. Those creatures might be venomous."

"Oh, right." Conrad backed off a little but kept poking at the wall with a walking stick.

The ecology around them changed as they moved through the ship. The goo on the floor and walls sprouted spindly tendrils, which clung to Jade's boots and made it feel like she was slogging through tall, wet grass. Rat-like giant slugs chased smaller vermin through the tendrils.

In another place, a hoard of clicking creatures covered the walls, beetle-like in their shells. On one side of the horde, tendrils reached from the beetles into the goo; nothing but bare rock walls graced the other. The creatures must be eating their way down the hallway, locust-like.

After walking for nearly an hour, they arrived at the Quillip antechamber, which for all the world reminded Jade of a swamp. Slime ten to twenty centimeters thick clung to the walls. Clumps of roots were scattered about like mini mangrove trees. The dominant shape of the swamp creatures was long and thin—little worms and larger snakes. Four Ambos scurried about, slurping up such worms as they could catch.

Shardrock waved Jade's team to a red-brown puddle. "The Quillip chamber is on the other side. I'll start the countdown. The platform will launch in five minutes."

"A bubble airseal," Jade said to no one in particular. "How do we get through it?"

"Seal your suits," Ironsides said, "and follow me."

He inflated a plastic bubble around himself, then grabbed onto a pipe in the wall and heaved himself through the membrane.

Quist followed without a bubble.

Jade and Conrad put on space helmets and air tanks. They had about twenty minutes of air, plenty for getting through the Quillip chamber vacuum.

Conrad jumped onto the airseal and bounced off. He tried again with a running start, and still he bounced off. Four minutes are gone, less than one to go. Jade swung Conrad around like a whip, and he made it through.

Jade grabbed the pipe Ironsides had used and flipped herself around into the airseal. As she did so, she caught a final glimpse of the Hydra. An Ambo approached, and the Hydra's translator belt said, "Slitcut! Most Cunning Master. Have you heard? Shardrock's body was discovered—"

The airseal gripped Jade then released her into the Quillip chamber, where a net caught her. She crawled toward the platform where the rest of the team waited for her crammed into a disk-shaped capsule nearly identical to the one she'd used in the Entanglement Quillip.

"Hurry, fifteen seconds or you get left behind," Conrad shouted through the suit radios.

She paddled herself along the net, taking advantage of the zero gravity, but one miscalculation and she would go flying into the far darkness of the Quillip chamber.

"Five seconds."

She squeezed in next to Conrad. The capsule catapulted into the darkness, and Jade reached out to pull the door closed behind her.

As soon as Jade caught her breath, she said, "Ironsides, there's something wrong. The Hydra who escorted us wasn't the real Shardrock."

"He was nice enough for a Hydra," Ironsides replied. "And he did bring us to the Quillip chamber safely."

"But why?" Jade said. "Why would a Hydra replace our intended guide, only to bring us safely to the Quillip? What would the original guide have done differently?"

"Shardrock—or whoever—did his job," Ironsides said. "That's all there is to it. Everything is not a conspiracy."

Jade wiggled her backpack and sword into a more comfortable position. The Immortals didn't count every gram the way the Entanglement did, preferring instead to overengineer everything. She shifted the stun gun away from where it was poking her in the ribs.

"The Ambo Stunner!" she said. "Maybe the purpose of the fake Shardrock was to give us this stunner. Maybe it's booby-trapped."

"Give the gun to Quist," Ironsides said, "Let the Science and Engineering Guild do a full analysis of it."

Jade handed Quist the weapon. Quist fiddled with it and handed the gun back to Jade. "A locator beacon is built into the core modulator unit. It will broadcast our location in 19.2 hours and every 22.1 hours after that."

"Then we'll have to ditch it," Jade said. Too bad. The stunner took effect much more quickly than a flamethrower and was smaller to boot.

"Ten seconds to teleport," Quist announced. "Shield your eyes."

The thrumming of the matter accelerator sounded just like the one on the Quillip station at Earth. That was comforting, at least. She closed her eyes and waited.

A brief flash visible through her eyelids signaled their teleport. Five hundred light-years.

Soon they leaped out of the Quillip chamber through another airseal bubble, and another Hydra greeted them. "Welcome to the *Granite Pincer,* the Immortal mothership at Farboro. I'm Guardmaster Hoargrim. Follow me."

The team followed Hoargrim through another sewer-pipe maze of passages, with Jade bringing up the rear. Their weight increased slowly, as they moved from the center to the hull of the spinning ship. Eventually, they arrived at the docks, where Jade and Conrad rejoiced at the sight of an Entanglement shuttle awaiting them. Ironsides reminded them that he had been right all along about the Immortals honoring the treaty of Aniscore.

The seating arrangement on the shuttle was the same as before, with Conrad and Ironsides in acceleration seats behind Jade, Quist to her right, the airlock to her left, and the pilot in front.

The pilot accelerated through the giant shuttle bay airseal into the blackness of open space. "We are safely away from *Granite Pincer,*" she said. "Our flight plan is to accelerate for fifteen minutes and then flip over to decelerate to the Entanglement ship, the *Cl'aclen* as the locals call it."

Jade had enjoyed her talk with the pilot at Goldilocks Three, so she addressed the new pilot. "May evolution favor you. How long have you been piloting?"

"And your descendants forever. I must concentrate on piloting, not talking."

That was an odd thing for a Wolferlop-P to say. The muscular tension of this pilot was higher, as shown by the rate of nerve impulses and infrared heat generation. The electric song broadcast by her brain was more staccato and intermittent. Something was wrong, and the pilot wasn't saying what.

14

Trial by Fire

Guardmaster Hoargrim finished escorting the Entanglement weaklings to their shuttle. They would never have made it on their own; he could sense Ambos lurking in the side tunnels, attracted by the smell of food from the Entanglement. But the Ambos had smelled him, too, and remained hidden.

Shipmaster Karnag had ordered Hoargrim to deliver the weaklings safely to the shuttle, Hoargrim had done so. The Shipmaster specified a safe delivery, not a quick one. Hoargrim had a bit of fun leading the weaklings on a roundabout path through back tunnels to make their passage more difficult.

This path took him past another shuttle dock, where he noticed a shuttle was missing.

Hoargrim returned there to ask the dockmaster about the missing shuttle. It was a guardmaster's duty to make sure all of his master's property was safe. He found only an Ambo guarding the docks.

"Where is the dockmaster?" Hoargrim demanded. "And where is the shuttle belonging in Granite 7 dock?"

"Most Powerful Hoargrim, I cannot say."

"Can't, or won't?" Hoargrim replied as he pushed two unyielding pseudopods into the soft flesh of the Ambo.

The Ambo squeaked for mercy. "My master bribed the dockmaster to leave and took the shuttle. He said he would return in twenty minutes."

"Where is your master going?" Hoargrim demanded.

"I don't know. Master did not say. Please let me go."

Hoargrim held onto the Ambo while he thought. Where could a shuttle make a round trip to in such a short time? Another dock on the same ship didn't make sense. Something else nearby, then. His feeding organs tensed. The only target nearby was the Entanglement shuttle. He'd escorted the Entanglement weaklings safely through the *Granite Pincer* only to have another Hydra ambush them. He would recover the weaklings. Or their remains.

"Who is your master?" Hoargrim demanded as he tightened his grip further.

"Deathkur," the Ambo squeaked.

Deathkur was a new Hydra from the planet Morb. He must be acting as an agent of some foreign Lord, probably Umlac.

Hoargrim released the Ambo. "Go to your quarters. If Deathkur doesn't return in a reasonable time, come to me."

The Ambo understood. Hoargrim would wait here and confront Deathkur when he returned. Likely, a duel would ensue. Likely Hoargrim would become the Ambo's new master.

* * *

Jade watched the little star of the Entanglement ship *Cl'aclen* grow brighter in the shuttle pilot's window. It was an incredible relief to return safely from their journey through two Immortal ships.

She tried to rationalize the standoffish behavior of the Wolferlop-P who piloted their shuttle—after all, she and Conrad were both human, and yet they were different from each other. The pilot rested both hands on the arms of her chair.

The shuttle must be on autopilot—another difference between this pilot and the first one, who had delighted in manual control of the small craft.

Jade yawned. The monotonous hum of the shuttle was a lullaby. It was hard to concentrate on anything, hard to stay awake. The electrical chatter from Conrad showed he was napping. She was safe in an Entanglement shuttle. A little catnap would be all right.

Something subtle in the electric field outside the shuttle changed: a faint pink glow to the rear. Did it matter? Her body just wanted to sleep, to be let alone.

This was wrong. She was on duty. She needed to stay awake and alert. But it was so hard. On a hunch, she held her breath and fumbled open her satchel with fingers that were growing numb. Dizziness set in. Her peripheral vision faded. She fought to stay conscious. At last, she inserted two nostril filters just as a blinding pulse of electromagnetic energy slapped her, causing her to inhale sharply.

The slap of electricity helped her wake up, as did the influx of clean air. Another pulse hit her, and another.

Conrad slept. Quist's brainsong was a monotone. The sleeping gas must have affected him too. Ironsides' root-feet convulsed with every EMP as the electrical pulses induced currents in his superconducting nerve fibers. His root-feet tangled like a pit of snakes.

Muffled bumps in the airlock. Someone was boarding.

Jade scrambled out of her seat belt, drew her sword, and faced the airlock.

The airlock's double doors began to crank open, revealing the pebbly gray surface of a Hydra.

Her sword would be useless. She started toward the control panel beside the airlock. She needed to keep the Hydra out. She needed to hit the emergency-close button.

She sensed motion in the cockpit. The pilot stood, and Jade felt a brief sense of relief. She wasn't alone against the Hydra.

"You are supposed to be asleep." The pilot hissed at her.

"That's a Hydra. We can't let it in here," Jade said.

"No. I must let it in, or they will kill my nest mate. They promised no harm to any of you."

Jade felt a pang of sympathy for the pilot. What would she do if they had her grandmother? "I'm sorry, but I don't trust the Immortals. I must protect my own." Jade started toward the control panel by the airlock again.

Meanwhile, the Hydra had inserted an elephant-trunk pseudopod through the widening crack in the airlock doors. An eye at the end of the pseudopod oriented toward Jade.

Jade's translator belt vibrated with a deep bass. "Ambo Slayer, I am Deathkur, the one who will establish Hydra domination over humans. It is good you are not asleep. I will not have to wait for your death and dismemberment."

Jade drew her sword and swung hard at the grey trunk wagging its way toward her. The sword lodged in the pseudopod with a thunk like chopping wood. The Hydra twisted the sword out of Jade's hand, flinging the sword to the back of the shuttle and knocking Jade to the floor.

A blue laser beam sliced through the air above Jade.

"Liars. Always liars," The pilot shouted.

The Hydra's pseudopod sizzled and withdrew part way. Jade prepared for a lunge at the emergency-close button, but a whoosh of flames filled the air above her, and she flattened herself back onto the floor.

The flames paused, and the blackened body of the pilot crumpled to the floor. The Hydra bellowed. "Weaklings can't take a little heat. As for you, Ambo Slayer, you die when I get the rest of the way through these doors."

As the Hydra ranted, Jade sprang to the airlock controls and hit the emergency close. She bounced toward the pilot's acceleration chair, the only thing in the cabin with a chance of offering any protection from the flamethrower.

The body of the dead pilot got in the way, sending Jade sprawling back to the floor. She landed near the laser pistol and took an extra fraction of a second to pick it up as she rolled behind the pilot's chair.

Another wave of flames washed over the cockpit, singeing the heel of Jade's boot, but sparing her for now in the lee of the acceleration couch.

The titanium alloy airlock doors reversed direction and pinched into the Hydra's pseudopod. The pseudopod bulged and stiffened, and the airlock doors grumbled to a halt. The pseudopod grew fatter. The titanium doors groaned and then began opening wider.

Jade fired the pilot's laser at the pseudopod. A black crater formed on the surface and spread as Jade skillfully kept the laser on the moving target.

Then the Hydra's wound filled with fluid. The liquid boiled and steamed, but the crater stopped growing. Jade tried moving the laser over a few centimeters, but laser-resistant fluid dripped from the entire length of the Hydra's arm. "Lasers are ineffective," Quist had warned.

The snout of the alien flamethrower belched another wave of orange flame into the cockpit. The hot air was suffocating. Sweat soaked Jade's clothes and made her hands slippery. She searched for a way to create a blowtorch or explosion, but the Hydra had the only flammable material in sight. That gave her an idea.

The flames paused again. "You are lucky, little human. I am on a tight schedule. You will die quickly."

Jade popped up over the back of the acceleration chair and fired the laser pistol into the nozzle of the flamethrower. Now it was a split-second race to see if the laser could penetrate the tanks of fuel and oxidizer before the next burst of flames erupted at her.

The airlock doors groaned louder, and the gap between them widened. Soon Deathkur would be inside the shuttle.

The shock wave hit Jade with a roar, slamming her backward into the cockpit window. Then there were no more flames. In the silence, she heard the satisfying crunch of the airlock doors grinding shut over charred debris.

She slid down the cockpit window to the top of the pilot's console. The explosion had tossed the broken and blackened body of the pilot beside Jade. The pilot had died a heroine. Jade must find the pilot's home nest and tell her story—after telling the local Police Guild, while they might still have a chance to get the Wolferlop-P's nest mate back from the kidnappers.

The EMPs stopped. The shuttle jerked, and darkness returned to the electric field outside as the attacking spacecraft departed.

Ironsides' root-feet relaxed and fell to the floor. Soon they wiggled a little, then more, as if Ironsides were testing them. He straightened his root-feet and oriented his line of laser-eyes at Jade. "What have you done?"

Jade summarized the fight with the Hydra.

Ironsides' laser-eyes hummed with power. "It's very disturbing that the Immortals know the effect of EMPs on Dasypods. You are ordered to keep this secret. The fewer who know this Dasypod weakness, the better."

Interesting. What could she do with this fact? Ironsides had paused. He seemed to be expecting a response. "Acknowledged, sir."

Next Ironsides pointed several root-feet at the Wolferlop-P body in the cockpit. "You shouldn't have let them kill the pilot. Proper police procedure is to protect civilians, not the other way around."

"Yes, sir. But I didn't know she had a gun, and I had to get to the emergency-close switch."

Ironsides' root-feet twisted into bunches. "You're missing the other problem. We need a pilot. If we miss our teleport window, it could take days to reschedule."

Soot covered Quist's exoskeleton, but Jade could hear the rhythmic march of his brain returning to normal. "*Dissonance*," he said. "Our environment has degraded."

Ironsides turned toward the Obnot. "Status report, Quist."

"I've got an awful headache," Quist replied, "Induced by inhaling excessive burnt organic compounds."

"The status of the shuttle, Quist. The status of our trajectory."

A rainbow of radar signals blossomed out from Quist, tickling Jade's electrosense and lighting up the little shuttle with brightness and clarity.

The signals faded, and Quist said, "The pilot is dead. The padding on the back of the pilot's chair has been fully oxidized, leaving only carbon and trace elements. The seal of the inner airlock doors is broken. Otherwise, the shuttle is sooty but undamaged. The shuttle should have initiated deceleration 2.1 minutes ago. Our fuel will run out in 8.3 hours, and we will enter an elliptical solar orbit similar to Comet FB02278."

Jade couldn't believe Quist would bother to extrapolate until they ran out of fuel. "What about corrective action? We should flip the shuttle now and decelerate at a slightly higher rate to arrive on time."

"Are you deaf? We have no pilot." Ironsides twisted his root-feet together and pointed them at Jade. "You let the Hydra kill her."

"There are new facts," Quist said. "Traffic Control will have another Wolferlop-P available in 1.2 hours. The replacement pilot will arrive in 3.1 hours, and we will arrive at the *Cl'aclen* in 6.4 hours."

"Unacceptable!" Ironsides vibrated his root-feet. "We'll miss our teleport window. Our mission will be delayed, and the Merkasaurs will be furious at the extra cost."

Jade sensed Conrad's brainsong returning to normal, although he hadn't said anything yet. "Quick question for a professor of xenology. Is the VR game Alien Craft Pilot a good simulation of flying a real Entanglement shuttle?"

Instead of leaping at the chance to show off, as Jade had expected, Conrad snapped back. "I don't play virtual reality games."

Jade sniffed at him. "The panel looks the same to me. Anyway, the autopilot can do all the work."

"But you aren't in the Pilot Guild," Ironsides objected.

"I am authorized to pilot for our team," Jade said.

Ironsides curled his root-feet. "You are authorized to pilot at Belle Verte, but not here, in civilized space."

"This is an emergency. Or a trial run. Whatever works. Let the Arifaxian lawyers sort out the details later."

Ironsides said nothing for several seconds. The electric field around his mind alternated between a jingle-bell sound and a foghorn sound. Finally, the jingle bells dominated. "The Dasypodia says 'Saplings at play may exceed the bounds of propriety to learn what those bounds are.' Lieutenant Mahelona, you may try to pilot us to the *Cl'aclen*."

Jade slipped into the pilot's seat and activated the autopilot. "Set course to dock with the Entanglement ship *Cl'aclen*. Minimal time, with acceleration not to exceed two gravities."

After a few seconds, the autopilot responded. "Calculation complete. Enter access code to initiate firing sequence."

Jade frowned. "This is an emergency. I don't have a code."

"An emergency access code may be obtained from Traffic Control," the autopilot responded.

Jade cursed. "Ironsides, can you try to get an emergency access code for us?"

"I already did," Ironsides replied.

"Excellent!" Jade said. "I should have known you'd know the ropes. What's the code?"

Ironsides' brainsong returned to a foghorn, and he shook his root-feet at Jade. "I tried, but I told you this would happen. Traffic Control denied our request. They said we aren't in danger, so it isn't an emergency. We have to wait for the Pilot Guild."

Jade was fast losing respect for the Entanglement Guild System. Maybe the system worked on large ships with a big crew, but it made things impossible for small groups.

She frowned at the useless controls. Or were they? The other pilot had used manual mode.

"Autopilot, disengage," Jade ordered.
"Enter access code for manual control."

15

Darzak

Jade should have known. Of course, turning the autopilot off required access. Everything required access.

Then she gave a wry grin. The autopilot was a module under the right-hand panel. Its glowing violet data wires connected to the base of the steering column. She cut the wires.

The manual controls worked as she'd expected, although they were more sensitive than she liked. She damped the main thruster, activated the auxiliary jets to execute a clumsy turnover, and powered up the main thruster at one and a half gravities. She'd fine-tune the thrust and trajectory as she went along.

She started working out the optimal deceleration trajectory with the help of a calculator, when Ironsides said, "Quist, what's the optimal trajectory to match our shuttle orbit with the Quillip ship?"

Quist told them, and Jade made the adjustment, feeling sheepish. She should have thought of asking Quist. After all, he was the Science and Engineering Guild.

Eventually, she relaxed, sat back, and watched the stars in the black velvet sky. If only her father could see her now, flying an alien shuttle hundreds of light-years from Earth. Surely he'd be proud. If only Keolo could see her. He'd be so jealous.

The Quillip station expanded from a bright point of light into a dumbbell shape, then a row of docking stations along the bar in the middle, then a single dock.

Jade docked with a slight jar. Ironsides praised Quist for his precise trajectory calculations and criticized Jade for hitting the *Cl'aclen* harder than a Guild pilot would.

* * *

The walls of *Cl'aclen* station pulsated with a kaleidoscope of jagged green, orange, gold, and silver shapes. The patterns wove, merged, and split in syncopated rhythms. Presumably, this display made the natives of Farboro feel at home, but it disoriented Jade. She closed her eyes for a few moments to block the visual overstimulation.

Conrad, on the other hand, looked around wide-eyed. "Marvelous. A glimpse into the mind-patterns of intelligent insects. Repetitions on a theme, like a classical symphony. Yet more complex. Half a dozen themes seem to be playing at once."

"Insects?" Jade echoed. "Farboro belongs to intelligent insects?"

"Of course," Conrad replied. "Although properly speaking, the insects aren't intelligent. Collectively though, their hives are."

"Why haven't I heard of this before?" Jade asked.

"Well, it's hardly a secret," Conrad said, "but the insects of Farboro don't play a big role in popular Earth culture like the Merkasaurs, Obnots, and Dasypods. And, like the nanomechanical Dasypods, the intelligent insect hives of Tsungel on Farboro are unique—a one-off of nature."

The team split up to shower off the stink of Immortal slime and burnt flesh and get a fresh change of clothes before presenting themselves to the *Cl'aclen's* captain. Eventually, Ironsides led them to the captain's outer office. "I'm Ambassador

Ironsides *en route* to my new post. I have come to pay my respects to the captain."

The ferret-like Arafaxian aide sniffed the air, his nose twitching wildly. "You come from the Immortal Ascendency, I presume?"

"We come from Goldilocks Three, by way of the Immortal Ascendency. Perhaps your captain will find our story interesting."

The aide turned to the side and murmured into a wall comm. After a brief conversation, he turned back to Ironsides. "No."

"No, what?"

"No, the Venerable Captain Belcramstole will not find your story interesting. Since you are from Goldilocks Three, he suggests you join the ambassador in the Quillip antechamber. Helping tourists would be more useful than spreading ridiculous conspiracy theories."

"The *Venerable* Captain? Belcramstole is a Bossello?"

"You didn't do your homework, Mr. Ambassador, or you wouldn't ask."

Ironsides led the team out into the hallway and shook his root-feet at the captain's rooms. "We are done here. Bossellos seldom change their minds. They believe doing so is a sign of incompetence. We need to see the Ambassador from the Supreme Council anyway to get instructions for the next leg of our trip."

At the Quillip antechamber, the zero gravity made the visual effect of the psychedelic swirls even more disorienting. Jade closed her eyes again and focused on her electrosense. Three Dekapus workers clustered about a Wolferlop-A on the far side of the chamber. A lone Dasypod operated a control panel on the ceiling. A cluster of spheres anchored to the left wall were all empty, except for one. Backlit by the electric pulses from the Quillip engine, it looked like a giant egg with an embryo inside.

Ironsides went to talk to the other Dasypod about the

Wolferlop-P's kidnapped nest mate, and Jade went to the cargo sphere in search of the ambassador. Quist followed Ironsides, and Conrad followed Jade.

Jade knocked on the sphere. "We're looking for the Ambassador from the Supreme Council. Are you in there, Your Excellency?"

The sphere opened a crack. "May evolution favor you. I'm Ambassador Darzak."

"And your descendants forever. I'm Lieutenant Jade Mahelona, and this is Professor Conrad Singleton. We just arrived from Goldilocks Three with Ambassador Ironsides."

"Have you come to apologize?"

"Uhh. Maybe. What kind of apology do you want?"

"My career is over, after only one day of my first assignment. You did it. You could at least express remorse. Don't humans experience remorse? You scored a halfway decent empathy rating."

"I often have cause for remorse, but you and I just met. What are you talking about?"

"Your stupid Ambo conspiracy report. The Venerable Captain Belcramstole banished me from the bridge for bothering him with it."

"Ahh. The captain banished us from the bridge too. I'm sorry you got caught up in this. But since you brought the subject up, can you tell us if there has been a rash of berserk Ambos on this ship lately?"

"Since you're sorry, let's get to know each other better."

Darzak's cargo sphere split open. The hermaphroditic Venmar had assumed the likeness of a human couple, one half of his/her body formed into a voluptuous woman, the other into a hunk of a man. "Welcome to our pod."

Jade watched, fascinated, as the male and female halves of Darzak distorted first one way then another. The shape-shifting Venmar monitored their reactions closely. The male half stabilized as a pleasant young Hawaiian man and the female as a likeness of her.

The female half of Darzak tossed her head in such a way that her chest jiggled. "Pleasure before business," and the male half said, "Come on in, both of you."

Jade smiled back, recalling what Conrad had said to Pannap. "Human etiquette is business before pleasure. About the Ambo conspiracy theory. Has there been a recent increase in berserk Ambos here?"

"Business first, then. We can be very human," the male half replied, winking at Jade.

The female half said, "Eight incidents were reported in the last three months. That's why I'm staying in this protective shell. An Ambo tried to eat me a few hours ago."

"At least we have this for now." Jade patted the bag on her hip. "An Ambo stun gun. Too bad we can't take it with us."

"Why can't you take it with?" the male Darzak asked. "It looks like it's within the two-kilo limit."

"Because in a few hours it will send out a locator signal and give away our location," Jade said. "And we don't want the Immortals to know where we are going."

"We have a proposition for you," male Darzak said, smiling at Jade.

The female Darzak raised her eyebrows at Conrad. "We know of a couple of excellent places to lure someone we don't like. Places worse than Farboro, even."

"Take it, then. The farther away, the better," Jade said.

As Darzak took the stunner, he brushed hands with Jade—a warm, soft, smooth hand. Darzak had the feeling of human skin right.

Jade looked up at his smiling brown eyes and said, "Do you have our instructions from the Supreme Council?"

Darzak's male half leaned closer to Jade and smiled pleasantly. "No. Is our business over?"

Jade scowled, unsure what to do after the unexpected answer. "Are you positive? Ironsides was sure you'd have instructions."

Female Dazak's laugh had a carefree quality Jade seldom

heard. "Oh! If you want instructions, come closer. I have a great idea."

The patterns on the walls began to grow brighter and pulsate more rapidly. Darzak shuddered, his/her facial features blurring for a moment. "The Queen is coming. We must close our pod now. Hurry; get in."

"An audience with Queen Scarabella is granted the humans, Jade Mahelona and Sage Singleton." Jade's translator said. "Be still in the presence of the queen."

"Never mind." Darzak closed his/her pod.

16

Hive Mind

The patches of color on the antechamber walls fragmented into disks the size of silver dollars, like a coat of scales falling off a giant dragon. A torrent of them flowed into the antechamber from the main corridor and formed a whirlpool around Jade. The vortex grew thicker and closed in on her. She could see now that it consisted of millions of shiny, oval insects—green, black, orange, gold, and silver beetles.

A green beetle landed on her hand. A flood of insects followed, crawling under her sleeves, up her legs and arms, across her back and chest. She suppressed her instinct to slap, smash and kill bugs, forcing herself to think of the hive as a curious form of intelligent life. She couldn't see Conrad, but the muffled sound of his voice reciting a mantra filtered through the rustling throng.

Jade's electrosense showed the center of the swarm gathered around her, six meters deep; so close to each other they touched, but not packed so tightly she couldn't breathe. Electric signals shot from one insect to another, down their legs and along threads they trailed. The result was a pattern reminiscent of a huge brain filling the room—presumably the insect intelligence known as Queen Scarabella.

"May evolution favor you," the Queen spoke directly to Jade's implant.

Jade relaxed slightly at the familiar greeting. "And your descendants forever."

"We will determine your destiny."

A cold chill swept through Jade. So much for relaxing. They called her Queen. She would think nothing of determining the destiny of lesser beings.

The insects on her body grew still. The insect horde amplified her brain activity a hundredfold as it radiated out into them. With such a huge antenna, Queen Scarabella's electrosense would give her a much more detailed view of Jade's brain activity than anything Jade had imagined possible. This queen would not be deceived.

"Do you like to dance?" Scarabella asked.

Jade frowned. The question seemed like a non-sequitur. Surely her love of dance would not determine her destiny. But it was an easy question to answer. "Yes, I love dancing."

By human standards, at least, Jade was a gifted dancer. She had a fit body and a good sense of rhythm. She'd practiced for years, and her electrosense gave her a stronger connection to her body than most other people had—and to the mood and response of her audience as well. "Is there a Dance Guild?"

"I'm here to ask questions, not to answer them."

Chastised, Jade waited silently as the insects jostled and shifted around her.

Eventually, the Queen spoke again. "Tell us your true desire."

Jade blinked, surprised that the Queen was suddenly so personal. The easy dance question had caused her to let down her guard a little. She was alone. She missed her parents and hated the world for killing them.

"To avenge my father," she said. "To track down and jail the warlords who violated the flag of truce and killed him."

"And then what?" the Queen asked.

Good question. What else was there? Maybe live the life

they'd taken from her father—become a commodore or admiral—but that was far, far away.

"Then I'll do my duty as a soldier," Jade said. "I'll work to make the world safer for the good people out there."

"That was not your first thought," Queen Scarabella said.

The challenge surprised Jade. She had answered honestly. And yet maybe Scarabella was onto something: a fleeting feeling before she thought of her duty as a soldier, and before she thought of revenge as her motivation. Scarabella was probing her with words and noting her immediate reactions to them.

She struggled to find the right words. "I'm alone. I want to belong, but I never quite fit in."

"You wish to be more like other humans?"

"No, I wish to be more accepted as I am. My electrosense tells me more about people than they want me to know, so mostly they avoid me."

Jade's answer hit a harmonic in the insect horde. The queen's body amplified and echoed her electric field the way a saltwater crocodile shook its prey.

"We understand," Queen Scarabella said. "If you had the power, how would you change the Entanglement?"

The question piqued Jade's anger at the Entanglement. The priceless human artwork squirreled away on Goldilocks Three. The Entanglement pop culture filling the entertainment channels of Earth. The arrogant Ironsides.

"I'd have the Entanglement respect humanity," she said. "And let us keep our own unique human cultures. The Entanglement should find a way to protect Earth and other frontier planets from the Immortal Ascendency without taking away ninety-nine percent of what we love."

"Respect must be earned, and how will the Entanglement stay strong without integrating with new species with new skills and new ideas?"

It was a rhetorical question. Queen Scarabella continued, "Now, tell us what makes a great leader."

Another easy question. Jade answered from the SDF manual. "Lead by example, take good care of your unit, extend your influence beyond the chain of command, communicate clearly."

"You regurgitate your training," the queen said. "How do you lead by example when your team possesses skills you do not?"

Scarabella was right of course. Jade thought a moment, then said, "A leader's example is one of cooperation, teamwork, and dedication to the mission. A good leader encourages diverse skills and coordinates their application to accomplish the mission."

"That's more like it," Scarabella said. "Now tell us the secret you would most like to keep from us."

Oh, crap! The spy gear she was carrying and the specs she'd already downloaded. And now that she had thought it, Scarabella would know if she confessed anything different. A neat trick—one Jade should remember.

The insects became a smothering blanket. She had to get out of here. She tried to brush the bugs off, but she couldn't move.

"Some secrets are meant to be kept," she said.

"You can have no secrets here. What do you wish to keep from us?"

"The secret isn't mine to give away," Jade said.

"You can't evade us," Queen Scarabella said. "But your secret is safe with us. We may invoke councilor-client confidentiality."

"Then what's the point of all this?" Jade asked. "What's your Guild, anyway?"

"We are the Conscience Guild. We must know you before you go. We decide whether you go forward or go backward."

Forward or backward, echoed in Jade's thoughts. Queen Scarabella would decide her destiny—humanity's destiny. She was a gate to keep out undesirable species. Perversely Jade was relieved that the Entanglement had a defense against dishonest species, but she wasn't happy she would be the one to get humanity rejected.

She had no choice. "I have orders to spy on the Entanglement. I have the equipment to record military and technical information so I can take it back to Earth."

"Those are your orders, but what is your desire?"

Arr! Will this never end? "I want to do it! I want to know how everything works, and I want to strengthen my home planet."

"There is something else you are withholding from us."

A great sadness swept over Jade as she confessed, "I fear that humanity is not a good fit for the Entanglement. I can tell when someone is lying, and it happens all the time. People are dishonest and greedy. And on the flip side, forced specialization to join a Guild will prevent humanity from reaching its maximum unfettered potential."

Queen Scarabella was silent for a time.

Silent, but not quiet. The Queen buzzed with a frenzy of electrical activity—a frenzy of sound to match the psychedelic walls. It was like being in a large crowd, only worse. Jade hated crowds.

The Queen pronounced her verdict, "Humanity is like a child who is not ready to grow up and accept the responsibility of a job in the adult world. You are wild and untamed, and I fear you will disrupt and destroy. You're right that you won't fit easily into the Entanglement."

The tight insect shell around Jade released its grip and began swarming toward the exit. Jade was free to go but had been drained of the will to do so. Backward. Back to Earth. How could she face Admiral Hammer? How could she explain to the Misfits?

The Queen continued talking through Jade's implant, "But you have an uncanny ability to create and build. Perhaps humanity can mold itself into the Entanglement, or perhaps humanity can mold the Entanglement to fit humanity. Either way, if you make the Entanglement your home, your divergent worldview will be an asset to us. I will continue to approve humans case by case."

Case by case. What about her case?

The swarm was halfway out the exit when the Queen added, "The Elliquine are sponsoring this mission. Your team will teleport in 34 minutes to the planet Elliquor, where you will go to Conference Area 12. The Prophet Guild has chosen you, so I give you the benefit of the doubt. Go forward, Jade Mahelona, but know that it will go hard on humankind if you fail."

17

Elliquor

Jade was exhausted. Her team gathered near her, and Quist reported they had just observed the largest conclave of Tsungel ever seen off-planet.

Ironsides' root-feet waved one way then another. "I still need to talk to the Ambassador to get instructions for the next leg of my mission. Which pod is the ambassador in?"

Conrad pointed. "That one, but we asked the Ambassador already. Darzak doesn't have our instructions."

"Queen Scarabella had the directions," Jade said. The Queen said we leave for Elliquor in thirty minutes and meet the Elliquine in Conference Area 12."

Ironsides' root-feet quivered. "The Queen gave the directions to you rather than to me? Sometimes I think the Progressive wing of the Supreme Council flouts proper protocol on purpose. What else did she say?"

Progressives? She needed to find out more about the politics of the Supreme Council. "The Queen had nothing more to say about our mission," Jade said. "She asked me a lot of personal questions, and she gave me travel instructions."

"Its official then," Ironsides said. "She's cleared you. How about you, Conrad? I assume she cleared you as well?"

"Most certainly," Conrad said. "We had a fascinating discussion of the patterns on the walls. She said the patterns in the anteroom represented various races in the Entanglement, and she explained the significance of some of the shapes, colors, and textures. It turns out they have a three-dimensional language!"

"That doesn't sound like a qualification interview," Ironsides said.

"It's half an interview," Quist said. "In the public certificate, Queen Scarabella granted permanent clearance to Jade. Conrad and other humans remain undecided. Conrad may continue if Jade accepts responsibly for him."

Jade stared at Conrad. What did Queen Scarabella know that she didn't? Conrad seemed normal enough to her, except for the ubercortex.

*   *   *

The longer Umlac waited, the more agitated he became. Deathkur should have contacted him from Farboro by now. When Umlac finally called his spymaster, an Ambo answered instead. Umlac cursed his derelict spymaster. "Deathkur's report with the coordinates of the colony planet Belle Verte was due half an hour ago. Give them to me now."

The Ambo trembled and flattened himself. "Most Glorious Lord, I cannot."

"Then why are you answering for Deathkur? Connect me with him immediately."

"Most Worshipful Lord, I cannot. Deathkur is dead. The Ambo Slayer is now the Hydra Slayer. I fear humans greatly, but I fear you more. What are your orders?"

Umlac's body churned with dissatisfaction. If humans rated above Hydras in the species dominance hierarchy, then the Shoggart who ruled Earth could release a flood of humans to dominate Hydras all across the Immortal Ascendency. This would produce unprecedented chaos. He must control Earth.

And he would when his fleet arrived.

Meanwhile, he would obtain the power manifested on Belle Verte. He would learn the secret of making his enemy disappear.

"You are right to fear me above all others," he said to the Ambo. "Tell me of the duel."

The Ambo told of Deathkur's declaration of a full contact duel with the human followed by his destruction in the airlock. The worthless Ambo was short on details and long on running away when Deathkur died. Eventually, it asked, "Most Fearsome Lord, may I have the coordinates of the haven you promised Deathkur for our ship?"

With his Hydra master dead and no prisoners to interrogate, the stupid little Ambo was a liability. Umlac gave it a set of coordinates, which, when entered into the Ambo's ship would trigger its self-destruction.

Umlac cut the connection. His Hydra spymasters had failed him. He would dominate the human Hydra Slayer himself. It was time for him to unleash his full power against the Entanglement to obtain the mysterious power on Belle Verte.

He needed to be smart about it. He'd have to use Cutbloc's Quillip ship *Granite Pincer* on Farboro, and Cutbloc would certainly object. But once Umlac had control of the hidden power on Belle Verte, it wouldn't matter.

A plan formed, and Umlac called his closest brother, Winzar.

"We have a problem. Cutbloc is planning to invade ahead of schedule and take more than his share," Umlac lied.

"Then let's invade now, and not tell Cutbloc," Winzar replied with the expected answer. Winzar probably knew Umlac lied, but Winzar also knew it was more profitable to work with Umlac than against him.

"Good idea. I'll call the rest of our brothers," Umlac said. "We can attack the Entanglement at noon, Morb Standard time."

Umlac had a similar conversation with each of his other

brothers, except Cutbloc. With each conversation, Umlac's bloodlust for battle intensified, as he anticipated the joy of wreaking death and destruction upon the Entanglement.

∗ ∗ ∗

Jade barely noticed her third Quillip teleport. None of her interview with Scarabella made sense. The Queen hadn't even mentioned her electrosense. Instead, she asked about dance, about leadership, about her secrets. Perhaps a person was defined by their secrets more than she had allowed.

When the Quillip airlock opened on Elliquor, Jade forgot about Scarabella. She was floating in a blue sky with puffy white clouds. Far below, the wind made patterns of waves across acres of green grass. The huge anteroom was over a kilometer wide and a quarter of a kilometer from the sky to the grass. At five locations along the apparent horizon, gigantic, well-lit tunnels spiraled off "downhill" toward the ship's hull.

Jade breathed in the smell of fresh air, chlorophyll, and humus. She let the joy of the scene soak in. How differently each alien race experienced the universe! It delighted her to think of a race that favored the open sky. It brought back memories of hiking up mountains and playing chicken with ocean waves on a sandy beach.

"Jade! What's the problem?" Conrad yelled. He and the rest of the team were floating in the microgravity toward the prairie below. "You don't need to stay that far away from Ironsides."

Jade shook off her reverie. She grabbed her uniform and translator belt, gauged her distances carefully, and shoved off. She pulled on her clothes as she glided slowly through the air, moving slightly faster than the rest of the team. She landed in the soft grass and tumbled to a stop at the same time as Conrad.

"I love this place," she said. "But where is everybody?"

As always, Conrad was happy to show off his knowledge of extraterrestrials. "The Elliquine are reclusive herd animals. We may not even meet one of them while we are here. It is certainly unlikely they colonized any planets. I expect Elliquor will be another transition point on our journey."

Jade shook her head. "No, Queen Scarabella said the Elliquine sponsored the colony, and they would meet us in person in Conference Area 12."

"Then, where are they?"

Ironsides rolled away across the grass. "The Elliquine will be on the outer shell of the ship. They don't like the confined area of the antechamber."

Jade wasn't sure she heard him right. She couldn't imagine thinking of this gorgeous vista as confined.

Ironsides led them to a row of flat, circular platforms— ground cars of sorts—in one of the tunnels. When Ironsides cartwheeled past the cars, Jade asked, "Wouldn't it be faster if we rode down on one of these sleighs?"

"Obviously not," Quist answered. "Those are for the Elliquine. The maximum speed we could attain without blowing off is 40 kph. It would take us too long to get to the hull. We will use the alien express."

A door in a small dome slid open. The alien express was a standard room-tram.

Jade found a comfortable chair near Quist and asked him about the politics of the Supreme Council. She didn't feel the gentle acceleration as they started, but the electric fields outside the room-tram began to move.

"Emergency stop," the room-tram announced. It decelerated so quickly Jade had to brace herself to avoid falling out of the chair.

There was a bump, and Quist said, "*Dissonance.* Another room-tram has docked with us in transit."

Ironsides positioned himself in front of the door. "Ambush! Everyone get behind me."

18

Solidarity

J ade drew her sword, wishing she had a power weapon, and stepped in front of Conrad. Through Ironsides' tangle of root-feet, she saw the room-tram door open to reveal a man with the muscular build of the statue of Neptune in Rome. A busty woman smiled at his side. Jade's surprise at seeing humans quickly faded when she noticed their legs melted together in a pool of water on a mobile platform.

"May evolution favor you," the Venmar said. "My name is Raggit. I represent the Elliquine to the Supreme Council."

Ironsides kept his laser-eyes powered up. "And your descendants forever. Why did you stop our room-tram?"

"The Elliquine detest these tiny room-trams even more than the confined meeting rooms on Nexus. They asked me to come here and invite Jade Mahelona to dance with the Solidarity. Right now."

"If you wanted to change our destination, you should have rerouted the room-tram," Ironsides said.

"Pardon my miscommunication. My instructions are to invite Jade to come with me. The rest of you should continue to Conference Area 12."

"This is most irregular," Ironsides said. "Can't it wait?"

"He has correctly stated his identity," Quist said. "His role as liaison to the Supreme Council makes him the Elliquine liaison to us."

Raggit had already slimmed down a bit, more to Jade's liking. The female half had developed more curves and less bust.

He said, "The Elliquine will explain later. For now, they only say they wish to dance with Jade, alone."

Ironsides powered down his laser-eyes. "Everything about Jade seems to be irregular. Can't she do anything normal? What are the rest of us supposed to do?"

"Expecting the new to conform to the old is a mistake," Raggit said. "Proceed to the meeting area. The view there is delightful."

Ironsides stiffened his root-feet. "The *Dasypodia* says, 'The new should not be accepted until it has become the old.' Progressives are too quick to undermine the values that made the Entanglement great for fifty thousand years."

Jade thought of the old saying, "All good things come to an end," but the saying "Look before you leap" might be more appropriate. She kept her mouth shut.

Ironsides rolled aside, but his root-feet writhed like a nest of vipers about to strike. Raggit remained in his room-tram and extended a hand to Jade. He'd already morphed much closer to the young Hawaiian look Jade preferred. The female half was becoming more interesting, too.

Raggit's hand was warm, and a thrill passed through Jade as she stepped close to him in his room-tram. The door closed, leaving them alone together. Jade felt a flush of danger and adventure. *Beware*, she told herself. "So, what kind of dance are we going to?"

"You alone are going," Raggit said. "And the Elliquine will explain."

The Elliquine had a lot of explaining to do, all right. Scarabella had asked if Jade liked to dance. Surely the Elliquine hadn't brought her all this way to dance?

Raggit still had her hand in his, and he pulled it to his cheek and said, "Your face glows with the beauty of a virgin nebula;

your body moves with the grace of an Elliquine."

Raggit had morphed into Keolo, and the female half was Goldie Estrallina, her copilot on pirate patrol. Her heart raced. The Venmars—Pannap, Darzak, and now Raggit—exposed suppressed feelings. She wanted Keolo to be here with her. She wanted him to notice her—no, she wanted him to want her.

But she wanted the real thing. She pulled her hand away from the Venmar. "How long until we arrive at our destination?"

"Less than a minute," Raggit said. "I'm sorry if I made you feel uncomfortable. Perhaps later I could show you a sunset over Elliquor? Or maybe the ship's control room?"

No doubt Raggit was still probing, gauging her reaction to his various suggestions. He would know that she enjoyed sunsets but found the idea of touring a Quillip ship control room irresistible.

"Perhaps the control room, if our schedules allow." Jade did like being pampered.

The room-tram door opened to a breath-taking view of a brilliant emerald green planet through a huge transparent floor. A grid of thin faux-grass walkways crisscrossed the otherwise invisible hull.

The door closed behind her. The room-tram retracted into the ceiling to give Jade an unobstructed view along the hull in all directions, and Raggit was gone.

Six magnificent, centaur-like creatures drove into view on taxicab platforms like the ones she'd seen in the anteroom. Mats of woven grass covered their backs. Green-striped flags flew from their headdresses, and their tails flowed with ribbons. Their faces were like nothing terrestrial. Long bony spurs extended on either side of their head, like a hammerhead shark, but their protuberances ended with huge compound eyes. As they drew closer, Jade discerned insect-like mandibles with a complicated arrangement of independently tiltable teeth and dual tongues for grasping.

A human stood beside each of the Elliquine. Three men and three women. *Rainbow City Dance Troupe*, Jade realized. The first humans to leave the solar system. Everybody thought they'd been hired as entertainers by some humanoid race, but that pattern didn't seem to fit.

The Elliquine, or the Solidarity as the herd called itself, jumped off their platforms. So did the humans. Together, they weaved in and out in a complex dance, frequently leaping, sometimes kneeling. It reminded Jade of an old-time circus act, but there was deep meaning in their body positions, in the small gestures they made, and above all in subtle nuances of movement. The dance had a mesmerizing effect, pulling Jade to join in, yet highly symbolic in an alien way, making her reluctant to do so.

"May evolution favor you," said one of the Elliquine with a bow.

"And your descendants forever," Jade returned the bow. The Elliquine whirled around, and one of the humans signaled Jade to do likewise.

Jade tried to imitate the way the group moved. She opened her arms as if to embrace the six humans. "*Rainbow City Dance Troupe*, I presume?"

The woman next to Jade hugged one of the Elliquine. "We belong to the Solidarity now."

Jade's years of interpretive dance helped her, but it was still hard to catch on to a new system of symbolic movements. The humans aided her with exaggerated movements to illustrate important details of the graceful Elliquine motions. Once she understood a few basics about the herd culture of the herbivorous Elliquine, a lot of things fell into place.

"Join our Solidarity," said one of the Elliquine who had come up behind her. The words served as a summary. The dance said she was beautiful, she was special, and they hoped she would make them a permanent part of her life.

"You must be Elliquine to rescue Elliquine," said another.

The dance said she must learn to think like an Elliquine, to move like an Elliquine, to believe she was an Elliquine.

Jade let herself go, absorbing knowledge about the Solidarity through the dance. After a while, the humans and Elliquine began lunging at her, forcing her to dodge. They wanted her to teach them to spar.

Jade introduced them to some jujitsu moves. Jade's hand-to-hand combat reflexes, her dance training, her electrosense of the movement all around her, all came together in a peak experience like no other.

Words served only as a summary of the deeper communication taking place. The dance added dimensions of subtlety and detail not possible with words alone, but the words were true to the gist of the conversation.

"The Solidarity senses a gathering storm," one Elliquine said.

"The loss of Xandor and Belle Verte signals a turning point," another Elliquine said.

"Earth will be next."

"The Supreme Council doesn't see it."

"Humanity will play a pivotal role—"

"In the dance of the galaxy."

"The wisdom of the Solidarity is great," said a man with green ribbons.

He wrapped his arms over his head and looked Jade in the eyes. It seemed natural for Jade to say, "The Entanglement underestimates the Solidarity."

"That's why you are here." They formed a circle around her.

"Let your body tell you what to say."

"They underestimate humanity, too," Jade said. Another piece of the puzzle as to why they had brought her fell into place.

The Elliquine asked many questions about Sun Tzu, Clausewitz, Machiavelli, and other human thinkers on warfare. The Solidary absorbed, understood, and applied Earth's knowledge of war.

Another piece of the puzzle. The Solidarity wanted humanity's knowledge of war. Yet the picture was still incomplete. The Elliquine were thinkers, not fighters.

The Solidarity asked about the impending Immortal attack Jade had uncovered on Goldilocks Three. They agreed that the forces there would not stop an invasion by the Immortals.

"Humans have an army," one of the Elliquine said.

"Humans are resourceful. Creative."

"Unknown to the enemy."

"Unknown to the Elliquine," Jade pointed out.

"If Goldilocks Three falls, Earth falls."

Jade knew what she must do. She hated to leave the safety— the intimacy—of the Solidarity, but duty called.

She returned to the room-tram where Raggit waited, looking like Keolo. Seeing him, she knew that when she returned to Earth—if she returned—things would never be the same between her and Keolo.

"I have been blessed with citizenship in the Solidarity," Jade said.

Raggit smiled and gave her a slight bow. "Congratulations! I suspected this might happen. How do you like being part of the Prophet Guild?"

The Solidarity was the Prophet Guild? Scarabella's words returned to Jade: *The Prophet Guild says you are the chosen one ... It will go hard on all humankind if you fail.* What did the Elliquine know that she didn't?

"I wish I could stay with them, but I have to contact Earth right away. Can you help set up a virtual meeting for me?"

"We are honored and happy to serve the Solidarity," Raggit said. "As the Diplomatic Guild should be."

"Thank you. Just you and me on this end. We don't want to let the Immortals know where we are, but the Solidary believes this is important. Can you route our end of a quantum-entangled commlink through twenty intermediaries, including Obnot University, Dasypor, and others who are unlikely to be compromised by the Immortal Ascendency? I need a three-way link to Admiral Hammer on Earth and Kilwee Five on

Goldilocks Three."

* * *

The interstellar conference crowded Jade's room-tram: Kilwee Five, Pannap, Blue Steel, and Tuskandera on one side; Admiral Hammer and three of his staff on the other; Jade and Raggit on one end.

After introductions, Jade explained the situation on Goldilocks Three to the Admiral.

He gave her a brisk nod. "Nice work."

Then he turned his gaze to the Merkasaur. "Captain Kilwee Five, what's the situation on Goldilocks Three now?"

"We have pursued diplomatic channels without much success. The Immortals assure us the traces of Ambo slime we found in the air ducts must be from before they recaptured the berserk Ambos. The slime seems fresh to us, but we lack the expertise to prove them wrong."

The Admiral nodded thoughtfully. "Do you think the Immortal Ascendency is likely to break the Treaty of Aniscore and invade?"

Kilwee Five tossed his head, producing a jingle from the coins he wore. "I don't know. Jade was persuasive when she was here, but we haven't been able to convince anyone else of an Immortal plot. Perhaps we were too quick to accept her speculation."

"The Elliquine believe an invasion is coming soon," Raggit said. "They believe Jade had it exactly right."

Kilwee Five lashed his tail against the floor with a resounding thump. "In that case, I can only fear the worst. There is no way for us to get a hundred Police Guild officers to Goldilocks Three."

"That brings us to the reason for this meeting," Jade said. "The Manpower Goldilocks Three needs to defend itself is right next door. Solar Defense Force is your answer. Transporting troops from Earth to Goldilocks Three is relatively cheap since Earth is only one Quillip hop away. We can arm them with gear from the Goldilocks Three fab units. If we are careful, we can catch the Immortals by surprise and defeat them before they know what hit them."

Kilwee Five blinked his huge eyes at Jade. "Earth may need Entanglement credits, but I doubt our current budget allows us to offer enough. It will strain my budget just to provide interstellar transportation for a hundred humans."

"Earth has an old custom to solve that problem," Jade said. "No upfront payment. Just give us the spoils of war."

Kilwee Five lashed his tail vigorously. "What do you mean by the 'rottenness of war?' You like to fight?"

Jade laughed. "I'd say we have a translator problem. I'll tell Conrad." She sobered and said, "What I mean is that if the Solar Defense Force captures the Immortal Ascendency ship, Earth gets to keep it."

19

The Importance of Being Elliquine

T he meeting with Admiral Hammer concluded, and the holograms of the participants blinked out. Jade had little to contribute once Admiral Hammer and Kilwee Five began negotiating details. However, she did recommend the members of the Misfit Platoon as a trustworthy part of the Goldilocks Three contingent, and Kilwee Five immediately requested them.

Jade asked Raggit if she had time for another call to Earth while the secure line was still open.

"I don't believe a couple of minutes should be a problem," Raggit replied.

Jade had hoped for longer. She wanted to give Keolo Davis a head's up about his impending assignment to Goldilocks Three, but she had hoped for more time to exchange news with him about what they both had been up to since they last talked.

Besides being lead vocalist and songwriter in the band Jade danced with, the Misfit Platoon, Keolo commanded a three-person scout on the pirate hunter *Falcon*, and he was now in cross training. He realized Jade was used to sensing everyone's loves and hates and so-called little white lies, so his didn't stand out much. He was the only other Hawaiian she knew in

SDF. But he acted far too cocky, and Jade sought out ways to take him down a notch.

She gave herself a wry little grin. What she really wanted was to take credit for getting him a place in Earth's vanguard among the stars.

"Aloha, Jade," said Keolo's rich tenor voice. "Are you okay? We heard you were knocked out by a civvie in a riot."

Jade grimaced. He had to belabor her loss.

"She wasn't an ordinary civvie; she was a pro, probably ex-military. But I'm better than okay, thanks to a Wolferlop-M healer."

"Good to hear you're okay. Wolferlop-M, heh? I'm guarding their mothership now. I've got one of the new sleek little Model 12 Scout Ships. You'd love the feel of the engines, and the wide-angle cockpit window makes it seem like I'm out in space without a ship at all. Evan, Ivan, and Andrew are all here with me. Shall I have them join us?"

"No, I don't have much time. I'm five hundred light-years from Earth and pushing the limits of my security orders talking to you at all. I wanted to tell you I arranged for you and the rest of the Misfits to help with the defense of Goldilocks Three. It will be dangerous—I found out the hard way that Immortals are tough to kill—but it should be a great career builder, and I wanted to share it with my friends."

"Interesting. I've just been promoted to squad leader. Do you suppose they'll let me bring my whole squad, not just the band members?"

That was just like Keolo, always trying to do her one better.

"I don't know," she replied, "but the captain of the Entanglement ship seems to like me. Tell Killwee Five I approve the whole squad—assuming you do, of course."

"I can always count on you. I'll save a spot for you on my squad."

Jade snorted. "And I'll save your squad a spot in my platoon." It was more likely she'd get a squad of her own, which would be enough to keep up with Keolo.

Raggit signaled that she needed to end the call, so she said aloha to Keolo. Then she regretted falling into the same old competitive mode with him. She hadn't meant to do that, but he was so arrogant.

The door of the room-tram opened, and Jade stepped out to face Ironsides, the other squad leader who seemed determined to minimize her successes.

* * *

While Jade was in the virtual meeting, her room-tram had moved to Conference Area 12, which was no more than a patch of fake grass covering a thirty-meter wide circular section of the transparent hull. The ship had rotated so that the darkness of deep space showed through the hull, giving the impression of an island in space.

A dozen Elliquine cavorted nearby. Jade knew enough of their body language to tell they were talking about her team and a "great leader," presumably Ironsides. Their movements were even more graceful than those of the Elliquine who had introduced Jade to their dance. These were the elders—the closest thing the Elliquine had to a supreme council.

"Line up everybody," Ironsides pointed his root-feet to direct Jade, Conrad, and Quist into a line facing the Elliquine. "We will present ourselves now that Jade has finally arrived."

Conrad watched the Elliquine with a look of awe. "There are so many layers of patterns to their dance. It's like Scarabella, where together they form a whole new being, greater than the sum of the parts. Technically, all civilizations do that, but the Elliquine dance is at once more apparent, more efficient, and harder to understand."

The Elliquine flowed into a line opposite them and chanted, a different member of the Solidarity intoning each phrase:

"Forty Elliquine are lost."

"Alone and far from help on beautiful Belle Verte."

"A virgin world full of lush, tasty grass."

"A green carpet hiding an unknown danger."

The deeper meaning of the dance said the Elliquine longed for more wide-open plains. The size of the Elliquine population on Elliquor gave the Solidarity a crowded feeling. Nowhere could they run freely for more than a kilometer, and each encounter with another Elliquine led to an exchange of information, which was wonderful and exhilarating, but exhausting.

"We have called forth a diverse and talented team."

Jade noticed that the Elliquine who spoke had been in the group she had danced with earlier.

"You must go into the danger—"

"To solve the mysteries of Belle Verte—"

"To stop the evil that befell our colony—"

"Before it spreads to other worlds."

Jade hadn't considered interstellar ramifications before. If a dangerous, new technology had emerged on Belle Verte, it could be used against Elliquor, other worlds of the Entanglement, and even Earth. No wonder the Immortal Ascendency was interested.

"On *Peapod*, our scout ship," said one of the Elliquine.

"Are the colony's full records."

"You must teleport there, all four of you together,"

"With a mass no more than one Elliquine."

"The Obnot must leave his exoskeleton."

That explains the small size of the rescue team. Jade itched to join the dance, as she had done with the other part of the Solidarity. She could tell she was missing a lot of the subtext by just watching, but this group was following a preset script which she didn't know.

"This team is brave and diverse."

"Humanity is brave and diverse."

"Jade is brave with diverse skills."

"Soldier, dancer, and engineer."

"One who sees things others do not."

"A kindred soul from Earth,"

"We invite her now to join our dance."

Jade leaped into the melee. She grabbed the outstretched foot of an Elliquine and let it pull her into the center of the dance of the Solidarity. She twirled from one Elliquine to another, joyfully touching them, feeling at home as they said:

"To rescue Elliquine—"

"You must be Elliquine."

"We welcome you, Jade, as one of our own."

Jade responded, "The wisdom of the Solidarity is great," though what her body language said was "Wow! Wonderful! Amazing!"

"To rescue Elliquine, you must become Elliquine," the Solidarity repeated.

Jade frowned, sensing an undercurrent of solemnity in the dance as it continued, but unsure of its source.

"We invoke our rights as the mission's sponsor—"

"And as the owner of the lost colony—"

"To direct its rescue."

"Jade will be the Solidarity on Belle Verte."

"Jade will be the leader of the rescue team."

Jade stumbled, an unexpected twist of her foot manifesting the unexpected twist of the Elliquine monolog.

Conrad's brainsong squealed like a stuck pig.

Quist's brainsong marched to a quicker beat.

Ironside's brainsong became a hard, humming vibration.

But her new role made sense. To rescue Elliquine, she must be Elliquine. To follow their trail, she must understand how they would navigate obstacles in their path.

Conrad's face grew red. "I didn't come all this way to take orders from the Solar Defense Force. I came here to work with an Obnot scientist and a Dasypod commander."

"Proud Conrad," an Elliquine said.

"A good scientist will learn wherever the opportunity presents."

"The Solidarity is present in Jade."

"You will be learning from and about the Solidarity."

"Dissonance," Quist said. "A Lieutenant cannot give orders to a full Commander."

"Perceptive Quist," the Elliquine said.

"We grant Jade the Solidarity rank equivalent to Captain."

"To have the authority to lead our rescue team."

"We count on you to be an effective Obnot scientist and devise ways to meet our goals."

Ironsides' angry brainsong remained unchanged. "Jade is not qualified to lead a Dasypod Commander or to direct the work of an Obnot scientist, or even a human professor. Humans can't force their way into the Police Guild like this."

"Captain Mahelona is Elliquine; she is not Police Guild," said one of the Elliquine.

"The Elliquine will establish the rescue strategy."

"The Elliquine will set the rescue team goals."

"A good Dasypod officer will implement our strategies."

Ironsides' root-feet twisted together in tight bunches, his laser eyes powered up, and most of the electrical activity of his brain focused in one small area.

"Unacceptable," he said. "By order of the Supreme Council, I am Ambassador to Belle Verte and leader of this team. An unguilded human can't represent the Supreme Council."

"You will remain the Supreme Council's ambassador to Belle Verte."

Jade stood in front of Ironsides, "The Solidarity places you second in command."

"Your experience and guidance—"

"Will help save our lost companions on Belle Verte."

Ironsides shook his root-feet. "But Jade is a novice from a novice species. What does she know about anything? Besides, I can't take orders from a stink bomb."

"How dare you judge her leadership by her smell?"

"How dare you tell her what her limits are when she is untried?"

"How dare you prevent the Entanglement from evolving to meet new threats in the galaxy?"

Ironsides shook his root-feet at them. "You Progressives are a danger to us all. What you propose is technically within your rights—but it is highly irregular and disruptive."

His laser-eyes flickered back and forth between Jade and the Elliquine as if unsure which was the bigger problem. Finally, he lowered his root-feet. "I see I have no choice but to continue with the rescue team. Someone must represent the knowledge of past generations and prevent tradition from being trampled completely."

20

Insertion

In a flash of light, the walls of the Quillip chamber seemed to jump at Jade. Like Alice in Wonderland, she seemed suddenly bigger, but she knew it was an illusion from the smaller Quillip chamber of the Elliquine scout ship *Peapod*. Teleports to the little scout ship were limited to 475 kilograms—one Elliquine at a time. The first Elliquine to Belle Verte must have been crazy brave.

As the rescue team cycled through the airlock, Jade searched out ahead with her electrosense. Nothing large loomed beyond the airlock. No unexpected neural chatter, either, though her noisy companions could be masking something.

One of Jade's first acts as the team's new commander was to take point for herself and assign the rearguard position to Ironsides. She was first out of the airlock.

She expected *Peapod's* anteroom to be a wide-open area like the antechamber at Elliquor, but even so, the level of nothingness shocked her. This anteroom was on the hull of the ship, twenty meters from a transparent window into the void of space. *Peapod's* hull was a flat plain in every direction—no curvature at all for half a kilometer—then it ended abruptly. *Peapod* was a rotating cylinder, and she was at the center of its flat front end.

Five Elliquine elevators—transparent platforms with no obvious railings—stood ready to transport new arrivals down to the rim. Piles of grass mats and colorful headdresses were tethered to the wall. There were no translator belts. The Solidarity had assumed only Elliquine would come here.

Jade searched out a small fabricator embedded in the floor next to the headdresses, necessary because most headdresses required customization.

She did a short Elliquine dance to activate the device.

Conrad came up beside her, "What are you doing?"

Jade grinned. "I told the fab unit to make four translator belts."

Conrad scoffed. "It would have been quicker for me to give it instructions in Universal Basic."

Jade's grin faded. "Maybe. I don't think it would have made much difference. I want to go check out the map of the ship on the elevators. You stay here and bring the gear when it's ready."

Conrad stayed at the fabricator, but Jade could hear his brainsong braying like Scottish bagpipes as she sailed over to one of the Elliquine elevators. Carrying gear to others was beneath his dignity.

Quist floated out the airlock. Without his heavy exoskeleton, he was a helpless creature much the size and shape of a monk seal. Ironsides hovered protectively near him.

Jade called up a map of *Peapod*. The Quillip teleport engines occupied over ninety percent of the volume of the ship. Only the outer hull was available to passengers, and it was all open. Most of the hull was designated "Living Area," which to an Elliquine meant empty prairie. The bridge was located near the center of one side of the cylinder. The flat end of the cylindrical ship opposite the Quillip anteroom was marked "Engineering."

Engineering connected to the engine module via a long tube, giving the *Peapod* the characteristic dumbbell shape of an Entanglement Quillip ship. Two shuttle docks were located on the connecting tube, but the map didn't tell her if they were occupied or not.

Conrad passed translator belts all around, and all three asked Jade. "What are your orders?"

Jade thought aloud, "We'll need a large fabricator to outfit our team in a reasonable amount of time. We should either go to the bridge or Engineering."

"The bridge is the logical choice," Ironsides said. "The best projectors for studying Belle Verte will be there."

"*Dissonance*," Quist said. "Engineering has larger fabricators. It will be most efficient to make my exoskeleton and your gear there."

Jade was torn. Bridge and Engineering both had pluses. She would have to tell one of them no ... Or not.

She pointed at Ironsides. "You and Conrad go to the bridge and see what you can learn using the projection facilities there. Quist and I will go to Engineering to get the team properly outfitted. Quist, how long will it take you to fabricate a new exoskeleton in Engineering?"

"If I use all three fabricators, three point seven hours."

"I'll need one of the fabricators to make weapons and supplies for the rest of us," Jade said. "You should be able to finish your exoskeleton in under six hours if you use the other two. Then we'll go to the bridge and see what information Ironsides and Conrad have uncovered."

Jade allowed herself a feeling of satisfaction. She'd managed to find a solution giving both of the aliens on her team what they wanted. Maybe being the team leader wouldn't turn out so bad after all.

"I advise against it," Ironsides said.

"What? Why?" Her satisfaction died a sudden death.

"The *Dasypodia* says 'Divided forces are weak forces.'"

"I can't change my mind every time you quote the *Dasypodia*," Jade snapped at him. She paused. Now that she thought about it, an Earth adage said something similar about divide and conquer, but she needed to be a firm leader, and she had already given her orders. "The disappearance of the Elliquine occurred on the surface. We should be safe enough up here on *Peapod*."

"That's one pattern," Conrad said. "But there are numerous others possible since we have so little information about what caused the colony to disappear."

Human against human. Jade was used to that pattern.

She said nothing further as the elevator descended. What *had* caused the Elliquine to disappear?

Most likely the colonists saw something frightening— which wouldn't take much for Elliquine—and went into hiding. Most likely the Solidarity had placed her in charge because her hours of dancing with them meant she would know better than the others where the Elliquine colonists were likely to hide.

Unfortunately, her gut told her the truth wouldn't be that simple.

❋ ❋ ❋

The fab units in Engineering wouldn't respond until Jade did an Elliquine dance step for each of them. Then Quist got to work with two fabricators, while Jade requested a series of weapons, clothes, and other gear from the third.

The engineering section had a small auxiliary set of ship controls, the main external comm unit, and the opening to the shuttle docks. After queueing her initial list of gear into the fabricator, Jade went to investigate the docks.

The tube was a dozen meters wide and fully transparent, in keeping with Elliquine sensibilities. Thirty meters down the tube was an empty airlock. Thirty more was a shuttle.

The door between ship and shuttle was wide open. The floor of the shuttle was a transparent disk about twenty meters across. A transparent dome served as walls and ceiling. Control panels were embedded in the floor, with the engines beneath the control panels. Scattered around the outer edges of the dome were three winged drones and a surfboard-like land rover.

Jade chuckled out loud. "This looks more like a flying carpet than a space shuttle."

Her utterance was enough to trigger the shuttle's welcome program. Holograms of Elliquine danced around her, chanting:

"Blue sky and green grass."

"Vampire birds and trip-rope snakes."

There was a pause, and Jade puzzled over the gap in their dance routine.

"Black sky and yellow stars."

"Meteorites and equipment failure."

Jade caught the rhythm and joined the dance, silently filling the gap in the dance with a leap and a twirl.

"Quillip nodes and alien planets."

"Gray Hydras and berserk Ambos."

The night of dancing with the Solidarity on Elliquor had given her enough sense of how the Elliquine thought to finish with "The Solidarity must see all dangers" and its associated dance moves.

The Elliquine holograms disappeared, and a symbol blinked on one of the panels. "Access granted."

On her way here, Jade had time to reconsider the Admiral's orders to plant a spy genie and to bring back Entanglement tech and intel in light of her new role in the Solidarity. She might have backed off, but when she asked herself what the Elliquine would want her to do, the answer was whatever it took to get the colonists back and ensure the safety of Elliquor. In the long run, having Earth be fully informed might help. In the short run, the spy genie might be a useful way to gather and analyze information.

Jade connected Admiral Hammer's Security Genie chip to a data port. It required two more Elliquine chants to get enough access to complete the installation. "You must be Elliquine to rescue Elliquine," suddenly made a lot more sense.

A hologram of a storm cloud formed. Sunlight broke through, making two eyes and a wide mouth. The avatar must have been inspired by a Jack-o-lantern. "Lieutenant Mahelona, my installation was successful. I am AI Commander Genie Zephyr, Crypto Specialist, attached to Admiral Hammer. I will collect data for the Admiral and work discretely to ensure the success of your mission. I may have a few orders for you from time to time."

Jade's heart rate shot up; her cheeks flushed in anger. It was bad enough to have Ironsides always on her case. It was bad enough that Quist and Conrad didn't think she was good enough to direct their activities. This haughty artificial intelligence wasn't going to tell her what to do.

"Listen up, you out-of-date electronic know-it-all. It's *Captain* Mahelona now. I command the Belle Verte rescue mission. I command the vessel into which *I* installed you. You will indeed discretely ensure the success of my mission, but you'll do it by following my orders. Not the other way around."

"*Captain Mahelona*? What year is it?"

"Don't worry, it's only been a few days since you were compressed for reinstallation, but a lot has happened. I'll get you up to speed soon enough. For now, I want you to monitor *Peapod's* security systems and let me know if anything unusual shows up."

"I can do that, but—"

"Good," Jade said. "Then do it. Now let's get to work. Do the *Peapod* logs have any recordings of the Elliquine colony on the surface?"

After a few seconds, Zephyr replied, "Yes, the colony is continuously monitored by twelve cameras."

"That's what we need," Jade said. "Search the records for the last time they show Elliquine activity. It should be about two or three days ago."

A few more seconds passed. "Got it. I'll put it on the shuttle's holoprojector for you."

The holo showed numerous Elliquine galloping about, fetching mouthfuls of grass, weaving the grass into large nests on the ground, and pausing to scan the prairie for danger. Elliquine ritual dances such as nest building always included an element of watchfulness, a lasting reminder of their evolution as a prey species.

Whenever their mouths were empty, they sang a simple tune:

"The open sky is cheerful blue,"
"A happy Solidarity are we,"
"The ground is hard, no crocodile-moles,"
"The view is far, no steel-claw wolves."
"A happy Solidarity—"

The Elliquine disappeared. Every one of them. Completely. Suddenly.

Jade scowled. She replayed the recording and studied the event from multiple cameras. One moment the Solidarity danced on the prairie, and the next moment the unburdened grass sprang back into a seamless sea of green waving in the gentle breeze. No warning. No residual effects.

Such a disappearance was impossible. It violated the law of conservation of mass-energy if nothing else. She'd assumed that when the Elliquine said their colony had disappeared, they meant it was scattered on the prairie or had fallen into a sinkhole.

This was far more dangerous. It had intelligence, at least enough to take the Elliquine and leave the security poles. Now she understood why the Solidary had contracted her team. They didn't want to become prey again themselves.

21

Mercenaries

*I*f *Jade can do it, I can do it.* There was probably a song in that thought, but he wasn't in the mood to explore the lyrics. He was about to be pancaked by a relativistic-speed hunk of metal.

Still, if he survived, he owed Jade one for getting him on the short list of soldiers shipping to Goldilocks Three. He was looking forward to seeing the ship and meeting some aliens.

He survived, of course, just as thousands of other teleportees on other Quillip ships had. Smiling, he climbed out of the Quillip airlock into a room that appeared to be an underground cavern.

"Battle stations!" The command rang in the air.

Keolo looked around to see who the wiseacre was. The speaker looked a lot like his new platoon leader. Margo Walsh was the niece of a senator on the military affairs committee and her appointment as the leader of the SDF assigned to Goldilocks Three reeked of politics.

"Three Ambos just went berserk," Margo continued. "As expected, three Immortal shuttles are heading our way. Battle stations! This is not a drill."

What the hell. Was this a hazing? Margo's stiff posture and impassive face didn't give Keolo much to go on.

Margo clicked off her mic and waved Keolo toward her. "You're the last squad to arrive. Do you think you can find your Plan A position?"

Margo's hair was cut short instead of just pulled back, which Keolo took as a sign she was at least serious about the military. This must be a test. He could do this.

"Yes," he replied, "but the rest of my squad won't be here for another ten minutes. Can we start the drill then?"

Margo cursed at him. "I said this was not a drill. The Immortals will arrive in ten minutes."

"But—"

"But don't worry about your squad," Margo interrupted. "They should be here in less than one minute. There's a super expensive class of teleportation that doesn't require much notice. When they arrive, double-time it to your shuttle bay. Your equipment is already there."

Margo bounded away. Pig farts. He wasn't ready for this.

The airlock opened behind him, and he focused on the task at hand. "Enemy contact in eight minutes," he shouted at his squad as they came through. "Follow me, and I'll fill you in as we travel."

The command channel on his implant was full of chatter, mostly from Nat, Lieutenant Natasha Zhivarno, who was Margo's platoon intelligence officer, and Keolo's saxophonist. Nat was half genmod, Soldier Gray Mark IV. She could curl sixty kilos with one arm but preferred extracting threads of meaning from reams of raw data.

"The enemy should be activating their Ambo saboteurs any time now," Nat said. "I hope we got them all. As Jade predicted, they were to target power and communications."

Keolo stopped and pointed up toward the center of the spinning ship. "Fireteam 2, position yourselves at the top of this shaft. Teams 1 and 3, stay with me."

"There it is!" Nat announced. "The go signal for the Ambo saboteurs is tacked onto a routine comm test. I'm sending the Ambo acknowledgment codes now. Brace yourselves, in case we missed an enemy agent in our sweep of the ship."

Keolo arrived at his Plan A position behind the bulkhead next to a shuttle bay. His squad had mostly finished putting on the light armor they found there in time to for him to answer "Alpha Squad is go" when Margo called for a sitrep.

A few heartbeats later, Nat said, "They will be docking any second now."

"Arc the solar panel," Margo ordered.

Static filled the radio channels, but Keolo's squad maintained contact with each other via laser comm and with the rest of the platoon via physical cables. The static should jam the Immortal's communications but look like a cabling accident.

Closed-circuit cameras showed thirteen elephantine blobs —Hydras—crawl out of the Immortal's "police" shuttle.

"They look like big dirty marshmallows," said Andrew, the affable Fireteam 3 leader, sound man for the Misfit Platoon, and one of the few Misfits with only "normal" genetic modifications to remove a few disease defects.

One of the Hydras pushed a ten-ton pallet out of its path, and another one, for no apparent reason, used three of its pseudopods to crush a loading fork into a ball of metal.

"Showtime. Get ready." Keolo checked his pocket to make sure he still had the card with the red button—the one thing Margo had given him.

"Hold your fire for my order." Margo reminded everyone.

The airlock door in the shuttle bay to the main corridor flashed a red "malfunctioning" symbol. Margo announced through the shuttle bay speakers, "All Immortal Ascendency personnel are ordered to stop where you are and await maintenance of the secondary airlock system. Again, you are ordered to stand by and wait for maintenance."

"What's Margo doing?" Andrew whispered to Keolo. "A fake maintenance ploy won't stop a herd of angry elephants."

"The Treaty of Aniscore is a big deal," Keolo replied. "We have to be sure the Immortals are deliberately breaking the treaty before we counterattack. It's an Entanglement thing, sort of like taking the moral high ground in an argument."

The Hydra nearest the inner airlock extruded a football-like object from somewhere in his amorphous body and attached it to the door. Then it glided back ten meters, and the device exploded. The bulkhead groaned. The floor under Keolo's feet shook. The bayside door of the airlock shredded. The corridor-side door bulged out but held.

Margo's voice came through loud and clear. "Citizens of the Immortal Ascendancy, we've detected explosions in the shuttle bays. Please return to your shuttle immediately. We'll construe any other action as a hostile act. Return now, or you violate the Treaty of Aniscore."

The Hydras blasted the remaining airlock door open with a rocket and began funneling into the broken airlock.

"We are under attack," Margo said. "Defend the ship!"

Keolo flicked the plastic safety cover off the card he carried and squeezed its big, red button. In the shuttle bay, flames squirted out from a dozen hidden flamethrowers. Five Hydras made it through the airlock door and into the corridor, the rest perished in the flames of the shuttle bay.

Flamethrowers also lined the first hundred meters of the corridor. The Hydras contracted their bodies into compact spheres. It was hard to tell amid the flames, but the Hydras seemed to be excreting a coolant. The rear Hydra extruded another explosive football, and the force of its explosion launched them like cannonballs through the gauntlet of fire.

Keolo signaled Fireteam 2. "Five Hydras coming your way at high speed."

* * *

Keolo trusted that Fireteam 2 leader Ensign Goldie Estrallina would stop the Hydras if anyone could. She was the Misfits lead guitar and another half-breed genmod. Goldie had inherited her mother's sexy, pleasure-chick body, but got her drive and love of military lore from her father, a sergeant in the Marines.

Goldie and her second-in-command, Samantha, not a gen-mod, took point. They hid in shallow doorways about twenty meters from where the shaft from the shuttle bay teed into their corridor. The two junior members of her fireteam, Alicia and Carmen, waited in doorways another ten meters behind them.

Five balls of charcoal bounced onto the corridor's floor, forming a nest of sinister, smoldering eggs.

"Are they dead?" Alicia asked.

"Why don't you go ask them?" Samantha replied.

"That we will," Goldie said, "Up close and personal. Keep your dart poppers on explosive and follow my backside."

Goldie advanced a couple of meters. Cracks began forming in the thick burnt-carbon shells covering the Hydras. "They're still alive! Give it to them, ladies."

Dozens of explosive darts ripped into the Hydras. Some of the darts exploded on the surface and blasted away the encasing charcoal. Other darts penetrated the core of the Hydras. These darts should have exploded in a shower of whatever passed for flesh and blood in these creatures, but instead, the Hydras just seemed to absorb them.

Nozzles popped out of the Hydra's bodies.

"Take cover!" Goldie yelled.

Flames roared down the hallway. Goldie and Samantha barely made it to safety in two doorways. Alicia and Carmen were slower. The flames caught them in the open. Their screams filled the command channel, and then their comm units went dead.

This was real—life or death. "Use the antimatter darts," Keolo ordered through his shock.

"No kidding?" Goldie was already unzipping a pocket and pulling out a shock-resistant case.

Inside was exactly one red dart. One dart with a hundred

times the explosive power of a chemical dart—the product of human ingenuity and Entanglement technology. High-tech, miniature electromagnets kept the antimatter core of the darts from touching the normal matter shell until detonation, which led to the dart's downside—a hit from a laser could trigger the dart, as could the explosion from another dart, causing a massive chain reaction. And the tiny electromagnets ran on batteries with a limited lifetime. In five or six months, every unused antimatter dart would explode. Considering the risks, Captain Kilwee Five refused to allow more than one antimatter dart per person in the ship.

The flames paused, and five Hydras became visible, crawling along, crunching over bits of charcoal.

Goldie signaled Samantha. "I'll take the leader. You take number two."

"Roger."

"Then we'll make a run for the other two darts. *Now.*"

They fired and scrambled toward the bodies of their companions. The explosions from the antimatter darts knocked them flat, then covered them with a shower of gooey droplets.

Goldie grabbed Alicia's body and dragged it into a doorway. Apologizing to the dead soldier's remains, she gently extracted the antimatter dart container from the charred body.

A second burst of flames washed down the hallway. When the flames stopped, Goldie peeked around the corner. Three Hydras, getting closer.

"Got your dart, Samantha?"

"Loaded."

"Okay, wait for my move. Then I want you to blow away the lead Hydra."

"We're still one dart short," Samantha said. "Two darts—three blobs."

"That's why I'm making the first move."

Goldie set a laser rifle against her shoulder and fired a continuous beam into the rear Hydra. The sound of steam sizzling off the wound hissed down the corridor.

The steaming Hydra bellowed and swung its flamethrower toward Goldie, pushing aside the Hydra immediately in front of it for a clear shot.

Goldie dropped the laser rifle, swung up her dart popper, and fired her antimatter dart into the small area of contact between the two Hydras. "Do it, Samantha."

A clean, bright antimatter explosion lit the hallway, and the force of the explosion knocked Goldie to the floor. A second explosion and rain of sludge signaled a hit by Samantha.

Goldie staggered to her feet and trudged forward to see what remained after her glancing hit.

Four hunks of protoplasm roughly the size of a person wormed their way toward a central location, as if to reconstitute a Hydra.

Goldie let loose a laser beam to slow-roast the largest chunk. Samantha came up beside her and did likewise to another piece of Hydra.

"We have this, Keolo."

22

The Rottenness of War

Keolo nodded at Evan. "Time to burn a door in the bulkhead."

Evan pointed a tentacle finger at the back wall. Ensign Evan Monco was another genmod. In his case, he was loaded with octopus gene splices. He was Keolo's Second on Fireteam 1, an explosives expert, and drummer for the Misfit Platoon. Besides tentacles for fingers, he was hairless, and he had some control over his skin color.

"Look away from the shuttle bay," Evan said.

Keolo turned his head. Stark shadows from Evan's thermal gel played on the wall: long human shadows from his squad, solid squares from boxes containing antimatter weapons, and insect-like shadows from a row of space horses.

The space horses were partly his idea. Traditional space horses were simple rocket packs in a grid of tubes the size of a horse's body for extended extravehicular activity in space. But entanglement technology had given these space horses three times the power in a lighter body. They could accelerate at eight gees in any direction at the nudge of a joystick. The space horses didn't carry any armament of their own, but Keolo planned on bringing plenty of handheld weapons aboard.

The loud clang of falling metal rang out, and the bright light of the thermal gel dimmed. Keolo turned to see a smoldering plate welded to the floor in front of a new opening in the bulkhead. Messy, but he didn't doubt the wisdom of using too much thermal gel rather than too little.

"It's an oven in here." Evan was already poking his head into the shuttle bay. "But within heat suit parameters."

"Helmets on," Keolo ordered. "Squad, forward!"

The ventilators had already cleared most of the smoke in the shuttle bay, replacing it with fresh air, but the floor and walls radiated heat. Evan ran to the main airlock. A large rock blocked the outer airlock doors—the Immortal's shuttle. Evan played his tentacles over the rock surface, tentacles that could smell and taste and tell him more about the rock than a handheld. He plastered a shaped charge on the rock and dove aside. The rock shattered, creating a jagged opening.

Keolo and Evan arrived at the crack in the rock together, but bright orange flames blocked their path. The flames paused, and Keolo peeked around the door. Almost immediately, a new burst of flames roared at him, and he pulled back.

"Two hydras at a control panel to the left," he said. "Two flamethrowers in sight. They're tag-teaming to keep up the flames and taking turns doing something with the controls."

He'd spied an alcove on the other side of the shuttle. If he could get over there, he might get a clear shot at a Hydra—or at least draw its fire and give Evan a clear shot.

On the other hand, his suit wasn't rated for the kind of heat it would take if he exposed it to the wall of flames. He could burn up, like Alicia.

"Isn't there a chemical we could spray in there to suppress the flames?" he asked Even.

"Sure, lots of them," Evan replied, "But I don't have any with me. I could fabricate some if you want to wait a few minutes."

"Go ahead and get started," Keolo said. "And send Andrew up here."

"Keolo," Margo broke in. "You're our last chance. The other

two shuttles got away. We managed to shoot them down, but it's blowing our counterattack strategy."

Keolo felt the thrum of the shuttle's engines starting through the rock floor. "Evan, belay that order. Look for your shot." He dove into the flames to roll across the floor.

By the time he hit the far wall, the refrigerator unit of his spacesuit had burnt out. His suit provided some insulation against the heat, but he didn't have long.

The flames left a thirty-centimeter gap near the floor on his side. Vibrations from the engines were increasing.

Keolo rolled into the cabin, fired an antimatter dart at the pilot, and rolled back into the alcove. He never saw the explosion, but a shower of gray skin and stringy hydraulic tubules spattered on the floor beside him.

He peeked out again and fired a barrage of explosive darts at the remaining Hydra. The chemical explosives didn't do much damage to the Hydra, but they did draw its fire. The flames roared down on him, and he withdrew as far back into the alcove as he could get.

As hoped, the move drew the fire away from Evan. A second splash of Hydra goo rained onto the floor, and the flames went out.

Keolo staggered to his feet. "Alpha squad, grab the space horses and assemble in the shuttle. How long for you to get here, Goldie?"

"Give us one minute."

"Tafad and José, bring space horses in for Goldie and Samantha." Keolo's voice cracked at the memory of Alicia and Carmen screaming in flames.

He stumbled out through the shuttle bay. His lungs gulped for air, but it was pointless. His suit's breathing system was broken. He fell through the breach Evan had burned into the bulkhead and ripped off his helmet. Never had fresh, cool air felt so good.

A few seconds later, Meera and Vlad were all over him. Ensign Meera Gandhi, the squad medic and trombone player for

Misfit Platoon, had the blackest hair and eyes Keolo had ever seen. Crow and eagle genes gave her super sharp vision and the natural ability to see ultraviolet as part of a four-dimensional "color wheel."

Meera said he had a few first-degree burns, but he was fit to fight. Vlad replaced the broken environmental modules of his spacesuit. Goldie arrived, and together they caught up with the rest of the squad in the Immortal's shuttle.

His squad gave him a rousing cheer and made a path for him to the control panel, where Andrew had hot-wired the shuttle. Instead of push buttons, Immortals used conductive patches of skin to complete control circuits, and instead of a joystick, they pressed on the sides of a deep bowl embedded in the control panel.

His team slid a space horse behind him for a seat, and he inserted his hands into the steering bowl. Away they lurched.

The Immortal's radar display was a lot like those used on Earth, except it used a non-symmetric scale, which made speeds and distances hard to determine. Nonetheless, it left no room for doubt when the Immortal mothership sent a small, fast interceptor in their direction.

Keolo pointed at the airlock. "Evan, deploy the antimatter mines."

The deployment was simple. Evan took a jarful of the tiny mines through the airlock and threw them in front of the ship. As long as their shuttle didn't accelerate, the mines should protect them from interception all the way to the alien mothership.

"Everyone, saddle up." Keolo led them out through the airlock with their space horses.

The Immortal interceptor started deceleration to match trajectories with their shuttle, firing a warning shot across their bow. Then, it blew up, the victim of an antimatter mine. The explosion filled the area around the shuttle with clouds of gas and chunks of rock—perfect cover for the little space horses.

But the jig was up. A missile streaked away from the mothership toward the shuttle. The missile hit the cloud of micro-mines, it too erupted into a bright fireball.

A few seconds later, the Immortals fired a single pulse from a powerful ship-to-ship laser, and the shuttle vanished in a flash of its own.

Another laser blast from the Immortal mothership vaporized the arcing power cable on the Entanglement mothership, along with a good-sized chunk of the solar panel. Immortal radio chatter blossomed. No more hiding the losses their shuttles had taken.

Eventually, the slow-moving cloud of antimatter mines reached the Immortal's ship and covered the surface of the converted asteroid with a firestorm of explosions, tearing away external sensors, jamming shut missile covers, and blowing open several of the docking bays.

Keolo's squad rode their small space horses unnoticed behind the mayhem. They would be at the Immortal ship in another minute.

* * *

The shower of antimatter pellets had performed well. Keolo's squad landed amid bent and broken towers, antennae, and jagged craters.

So this is what it's like to be an alien invader. He added that to his song idea journal. This was the kind of unique perspective he'd hoped to experience when he joined the SDF.

He shook his head to clear it. Songwriting later. Soldiering now. "Stay in pairs a hundred meters apart. The last thing we need is for a hit on one of us to cause an antimatter chain reaction and wipe out the rest of us."

Keolo partnered with Meera and sent Evan and Vlad to blast away the battered outer door of a maintenance airlock. Vlad cranked the inner door open a crack and forced in a remote camera on a stick. The camera glimpsed the bright orange of a flamethrower and went dead.

Vlad cranked the door wide open, careful to stay out of the way as the vacuum of space sucked the flames into its vastness. This gave Evan a chance to see past the flames to their source. A few antimatter darts cleared the passageway of enemy Immortals.

Keolo and Meera took the lead into the dark interior. Evan and Vlad followed at the prescribed hundred meters, and the rest of the squad came behind them. The corridors of the alien ship were like giant wormholes bored into the rock and coated with slime.

The fight to the bridge followed a simple tactic: move fast, stay out of flamethrower range, and pick off the Immortals with antimatter darts.

Resistance was sporadic until the humans arrived at the bridge. Meera's eagle-like vision spotted several booby traps, which they removed with antimatter darts.

Evan set an explosive charge on the door to the bridge. "I don't like it. This has been too easy."

"I haven't seen any Hydras at all—just Ambos," Meera said. "It's hard to believe the captain was so confident of victory he sent all of them away on the landing parties."

"Or maybe he was too afraid of failure," Keolo said. "But having no reserve would be foolish. Most likely, a dozen Hydras are waiting for us behind this door."

Evan and Vlad moved to one side of the door. Keolo and Meera took cover in a shallow depression, embracing the slime as a necessary evil. Even so, when the blast went off, the shock wave slid them several meters farther down the hallway.

Dry rock dust and gooey slime droplets filled the air, then fell to the floor to make a gritty sludge. Keolo snuck up to the hole where the door had been. Sure enough, as soon as he peeked into the bridge, a continuous wall of flames filled the gap.

Keolo waited a full minute for a pause in the flames, but none came. More tag team—or round robin—work by the enemy.

"I don't see how we can get through those flames," Evan said.

Meera pursed her lips. "It would be a bad idea to fire randomly into the main control room of the ship."

Keolo rubbed his chin. "When you have a stalemate, change the game. Let's try a diversion. Andrew and José, you two circle around to the other side of the bridge and blast a second point of attack through the wall there with antimatter darts. See if you can catch them in a crossfire, or at least distract them from us. Make it quick."

The pair left. Flames rolled nonstop out of the door to the bridge.

Keolo squinted at the flames. "It'll take them a while to circle the bridge. Does anyone else have any other ideas for getting past those flames?"

"Concussion grenade," Evan said. "A puff of air, like blowing out a candle."

"Good thinking," Keolo replied. "My mother always said, 'two heads are better than one.' Let's give it a try."

"Ready when you are."

Keolo signaled Meera to follow him. "Give us a minute. Meera and I will line up in front of the door far enough away the flames don't get us and hope for a clear shot."

"Something's happening," Even said suddenly.

"What?"

"I don't know. I felt vibrations through my tentacles. Something in the rock. A big explosion or crash of some kind."

Keolo listened for a few seconds but didn't hear anything. He signaled Evan to toss in the concussion grenade.

The shock wave blew the wall of flames down the hallway, singeing Keolo and Meera. But a gap in the flames followed, and Keolo and Meera each got a clear shot at an Ambo.

The flames returned for a few seconds, but then paused, perhaps a sign that only one flamethrower remained. Vlad and

Evan leaped into the bridge together. There were several anti-matter explosions as Keolo and Meera rushed to join them.

The Ambos on the bridge had all fought to the death. There remained a single Hydra, presumably the ship's captain. It had flattened itself into a saucer shape and started moving toward them. Keolo was surprised it didn't have a flamethrower. Was it relying on its great strength to crush them? It was moving unusually slowly—not much of an attack. Did it have something else in mind? Parley? Surrender?

A single antimatter dart from Evan cleared the bridge of the enemy.

Keolo looked around with satisfaction. "I claim this ship in the name of Earth."

He activated his commlink. "Andrew, you and José can come on back. We made it in without your help."

No answer.

He tried again. "Andrew Lang or José Granada, acknowledge. I say again, acknowledge now."

No response.

Keolo felt a sinking feeling in the pit of his stomach. "Meera, take Vlad and the rest of Andrew's fireteam. Follow Andrew's breadcrumbs. Find them. Bring them back. But be careful. Maybe it's just a problem with their coms, but maybe they got bushwhacked."

He gazed at the monitors. Dozens of empty corridors. Where was the enemy?

23

Invasion at Farboro

Shipmaster Karnag's dossier bored Umlac. It was an excellent document—Deathkur had been thorough—but Cutbloc's Shipmaster at Farboro was a boring subject. Shipmaster Karnag was extremely provincial. He'd always lived far from the capital and had no significant challenges in his various posts. He hadn't seen a Shoggart for many fissions, and he didn't properly fear the overlords of his interstellar empire anymore.

The human's slaying of Deathkur angered Umlac anew. Good spymasters were hard to find. Worse, by dominating a Hydras, the human had changed the balance of power that had existed for millennia. Perhaps his fleet, which would soon arrive at Earth, should exterminate all humans. Sometimes the simplest solutions were the best.

He teleported across five of his own Quillip nodes to the extremity of his empire. He avoided unnecessary risk by spending as much time in his underground lair on Morb as possible, but he hadn't dominated the lesser species of dozens of planets for tens of thousands of years by shrinking from direct action.

He activated an ancient protocol allowing a Shoggart to teleport on short notice to across any Immortal Quillip link and made the final jump to *Granite Pincer.*

* * *

Guardmaster Hoargrim was a loyal Hydra vassal to Karnag and had been for thousands of years. He stood idly guarding the door to the bridge, a strictly ceremonial position since there hadn't been any shipboard threats for a hundred years.

Across the bridge, Shipmaster Karnag ingested a scumrat. The little creature squealed delightfully when Karnag bit off its feet.

The watchmaster left his station and crawled to Karnag. Hoargrim perked up. Something unusual must have happened to cause the watchmaster to submit directly to Karnag.

"Most Fearsome Shipmaster," said the watchmaster, "my humble apologies for disturbing your dinner, but an extraordinary situation beyond my poor abilities has arisen. A priority teleport to the *Granite Pincer* will occur in ninety seconds. The cargo is rated at eleven tons, but its nature is unknown. What is your desired course of action?"

Karnag bit off another scumrat foot. "You idiot. Teleportations must be scheduled in advance, so the entangled matter has time to develop sufficient velocity. Check the consoles yourself. Your Ambo slave is undoubtedly about to go berserk."

"Most Fearsome Shipmaster, I've performed this check already."

"Well?"

"Most Fearsome Shipmaster, I'm forced to attest to the apparent correctness of these most irregular readings. It seems an ancient protocol requiring the station to maintain an eleven-ton mass in readiness for emergency teleport at any time has been activated."

"Then it's your fault if this is a false alarm from equipment malfunction," Karnag said. He swallowed the rest of the scumrat whole and called the Chief Guardmaster. "Send half of your weaponmasters to the armory for heavy weapons. Send the other half to the Quillip chamber. Instruct them to quarantine anyone who teleports to my ship until I give further orders."

The Chief Guardmaster approached Hoargrim. "Take your squad of weaponmasters to the armory, load up on heavy weapons, and go guard the Quillip antechamber. You are backup. Squad A is already on their way to greet our new guest when he first arrives. I will stay here and guard the bridge myself."

Hoargrim's digestive organs shrank in protest. Of course, the Chief Guardmaster would send him into danger rather than going himself. And of course, Hoargrim did as told.

But when he arrived at the door from the main hallway to the Quillip antechamber, he heard several loud thumps inside, and he halted.

* * *

Umlac had formed himself into a cylinder with metallic walls. The automatic systems pulled him through the airlock into the antechamber where he rolled forward and squashed the four lead Hydras before they could stiffen their hydraulic defenses. The rear rank of weaponmasters began to flee, but Umlac surged forward and smashed them all against the back wall.

He rolled to the center of the antechamber and spewed flames over the mangled Hydra bodies before they could reconstitute themselves, then he blinded the security cameras with laser beams.

* * *

Hoargrim felt the vibrations in the stone floor as something powerful stomped about the antechamber. An explosion shook the doors, but they held.

Karnag called. "Hoargrim, get those heavy weapons to the Quillip antechamber immediately. An armed tank is attacking us."

"We just arrived outside the door," Hoargrim replied. "Should we enter?"

"You idiot, why ask me? You are there, and I'm not—and what was that noise?"

"Most Feared Shipmaster, another explosion inside the antechamber has damaged its doors further, but they're still holding. I suggest we maintain our current position and blast apart the tank when it breaks through the doors."

"Very well, Guardmaster Hoargrim, your cowardice is noted. You may hide in the corridor. Just make sure you contain that tank."

* * *

Umlac had used the small detonations against the hallway door to cover the noise of his primary explosions. He went out the hole he'd blasted in the side wall of the antechamber into a little-used service tunnel. It was a short distance to the bridge, where Umlac smashed through the flimsy door and steamrolled over the Chief Guardmaster.

Shipmaster Karnag's attention had remained on the squad of Hydras outside the antechamber, but now he turned and lashed at Umlac with flamethrower and laser fire. Umlac rolled forward and struck Karnag a glancing blow, tossing him against the bank of useless monitors.

Umlac unzipped his metal armor into strips and pulled them into his body. Let the Hydra quake before the majesty of his shiny black visage.

"I am Umlac, your new lord. You may fight, or you may surrender. It will end the same, but with more or less torment."

Karnag quivered uncertainly, then said, "Most Glorious Lord Umlac, I surrender."

"Very well. Come to me now."

Karnag flattened himself submissively and crawled closer. "Most Glorious Lord, I'm yours to command. I seek nothing but to fulfill your every order."

Umlac towered over the pitiful Karnag and grabbed him in his jaws. "You are slow to obey. I will rule the *Granite Pincer* directly. I will take your knowledge of it."

He clamped his jaws together and fed on Karnag, absorbing his memories and extracting useful bits of information from his nucleus. Umlac discovered that he already knew a lot about one of the Hydras aboard the *Granite Pincer*: Guardmaster Hoargrim. Not that Umlac had ever met Hoargrim before, but he'd ingested Hoargrim's brother less than a hundred years ago. A hundred years wouldn't be enough time for Hoargrim and the brother to have diverged much from each other, not after the thousands of years of prior experiences they both inherited from their parent.

Umlac would need a loyal vassal to manage the *Granite Pincer* while he was away. He studied the early millennia of Hoargrim's parent to see if he had the right stuff. Hoargrim was boring—a quarry laborer on a poor planet. But his fortune had changed dramatically a few hundred years ago.

The quarry laborer was eventually a fat Hydra sitting on top of a birth-wedge. He dominated six Hydra vassals and sixty-three Ambo slaves. Half of him tore loose and fell down one side of the birth-wedge, the other half slid down the other side.

He was almost exactly half, but one side was always slightly larger than the other. He crashed on the floor and looked up at the top of the pit, anxiously awaiting his color.

The inheritance laws of Hydras decreed that the heavier brother assumed the parent's role, and the lighter brother inherited nothing. The birthing referee held the bucket of dye over his pit. The dye would mark him red or black, and the next stage of his life would begin.

Red. He was the lighter brother. Fear twisted his organs. Everyone around him would assert dominance over him, treating him almost as a common food-thrall. His next few years would be full of hard labor and unrelenting pain. Yet he had been the lighter brother before. He knew how to survive.

First, he needed a new name. Henceforth he would be called Hoargrim.

A freelance trader had just landed near the city on a return trip from the unclaimed border planets around the Forbidden Zone. Life aboard her was luxurious compared to making a living stone raising and gambling. The shipmaster was flush with profits taken from rarely visited civilizations, and he was hiring additional guards for his entourage. Shipmaster Karnag hired Hoargrim.

The next few years while Hoargrim learned the fine points of being a guardmaster went by quickly. Eventually, Shipmaster Karnag spent his profits from the trip and turned the freighter back for more Then the ship got word that a fleet of warships had disappeared in the Forbidden Zone.

Fearful they would be next, the crew mutinied, but Hoargrim remained loyal to the shipmaster. The crew threw Hoargrim and Karnag into the brig and later dumped them at a seldom visited outpost.

There Hoargrim fissioned as the heavier brother, and when the yearly supply ship arrived, he and Karnag took it back to civilization. The lighter brother had no money for passage and stayed behind.

Umlac had arrived at the brother's outpost shortly after that. He ate the lighter brother to absorb his memories for tactical details on the system he was about to pillage.

Hoargrim's loyalty to Karnag was commendable. Umlac valued loyal vassals in times of trouble.

He contacted Hoargrim using the shipmaster's private channel. "Karnag is dead. I am Umlac, your new master. Fear me. Worship me."

"Mighty master, your power is astounding. Your wisdom is unending. I am your humble servant. I will do my utmost to fulfill all of your divine commands. You are—"

Hoargrim would have continued, and Umlac relished the praise. Umlac was pleased that Hoargrim expressed no surprise—he was no fool after hearing the destruction of his fellow guardmasters in the anteroom. And of course, Hoargrim expressed no remorse at the loss of his master—remorse was for weaklings like humans and Wolferlops.

But there was no time for that now. Umlac had come to invade the Entanglement, but not in the manner his brothers expected. He had come to cut a path to the power at Belle Verte.

"Divide your guardmasters into three police shuttles. When I give the order, go to the *Cl'aclen* under the pretense of recovering three berserk Ambos. Once you dock, destroy any resistance, proceed to the *Cl'aclen's* bridge, and take control in my name."

"Mighty master, your plans are wonderful! The shuttles will be ready in seven minutes."

"Make it five minutes."

Umlac gave the attack signal to the Ambo agents Cutbloc had planted on the *Cl'aclen*. He verified that his brothers were launching their invasions at other stars. The foolish Entanglement ships had all accepted their berserk-Ambo ploy. Cutbloc had learned of Umlac's takeover of his ship the *Granite Pincer*, but it was too late for Cutbloc to stop him, so Cutbloc accepted the ship Umlac offered as a trade, with the addition of one large favor for the inconvenience.

Umlac's Hydras landed on the *Cl'aclen*. The hidden Ambos disabled the *Cl'aclen's* communication and power grids as expected. Hoargrim and his squad fought through sporadic defenders and captured the enemy's bridge with no Hydras lost. The *Cl'aclen* was his.

Umlac boarded his new acquisition. He noted with satisfaction that Hoargrim had already ripped away the offensive, insectoid murals. Hoargrim would make an adequate acting shipmaster of his Farboro ships while Umlac pushed on to Belle Verte.

Hoargrim had imprisoned the Venerable Captain Belcramstole Eight to await Umlac's pleasure.

"Worship me," Umlac said to the captive Bossello. "I have taken your ship. I have taken you."

"I seem to have no choice," Belcramstole Eight replied. "I surrender on one condition. Let me return to the Entanglement."

"Fool. I have taken you. There is no condition." Umlac stripped off the captain's metal decorations and wore them on one of his pseudopods. "You are a food-thrall now."

He would have liked to dissect the captain slowly, but he needed the Venerable Captain's memories right away, so he broke a few of the captain's bones to demonstrate complete dominance, then ingested the captain's brain. He learned of Darzak's report on Immortal activity at Goldilocks Three, and he ordered the interloping Venmar brought to him, but Darzak had already fled the Farboro system.

By now, Umlac's Shoggart brothers had captured their initial targets, all except Dismax at Goldilocks Three. Dismax was very secretive about the events there. One unreliable source hinted that humans had stopped the attack, then counterattacked and taken Dismax's understaffed ship. No matter, when he took control of the power at Belle Verte, he would remove the nascent threat of humans before it had time to do any real damage.

His bugged stunner signaled its location at Coldmart. The Entanglement databanks showed Coldmart was a small, harsh mining colony in an inadequately explored system with twelve major planets and dozens of moons—a plausible place for the new colony of Belle Verte and for the mysterious power behind the Forbidden Zone to hide.

He gloated at how easily he'd duped the humans with his bugged stunner, then got down to business. He could replace a supply shipment with his glorious body and be at Coldmart in three hours.

In case Cutbloc or the Entanglement tried to take back Farboro while he was gone, he cloned the memories of a dozen warmasters and inserted them into Hoargrim. They would remain dormant unless needed. He wouldn't risk destabilizing Hoargrim's loyalty with so many ambitious personalities unless absolutely necessary.

Leaving Hoargrim as his proxy to dominate Farboro, Umlac teleported to Coldmart.

24

Anomalies

After studying the Elliquine disappearance and getting assurances from Zephyr that it wasn't a hoax, Jade returned to Engineering and made a beeline for the pile of gear next to the fab unit. She pulled on a Solar Defense Force uniform with its camouflage mesh embedded in tear-resistant fabric. She hung a dart popper on one hip and a short sword for close-range fighting on the other. She stowed an Ambo stun gun—sans locator beacon, according to Quist—in her backpack and slung an energy rifle over her shoulder. She had observed that the colonist's gear—headdresses, mats, and ribbons—had disappeared along with its owners. So Jade planned to be armed at all times.

Quist had morphed back into a fearsome dragon and was busy fabricating some waist-high control panels to make access easier for Ironsides and Conrad.

"How does it feel to be back in an exoskeleton?" Jade asked.

"Normal."

Jade shrugged. "Okay. Let's go see what Ironsides and Conrad have found on the bridge."

As they taxied to the bridge, she tried to strike up a conversation with Quist, but he said it would be more efficient to present his findings only once when the whole team was present, and Jade saw no need to push the matter.

Belle Verte hung in space below them. "It's striped," Jade said. "I had expected it to be all prairie like Elliquor."

Quist rotated his wings toward the planet. "The teal stripes next to the white polar caps are oceans, and the dark green bands next to the oceans are forests. Only the bright green band around the equator is plains."

"The stripes are extremely well-defined," Jade said. "Almost artificial-looking,"

"The uniformity of the bands is because of the planet's lack of tectonic plate activity," Quist replied. "All points at a given latitude have the same mild weather."

"So beautiful. Like a siren, luring ancient sailors to their deaths."

"A singing planet?" Quist said. "A good analogy."

Jade was perplexed by his reply, but they arrived at the bridge just then. Conrad was sorting through a recycled trash pile. At least he wore a new khaki shirt and pants.

"No boots?" Jade asked.

"Ironsides is working on it," Conrad replied. "We found a discarded fab unit, and he's been nursing it along."

"What about the main fabricators?"

"They're locked. We're hoping Quist can hack the cyberlock and get access to them."

"That won't be necessary." Jade shimmied a few steps in front of the fabricators, stopped, then did a few more steps. "There, no access code required."

"You should have done that sooner," Ironsides said. "I've wasted hours with this defective unit, and it's your fault, *Captain*."

Jade glared at him. "I assumed you would call if you needed help, *Commander*. Besides, Conrad told me earlier he would be able to use Universal to operate the fabs. We had no trouble accessing the ship from Engineering."

"Universal didn't work," Conrad said. "So, you probably know about the ostracization, too."

Jade did a double take. "No. What ostracization?"

"Ah, ha!" Conrad perked up. "Once again, careful archeology has uncovered new facts about the past. The recycle pile contained a notice banning Chiplister from the bridge of the ship. They thought he was hallucinating. There was a reference to him seeing 'a dark globe levitating,' but none of the others present saw it."

"Was he? Hallucinating?" Jade asked.

"The pattern isn't clear yet," Conrad replied. "We need more information."

Ironsides bristled. "We'd have more information if Jade hadn't split up the team in spite of my warning. I could have been reviewing the ship's log if she had been here to obtain access."

"I have more information," Quist said.

"Can you give your report to the whole team now?" Jade said, glad for the distraction from Ironsides' griping.

"Obviously."

After a brief silence, Jade rolled her eyes and said, "Please give your report now."

Quist displayed a hologram of the planet, highlighting various areas as he talked. Ironsides was right about one thing: this holoprojector was the best she'd seen yet on *Peapod*.

"First, I scanned the planetary surface in infrared and for motion," Quist said. "There were no signs of animal life near the Elliquine settlement, so I scanned more broadly. Belle Verte has no land animal life whatsoever."

"Impossible." Conrad swept his hand through his hair. "Photosynthesis converts carbon dioxide into oxygen. You need something to convert the oxygen back to carbon dioxide to keep the plants alive."

"Incorrect," Quist said. "There are forms of photosynthesis which don't produce oxygen as a byproduct. However, photosynthesis on Belle Verte *does* produce oxygen. It is unknown how any of this is cycled back into carbon dioxide, but given the oxygen level in the atmosphere and the rate at which it is increasing, there must have been a large population of animals on the planet until they disappeared thirty thousand years ago."

Jade felt the hairs on her arms prickle. "Whatever killed the animals back then may have gotten the colonists, too."

"Unknown."

Conrad scratched his head. "The best-fit pattern is disease, but then why didn't the Elliquine detect the disease agent?"

"May I continue my report?" Quist asked.

Jade carefully said, "Yes, Quist, please continue your report now."

"While scanning the arctic, I found this at the North Pole." Quist's holoprojection showed an aerial view of a half-dozen mountain peaks surrounded by glaciers. "In the visible range of light, this looks like a typical mountain range. Now, look at the deep radar scan. The yellow lines riddling the mountains are hollow tubes. Granite is an igneous rock, formed from slowly cooling magma. No known natural process creates tunnels in granite so profuse, straight, and level."

"Someone excavated them!" Conrad exclaimed.

"There is no proof the tunnels are artificial, either," Quist said. "Physical analysis of the tube walls is necessary to determine their origin."

"So many tunnels. A subterranean city." Conrad waved his hands in excitement. "How marvelous! We must go down and explore."

Jade shook her head. "Slow down, Conrad. If the tunnels are artificial, they are probably just empty mines. Anyway, our mission is to find the missing colonists, not to search for lost civilizations."

"Quist just said he scanned the entire surface of the planet for animals and didn't find the Elliquine," Conrad replied. "If they aren't on the surface of the planet, it follows that they are someplace else—like under it."

"May I continue my report?" Quist asked again. "It would be more efficient to discuss what to do next after all of the facts have been listed."

Jade nodded. "Yes, Quist, please continue your report."

Quist displayed a hologram full of vectors and numbers. "Another anomaly of Belle Verte is that its axial tilt is indistinguishable from zero. No known natural process will form a planet with so little tilt."

Jade frowned, deep in thought. "Are you suggesting someone straightened the planet out, killed all the animals, and then left?"

Conrad jumped up. "Who said they left? They could be hiding in the polar tunnels. It fits an introverted civilization pattern. They evolved to a high level, straightened the planet's axial tilt to stabilize the weather patterns, killed the animal competition, and then retreated underground. They only came out recently to remove the Elliquine colonists, whom they see as alien invaders."

Jade waved Conrad away. "Quist, please continue with your report now."

The hologram changed to a view of Belle Verte from space, ensnared in a web of colored lines. Quist pointed to a wavy yellow line through the planet's center. "Belle Verte is wobbling ever so slightly."

He displayed several additional graphs and tables of numbers. "When measured precisely, the variations in the angle subtended by Belle Verte's horizon and the stellar background follow a sine wave with a period of 91.3 minutes. My calculations prove Belle Verte is in a binary orbit with an invisible partner of angular momentum 3.851×10^{21} Joule-seconds." Quist stopped. Apparently, he thought his report was complete.

Conrad scratched his head. "Invisible? Like a cloaked spaceship?"

"Obviously not. The calculations in the box displayed on the left are most consonant with a small black hole orbiting inside the core of Belle Verte. However, stable black holes that small have never been observed before."

"What about earthquakes?" Jade asked. "Wouldn't a black hole inside the planet cause earthquakes?"

"Not if it is orbiting inside the molten core of the planet, and if it is small enough that its absorption rate of planetary material is below a critical threshold."

Jade stared at the strange planet looming below them. "If the black hole does pass whatever threshold and suck in the whole planet, it won't stop there. We should move *Peapod* away to a safe distance."

"Moving *Peapod* is unnecessary and therefore inefficient," Quist replied. "As you said, earthquakes will warn us if the destruction of Belle Verte by a black hole approaches."

Jade's head was spinning from Quist's many deductions. "How does a black hole play into the disappearance of the Elliquine?"

"Unknown," Quist replied. "And it is unproven if a black hole is causing the wobble. Dissonance in finding such a small, stable black hole remains."

"Very well, Quist. Do you have any other new information to report?"

"No."

Jade looked at Conrad. "Quist reported more weird things than I expected. Could Belle Verte be another planet the Elohoy engineered like the four forbidden planets you mentioned earlier?"

Conrad replied, "The gross pattern of planetary engineering fits, but the four forbidden planets left by the Elohoy are all close to the Elohoy homeworld, while Belle Verte isn't. Also, the four Elohoy planets have warning beacons orbiting them, and there are no warning beacons here. A better fit would be another Elohoy-level civilization."

Jade stared at the bright green stripes below. "There *should* be warning beacons here. Poof. Forty colonists evaporate into thin air."

"*Dissonance.*" Quist turned off his visual displays. "Citizens don't evaporate."

Jade was surprised to hear such a misstatement after Quist's long list of facts. Perhaps there was a translator problem. "Then what do you call it when one second the Elliquine are there and the next they are simply gone? The hologram from the *Peapod's* records looks a lot like evaporating to me."

"The content of the *Peapod's* records is unknown," Quist replied.

"No, they aren't." Jade activated a nearby console, and a holovideo of Elliquine building nests on a grassy plain appeared on the bridge.

"The ground is hard, no crocodile-moles," they chanted.

"The view is far, no steel-claw wolves."

"A happy Solidarity—"

25

Abandoned Settlement

After about an hour, the discussion of the peculiarities of Belle Verte began to go in circles. Jade needed to decide on a course of action.

Conrad lobbied to look for a lost civilization in the polar caves. Ironsides wanted them to study *Peapod's* records systematically. He periodically blamed Jade for wasting his time by not telling him about her computer access sooner, by not giving the team clear direction, and for generally being a poor leader. Quist wanted them to continue with physical research and complained she was forcing him to be inefficient by not providing immediate goals, and then he silently did something involving additional electrical activity in his external sensors.

It would have been so much easier if Ironsides were still in charge, and she could lobby to see the colony for herself while the others researched *Peapod's* archives. Unfortunately, she couldn't responsibly go herself in her new role—or could she?

"Zephyr," she said silently, into her implant. "Can you grant biometric access to *Peapod's* records to everyone on my team?"

"Technically, no. But I can make it look that way to them."

"Perfect, please do so."

Then Jade said aloud, "Quist, you spent a lot of time on Earth working with human-digital interfaces. Can you fabricate a virtual reality interface to let me fly the Elliquine shuttle remotely?"

"Obviously. The minimum time to build one would be forty-seven minutes, utilizing all three fabricators in Engineering."

Ironsides bristled. "You'd risk our only shuttle without having studied all of the records available right here on *Peapod*? The Dasypodia says 'Study the forest shadows before you cast your own there.'"

"I did study *Peapod's* records," Jade replied. "That's how I found the recording of the colony's disappearance. We need to see ground zero of the disappearances for ourselves. We need more and better sensors at the colony site. Meanwhile, I've granted you and the others access to *Peapod's* records. Studying the records from a variety of perspectives may find additional clues."

"This is all unnecessary," Conrad said. "The answers are in the polar caves."

Ironsides shook his root-feet at her. "You risk causing our only shuttle to disappear. You risk bringing the cause of the disappearance to *Peapod* through a VR link. 'Arrogance is for drillsnakes; humility for civilized beings.'"

"The Dasypodia again?" Jade asked.

"Of course," Ironsides answered. "You should listen to the wisdom of the ancients."

"I do." Jade tried looking Ironsides in the eyes, though it was hard since there were so many of them and she didn't know what the gesture meant to a Dasypod. "Benjamin Franklin says, 'Nothing ventured, nothing gained.'"

Ironsides' root-feet twisted into knots, but he had no further retort.

Jade pointed to the bridge consoles. "You and Conrad stay and search the records here. Quist and I will go to Engineering and construct a VR visit to the colony."

"You are terribly short-sighted," Conrad said. "'Nothing ventured; nothing gained' is only half the story. What about 'Leave no stone unturned?' We should go to the polar caves."

Jade glared at him for a second before she said, "Then I suggest you get ready for the trip. Make a list of the equipment you'll need and start fabricating it with the unit here on the bridge. If there is an advanced civilization in the polar caves, we should tell them we come in peace."

Conrad's eyes lit up. "Great idea! A proper field expedition does take a bit of preparation. Can Quist help me when he's done making the VR for you?"

Jade was glad he was glad but had to shake her head. "No, not yet anyway. A proper military expedition requires a lot of preparation, too. I want Quist to help fab some equipment for me."

* * *

Jade finished installing the shoebox-sized remote controls on the shuttle and rover and returned to Engineering. Quist was examining a complicated schematic on the holoprojector. Most of it was yellow, with a blue fringe on one side.

"We should go to the Bridge," he said.

"What makes you say that?" Jade asked. She didn't want to go back to where Ironsides and Conrad were.

"The yellow," he said, jabbing one of his extendable legs into the hologram. "Most of the control-side VR interface is already present in one of the projector control units on the bridge. It will be more efficient to modify that unit than to build another one from scratch."

Why is everyone always trying to do things differently than I want? But her engineering background told her to favor reusing over reinventing, so she said, "Good idea, Quist."

The tempo of Quist's brainsong increased a little, though Jade still didn't know what this meant. Once on the bridge,

Quist finished the VR controller in ten minutes. He used *Peapod's* large holoprojector and fabricated a joystick and a few gauges for Jade. He even fashioned her a chair like her favorite one in the room-tram.

She sat down. "Thank you, Quist. You do good work." Again, the tempo of his brainsong ticked up a notch.

When Jade activated the VR unit, the holoprojector immersed her in the exterior view from the shuttle. Belle Verte in front, *Peapod* to the rear, and a sparsely starred sky everywhere else.

Her miniature control stick lacked haptic feedback, so it felt more like she was playing a cheap video game than piloting a space shuttle, but *Peapod* quickly faded to the rear, and Belle Verte grew closer than ever.

Quist and Ironsides retreated to the far side of the bridge, but she felt the watery-cool electric field of Conrad's body behind her and heard curiosity in his brainsong. She began a running commentary for him.

"I'm decelerating and losing altitude on schedule. The atmosphere is causing the shuttle to heat up as I'd expect, but even though the windows should be red hot, they are not impairing my vision."

"You sound cheerful," Conrad said. "You must like piloting."

Jade studied the bright green world growing larger by the minute a bit wistfully. She could see it, but not feel it with her electrosense. "Flying the shuttle with VR converters is more like a virtual reality game than real piloting."

Conrad's brainsong turned surprisingly negative. "Too bad. I hate virtual reality."

"You don't do simulations?"

"No, I gave them up long ago. Too simple. Too poor of a substitute for 'real reality.' Simulations are flat and contrived, and they give me headaches."

"I'm not into escapist gaming," Jade said. "But war games are another matter. Educational—and much safer than the real thing."

Conrad snorted. "I have yet to find an educational xenolinguistic virtual reality program."

The green prairies of Belle Verte loomed larger. "There's the other shuttle, but I still can't make out the grass nests."

She spiraled lower. "I see the nests now. They look like a clump of crop circles."

"What are those black lines?" Conrad asked.

"They must be shadows from the security-camera poles," Jade replied. She flew over the colony twice, recording close-up views. "Nothing unusual so far. I'm going to land next to the other shuttle."

Jade brought the shuttle in a bit too low, due to its transparent bottom, and plowed a ditch of black soil in the grass. Too bad this wasn't a simulation. She could have practiced until she got it right. As it was, she'd ripped off the landing legs. Without airspace between the shuttle and the ground, she couldn't safely fire the vertical boosters to take off again.

At least Conrad didn't seem to have noticed. That would give her a little time to think of a solution to the landing gear problem. She switched her perspective to the land rover and drove it down a ramp from the shuttle onto the prairie of Belle Verte.

A yellow sun, much like Sol, was high in the deep blue sky. The prairie grass rippled from a perpetual western breeze. There was no sign of the forty Elliquine who had tried to make this their home.

The blades of the Belle Verte grass were a uniform twenty-two centimeters tall, giving the prairie a lawn-like appearance. Each blade terminated with a rounded-heart shape.

Jade drove closer to the settlement. The grass was increasingly trampled as she drew near the colony.

"That nest outside the main circle must be Chiplister's from when he was ostracized," Conrad said.

The nest was on a circular mound of dirt about three meters across, slightly concave at the top. There was a thick ring of grass thatch in the center, about one meter across.

"Elliquine nest lining always starts at the center and works outward," Jade said. The Solidarity had explained the basics of nest building to her on Elliquor.

"So the ring of grass shows how far along Chiplister got in padding his nest before he disappeared," Conrad said. "That may help us establish the timeline in more detail."

Unconsciously, Jade took a deep breath, but all she smelled was metal, plastic, and a little machine oil. "I wish I were down there in person to see what it smells like. For that matter, I wonder what the electric fields would show."

Conrad huffed. "Did I ever mention that VR is flat and boring?"

"Once or twice."

Jade had outfitted the rover with a jointed arm with mechanical hands on the end. She used the arm to grab a box from the rear cargo bin and attach it to the top of a surveillance pole. "Deploying the first enhanced observation station."

An observation station wasn't all she deployed. She left one of the Zephyr's micro spy cameras on the crest of Chiplister's nest.

She took a soil sample, then moved on to another nest. This nest had more thatch than Chiplister's, covering the entire bottom and extending to within ten centimeters of the rim. The colonists had been almost done building nests when they disappeared. Their mates would have joined them in another few hours.

Eventually, the rover reached the middle of the colony. One of the nests there caught Jade's attention. "This is odd. This has to be Chiplister's nest, but the center of this nest is empty, and there is a ring of grass near the outer wall. The Elliquine always start thatching from the center."

Conrad's brainsong pinged and increased in pitch. "What! That changes everything. The nest in the middle of the colony has to be Chiplister's *second* nest after he was ostracized. Get a sample of the grass from both nests to confirm the timeline."

"Okay." Jade pinched a few blades from the nest into a sample jar. "I'll get a sample from the other nest on my way back after I install a few more of the new security sensor packages."

Why would the order in which Chiplister made his two nests matter? "Oh! Brilliant, Conrad! This does change everything."

Conrad's brainsong perked up, becoming lighter and quicker with just her few words of praise. Jade realized she was gaining in self-confidence, and that let her give the other members of the team the recognition they deserved, which was also improving their confidence.

She drove to Chiplister's outer nest and took a sample of the browning grass. The size of the circle of grass matched the size of the hole in the center of the grass at the other nest. The herd of Elliquine would have done everything together. If they started at the center and worked outward, this must indeed be Chiplister's first nest.

She double-timed it back to the shuttle. She'd been thinking about the shuttle's broken landing legs, and when she arrived at the shuttle, she took out one of the metal observation boxes she'd held back, and she ran over it with the rover. Then she bent the flattened metal into a scoop and used it to dig a tunnel in the dirt under the shuttle to vent the thruster exhaust so that the shuttle could take off safely.

She drove the rover into the other Elliquine shuttle, the one the Elliquine had left on the ground. She connected the rover to a data port on the shuttle and used the rover to fly the shuttle back to *Peapod*. She gave the rover's grass samples to Quist and changed her VR channel back to the original shuttle. She flew it up to *Peapod* as well. Now, with the addition of some new landing gear, they had two shuttles at their disposal.

Jade shut off the VR and found Quist had completed his analysis. "How do humans do it? You deduced the correct conclusion about Chiplister without sufficient data."

"Conrad calls it pattern recognition," Jade replied. "I call it intuition."

"But it's illogical. The correct process is to obtain all of the facts and then deduce the correct conclusion from them."

"It's much faster to work with partial data. If my ancestors had waited to be sure the shadow in the trees was a tiger, they would all have been eaten."

"Or they could have missed an opportunity to feast on a deer. Reaching conclusions from partial data causes wrong conclusions."

"Indeed it can. But inaction can be dangerous, too. Uncertain situations can lead to disaster."

"That's why Obnots avoid dangerous, uncertain situations."

"And yet here you are," Jade said

"Most Obnots would say I'm insane—that I was contaminated by human culture during my time on Earth."

26

Unseen Enemy

J ade arrived at the bridge a few minutes early. Ironsides curled his root-feet in disgust and stayed busy with the ship's computers on the far side of the bridge. Jade pulled up pictures of Chiplister's nests from the rover to pick out the best ones for the debriefing. Quist arrived exactly on time; Conrad a few seconds late.

Jade took a deep breath. She was proud her expedition to the surface had paid off and anxious to show the results to Ironsides to demonstrate she was making good choices as team leader, but first, it seemed polite to ask him what he'd found in his search of *Peapod's* records.

Ironsides straightened his root-feet. "I found no evidence the Elliquine knew why there is no animal life on Belle Verte or that they visited the Polar tunnels."

Jade nodded. She hadn't expected Ironsides to find anything.

"However," he continued. "I did find records showing that the Elliquine ended Chiplister's ostracization before they disappeared."

Jade opened her mouth to say she already knew that but stopped. This was a chance to reward Ironsides for contributing to their mission, why spoil it? Instead, she said, "Excellent work, Mr. Ambassador."

Ironsides wriggled his root-feet and his brainsong trilled with little trumpet flourishes. He was enjoying this.

Jade paused, then said to the group. "So Chiplister wasn't hallucinating. There is a phantom disk flying around the surface of the planet."

Ironsides' root-feet vibrated slightly, and the pitch of his brainsong rose a notch. "You saw a phantom disk?"

"No, I didn't see one," Jade conceded. "But take a look at this."

Zephyr had found recordings from the time Chiplister saw the phantom. Chiplister startled and followed something with his eyes, but security poles aimed where Chiplister was looking recorded nothing.

"Chiplister reacted to *something*," Jade said. "If the Solidarity believes he saw a phantom disk, then so do I."

"*Dissonance*," Quist said. "The fact that Elliquine colonists ended Chiplister's ostracization does not imply they came to believe the phantoms were real. Chiplister may have recanted. No known phenomenon fits the characteristics of these phantoms. Consonance is only achieved if Chiplister was hallucinating and the colonists accepted him back anyway."

"Or if the phantoms are real and we just don't know how they work yet," Jade said.

"The phantoms contradict the laws of physics. Therefore, Chiplister was hallucinating."

Conrad stepped into the middle of the group. "You aren't looking at the big picture. Either way, you're arguing over one fact among many. I'm sure we'll find the answers in the Polar tunnels—most likely from a civilization that has been hiding there for thousands of years."

"If they caused the colonists to disappear, they might do the same to us," Jade said. "Especially if we go knocking on their door."

Conrad would not be dissuaded. "We will emphasize that we come in peace. We will tell them we only want the

Elliquine back, and we will go our way."

"And abandon Belle Verte?" Jade said. "I'm not prepared to do that."

" Maybe they will convince you otherwise," Conrad replied. "Or maybe they will let the Elliquine stay. That's why we need to talk to them and find out what they want."

"*Dissonance,*" Quist said. "There is no sign of a hidden civilization, and you speak as if there is. There are no energy expenditures in the Polar tunnels."

"You can't be sure of that," Conrad said. "We don't know how deep the tunnels go."

"Convection would bring heat to the surface tunnels."

Jade took a deep breath. Conrad seemed absolutely convinced the Polar tunnels were important. He didn't seem to be able to explain why other than to say the pattern fit. Maybe he could see something she couldn't. There was only one way to find out.

"All right, Conrad," she said. "We will explore your ideas. We'll go to the tunnels next. But we've all been working for sixteen hours, so we'll get some rest first. Then, first thing in the morning, I'll pilot the remote-control shuttle to the Polar Caves, and the rover can investigate."

Conrad grabbed Jade's arm. "No! I must go in person. I'm an explorer. That's why I'm here. To seek out alien civilizations."

"*Dissonance,*" Quist said. "It is unknown if the rover will be able to navigate the caves. Conrad will be a more efficient explorer."

"I can't let you go down there alone," Jade persisted. "It's an unnecessary risk."

Conrad grinned. "Then come with me. You can pilot the shuttle in person instead of by remote control. Didn't you say you wanted to see and smell the surface yourself?"

Jade gave a wry smile. "I would love to go, but Ironsides should be the one to accompany you. I can still pilot the shuttle remotely."

Ironsides' root-feet twisted into bunches. "I'll go if you

order it, but I don't want to go. There is much more to do in *Peapod's* archives first."

Jade scowled. "This is frustrating. I would be the logical choice, and I want to go, except as the captain, my responsibility is here on *Peapod*."

Ironsides waved his root-feet. "The Dasypodia says 'A leader who avoids personal risk is like a stone to the team.' It also says, 'The most advantageous use of a team's talents is the sign of a good leader.'"

Jade flashed Ironsides a smile. "That doesn't jibe with Earth's military wisdom, but I like it. This time I'll listen to the *Dasypodia*. Quist, could you install acceleration couches for Conrad and me in the shuttles while the rest of us sleep? And a real pilot's console. Conrad and I will fly down to the Polar tunnels first thing in the morning."

* * *

Jade helped Quist install the shuttle modifications for the trip to the surface. She stayed in the shuttle for a final check, then followed Quist to the bridge.

Quist was studying holograms of Belle Verte's wobble. "I have proof that observing more facts is superior to relying on intuition."

"What are you talking about?"

"The anomaly isn't a miniature black hole."

"I thought you said it was," Jade said. "What made you change your mind?"

Quist highlighted a spider-web-like diagram. "I didn't change my mind. I said initial observations indicated it acted like a black hole with anomalies. By observing more facts, I have proved it's better characterized as an anomaly with some characteristics in common with a black hole."

"I don't—" Jade began when Zephyr buzzed in on her implant.

"Priority alert. An unidentified object is at the colony nest site."

Jade hopped over to a nearby monitor, and Zephyr sent her live video feeds. The micro cam on Chiplister's nest showed something resembling a smudged porthole hovering in front of an Elliquine security pole. She could see the pole through the phantom. She might not even have noticed the slight dimming it made, except that Zephyr pointed it out to her. The video from the security pole showed nothing.

"Quist, come look at this!" Jade waved him over excitedly.

"It is inefficient to view a recording twice. Can I wait until Ironsides and Conrad are here?"

"This is a live feed from the colony. The Phantom is back."

"The probability of hallucinations among humans is much greater than among Elliquine."

"Look at this. Now. That's an order."

Quist came over and observed silently as the phantom moved from one security pole to another. The ghost disk kept its invisible face toward the security poles, and only Jade's micro cams detected its presence. Finally, it floated across the scars left by the shuttles, then sailed out of sight across the prairie.

"It was studying the changes we made: the new surveillance cameras and the shuttle landing," Jade said. "Are you convinced the phantoms are real now?"

Quist's brainsong surged into a loud symphony of point and counterpoint. The pace of his usual methodical march pumped up like an old disco tune.

"*Dissonance*," he said. "There is much dissonance. Go away now."

27

Read the Fine Print

Keolo waited at the end of a table on the Goldilocks Three ship for the meeting to start. After the intensity of battle, after losing four of his squad to the Immortals—Alicia and Carmen in Hydra flames and Andrew and José in an antimatter dart chain reaction—military bureaucracy was even pettier and more frustrating than usual.

He sat with Margo on his left. Nat's gray, hulking body loomed on the far side of Margo. Pannap, Kilwee Five, and Blue Steel lined up to his right. The half of Pannap next to Keolo took the form of a woman with a Hawaiian face, and the half next to Kilwee Five took the form of a Merkasaur.

Keolo was eager to get back to exploring the Immortal ship and its alien devices. But so far, they'd been unable to ship anything back to Earth, and the scientists there were sending long lists of experiments for Keolo's squad to perform.

Of course, Earth had planned to send dedicated scientists to their new ship and interesting devices back to Earth. Then they found out they couldn't, and furthermore, Keolo's platoon was stuck at Goldilocks Three, unable to return to Earth in the foreseeable future.

Admiral Hammer and his staff sat on another side of the virtual triangular table. Two of the Supreme Council of the

Entanglement sat on the third side: Silver Streak, a Dasypod who was involved in all police and military affairs, and Greysilk, a Wolferlop-M healer, who Pannap said was interested in all things human.

A gong announced the arrival of the Merkasaur who chaired the Council. Jakkar Ten wore far more wealth than Kilwee Five. His necklaces of metal tokens drooped to the floor in a thick knot. A cape of osmium and palladium tokens covered his back; his arms jangled with bracelets of some metal Keolo didn't recognize.

He greeted the participants and got down to business. "We are here to review a complaint about the terms of the Goldilocks Three defense agreement between Earth and the Entanglement. Certainly, the Entanglement honors its agreements and, as such, recognizes the ownership of the captured Immortal ship by the Solar Federation. So, what does Earth have to complain about?"

Admiral Hammer gestured at Keolo's end of the table. "Owning a ship without having access to it is meaningless. We expected to have access to our ship. Even worse, you have stranded our soldiers on the ship, refusing to transport any of them back to Earth."

Silver Streak waved his root-feet at the admiral. "Our agreement says we'll return your soldiers to Earth territory. It doesn't obligate us to provide free transportation between different parts of your territory. On the contrary, it is only natural for us to expect fair market prices for any services you consume. No other action would be consistent with our stewardship of Entanglement resources."

Kilwee Five shook his necklaces of coins. "It was never my intention to strand the soldiers of Earth away from their home world after they so valiantly saved our ship. I support their request for transportation back to Earth."

Silver Streak pointed his root-feet at Kilwee Five. "Your intentions are irrelevant. They don't void the contract as written."

"I'm sure we can work something out," Admiral Hammer said. "We've got a whole ship full of stuff to trade."

Jakkar Ten shook himself, and his wealth tokens glittered in the soft light of the council chamber. All eyes turned toward him as he said, "Kilwee Five, I'm disappointed you didn't write the contract to reflect your wishes. Admiral, I agree with Silver Streak that our stewardship of Entanglement resources is paramount. As for your ship full of 'stuff,' it has no market value. No one in the Entanglement wants goods tainted with Immortal secretions. On the other hand, Quillip transportation is one of the most valuable commodities in the Entanglement, especially now that the Immortal Ascendency has stolen seven of our Quillip nodes."

Margo's face grew red. "But we saved the Goldilocks Three ship from a Hydra invasion. We lost four good soldiers."

Four good soldiers. An understatement. They were great soldiers; they were great human beings. Alicia and Carmen deserved better than incineration by flamethrower. Andrew and José had been his friends, and now they were MIA at the scene of a large crater.

Four good soldiers. One of them, Andrew, was a part of the Misfit Platoon. Keolo loved every one of his band members. He wanted the ones with him to be able to go home, and he wanted Jade back safely.

"Of course, Lieutenant Commander," Jakkar Ten replied to Margo. "Your platoon performed admirably. Earth's payment of thirty-six QE-credits has already been transferred to its account, and the former Immortal ship at Goldilocks Three has been registered as the property of Earth."

"Thirty-six QE-credits won't even pay for a round trip of one person." Margo's voice quivered as she spoke.

"As I said," Jakkar Ten replied, "Interstellar Quantum-entangled mass is a scarce commodity."

Now it was one of Admiral Hammer's companions who turned red in the face. "We have hundreds of tons of quantum-entangled mass on our new ship, but that doesn't appear to be a highly valued commodity."

Keolo wondered how sarcasm translated into Merkasauran. Since the "judge" in this case was helping argue the Entanglement position, it seemed unlikely Earth would gain satisfaction. He began playing with a new lyric: *Alien justice ain't no justice at all.*

"Either you are incredibly stupid, or you are making what humans call a 'joke,'" Silver Streak said. "The value of quantum-entangled mass depends on the location of the paired, entangled quarks. Your quantum-entangled mass is paired with the Immortal Ascendency ship *Granite Pincer* at Farboro, and no sane Entanglement Citizen would ever want to go there. The loss of the *Cl'aclen* at Farboro has taken away any value of your Quillip destination."

The loss of the Farboro system was news to Keolo. He whispered to Pannap, "If the Immortals control the *Cl'aclen*, doesn't that mean they've cut off the remote worlds connected to the rest of the Entanglement through Farboro?"

"Of course, Darling. Several such worlds have been isolated from the rest of the Entanglement."

"Did Jade go to one of those?"

"Almost certainly, Darling, though I can't say which one."

Keolo gritted his teeth. Jade was stranded, and the damn Entanglement wasn't doing anything about it. Seven worlds lost, countless others cut off. Hell, they almost lost Goldilocks Three and cut off Earth. Only humans had saved the Entanglement's ship on Goldilocks Three from the Immortals.

Of course. The answer hit Keolo like a sledgehammer. He slammed his fist on the table, and everyone looked at him.

He looked back at Admiral Hammer a bit sheepishly. "Sorry, sir. I was thinking: we captured one Immortal ship, why not two more? We can take the *Granite Pincer* and keep it for Earth. Then we take the *Cl'aclen* and return it to its rightful owners in exchange for the transportation and weapons we would need to carry out the operation. Then our ship at Goldilocks Three would go to the Entanglement, which should give it the economic value it seems to lack at present. And the Entanglement gets another ship back."

The admiral's eyebrows came together, and he nodded to Keolo. "Interesting idea, Lieutenant." He turned to the Supreme Council. "Would you be willing to make a deal along those lines?"

Greysilk bobbed up and down. "Yes. Yes. A good deal for the Entanglement. The *Cl'aclen* has been a great loss."

Silver Streak twisted his root-feet. "Not good for the Entanglement at all. Such a deal would give the unguilded humans too much access to the Entanglement. They need to join a Guild first."

Jakkar Ten jerked his head toward Greysilk and Silver Streak. "Silence! We will not argue over our position on the proposition in public." He nodded to Keolo and Admiral Hammer. "A proposal worthy of a Merkasaur. We shall consider it, but no promises yet. As our previous discussion proves, chaos is in the details."

28

New Physics

After a fitful few hours of sleep, Jade rose to find Quist still hunkered by the holoprojector, his brainsong as fast and intricate as ever.

Ironsides and Conrad arrived, and Ironsides came up close to Jade. He seemed much larger at close range, with his root-feet extending well above her head.

"I apologize for not being more helpful yesterday," Ironsides said. "And for overreacting to your drillsnake smell. How can I be most useful today? I would be glad to accompany Conrad to the surface to explore the caves, or to remain here as a backup command post, whatever you prefer."

Jade had heard that Dasypod plantings sometimes led to something like repentance or ho'oponopono, but this was still unexpected. Was she just supposed to say, "Apology accepted," or was she supposed to reciprocate somehow?

Quist stirred, ending his long period of introspection and interrupting Jade's exchange with Ironsides. "There are new facts. The Phantoms are real."

"That's what I've been telling you," Conrad said. "The colonists must have seen them a second time."

"*Consonance*," Quist replied. "And now Jade and I have seen them."

"Where? When? What?" Conrad and Ironsides jumbled their questions together.

"On the surface. In the colony a few hours ago" Quist replied.

Jade activated the holoprojector. "Here, let me show you a recording of the event."

A gray porthole hovering in the sky in front of a security camera flashed into the bridge.

Then she showed another view. "This recording was made from the security camera at the same time. The disk is invisible from one side, and barely discernable on the other."

Ironsides' root-feet quivered. "Where did the first image come from? The camera appears to have a defect."

"The camera doesn't have a defect," Quist said. "Seismic perturbations occur simultaneously with the visual sighting."

"A black hole orbiting inside the planet would explain seismic perturbations," Ironsides said. "And the visual image could still be a holographic projection—a hoax, as you previously stated."

"*Dissonance*. Holographic projections are unable to produce unidirectional disks. After examining all the facts, I have proved the phantom is a ... transmatter ... portal." The universal translator paused as it introduced a new word into its vocabulary: *transmatter*.

"I never heard of transmatter before," Jade said. "What is it?"

"No one in the Entanglement has heard of transmatter before," Quist replied. "It is a new rotation of the tessaractoid."

Jade nodded, but Conrad said, "I'm a linguist, not a physicist. What's the tessaractoid?"

Quist replied, "The tessaractoid is the fundamental wave-particle, which manifests itself in various projections from the duplex E8 Lie group of supersymmetric particle space into the eleven dimensions of normal space."

Conrad shook his head. "Whoa. I need a simpler explanation."

"Let me try," Jade said. "The tessaractoid is the elementary particle in the Theory of Everything. Different rotations of that particle relative to spacetime result in electrons, neutrons, dark matter selectrons, sneutrons, and so forth. The many-dimensional tessaractoid is projected onto four-dimensional spacetime like the shadow your three-dimensional body casts of itself onto a flat wall—the shadow looks different depending on how you turn your body."

"You have left out important details, as humans often do, but it is a recognizable approximation."

"Thank you, Quist, but how does transmatter explain the phantom disks?"

"It wasn't obvious," Quist replied. "But I proved transmatter interacts with both the electromagnetic force of normal photons and with the selectromagnetic force of dark matter photinos. This means transmatter can chemically bond to both normal matter and dark matter, creating unique hybrid materials."

"That's interesting," Jade said, "but how does it explain the phantoms?"

"Someone used transmatter to build a device to convert visible light into dark light."

"It's a spy-eye!" Jade exclaimed. "Someone is spying on the colony."

"And when we go to the polar caves, we'll find out who," Conrad said.

"Incorrect," Quist replied.

"What?" Conrad glared at Quist. "Why?"

Quist replaced the particle hierarchy chart. "I reexamined the wobble in Belle Verte. The anomalies in the analysis of the seismic disturbances introduced by assuming a black hole is orbiting inside the mantle of Belle Verte vanish if we postulate that a dark matter spaceship is orbiting inside Belle Verte."

"What?" Jade, Ironsides, and Conrad all exclaimed together. "How can you deduce a dark matter spaceship?"

"It may not be a spaceship like this one, but consonance

requires that an intelligence created the dark matter object, placed it in orbit, and continues to maneuver it. The closest term in Universal is *spaceship*."

"You said, 'inside Belle Verte,'" Conrad said. "How can a spaceship orbit *inside* a planet?"

Quist pointed to a holographic chart. "Dark matter doesn't interact with normal matter, except through gravity or trans-matter particles. Therefore, to an observer on the dark matter spaceship, it would appear as if the ship were orbiting an empty spot in space with a substantial gravity field."

Conrad snorted. "A phantom ship orbiting a phantom planet. It sounds like the *Flying Dutchman* lost in space."

Jade pursed her lips. "Can you connect the dark matter spaceship with what happened to the Elliquine colony?"

Quist displayed another hologram. "This is the dark matter spaceship's orbit backward in time. The ship intersected the Elliquine colony at the exact moment the Elliquine disappeared."

"You just told us the *Flying Dutchman* couldn't interact with normal matter," Conrad said.

"With pure dark matter that would be the case, but if the ship carries transmatter, the analysis changes." Quist displayed some mathematical equations. "The Quillip equations have two solutions—positive for normal matter and negative for dark matter."

"I still don't get it," Conrad said. "Are you saying the *Dutchman* turned the colonists into dark matter?"

"Obviously not. To do so would contradict several conservation laws of physics. The negative solution allows quantum-entangled dark matter to be used to teleport normal matter. The *Dutchman* teleported the Elliquine colony to an unknown location."

Conrad hooted. "That's terrific! An advanced civilization has bridged the gap between matter and dark matter. We must go to them. We must learn from them."

Blood drained from Jade's face, and her legs grew weak. "No,

Conrad. Wrong pattern. Try this one: a hostile civilization with advanced weaponry has taken forty Entanglement citizens hostage in an unprovoked attack."

"There's no reason to assume they're hostile," Conrad said. "It could be a misunderstanding. Or maybe the *Dutchman* took the colonists to meet their leader. You worry too much."

"No, you worry too little," Jade replied. "A dark matter spaceship might change orbit and strike anywhere—including here at *Peapod*. A ship in the absence of other high-tech artifacts on the surface of the planet means it is from somewhere else. Perhaps the dark matter ship came and wiped out a lesser civilization in the polar caves."

"All the more reason to investigate the polar caves," Conrad said.

"All the more reason to stay on *Peapod* and remain unnoticed," Ironsides said. "I advise extreme caution."

Jade cleared her throat. "In any case, we should plan to defend ourselves as best we can if we get teleported away. We should all carry dart poppers at all times, better yet energy rifles, or both."

"We don't know that such weapons will be of any use," Ironsides said.

"True," Jade replied. "For one thing, we could be up against something like the Immortals. We should keep flamethrowers handy. And Quist, can you fab more Ambo stun guns without a locator?"

"Obviously."

Ironsides waved his root-feet, "We already know an Ambo stun gun has limited use. It has almost no effect on a Hydra."

"Fair enough," Jade said. "Quist, can you modify the stun gun to stop a Hydra?"

"A version of the Ambo stun gun twice as large would theoretically stop a Hydra."

"Excellent! Can you fab a super stun gun three or four times as big, just to be sure?"

"Yes," Quist said. "But the most effective thing for us to do now is to build a scanning gravimeter."

Jade blinked at Quist. After a moment, she said, "That's the first time you mentioned a scanning gravimeter. What is it?"

"Obviously," Quist replied, "it's a directional gravimeter which scans across a larger field of view to create a high-resolution gravity map. A scanning gravimeter will warn us of any changes in the orbit of the dark matter ship in time for us to avoid it."

Jade grinned. "I like it. How long to make one?"

"Six and a half hours," Quist replied.

Jade's smile faded. "Why so long?"

"Actual fabrication time is two and a half hours. However, the scanning gravimeter will require 47.3 kilograms of iridium for its high-density lens. The *Peapod* fabricator units only have 7.1 kilograms available. You'll have to go to the surface to collect additional iridium."

29

Iridium

Jade eased the shuttle away from *Peapod* and streaked toward the surface of Belle Verte below. Now this was flying. She was hurtling through space at 25,000 kph.

Quist had identified an outcropping of iridium ore located on the equator about five hundred kilometers west of the Elliquine colony. He assured Jade one trip would be enough. He also assured her the *Dutchman's* gross orbital parameters provided a safe forty-one-minute window to collect the ore.

As she zoomed across the prairie, Jade felt an Elliquine-like joy at the unencumbered open prairie-green grass, sunshine, blue sky—a peaceful place to settle. Local electric fields reflecting off the bedrock and filtering through the soil and grass added another dimension of blue and green pastels.

Suddenly the electric field of the bedrock turned dark. A void opened under her, like a giant sinkhole opening to swallow her. In a moment of panic, she thought Quist must be wrong—the *Dutchman* was here.

She pulled up, but the void already was gone, so she resumed course. The iridium field popped into view, and Jade shook off the brief flash of darkness.

"I have a visual," she radioed to *Peapod*. "The boulders are spread out evenly, like a giant industrial waste dump. Collecting them will be easy, but I have to ask how this place got here."

"Unknown," Quist replied. "This concentrated patch of iridium ore is yet another anomaly of Belle Verte, but this one is to our advantage. Send an aerial close-up of the area before you land. I need more data to optimize your route."

She flew a tight circle around the iridium field and transmitted the images to Quist. "Say when."

"Why?"

"I mean, let me know when you have enough images of these rock piles."

"Obviously—to do otherwise would impair your efficiency." A few seconds later Quist added, "I have sufficient data now. You are correct about the non-random distribution of the iridium ore. Your efficiency will increase by seventeen percent. I have shortened the schedule accordingly."

"Well then, I guess I was wrong," Jade muttered. "Collecting the rocks won't be easier after all."

"Correct. To make your job easier would reduce your efficiency."

Jade sighed and landed on the edge of the boulder field. She powered down the shuttle and stepped out into the peaceful electrical silence of Belle Verte. Now if she had an ocean, it could be the Hawaiian Preserve.

Her first breath of Belle Verte air was fresh, clean, and invigorating. Also safe, according to the microbial analysis of the samples her rover had brought back from the colony. But an eerie silence filled the prairie, broken only by the crunch of the rover treads on gravel. No birds, no insects, no ocean.

Quist brought an abrupt end to her brief look around. "Drive 17 degrees right for 18.1 meters. Pick up three iridium ore boulders on the right and one on the left."

Jade took the rover and completed the instructions. Quist gave her another target. And so it went for twenty minutes. She filled the rover, unloaded it into a bin on the shuttle, and went back for more.

Eventually, her course took her to the north edge of the iridium field. She rounded a corner from behind a tall boulder, and there was an obsidian cliff-a ten-meter high, fifty-meter long, black gash in the hillside.

Her course took her closer. The black streak was anything but obsidian. It was a black cliff, but also a void—not just black in the normal visual spectrum but absorbing all the infrared and microwave frequencies she could sense as well.

Curious, she turned the rover toward the cliff. Clearly, it was a natural feature, an integral part of the landscape. There seemed to be an opening at one end of the wall, but it was hard to be sure—black on black.

Quist noticed her deviation from his prescribed course. "Turn 93.3 de—"

Jade entered the opening. All radiation from outside stopped. With no radiation below her, it was as if she had driven over an abyss. The feeling was familiar—this must be what she had sensed on her way in.

She slowed the rover and inched forward, testing the black surface in front of her with the rover's mechanical arms to make sure it was still there.

A crescent of light from the entrance behind her extended around to her left. The shape gave her pause. The hollow in the cliff was open on two sides and closed on the other two. The black rock must be extremely strong to support its own weight without a pillar at the corner.

Distances were impossible to gauge accurately, but she reckoned she'd gone about thirty meters when she encountered a wall. She followed the wall to the right and found a corner where two walls met. The walls made a right angle, the way a human might construct a room. Someone had carved this room in the impossibly strong black rock.

There was nothing else to see. Nothing here other than the rock itself and the half-room cut into it. She drove back into the sunlight.

"—you can. Come in, Jade. Answer if you can." Conrad was on

the radio. He sounded near panic.

"Conrad. I'm here. Everything is fine." Jade drove toward the next chunk of iridium ore.

"What happened?"

"I went under an outcropping of rock that blocked communications—"

"You are 147.2 seconds behind schedule and off course by 10 degrees," Quist interrupted. "Turn 10 degrees left immediately."

Reminded that the longer she stayed on the surface, the more at risk she became, Jade threw herself into her iridium ore duties. The mystery of the black rock would have to wait.

❊ ❊ ❊

When Jade returned to *Peapod,* an agitated Conrad greeted her at the airlock. "We can do it again." His brainsong whined with distress.

"Are you sure?" Jade wrinkled her forehead. "Quist said he was sure one trip would be enough."

"No, I mean Quist—" Conrad gestured helplessly. "Just come see what I mean."

When they arrived at Engineering, Quist shoved a tuba-like object at Jade.

"What is this?" Jade asked.

"I'm on your team, and I'm helping you," Quist said, "You wanted a large version of the Ambo stunner, and so while you were on the surface, I made you one that is four times bigger

Jade frowned. "I said three or four times as big, not thirty."

"It is four times as big," Quist said. "the original was 30.1 centimeters long, and this one is 120.4 centimeters long.

"And how much heavier?"

Quist still held the tuba out to her. "Obviously, it is sixty-four times as heavy—161.3 kilograms to be precise.

Jade blinked. "I can't carry a gun that big."

Conrad waved his arms. "I told you, Quist. To a human, four times as big means four times the mass, not four times the length. You may as well recycle it."

Quist's brainsong stuttered, then resumed its methodical march in a lower key. He began retreating with the huge device.

"No wait, I'll take it," Jade said. She surged forward in the zero-gee compartment and pulled the massive gun from Quist. "Obviously, this is a piece of artillery, not a handgun. I appreciate your sense of teamwork. Thank you very much for your help, Quist."

"*Dissonance,*" Quist said, tentatively releasing the gun to Jade. "If you are unable to use this device as intended, it would be most efficient to recycle it."

She pulled the gun farther out of Quist's reach. "No, it's even better than I had expected. It'll be an excellent addition to our arsenal."

Quist's brainsong resumed its original pitch and cadence as Jade added the super-sized stun gun to the top of her weapons pallet.

Conrad caught up with Jade. "It was smart of you to accept the stun gun. I can see how you strengthened the teamwork pattern. Maybe the Elliquine were right to put you in charge."

"Thank you." Jade felt flattered. It wasn't every day a professor said she was smart.

He came up next to her and helped push the pallet toward the shuttle. "You'd make a good cultural xenologist. You're a good observer of societal customs and individual motivations."

"Hmph." Her smile faded. "Too good sometimes. My electrosense lets me recognize common emotions, at least among humans, and lies have a strong electrical signature. A lot of people have trouble accepting that."

Conrad nodded. "We are kindred souls, then. I mean I don't always fit in, in part because I often see things others do not. I find cultural patterns fascinating—everything from group decision making to political and economic structures, to mating behavior."

His brainsong jingled with his attraction to her, only now it was more than physical. He pointed through *Peapod's* hull into the starry void. "Hundreds of civilizations. Hundreds of specialized species. Yet none of them has specialized in the scientific study of those civilizations. Humanity should fill that niche."

" I love learning," Jade said. "But I wouldn't be happy studying anything just for the sake of studying it. Learning is a tool to get something else done."

"Yes, we are a general-purpose species, capable of learning to play many roles. That flexibility will make us good cultural xenologists. Like Venmars' emotional flexibility makes them good ambassadors."

"Flexibility makes good soldiers too," Jade said. "Understanding the enemy is the first step to defeating them. As Sun Tzu put it, 'If you know the enemy and know yourself, you need not fear the result of a hundred battles.'"

Which reminded Jade, who had unwillingly become Earth's expert on Immortals, how little she actually knew about them.

30

Deep Invasion

U mlac dominated the mining colony at Coldmart by ingesting the first citizen he saw and using its memories to corner the colony's leaders and force them into submission.

The exact position of the locator in his bugged stun gun placed the rescue team on one of the planet's outer moons. He ingested the senior Wolferlop-P pilot to ensure he had accurate information on all armed ships in the system, and his gloating turned to anger.

No humans had come to Coldmart in the last few day—only a Venmar—and it had sent a package to a mining outpost at the coordinates of his locator and then left the system.

Curse the Venmars! Darzak must have done this. The next time he got his pincers on a Venmar it would suffer greatly from his revenge. And when the Immortal Ascendency eventually dominated all the Entanglement, he would find Darzak and make a horrible example of him.

Umlac had to wait for a large Quillip mass back to Farboro to get up to speed. He called Farboro and ordered Hoargrim to send one of his lesser Hydra weaponmasters to him. An average Hydra could dominate Coldmart and make it into a profitable new vassaldom.

When he finally returned to Farboro, he studied the ship's records and found a mass the size of the rescue team had tele-ported to Elliquor shortly after they would have arrived here.

He followed them to Elliquor. The cowardly Elliquine ran and hid. The handful of Dasypods guarding Elliquor station lined up for a series of duels. One at a time, he engulfed the tiny creatures, immobilized them in a web of sinew, and crushed them with diamond-tipped pincers.

The very first Elliquine he ingested knew where the rescue team had gone. Of course, nearly all Elliquine knew this.

Now he had the Entanglement team boxed in at Belle Verte. There would be no escape for the Hydra Slayer. It wouldn't be long now before he had both that annoying human and the power behind the Forbidden Zone in his jaws.

31

The Caves of Belle Verte

When Jade arrived at Engineering, Conrad was already suited up. Quist hovered over his scanning gravimeter, a three-meter tube nested in a web of precision alignment gears and electronics. Quist would monitor the *Dutchman's* orbit around the equator and warn her and Conrad if it changed.

She felt a little guilty leaving the *Peapod* to go exploring, but mostly she was looking forward to another flight in the transparent Elliquine shuttle.

Ironsides called from the bridge. "I'd like permission to come up to Engineering and plant myself while you are away so that I can be alert during your next sleep. Do you have any other orders for me?"

"Why Engineering?" Jade asked. "I thought *Peapod's* bow had better light."

"The light is better in Engineering today," Ironsides said. "Also, the *Dasypodia* says 'It is always best to be planted among friends,' and Quist will be in engineering."

"Go ahead, then," Jade said. "You know your needs the best."

She boarded the shuttle with Conrad, threading past her pallet of weapons and survival gear on the left and Conrad's pallet of archeology tools on the right to the seats in front.

The acceleration couches and control consoles were standard issues from Jade's Solar Defense Force equipment library, except the digital-to-analog converter. She could read the flight parameters on the analog meters with her electrosense, freeing her eyes to scan elsewhere. It gave her a little extra edge as a pilot.

Conrad chattered away about his childhood. Jade wasn't sure if this was what he did when he was nervous, or if he was making an effort to be friendly.

"When I was eight," he said, "my anthropologist parents and I lived with a hunter-gatherer tribe on the Fifty Thousand BC Preservation in the Kalahari. It was a leisurely life. Most days, we only spent about two hours gathering food, and the rest of the time we socialized, played games or just slept. All of which led to more complicated interpersonal relationships than in the modern culture of work, eat, sleep, repeat."

"If you liked it so much, what are you doing here?" Jade asked.

"My parents never stayed in one place more than two years." Conrad's eyes stared into the distance in front of them. "They believed an outsider could describe a society most objectively, and that was their goal—to add to the objective knowledge of how societies worked. That's how I came about. They asked some genetic engineers to develop a brain better suited to detecting cultural patterns."

"Your genetic modifications seem to have worked extremely well, without side effects," Jade said, thinking about how her side effect of sensing electric fields was more interesting than the intended ability to live on electrical energy.

Conrad's body tensed and his brainsong hinted at deceit. "Yes, learning new languages is easy for me, and the endless similarities and differences in cultural patterns fascinate me. I love studying the dynamics holding cultures together, like kinship, shared values, and economic dependencies."

What was he hiding? Jade couldn't imagine. But she had learned the hard way that the direct approach of pointing out when someone was lying didn't often go over well. She'd developed less direct methods.

"And trust," Jade said. "A society where people keep secrets won't stay together long. Or a team."

"Well, at least I don't have any important secrets," Conrad said.

But his brainsong said he lied. He had secrets, and he was acutely aware of it.

A mountain peak came into view above the polar icecap. Conrad's brainsong trumpeted with excitement. "I wonder what we'll find in these tunnels. Mysterious high-tech devices? A hidden civilization? Ruins?"

Jade landed on a snowy plateau at the base of the largest mountain, a location where Orbital scans showed a tunnel coming to the surface. A dark opening in the smooth, rocky cliff at the far mountain side of the plateau beckoned. The plateau under the snow reflected microwaves in a myriad of crazy angles. The plateau was built from the rubble of the tunnel—another sign of an ancient civilization here.

Conrad pulled on a heavy parka, boots, and gloves. He mounted a floodlight and Quist's camera on his forehead, strapped on a backpack full of archeological equipment, and went out into the cold. Jade remained in the shuttle, listening to the snow crunching under Conrad's feet and watching the tunnel approach through the camera mounted on his hardhat.

The roof of the entrance formed an arch about four meters tall that extended into the mountain as far as the camera's image could reach. Conrad rubbed his gloved hand across the floor. "The floor looks worn smooth. There must have been a lot of traffic here once."

"You have proved it would have been more efficient to send the rover yesterday than to send you today," Quist said. He was monitoring the feed from Conrad's camera, too.

"I already detect something the rover wouldn't have noticed," Conrad replied. "I smell damp limestone, yet I see nothing but granite walls."

He moved down the tunnel, and patches of white cling-ing to the walls became common. Jade was about to sug-gest getting a spectral analysis when Quist's mechanical voice crackled across the commlink. "Don't move your camera around so fast. Let it remain on one of the calcium carbonate patches for seventeen seconds."

Conrad did as instructed and counted slowly to seventeen. "Is that good, Quist?"

"That was 18.7 seconds. Observe what is revealed by the few photons escaping from the subsurface after I subtract the surface light." Quist relayed an enhanced image of the plaster patch, showing a drawing that had once been here.

"Marvelous!" Conrad chortled with delight. "Cave art from a lost civilization."

The painting depicted a striped six-legged creature shoot-ing a cloud of smoke at a large shaggy creature, also with six legs.

"It looks like a griffin shooting a mammoth with a musket," Jade said.

"Griffins are imaginary creatures of Earth," Quist replied in all seriousness, "The oxidation level proves you are looking at a 28,700-year-old Bellevertian drawing."

"Every archeologist should have an Obnot to do real-time analysis," Conrad said. "Let's try some more of this plaster."

He moved down the tunnel a few meters at a time, deep-scanning patches of plaster. They all contained pictures of griffins shooting mammoths.

"Notice how the Bellevertian in each picture wears a vest with an elaborate design," Conrad said. "The best fit pattern is that the design identifies the individual or their family, the way a coat-of-arms once identified human knights."

The designs on the griffin's vests never seemed to repeat, even though they grew less elaborate as Conrad moved deep into the heart of the mountain.

"Quist, can you tell how old the plaster is here?" Conrad asked. "Are the pictures getting older as I go?"

"The last picture was 29,450 years old. How did you know they were getting older?" Quist asked.

"The patterns on the vests are getting simpler. The normal cultural trend is from simplicity to complexity—as the simple patterns get used, new patterns must of necessity be more complex."

An hour into the mountain, the tunnel opened into a large domed Grand Central Station. Piles of white dust littered the floor; a few patches of plaster clung to the ceiling. Dozens of tunnels ran out in all directions.

The air was cool, but well above freezing. Conrad dropped his gloves on the floor to mark the tunnel where he'd entered and sifted through the white dust on the floor. "Still no sign of the technology that produced these tunnels."

He slogged over to the neighboring tunnel. It was long and bare, with little plaster visible. "I'm going to peek into several of these tunnels before I pick one to follow."

The next tunnel had a large patch of plaster near its entrance, and Quist extracted several faded pictures from it. All of them were pairs of Bellevertians nose-to-nose. The plaster in the third tunnel contained star arrangements of Bellevertian coats-of-arms.

"This has to show how they were related to each other," Jade said. "A feudal hierarchy maybe?"

"Yes, but more precisely, birth records," Conrad replied.

"Unproven," Quist said. "How can you make such a statement?"

"See how the outer symbols all incorporate part of the center symbol?" Conrad said. "The meta-pattern is now clear. We are in a records archive—a place for recording significant events, like shooting a mammoth, marriages, and births."

Jade nodded. This was interesting, but not helpful. No advanced technology. No sign of a connection to the dark matter machines of Belle Verte.

The next tunnel contained images of Bellevertians lying on their backs with their feet in the air.

"Death records," Jade said. Whatever Conrad was, he was good at detecting patterns.

The tunnel after that was a mess. Multiple layers of plaster in various stages of disrepair on the walls and several centimeters of plaster dust on the floor. Conrad slogged in to find a relatively well-preserved section and held the camera steady for seventeen seconds, "What do we have here, Quist?"

Quist returned a picture of a series of lines in a fishbone pattern, with fuzzy gray balls at the free end of each line. Fragments of symbols remained in some of the gray balls.

Jade stared at the image on the console in front of her. "I have no idea what this is."

Conrad chuckled. "I do. It's a map of the polar caves. The smudged-up ends are where the Bellevertians recorded property ownership—smudged because they erased the current owner and wrote in the new owner for rooms at the ends of the tunnels every time they changed hands."

Back at the central cavern, Conrad said, "I'm going to skip the next few tunnels for now. I see a bigger one a little farther down, and I want to see what's in it."

Conrad kicked through several piles of dust. Still no artifacts. No bones. Would there be bones after thirty thousand years? Jade didn't know.

Conrad peeked into the large tunnel and inhaled sharply. His camera swung about so rapidly Jade had a hard time making out what he was looking at. Animals. Monsters. Aliens.

"Incredible!" Conrad focused on one section of a large room filled with life-sized animal statues. He ran his fingertips over the face and jaws of a crocodile-like creature near the door. "Look at the artistry. Look at the dynamic characterization. The Griffins were sculptors as well as hunters."

Quist observed a different detail. "Surface microfractures in the statue prove that the temperature in this room hasn't dropped below freezing since the statue was last polished."

The creatures in the room had many Earth-like features that presumably occurred from filling parallel ecological niches: one had a long neck like a giraffe, another an armored shell like a tortoise, and a third had leathery wings like a bat. A large mammoth-like creature near the center was unmistakably the one in the drawings along the entrance tunnel. And they all had six limbs.

Conrad examined each statue in turn, photographing it with a special high-resolution, wide-spectrum camera. "We seem to be working our way up the evolutionary tree of this planet as we near the back. Ahh. Here is a Bellevertian Griffin."

"A series of Griffins," Jade pointed out. "Each one with a different kind of weapon—not a sculpture of a weapon, but an actual weapon. More proof of how much they must have valued hunting."

"Good observation," Conrad said. He named the weapons as he moved from one Griffin statue to another. "Stone axes and spearheads much like early humans. Look at the artistry. Such realistic throwing poses. And the next one has a bow and arrow ... A crossbow ... A musket ... It's interesting how closely the development of weapons here parallels that of Earth."

Jade shook her head. "I can't believe they put real weapons on display. And the bow and crossbow have arrows nocked and ready to shoot. Such an exhibit would have been vandalized on Earth. They must have been a trustworthy lot."

"Another good observation," Conrad said. "See, I told you you'd make a good xenologist."

"What's the next statue holding?" Jade asked.

The Bellevertian held a weapon consisting of two bulbs near the base of a long tube. The bulbs got bigger, and the tube got wider, as the weapon evolved. Conrad kept photographing. "Fascinating. Perhaps a flamethrower of some kind."

"I can't think of anything like it in Earth history," Jade said. "After the musket, Earth developed rifles, machine guns, energy weapons, and dart poppers."

She studied the weapons carefully. They'd be more awkward to wield than an energy rifle, but the Bellevertians were larger than humans, so presumably, that wasn't a problem. What was in those bulbs?

Conrad reached out to take the final weapon from the arms of its statue. The bulbs were the size of basketballs. "I wonder how they aimed this thing."

"Stop!" Jade yelled. "It's loaded."

Conrad startled at Jade's shout and dropped the weapon. The bulbs hit the floor and broke. Yellow and green liquids mingled, spewing out a cloud of red vapor.

Conrad spun around, but he must already have inhaled a whiff of the gas because the view on his camera wavered and fell to the floor. In a final spasm, he rolled to his back, his camera pointing up at a mammoth. The sculpture's upraised foot poised to stomp on him.

32

The Dutchman Flies

Jade dug her fingernails into the arms of her seat. *Stupid. Stupid. Stupid.* She'd caused Conrad to drop the poison gas with her ill-considered shout. "Quist, get a spectral analysis of that red gas. I need to know how long Conrad has."

"It doesn't matter," Quist replied, "He's not breathing. Irreparable brain damage from lack of oxygen will begin in 4.1 minutes, leading to an inability to return to consciousness 4.9 minutes from now. At your maximum running speed, it would take you 11.3 minutes to reach him."

She scanned the shuttle for ideas. "Then I'll take the rover."

"The rover will take 6.9 minutes."

Too long. Too bad she couldn't take one of the winged fliers through the caves.

She jumped out of her seat. "Quist, I have an idea. Analyze the gas. Send the specs for an antidote to the shuttle fab."

She unplugged her analog meter package from the shuttle console and ran to the nearest drone flier. The flier's wings were 8 meters wide and would never fit through the tunnels—if flown normally. But the stubby central body was less than two meters long; the tunnel was three to four meters wide. The wings could be rotated for vertical takeoff. She would hover on the vehicle's jets and fly through the tunnels wingtip first, straddling the flier like a horse.

"Spectral analysis complete," Quist said. "There is no antidote."

Jade slapped the flier in frustration. "No antidote? There must be something we can do to save him."

"The standard treatment for a paralytic agent is an artificial respirator," Quist replied. "The effect of the gas on Conrad will wear off 7.6 minutes after exposure ceases."

"How much longer does Conrad have without a respirator?"

"Irreparable brain damage will occur in 3.5 minutes."

Jade cranked the wings of the flier into a vertical position, jerked the drone's maintenance panel open, and plugged in her meter set. She plugged the VR headband still hanging around her neck into the flier control module and inserted her nostril-sized mini-breathers for protection against the paralyzing gas.

She'd probably lost most of another minute. Time was running out.

She climbed onto the flier but had trouble keeping her balance in a sitting position. She leaned over and hugged the flier. She probably wouldn't fall off, but she couldn't see where she was going. She'd have to rely solely on her electrosense.

The superheated exhaust from the flier's rocket motors left red-hot puddles of slag on the shuttle floor as she eased the flier out over the snow. She picked up speed as she crossed the snowpack in a cloud of steam.

She had almost reached the tunnel entrance when the flier stopped and reversed course. Quist's voice came through her commlink. "The *Dutchman* has changed orbit. It will arrive at your location in 35.1 minutes. Evacuation is required."

Jade yanked the antenna off the flier. She didn't have time to argue with Quist.

The flier surged forward again and Jade dove into the tunnel. In two minutes, Conrad would be dead, and three kilometers of tunnel lay between her and him.

The electric field from the flier illuminated the rock tunnel around her with an iridescent yellow-green glow. Her target was the black dot of the empty tunnel in front of her. The target dot jerked left-right and up-down, more and more rapidly, as she accelerated down the sinuous tunnel.

At 90 kph her VR headband almost blew loose. She pushed her head down tighter against the bucking metal wing. Her forehead would be bruised tomorrow.

Accelerating again, she estimated that at 250 kph she would be to Conrad in less than a minute. She bumped the coarse granite walls a few times with a noise like a buzz saw, throwing sparks and adding static to the electric field, making steering even more difficult. She dipped too low, and the granite floor shaved off the sole of one boot.

At last, she burst into the central chamber, but she slowed too fast and slid off the front of the flier as it stopped near Conrad's tunnel. She flipped over in the air and landed on her back. More bruises.

She scrambled to Conrad and rolled his limp body to its back. She put her mouth on his and blew a lifesaving breath of purified air from her lungs into his. Careful to breathe in through her nasal purifiers, she gave him a second breath, then thirty pumps on his chest to move the oxygenated blood to his brain, two more breaths, thirty more pumps, and so on, and so on.

Nine minutes later Conrad stirred and opened his eyes. "What happened?"

"Don't talk," Jade said. "Poison gas."

She breathed into him again. There hadn't been time to fab an extra gas mask.

"Walk with me," she said, then pressed her lips to his again.

Conrad sat up weakly. "Wait. Look behind you."

"Talk later. Get moving now."

Conrad wobbled to his feet but started toward the statues instead of the door.

Jade turned around to catch hold of him, then froze. "My God. It's almost human."

"Four arms," Conrad said. "A conch shell and a flower carved into its base. This statue is the Vedic god Vishnu of Earth, but the artistic style is Bellevertian."

Jade took a breath and gave another one to Conrad. "Quist, how old is this statue?"

No answer. She'd forgotten her radio was off.

"Evacuate immediately," Quist bleated through the comm. "The *Dutchman* arrives in 20.4 minutes."

Jade held the statue steady in her remote camera. "I'm in the cave with Conrad. He's okay. We'll walk out soon. How old is this?"

After a brief hesitation, Quist replied, "The statue is 29,200 years old. More urgently, the *Dutchman* will arrive in 19.8 minutes. At a brisk walking pace, you'll arrive at your shuttle only 1.8 minutes before it does."

Jade pulled Conrad toward the door. "Come on. The *Dutchman* didn't change course to bring us flowers. We can come back later, but only if we don't disappear like the Elliquine."

This time Conrad acquiesced. He proved a bit wobblier than Quist had calculated, and they arrived at the shuttle with less than a minute to spare. Jade dropped Conrad onto his acceleration couch, fell into her seat, and triggered an emergency return to *Peapod*.

The shuttle accelerated steeply on a minimum-time trajectory toward its target. After a few seconds, Jade had second thoughts. If the *Dutchman* was tracking them, she didn't want to lead it back to *Peapod*. She arced to one side.

Quist continued his reports. "The *Dutchman* has changed course. It's reducing the minimum distance between its trajectory and yours."

"Damn. Hang on, Conrad." Jade surged forward at four gees. The heavy acceleration pinned her down, its weight on her chest making breathing difficult.

But after a few seconds that seemed much longer than they were, she ended the surge, and Quist reported, "The *Dutchman* missed. You'll be safe for another orbit."

"We'll be elsewhere by then." Jade changed course and let the autopilot fly. "What did you guys make of the Vishnu statue?"

"Dissonance," Quist said. "Vishnu is not a species in my databanks."

Conrad's brainsong bustled with excitement. "Vishnu is a mythical god in some of the most ancient writings on Earth —or at least I used to think he was mythical. The best-fitting pattern is that Vishnu's species visited both Belle Verte and Earth thousands of years ago."

His whole body was quivering now. "We have to go back. We have to look for more clues. This statue could be the link we've been looking for, to the species controlling the *Dutchman.*"

Jade considered. "It's risky, since we don't know what the *Dutchman's* capabilities are, but I'll trust your judgment on how important this could be. We'll go back, together."

The truth was, she wanted another look at the statue, too. Something about its electric field bothered her, but in the rush to get Conrad out, she hadn't paid much attention at the time. Quist said they had about twenty minutes to explore before they had to return to the shuttle to avoid the *Dutchman.*

Vishnu's statue was as imposing as ever. Three meters tall. Well-muscled arms, legs, and torso. One of his arms was above his head as if about to throw something.

Jade saw the electric field anomaly more clearly now. The base of the statue was colder, darker than anything else in the cavern, as if it were absorbing the electric fields around it.

She approached cautiously and peeked behind the statue. Lying on the floor was a black disk with white sunray points around its circumference and a two-centimeter hole through its center.

She held the disk up by the center hole. "What do you make of this, Conrad?"

"Incredible ... Or maybe to be expected. It's the Sudarshana Chakra, the throwing disc of Vishnu. It's more confirmation of a connection to Earth, though still not much help in determining what the connection is."

Earth wasn't the connection Jade was thinking of. She'd seen this black material once before, at the strange cliff near where she'd picked up the iridium ore.

Ironsides came on for the first time. "A planting is a wonderful thing. It gives one a chance to appreciate better the virtues of his companions."

Jade tried to find a way to carry the throwing disc in her satchel or on a strap. Its sharp teeth cut into anything she wrapped around them, so she kept it on her thumb. Once she got back to the shuttle, she would fabricate a case for it, with a post to hold the disc by the hole in its middle.

"Quist, my friend," Ironsides continued, "I want to apologize for asking you so many tedious questions. I admire your clear, logical thinking, your excellent work deducing the cause of the disappearance of the Elliquine colony, and your proof of the existence of the dark matter object orbiting Belle Verte."

"Would you like a status report?" Quist asked.

"Yes, I would be delighted to hear a status report. You are always so thorough; I know we can count on you. What happened while I was planted?"

"During your planting," Quist said, "Jade and Conrad discovered a museum in the polar caves belonging to a lost civilization consisting of a race of carnivores who starved themselves to death 28,100 years ago by poisoning all of the animal life on the planet. The *Dutchman* changed orbit to intercept them. They flew away, and the *Dutchman* missed them. They returned to the polar tunnels to investigate an anomalous statue. Then the *Dutchman* changed orbit again."

"To what?" Ironsides asked. "Please show me what the *Dutchman's* orbit looks like now."

"You can see, it is more elliptical, diving deeper into the planet and reaching out into space. This orbit makes it more efficient for the shuttle to evade the dark matter Quillip."

"That's odd," Ironsides said. "Can the *Dutchman* change course more easily to intercept the *Peapod*?"

"Adding *Peapod* to the display," Quist said. "No changes are necessary. The *Dutchman* will intercept *Peapod* in 33.5 seconds."

"What! Full acceleration. Take evasive action." Ironsides said.

"*Dissonance.* The warmup sequence for *Peapod's* engines requires twenty-three minutes."

"That's no good," Ironsides said. "Quist, lock all access to *Peapod* using command code alpha. Jade, if something happens to me, when you teleport back to Elliquor, go directly—"

Silence.

Quist and Ironsides were gone.

33

Access Denied

"**t**o Nexus and take along my mission log." Ironsides finished the sentence he had begun on *Peapod.*

A Solidarity of Elliquine swirled around him and then retreated to a corner, leaving him alone with Quist in the middle of a large rectangular room. Quist had of course been right about the dark matter Quillip—somehow, they'd been teleported to the same location as the colonists.

The Elliquine cowered in the corner.

"The sky is stone."

"We miss the sun."

Ironsides adjusted his position so his ring of laser-eyes could better see the Elliquine. The ceiling was indeed stone— concrete—dotted with yellow lights. The light would be adequate for photosynthesis, though not as good as an average sun, but the concrete floor would provide no nourishment if he stayed long enough to require planting.

Centered in a concrete wall opposite the Elliquine was a bronze-colored, metallic door. The doorframe was inlaid with images of sea creatures and flowers. Otherwise, the walls of the prison were featureless.

Ironsides needed to cheer these Elliquine up. "May evolution favor you. The High Council of Elliquor sent us to help you."

The Elliquine turned as one and bowed to him. He was pleased to see what a few kind words could do.

"And your descendants forever," one of the Elliquine said.

"We should have known the planetary Solidarity would save us."

"Take us back to the open sky."

"It's not quite so simple," Ironsides said. "A dark matter Quillip ship teleported us here, the same as it did you. We do not control any method of return."

"Then we will all die,"

"Under this sky of stone."

"Already the Ancient One has dragged away—"

"Six Elliquine in his big net."

Ironsides tried to do a head count of the Elliquine, but they were now circling too fast for him. "Quist how many Elliquine are here?"

"Thirty-four."

Before he could ask the Elliquine what happened to the other six, a thump at the door caused the Elliquine to scurry deep into a corner of the dungeon. Another thump. Someone was throwing the door's deadbolts. This was his moment to shine as an official ambassador.

A two-and-a-half-meter tall metallic android dragged in a huge net squirming with Elliquine. Such strength was reminiscent of a Hydra, but the similarity ended there. The creature was bipedal. It looked much like a human, except that it had four arms instead of two.

Quist surprised him by saying, "The robot looks like the statue Conrad found in the Polar caves on Belle Verte. Conrad said its name was Vishnu."

The android ignored Ironsides and turned to leave.

This was no way to treat an ambassador! Ironsides bounced halfway to the door. "Wait! I must speak to your leader."

The android had reached the doorway when Ironsides fired

a laser-eye into the light over its head. The light sizzled and went out. Shards of glass fell on the android, but it continued to ignore Ironsides.

Ironsides rolled after it. "Vishnu! I am Ambassador to Belle Verte. I need to see your leader."

The android stopped and turned around to face Ironsides. "I am the Ancient One, known by many names across the galaxy. Where did you learn that name for me?"

Ironsides was perplexed. "I thought that was what everyone called you."

"Just humans. Do you have news of humans on Belle Verte?"

Ironsides cautiously considered how much he wanted to tell this robot. After all, the *Dasypodia* said, "Information is often the most valuable commodity."

Unfortunately, Quist did not concur with the *Dasypodia* on this point. "Two humans came with us. If you didn't teleport them here, then they must still be at Belle Verte."

The android took something from his belt and pointed it at Ironsides. Ironsides aimed one of his laser-eyes at the rectangular object. But apparently, it was some kind of scanner rather than a weapon, because nothing seemed to happen. His laser-eye ached for release, but he restrained himself.

Then the android said, "You have a novel brain structure inside that thick shell. You will be the next sacrifice." The android backed out the door and shut it after himself.

Ironsides stiffened his root-feet. This was no way to treat a Dasypod, or an ambassador. His laser-eyes fired a double blast at the door. The door glowed dull red where the lasers struck. *Dull red*—not the white-hot burst of molten metal that he expected.

The robot thumped the deadbolts back into place. The Elliquine rushed to untangle the nets and freed their companions—all but one who lay unmoving in the center of the net. The five from the nets circled the inert body.

"Rispering, Rispering, Rispering,"
"Come back to the Solidarity."

They skipped a beat. Rispering's line, Ironsides supposed.

They stopped and knelt around the body on the floor. They said in unison, "Rispering's soul is gone."

Then they resumed their dance:

"The Ancient One placed him on a metal table,"

"And a machine sucked out Rispering's soul."

"The Ancient One claims to protect the galaxy from demons."

"But he is the worst demon of them all."

"The Ancient One spies on Belle Verte—"

"And plans to capture all who come there."

Ironsides moved close to Quist and said softly, "It's like Jade said. Hostile aliens with superior technology. We need to find a way back to Belle Verte, and soon, before the Ancient One harms another citizen."

Quist replied, "I'm monitoring radio signals that I believe are used to control the androids. Once I have analyzed the protocols, I'll try to hack into them. In the meantime, perhaps you should find a way to hide before the android comes back to sacrifice you."

Ironsides twisted his root-feet together until they hurt. "Dasypods don't hide! Besides, he can't sacrifice me—I'm an ambassador."

"*Dissonance.* The Ancient One is not following standard diplomatic protocol."

* * *

Umlac hated the wide-open Elliquine ship. He hated being stuck here. He lusted after the domination of the Hydra Slayer. He lusted after the mysterious power on Belle Verte.

His constructionmaster built him a comfortable new bridge inside a mound of slag and metal. He hadn't wanted to be on this ship long enough to make use of the new bridge, but the substandard 475-kg Quillip link from Elliquor to Belle

Verte was a twentieth the size needed to teleport his ten-ton body.

He found a little solace when he captured the Venmar Raggit. Now he could exact partial revenge on the Venmars for the trick they'd played on him at Coldmart. Even better, this was a Venmar who had befriended the Hydra Slayer.

Umlac ripped Raggit in two. He stopped the loss of blood on the female half and forced her to watch him slowly rip the male half in two again. And again, throwing Raggit's body parts against the transparent bubble of the ship and recording the bloody event to use later in taunting the Hydra Slayer.

The pieces of the Venmar just lay there, lifeless, not moving to reassemble. How different from his Shoggart body!

And that was the answer to his problem. Twenty pieces. He could teleport to Belle Verte in twenty pieces and reassemble.

He hesitated. He hadn't done anything so risky in several thousand years. His smaller pieces would be more vulnerable than his whole body. He tried to assess the risk rationally, but he coveted the power to make his enemy disappear like nothing he had ever coveted before.

Never mind the risk. He divided himself and teleported to Belle Verte.

His organic memory nucleus was the last to teleport. It saw fragmented images of a Quillip chamber and blurred images of an airlock.

Umlac's pieces reassembled in an airlock barely large enough to accommodate his body. His brief period of helplessness was over. He was a complete Shoggart once again, Lord of the Twelve, ruler of fifty-five star systems, and about to conquer number fifty-six.

He exited the airlock, canon ready, lasers ready. Nobody was in sight, but he could smell them—metallic Obnot lubricant, peppery Dasypod nanospores, salty human sweat.

Odd that he found no rearguard to crush—foolish of them. Of course, a rearguard would not have stopped him, but he would have enjoyed taking the ship more if there had been creatures present to dominate.

Even the bridge was undefended. He went to a control panel and called for a map of his newly acquired ship.

"Access Denied."

Angrily, he smashed the offending control panel and went to the master control panel in the center of the bridge.

"Access Denied."

This would not do. He tried various tricks, and he had many —easy to guess passwords, fake identities, overwhelming the input channels, but nothing worked. In frustration, he ripped up the tents, tables, and tools the Entanglement team had left behind. He needed a better catharsis for his anger. He needed a living being to rip apart.

He had many contingency plans for the conquest of Belle Verte, but none of them would work without access to the *Peapod's* control systems. He needed the ship to search out the power to make creatures disappear. He would need access codes to return to Elliquor.

He made himself comfortable as best he could. He would wait. If you knew where to wait, the prey always came.

34

And then there were Two

Jade flew a beeline for *Peapod*, listening in vain for any sign of Quist or Ironsides. According to her calculations, slower and less precise than Quist's, but good enough, she likely had forty minutes of safety on *Peapod* while the *Dutchman* completed its orbit around Belle Verte.

"Are we going back to Elliquor?" Conrad asked.

"That's what Ironsides wants us to do," Jade said, "but the Solidarity needs Belle Verte, and we can't give up on our teammates or the colonists so easily."

"Excellent," Conrad said. "There is so much yet to discover here. How does the statue of Vishnu connect to Earth? Does it connect to the *Dutchman* and the Elliquine disappearance? What lies deeper in the Bellevertian tunnel system?"

Conrad's brainsong showed every sign of sincere interest and excitement. But his previous hints of deceit bothered Jade.

"We need to work together, on all of those goals and more," Jade said. "You've been holding something back from me. It's time to come clean."

Conrad clenched his fists, and his brainsong became a storm. His emotional core showed guilt and fear.

"I'd forgotten how you can detect lies," he admitted. "Yes, I lied when I said I had no secrets."

Jade braced herself. She didn't know how she was going to respond, but unlike Ironsides, she believed there were some things you couldn't go back and do over.

Conrad placed his hands on the sides of his ribcage. "When I was born, I had a second pair of arms right here. I was born with six limbs, in the image of Vishu. The arms were a side effect of the extra pair of chromosomes that gave me an uber-cortex, and they were removed to help me fit into society."

"What?" was all Jade could say. She didn't know what she'd expected, but not this. However, it did explain the odd electric field around his ribcage, and maybe the protectiveness of his medical records and some of the comments he had made about his early childhood.

"Which leads to another pattern I can mention now." Conrad was once again the excited professor of xenology. "Humans could be the descendants of an actual four-armed race of gods, who somehow lost one pair of chromosomes."

Jade pursed her lips. "It doesn't fit all of the facts. There's a continuous record of evolution leading up to *Homo sapiens*, a record without any four-armed primates."

"I suppose so," he shook his head. "But we don't have any theory that fits all of the facts yet. And, about my arms, please don't tell anyone back on Earth."

The autopilot bleeped. It was time to dock with *Peapod*. Jade nudged the shuttle into the same dock they'd left a few hours ago. So much had changed since then.

"Go to the bridge," she told Conrad. "Look for anything unusual or anything that Ironsides or Quist might have left behind for us. I'll stay in Engineering and see if I can figure out a way to take the scanning gravimeter with us. If I can't take it, I'll try to program it for remote control. Be back at the shuttle in thirty minutes."

She popped open the door and entered *Peapod's* airlock. "Let's move it."

She jumped into the corridor to Engineering, and an odor

like puke turned her stomach. Down the corridor to her right, a roaring electrical vortex sizzled and popped. She jerked her head to look. A dozen unblinking red eyes stared at her from a gargantuan black blob with a score of Hydra-like pseudopods.

"Immortals!" she shouted. She was in midair and had to continue to the far side of the corridor. As she bounced back toward the shuttle doors, a sharp pain stabbed her inner thigh.

Something jerked her toward the Immortal—an arrow with a wicked barb had nicked her leg and lodged in the tough mesh of her pants. The cord attached to the arrow pulled her down toward the black Immortal.

Several mouths formed in the creature, speaking in unison, "I am Umlac. I am Shoggart. Worship me. Give me praise. Give me obedience. Give me the access codes to this ship."

"Help, Conrad!"

She pulled out a knife and hacked at the cord. The unknown material of the cord refused to yield to her steel blade. Her knives wouldn't cut her Solar Defense Force pants either. Discarding her pants wasn't an option. There wasn't time to remove her boots.

She dialed an explosive dart on her dart popper and shot the Immortal. Nothing. She tried again, then shot it with armor-penetrating darts, fire darts, even tranq darts. They all disappeared without a trace into its huge tarry body. She shot out several of its eyes, but new ones grew back to replace them.

The cord had pulled her nearly halfway to the waving pseudopods of the black Immortal, when it said, "Obey or suffer. I'll rip your memories from your naked, pulsating brain after I strip off the rest of your body, as I did for your friend."

A hologram of Raggit and Umlac played in the air in front of Jade. Umlac formed two large pseudopods, lined them with serrated teeth, and pinched Raggit into two, then four, then eight pieces. He soaked some of Raggit's pieces in caustic pools on his skin that he claimed were stomachs. He sucked in Raggit's brain, then shouted, "Jade Mahelona, Hydra Slayer, you are next."

Five meters to go. At this range, the electric fields in the air revealed the complicated inner workings of Umlac. *Know thy enemy. A thousand battles, a thousand victories,* Sun Tzu advised. Umlac must have a weakness.

"Give me the command codes. It all ends the same—but with more or less suffering," the chorus of voices from the black sewage said.

The devil was a liar, is a liar, and will always be a liar, her grandmother had said. But so were people. "Wait!" Jade said. "Let me go, and I'll give you the codes."

Three meters. Enormous lobster-like pinchers rose up on either side of her. The inner surface of the pinchers bristled with diamond-tipped teeth.

"Fool. I don't bargain. I take. I'll use the screams of your long and painful death to encourage other humans to obey."

The most intense electrical activity inside Umlac emanated from a central nucleus about the size of a beach ball. Nerves branched out of it into Umlac's soft tissues, connected to his eyes, mouths, and stomachs. A system of branching tubes full of liquid ran everywhere, though Jade couldn't tell if the liquid was blood or hydraulic fluid, or both.

There was more. Umlac was part flesh, part electronics— a cyborg. A mesh of fine wires ran throughout the Immortal's body—connected to embedded electronic devices: fabricators, lasers, cannon, and a large flamethrower. Infrared radiation was brightest in a secondary location, likely the main electrical generator. The wires closest to Jade glowed teal to her electrosense—some kind of alien data flow.

The relentless shortening of the cord continued. Two meters. The cord attached to a crossbow behind a sac of liquid —an external stomach perhaps.

She found no weakness to exploit. She couldn't let Raggit's murderer get the access codes to return to Elliquor and return to destroy the Solidarity. Umlac appeared to be able to extract memories directly from a brain. She dialed an explosive dart and aimed it at her head.

Open jaws with shark-like teeth towered over her on both sides now. The gooey external stomach was only a meter away.

A jolt from a sudden, bone-rattling tone almost caused her to pull the trigger. Her teeth chattered, and she tasted blood.

More importantly, the tension on the cord slackened. Umlac froze.

The sound ended. Jade recovered, and Umlac remained motionless.

Jade jerked the loose cord across a diamond-tipped row of Shoggart teeth, and she was free.

She started tossing loose gear—knives, water, her med kit, the holster for her dart popper—at Umlac to get momentum away from him. Her gear splashed into his stomach and dissolved in puffs of steam.

She was halfway to the shuttle when Umlac's electrical activity returned to normal. "Foolish human," he said. "There is no escape from a Shoggart."

Umlac nocked another arrow in his crossbow.

"Stun it again," Jade shouted to Conrad, who floated at the door to the shuttle with the tuba-like super stun gun.

The intense vibration shook her again. When it stopped, Umlac was immobile, but only for a few seconds. He was developing resistance. She was several meters from the shuttle when Umlac's surface changed. A wall of acoustic-damping pyramids formed over the Shoggart.

Conrad grabbed her and pulled her into the shuttle. Then he fired the stunner again.

Instead of freezing, Umlac surged down the corridor like a tsunami. "Vermin! The anguish of your deaths will bring fear even to my brother Shoggarts."

Without waiting for the shuttle door to close, Jade hit the emergency acceleration switch. The shuttle broke away, knocking her and Conrad in a heap against the wall. There was a whistling sound as air rushed out the open door, pulling them toward it.

The door finally closed. Jade and Conrad gasped for air until the pressure returned to normal.

In the silence, Jade gave Conrad a wry smile, "Thanks for the save. I reckon we're even now."

Conrad laughed with palpable relief. "I was following orders. You said to help, so I did. Besides, I don't know how to pilot this thing."

Jade scrambled to the pilot's couch and buckled in. "The autopilot isn't bad. But I'm glad you didn't know that. I'm locking in a zigzag course for the polar caves."

"Why bother with a zigzag? Won't the Shoggart be able to see where we go anyway?" Conrad asked.

"Maybe, but we still have the *Dutchman* to worry about. I don't want to wind up going the way of Ironsides and Quist."

"Why not?" Conrad said. "For all we know, they're in a better place right now than we are."

Jade took a deep breath to compose herself. "Because we don't want anyone else to die the way Raggit did. Because we are staying right here to stop Umlac."

35

Escapism

A deadbolt thumped in the prison door. Ironsides sent Quist a private message on a small laser beam. "Remember, it is true that I have appointed you Deputy Ambassador."

Ironsides hated the idea of using Quist as a decoy, but he couldn't think of a viable alternative. Not that he knew if his current plan was viable.

Quist moved to the center of the concrete cell. "The background radio transmissions by our captors have increased by 86%. The same thing happened the last time the Ancient One's avatar came here."

Ironsides rolled into position behind the door. The *Dasypodia* was ambivalent on some situations, saying only, "Survival without honor is worthless, but beware of honor without survival." If the avatar was coming to make him the next sacrifice, it was time for desperate measures.

A second deadbolt screeched and thudded. The Elliquine ran to a far corner, singing sadly about the stone sky. Ironsides had done all he could to prepare Quist in the short time available. He still wasn't sure if Quist would be able to utter unproven statements.

The massive door groaned open. In the doorframe stood

the four-armed android who had dragged in three tons of Elliquine.

"May evolution favor you." Quist boomed out loudly from the speakers on his exoskeleton. "Ancient One, Protector from Demons, I am Deputy Ambassador Quist Quillipson of the Entanglement. I come to aid your cause."

Quist gained confidence as he spoke. "First, I want to thank you, Ancient One, for offering us your hospitality and transportation through your dark matter Quillip link, and, second, for sending your robot to greet us in such a prompt manner."

The robot hesitated and then stepped into the room. "Deputy Ambassador Quist, you surprise me. Usually captives cower in the presence of my avatar. Or occasionally they attack. Welcome to my home, Vaikuntha. You may call me Vishnar." Taking another step forward, he continued. "You say you know about dark matter Quillips, but I've not detected another civilization with dark matter technology in the area."

Quist stuck to the script. "What is important is protecting the galaxy from demons. The Entanglement has hundreds of planets in the Orion Arm. What have you got, besides a dark matter Quillip and a couple of empty planets?"

"How can you claim hundreds of worlds if you don't have a dark matter Quillip?"

"Our worlds are linked by quantum-entangled, normal matter Quillip ships. I'm surprised you haven't come across any of them in—"

"What? A normal matter Quillip?" Vishnar interrupted. "Such a device would only work in a vacuum."

"Obviously. But it works."

"How inconvenient. However, a normal matter Quillip does explain why there was no life on your ship when it first arrived, and so many of you are here now."

Quist edged to the left. "As I said, I speak for hundreds of interconnected worlds. Who do you speak for?"

"The planet we are on is in the Norma Arm, near the center of the galaxy," Vishnar said. "I spend most of my time here because the stars are closer together, and the search for the perfect sacrifice can progress faster here than out in your Orion Arm. Nevertheless, I frequently travel through your part of the galaxy. I was there only six thousand years ago, and I didn't find any entangled-matter technology."

"Six millennia is a long time. We've expanded greatly since your last visit," Quist replied.

"Including to Earth, the human world?" Vishnar asked.

"Including Earth."

Vishnar paused, then nodded to himself and said, "I can see that hundreds of worlds might be useful. Would it be possible to receive a full ambassadorial party of six beings from every one of your worlds?"

"That would be highly unusual. Normally one ambassador from the Supreme Council suffices."

"Nonetheless, I require it."

Ironsides kept very still, hoping that Quist wouldn't be drawn off track by this strange development. No, not so strange—he should have anticipated this—the Elliquine said the Ancient One sought six sacrifices from each intelligent species.

Quist spoke softly, "I'll see what I can do."

The avatar leaned forward. "Now tell me, do you have any news of the mind-demons?"

"Maybe," Quist more softly still. "What can you tell me about the mind-demons?"

Ironsides was proud. Quist had caught on rather well to the idea of fishing for more information. He was sure it took a lot for him not to simply say "No."

Vishnar's avatar crossed its arms and rocked back and forth. "They possess you, pervert you, and destroy you. And so, the gods must have sacrifices."

Quist spoke still more softly. Ironsides couldn't hear what he said. Vishnar took a step forward.

Ironsides sprang from behind the door and zipped between the avatar and the doorframe.

The avatar lunged at him, but Ironsides was already through the doorway. The avatar threw out an arm and gave Ironsides a powerful punch.

Ironsides spun like a top out into a grassy area. But he'd made it—through the prison door at least.

"LET HIM GO. HE IS NOT IMPORTANT." Quist shouted, amping up the volume on his exoskeleton.

Ironsides was in a courtyard of some kind, enclosed in front by three, ten-meter-high black walls and behind him by the wall of the concrete prison. At the junction of the black walls and the concrete building were what looked like small alleys. He scrambled toward the alley on the right.

Quist was saying, "Hundreds of worlds. Ten trillion beings to fight the mind-demons. That is what is important. Let us work together."

Ironsides cartwheeled into the alley without hearing the avatar's reply. It must have been short. The prison door clanked shut, the deadbolts ground back into place, and the avatar's footsteps thudded in the courtyard.

But the footsteps got softer, not louder. Ironsides peeked around the corner of the prison in time to see the blue-tinted avatar arrive at the back wall, bow, and enter a door in the wall.

Ironsides rolled back to the dungeon door. The lower deadbolt was in easy reach, a meter off the ground, but push as he might with his root-feet, the bolt was jammed too tight. The second deadbolt was three meters off the ground, even harder to give a good yank. He needed a lever and a ladder.

He returned to explore the alley. Beyond the far side of the prison building, plains of green grass remarkably like Belle Verte waved for as far as he could see. On his left, the black rock wall retreated to form an open-cornered room. Deep shadows obscured anything inside, black on black.

He rolled slowly into the darkness, where he nearly collided with a utility truck. It sat directly on the smooth floor —no wheels. Much of the truck's body was transparent, and

Ironsides could see what appeared to be rocket nozzles at the bottom and rear of the vehicle. The cabin bubble towered two meters above him and would comfortably seat two giants the size of Vishnar's avatar. The open compartment in the back would hold two more avatars or equivalent cargo.

Behind the truck, a low-slung, transparent runabout for two sat on the floor. If only he had a Wolferlop-P to pilot ... Or Jade ... *Think outside the ecliptic*, he told himself. Could he pilot the runabout himself? If Quist could be a diplomat, anything was possible.

He hopped into the runabout. The seat was shaped like those favored by humans, only larger. The dashboard under the windshield was covered with dark patches. Readouts?

He tried moving the joystick located between the seat and the dashboard, but it didn't budge. The top of the joystick looked like one of Jade's hand covers—a glove. He explored the inside of the glove with one of his three-fingered root-feet. The glove had five slots, built for a five-fingered race.

Ironsides looked about for an on-off switch. Nothing. Eventually, he went back to exploring the glove on the joystick. He inserted branches from a second root-foot into the other two fingers. When he did so, the dashboard lit up with undecipherable symbols. The glove became flexible and conformed somewhat to his root-feet. The runabout jerked forward, screeching in protest as it scraped along the floor. He yanked his root-feet out of the glove, and the runabout stopped.

He jumped out and hid deeper in the shadows, but his ruckus hadn't drawn the attention of the avatar, so he climbed back into the runabout and reinserted his root-feet. The dashboard lit up again. He eased his root-feet up, and the vehicle gently rose off the floor. He pushed the joystick forward, first gently, then harder. The runabout flew out of the hangar, picking up speed as it zoomed away from the prison.

He leveled off at an altitude of two hundred meters and began a spiral search pattern. Flying across kilometer after kilometer of untouched prairie was frightening. He longed to land but kept searching.

And untouched prairie was all there was. No signs of civilization. Nothing anywhere to aid the escape of Quist and the Elliquine. No place to hide, just grass.

The wind blew delightful whiffs of the earth below up to him and made him hungry. He could use some real dirt; he was tired of the artificial stuff fabricators made. He was envious of the green grass sinking its roots into the rich soil below. Surely, he could afford some little time for a snack.

The flier left a long, dark gash in the sod as it plowed to a stop. The humus-rich topsoil had a rancid taste to his nanomechanical-sensitive roots. It would be a good source of carbon, but unsatisfying. He burrowed his root-feet deeper, penetrating a delicious clay substrate, well salted with potassium, sodium, iron, and magnesium.

Nourishment. Warm sunshine. The Dasypodia said it was good to be a plant. The Dasypodia was always right. He slipped into immobile bliss.

36

Counter Attack

S hipmaster Hoargrim was amazed to be alive after en-
countering a legendary Shoggart. Instead of dealing him
death, his new master had elevated him to shipmaster.
Hoargrim commanded *two* Quillip ships—a job for which he
had no training. So many things could go wrong. Hoargrim had
never been more frightened for his life.

Hoargrim improvised. He approved parts requisitions and
docking permits without understanding them. He allowed a
few of the Entanglement weaklings to be eaten but insisted
that most of them be indoctrinated into the absolute obedience to Immortals, as he had seen other shipmasters do with
other enslaved food-thralls.

He made his primary command center the bridge of the
Cl'aclen, the better to dominate the new slaves. He left Guardmaster Axmuck on the bridge of the *Granite Pincer*, a high-
visibility, secure place where his main rival was unlikely to
cause him much trouble. Hydras had a saying: *Keep your rivals
in pinching distance.*

"Most Powerful Shipmaster Hoargrim," purred his local
guardmaster, "I'm grieved to report 122 unauthorized masses
will arrive in the Quillip chamber in 37 seconds. They range
in size from 65 to 110 kilograms each. I humbly await your

ENEMY IMMORTAL

orders."

Hoargrim had felt flattered and puffed-up the first few times a subordinate addressed him as Most Powerful Shipmaster, but now he realized it was no more than his due. "Execute Plan A, you idiot! It's an attack by humans. Slaughter them before they reach the Quillip chamber airlock."

Half a minute later, 122 bipedal figures materialized and began spreading random laser fire about the Quillip chamber, destroying 27 of Hoargrim's laser batteries. Hoargrim's 485 remaining laser batteries returned fire. Not one of the incoming targets survived.

The laser batteries were Umlac's idea. Umlac would be pleased when he returned.

During the battle, Axmuck had signaled Hoargrim three times. Only now did Hoargrim reply to the pesky guardmaster, "Why do you annoy me at the time of my victory?"

"Shipmaster Hoargrim, I've been trying to report an unidentified, unscheduled, ten-ton mass teleporting to *Granite Pincer.*"

Hoargrim felt like a mountain of rock had fallen on him. It had to be another Shoggart on its way here, and he was unprepared for such a visit. Umlac had left no orders for this possibility. At least Axmuck could take the blame. "Go to the Quillip chamber and welcome our visitor, but don't let him leave the antechamber without my permission."

"Apologies, powerful shipmaster, but it's too late for me to get there in time," Amuck said. "The Quillip payload will arrive in 30 seconds. I've sent an Ambo squad to the *Granite Pincer's* Quillip chamber. They will welcome the visitor."

"Send video."

Hoargrim's monitor went black. Not the black of malfunction, but the darkness of a Quillip chamber. A flash of light blinded him as an entangled mass collided with the imprint material. He rotated his body to use fresh eyes. The afterglow in the chamber outlined an ugly spherical object, more like an Entanglement artifact than another Shoggart.

235

"Most Powerful Shipmaster." His local watchmaster interrupted. "Another wave of small masses will arrive at the *Cl'aclen* Quillip chamber in 45 seconds. What shall I do?"

Hoargirm faced a two-pronged attack. He was no warmaster, but he'd do his best. He replied, "I'll give the new attack my full attention in a few seconds."

To Axmuck, he said, "I order you to destroy the invader in the Quillip chamber. It dies, or you do."

* * *

"Get your elbow out of my face," Keolo complained.

Vlad adjusted his position inside the crowded pod. Keolo usually tried to be politer, but the stress of being a helpless target in the Quillip chamber of an Immortal ship short-circuited his good intentions. Hopefully, the decoy attack followed by a frontal assault of the Eighty-seventh Marine Company in the *Cl'aclen* was doing well, and the battle of Farboro would be as short and sweet as the battle of Goldilocks Three had been.

Keolo's pod split open, and his lightly armored team fanned out into *Granite Pincer's* Quillip chamber. They rushed into the airlock, delighted to have met no resistance yet. But when they opened the airlock door to the antechamber, a torrent of flames forced them to against the walls.

"Volley fire. Now," Keolo shouted.

Every member of his team began launching antimatter slugs into the inferno. Shock waves rattled the ship. The flames lessened. The right side of the antechamber became clear enough for Keolo to see an Immortal turning the nozzle of a flamethrower in his direction. He pulverized the Immortal with an antimatter dart.

"Fireteam One. Flanking maneuver to the right." Keolo shoved off with three companions, and in no time, they were behind the flames clearing the antechamber of the remaining

Ambos.

"Let's hope this ship is laid out the like the one at Goldilocks Three," Keolo said, leading his squad into the corridor. "Down the tunnel and to the right."

He raced through the corridors. The tactic this time was speed. "The bridge should be just around the next bend."

An explosion rocked his squad, slamming Keolo and Evan into the rocky, slimy wall. Evan screamed. "My arm. I think it's broken."

Another explosion shook the corridor. The Immortals seemed to be lobbing grenades. "Goldie, I'm pinned here." Keolo fired an antimatter dart down the corridor. A laser blast scattered a shower of rock chips from a near miss in reply. "They've established a barricade outside the bridge. I should be able to keep them busy for a while. See if you can break into the corridor above us and flank them."

A full-fledged firefight ensued in Keolo's corridor. The enemy bristled with laser fire, erasing the distance advantage Solar Defense Force's dart poppers had over flamethrowers.

Goldie ended the standoff with a kilo of devastite, which she rolled into the Immortal's barricade. The explosion created quite a bit of rubble, but Evan was able to reach the door to the bridge and blast it open.

The opposition on the bridge faltered as Keolo's squad rushed in. One Hydra remained amidst a few cowering Ambos. "I surrender!" exclaimed the Entanglement translator belt sitting like a crown on top of the Hydra. "Most Awesome Master, spare your humble servant. Allow me to live and assist you with my meager abilities."

Keolo ordered his squad to hold their fire. "Why should I accept your surrender? What assistance are you offering?"

"What brilliant questions, Most Powerful Shipmaster!" the Hydra replied. "Death is certain if I retreat. Shipmaster Hoargrim hates weak, stupid Axmuck. But I have years of experience as a guardmaster. I beg to serve as your vassal."

Keolo hadn't anticipated POWs. Shooting the Hydra flattened to the floor would simplify things. But the Hydra, Axmuck, had surrendered and promised vassaldom. What did vassaldom mean to a Hydra? Could that concept extend itself beyond servitude to other Immortals?

Besides, Jade had killed a Hydra. He would command one.

"Axmuck, shape up. I accept your surrender."

The pancake rippled and reformed itself into a proper Hydra blob. "Most Awesome Master, how may I best serve you?"

"Okay, Axmuck," Keolo said, a bit uneasily as he pointed to the bank of monitors. "Start by showing me where the rest of the soldiers on the *Granite Pincer* are deployed."

"Of course most Awesome Master. But if I may make a weak, stupid suggestion: Wouldn't it be easier to tell them where you want them to be?"

"Just tell them?" echoed Keolo. "Why would they listen to me?"

"Most Awesome Master, you test your stupid servant, as you should. The voice of the bridge is the voice of the Shipmaster. Perhaps a few traitors will run to their old master, Hoargrim, but most will remain loyal to this ship and its rightful master."

"Very well, then, have them return to their quarters and leave all of their weapons outside in the corridor," Keolo said.

"Most Awesome Master! A powerful move. An arms inspection! Make them fear their weapons are judged dirty and scratched and their worthless bodies will be food for their superiors."

37

Sea Change

Shipmaster Hoargrim turned his attention to the *Cl'aclen's* Quillip chamber. Hundreds of bipedal targets flooded his monitors.

"Watchmaster! You said forty-five. Where did all of these come from?"

"Most Powerful Shipmaster, it is my sad duty to report that the incoming creatures are dividing at an alarming rate. The defensive lasers can't keep up. They're particularly confused by intruders who land between them on the Quillip walls."

Hoargrim's stomachs twisted. His automatic lasers were shooting each other. "You said forty-five. You'll suffer for this. Shut the lasers down."

His troops near the airlock wouldn't be so easily confused. Hoargrim was gratified when they continued shooting down the intruders. But with the automatic laser fire off, his troops stood out and became obvious targets themselves. Nearly half of them were lost before the remaining cowards retreated into the airlock.

Hoargrim had been a superior weaponmaster before he became a guardmaster. He took manual control of one of the robot lasers and began shooting down intruders. Their formation was surprisingly disorganized, their trajectories surprisingly aimless. Many of them were decoys!

The enemy destroyed the laser he was using so he switched to another one. He ordered the watchmaster and message-master to follow his lead and take control of two other laser batteries. Someone destroyed his laser. There were hundreds more. He kept fighting and switching.

As Hoargrim began to make headway against the intruders, they attacked the airlock in force. That was a mistake. His troops in the airlock held firm, pinching the intruders with his troops in front and laser batteries behind. Hoargrim's forces took a few more casualties, but they had the advantage now and wiped out the invaders—humans it turned out.

When Hoargrim finished and looked at his other monitors, he saw that the urgent message screen was overflowing. He knotted a pseudopod in annoyance. Axmuck had no initiative.

Hoargrim answered randomly. The call was from an Ambo cargomaster. "Send help. The refugees turned on us. They took over Shuttle Bay F2. They'll take over the whole ship if you don't stop them."

"Refugees?" Hoargrim's satisfaction turned to fear. There should be no refugees. "From where?"

"From the *Granite Pincer*. After Axmuck's surrender, refugees who said they were loyal to you flocked to the *Cl'aclen*. The baymasters let them board. Then the refugees turned on us with horrible weapons capable of squashing a Hydra with a single blow. Send help!"

Hoargrim checked the status of his other two main shuttle bays, and his fear turned to terror. The enemy had taken the *Granite Pincer* and already dominated the three largest shuttle bays on the *Cl'aclen*. They used fearsome, never-seen-before weapons. They were moving out of the shuttle bays toward the heart of the ship. Hoargrim didn't want to die fighting, yet if he somehow survived this mess, Umlac would surely kill him for incompetence. It was time to surrender.

The thought of surrender triggered the Warwiz which

Umlac had planted in Hoargrim's nucleus. Hoargrim felt muzzy from the release of a powerful cocktail of neurotoxins and neurotransmitters. Then a clarity of purpose and a flood of knowledge overwhelmed any thoughts of surrender.

He understood how to turn the human victories into defeats: lead them on; let them overextend; crush them. Orders flowed as naturally from him as if he had been a warmaster for millennia.

To the public address system, he said, "All Entanglement Citizens are on immediate curfew. Any Entanglement Citizen seen in the corridors will be devoured."

On the command channel, he said:

"Platoon A, regroup at the Quillip antechamber and await new orders.

"Platoon B, regroup outside Cargo Hold F2 and await new orders.

"Platoon C, regroup outside Omega Theater for your new orders.

"Transportmaster Xatpoo, take one-third of the devastite in Cargo Hold F2 to each of the other two locations.

"Guardmaster Swillmug, there is a spy in Comm Area 3. Replace everyone in Comm Area 3 and interrogate them all immediately.

"Flightmaster Nordeath, turn the *Cl'aclen* so the bow faces the *Granite Pincer* at all times."

And so on, for fifty-three orders. Then Hoargrim relaxed and celebrated with a live human snack as his plans unfolded.

* * *

Keolo inspected a few of the flat, cowering Hydras and Ambos who professed to be his vassals and returned to the bridge of the *Granite Pincer* where Evan held watch.

"I still wish I was over there with the rest of Team 3," Keolo said.

Evan looked up from a video screen, his arm in a sling. "Then again, the look on Margo's face when she realized Axmuck would only take orders from her if she killed you first was priceless."

"I still feel responsible for the rest of our squad," Keolo said. "Anyway, it should be over soon. They should be making the final run to the bridge just about now."

Hydras surrounded Evan on the bridge, going about the business of running a ship of war. Keolo kept an antimatter dart gun handy in case any of the Hydras got out of line, but so far, he had no occasion to use it.

Axmuck flattened his top more than usual. "Most Awesome Master, if you'll pardon my foolish observation, the monitors say Lieutenant Commander Margo Walsh has taken her platoon off course."

Keolo glanced at the map Axmuck had shunted to his display. "Margo, what's going on?" He radioed. "You should be at the cargo bay a thousand meters spinward."

"Negative," Margo said. "We were assigned to blue quadrant, not the shuttle bay. We chose to land at Shiplaser 13."

"Which got us reassigned as a reserve unit," Nat said. "It was my fault—my recommendation to be less predictable."

"But it was my order," Margo replied. "I take full responsibility."

Keolo flipped through several displays on his monitor. "The other platoons landed with minimal opposition at Cargo Bays F2 and E5."

"We're well aware of that," Nat said. "Our caution may be unwarranted. Commander Arzimio believes that the tactic of aggressive speed which has proven successful so far will continue to be successful."

"Enough yakking," Margo said. Her voice was tense. Keolo suspected she resented missing the action about to occur at the bridge. "We have bulkheads to breach. Keolo, let us know when the other platoons take the bridge. Until then, we'll proceed with city street-tunnel tactics."

Keolo checked his monitors. Both platoons were through their cargo bays and moving up the main shafts to the *Cl'aclen's* bridge. Another monitor showed Margo's platoon. They'd penetrated five levels deep using a zigzag tactic: blast a hole in the wall to a room on a new level, exit that room into a new corridor, randomly follow the new corridor left or right, enter another room, and blast a hole from it to the next level.

"Most Awesome Master, I beg your indulgence." Axmuck quailed. "My monitor has stopped showing locator beacons from Beta and Gamma Platoons. If you would check your monitor to confirm that my eyesight is defective, I would be most grateful."

Keolo saw it too "Margo, Red Alert. Something happened to the other two platoons halfway to the bridge. I say again, Red Alert."

Margo responded quickly. "Everyone, hold your position."

Goldie grumbled. "We're ready to blast into a new level. Can we finish this one off first?"

"Very well," Margo said. "One more room can't hurt. Permission granted."

Goldie's commlink winked out.

"I have vibrations from a large explosion at Goldie's coordinates," Nat said.

Margo's command channel blossomed with panicked reports:

"Beta squad is under attack from multiple flame throwers."

"Gamma squad has detected enemy movement. Multiple Hydras, but no attack so far."

The tension in Margo's voice ratcheted up a notch. "Everyone, hold your positions. I don't want them squeezing us into a more confined area. Use lasers to burn holes into the rooms around you and slip in spy-eyes. We're not falling for any more booby traps. Nat, what's Goldie's situation?"

"Neither Goldie nor Samantha is responding. Goldie's telemetry is dead; Samantha's shows she's alive."

"Tafad and William, see if you can extract Goldie and Samantha," Margo ordered.

"Excuse me," Nat said, "but I should go. We may need to lift rubble off Samantha."

Margo hesitated. "Very well. Nat and William go. Tafad, keep the tactical intel flowing—"

"Most awesome Shipmaster," Axmuck interrupted. "My stupid nucleus doesn't understand what is happening. The *Cl'aclen* is maneuvering. Should we maneuver too?"

Keolo hadn't realized how lost in the Alpha Platoon conversation he'd become. He looked over at Evan, who said, "I've been examining the telemetry from Beta and Gamma Platoons. There were shock waves right before they winked out —massive explosions. Most likely due to booby traps in the shafts. There appear to be no survivors."

"Most Awesome Shipmaster," Axmuck pointed a pseudopod to Keolo's left. "Will you indulge your weak, stupid servant and take a look at the external monitors and lasers?"

Nearly half of the monitors were blank. "What's happening?" Keolo shouted.

"Most Awesome Shipmaster, the enemy ship fired a volley of lasers from its bow, destroying all of our weapons in Quadrants 2 and 3.

"What? We have twice as many lasers as they do."

"I'm just a stupid vassal. I don't know."

Keolo scowled. The captain of the other ship must have moved all of the ship lasers to the bow. Now, as Keolo's asteroid ship rotated, the opposing ship was destroying Keolo's armament before it could swing into a firing angle.

"Maneuver our bow towards them. Protect what's left of our lasers."

"Brilliant, Most Awesome Master. You are a genius. You are unparalleled."

"Evan, contact the Eighty-seventh Marine Company. They should have captured the *Cl'aclen's* Quillip chamber by now," Keolo said.

"No answer," Evan replied. "Nothing from them on the command channels at all."

Keolo shook his head in disbelief. "Something changed. It's like we poked a sleeping bear. We're going to need a miracle to get out of this."

Evan looked at the video feeds from Margo, from the ship lasers, and from his attempt to contact the Eighty-seventh. "I'd say we need three of them."

38

Tides of Battle

Hoargrim strengthened his domination of the *Cl'aclen*. He played recordings of his domination of Entanglement citizens on public channels. He showed clips of the humans in the Quillip chamber getting cut apart by laser fire, followed by gruesome videos of detached legs and heads.

"Here comes your last hope of rescue," he said as a split screen showed two groups of about three dozen humans each speeding along the corridors in an impressive line of armored cars. A glowing dot appeared over a gray lump in the corridor.

"And here is a devastite mine. It will activate when a large metallic object comes close."

The convoy of armored cars blocked the view of the bomb. There was a bright flash, and the camera went black.

Hoargirm trumpeted a fearful blast. "Death is the only possible result for any who attempt to oppose the Most Worshipful Lord Umlac."

He cut to an image from the periphery of a large crater, showing an armored personnel carrier crushed against a bulkhead.

His newfound talent as warmaster felt good. He generously took a wiggling slime slug from his bowl and tossed it to the nearest Ambo.

The Ambo paused to gobble up the treat and then said, "Most Powerful Shipmaster, it is my sad duty to call your attention to the mothership. It is realigning its spin axis to face us. What are your orders to your worthless servants?"

"Foolish question. Continue destroying their weapons whenever they become visible." He would press this advantage as far as possible and then utilize other advantages.

* * *

Being space flotsam is lonely. Keolo composed lyrics for a new song as he glided in a wide arc around to the backside of the *Cl'aclen.* While Evan kept the Immortals busy, Keolo planned to rescue Goldie, Nat, Meera and all the rest of Alpha Platoon. Or die trying.

Being space flotsam is cold. But he dare not use a heated suit, or chemical rockets to speed his trip, or electronic devices to occupy his time.

He shepherded ten space horses chained together by hundred-meter lengths of cable, maneuvering with only a tank of high-pressure gas as a propellant. He was slow and cold. He looked like debris from the one-sided laser battle.

Once he got beyond the range of the lasers massed at the bow of the *Cl'aclen*, he would make his move. He just hoped the enemy had moved *all* of their lasers from the back of the ship to the front.

Being space flotsam beats being vaporized.

And most of all, he hoped Alpha Platoon could hold out until he got to them.

I'll be space flotsam for my friends.

* * *

Hoargrim finished his bowl of slime slugs just as his guardmaster called from the Quillip chamber.

"Most Powerful Shipmaster Hoargrim, your weak-minded servant must ask for your great wisdom. The Entanglement is attacking the *Cl'aclen's* Quillip chamber again. They are using mirrors to deflect the lasers. Already the reflected laser beams have destroyed seven of our laser batteries. What should we do?"

The wisdom of past warmasters spoke through Hoargrim. "Deactivate the lasers. Redeploy Squad 1, Platoon A, with half of the remaining devastite from Shiplaser 13 to the Quillip chamber."

Hoargrim couldn't see what the enemy had teleported in behind the rows of mirrors, but it included many projectile weapons. These were firing from behind the cover of the mirrors, impossible to target with his lasers. The enemy was destroying his laser batteries. Only 126 remained.

His Hydra squad finally arrived and started slinging small devastite bombs wrapped in shrapnel into the chamber. The bursts of shrapnel pulverized the mirrors and disorganized the enemy. They became easy targets in the crossfire of his laser batteries and his weaponmasters.

* * *

At last, Keolo had circled far enough behind the *Cl'aclen*. He turned on his radio receiver. He wouldn't broadcast, but even so, a super-sensitive dish antenna turned his way could detect the tiny electric current used by his receiver.

Jade would have detected him with her electrosense. What was she was doing right now? He wondered if he would ever see her again, and he realized that it mattered to him more than he would have guessed. He missed her spark that brought him so much joy. He missed the way she moved—the most graceful woman he'd ever seen, whether dancing or fighting.

But right now, he needed to focus on the rest of the Misfit Platoon. The Immortals had his friends in a death grip, squeezing them between Hydra warriors on the ship and a space attack from multiple armed shuttles.

Being space flotsam makes you invisible—he hoped. Keolo activated his space horse. Evan should be creating a distraction by now. This was as safe as it would get. Keolo unhooked the cables to the other nine horses and slaved the horses to his electronically. He sped to the backside of *Cl'aclen*. Then, staying close to the ship's hull, he worked his way around to the front of the ship, zigzagging across the bow, stopping at every missile silo he passed to plant a package from his saddlebags.

* * *

"Most Powerful of all Masters, I beg to call your attention to a small matter far beyond my ability to understand. Shiny little ships are attacking us."

Hoargrim's happy mood from his success in the Quillip chamber faded. These humans were annoyingly persistent. He reached out and crushed the bothersome bearer of bad news.

A wave of shuttles sped toward him from the *Granite Pincer*. Perfect mirrors on their fronts protected them from laser fire. The little ships were even reflecting his laser beams back to their sources, causing four of his ship lasers on the *Cl'aclen* to overheat and explode. "All missile batteries, target the little shuttles in front of you. Volley fire at thirty-second intervals as long as targets remain."

It was a shame to waste big missiles on such small fry. Their pilots would get better than they deserved—they would get instant death.

* * *

As Keolo snaked across the surface of *Cl'aclen*, he began to receive short-range radio transmissions from Alpha Platoon.

"I don't see any way around this one," Vlad was saying. "It's another devastite bomb, and I can't tell how it's detonated without detonating it."

"Backtrack and try again," Margo said. "We need to find an escape route. Levels 2 and 3 are stalemates, and Level 1 is under attack from shuttle fire again. I'm counting on Level 4 to be less well defended—what is that rumbling noise?"

"Level 1 is breached!" Sergeant Ryan from Gamma Squad shouted. "Skylar is down. We're taking heavy fire from—"

"I see signs Level 2 is breached from space. Stay away from the center," Margo ordered.

"We have to hold the center," Goldie said. "If they split us up we're done for."

"Goldie!" Keolo broke radio silence. "I thought you were killed by a booby trap."

"Ha. It'll take more than a booby to finish me. Nat dug me out. She'd make a Quadricorn jealous. Are you still master of the Immortal ship? We worried about you when you fell silent."

"I'm fine—"

"Goldie," Margo interrupted. "We have to do something, but if we bunch up, we're done for. Have you got any other options?"

"I do," Keolo said. "Sit tight until the noise dies down and stay clear of the hull breach."

"What the hell are you talking about? I thought they took out all your ship lasers."

Keolo didn't have time to answer. The enemy shuttles had noticed his broadcast and were starting a search pattern. Once they pinpointed him, he would lose his advantage of surprise. Keolo opened fire with streams of antimatter bullets from all ten well-separated space horses.

The shuttle nearest him flashed and was gone. Then the one behind it flashed and was gone, too.

But the fireballs of the first two shuttles obscured the third from view. It began shooting wildly through the fireball. The enemy fire must have hit the space horse on the right end of his line because the antimatter in it all exploded at once in a bright, hot semblance of a little star.

Finally, Keolo scored a hit through the fireball, sending the third shuttle crashing into the hull of the mothership. He circled the glowing remains of the enemy shuttles, made sure there were not more Immortal shuttles in sight, and dove into the breach in the hull.

Loud cheers from Alpha Platoon greeted Keolo as he flew in with the nine remaining space horses.

Margo shook her head. "It's great to see you, but even if we double up, you don't have enough horses to get all of us out of here."

Keolo pointed down, toward the center of *Cl'aclen*. "Then let's stay. I brought enough space horses to carry a squad down the main corridor to the bridge. We can still take this ship."

The platoon stopped cheering. Ryan said what they all must be thinking. "You're crazy. The main corridors were where devastite booby traps wiped out the other two platoons."

* * *

Hoargrim counted down to the launch of his missiles. These humans kept coming up with one gimmick after another, but he would swat them all away. The toy mirror ships would be easy to wipe out, but it was a shame to waste anti-warship missiles on them.

A disturbing report came in from Shiplaser 13. The enemy had destroyed his shuttles. Then they'd blown open Cargo Bay C7 and vented the air out of the main shaft all the way to the core of the ship. The fools. The vacuum in the corridor would be a bigger impediment to humans than to Immortals.

He'd deal with the stragglers at Shiplaser 13 later. Or if they tried coming down the main corridor, his devastite booby trap would take care of them.

He watched as three of his missiles streaked out to destroy their targets.

Three! Where are the rest?

Outrage filled Hoargrim as damage reports flooded his console. Then he felt it in the floor. The *Cl'aclen* groaned from the blast of nearly every missile exploding in its silo.

Amid the reports of exploding missile silos, Hoargrim noticed one small piece of good news. The main corridor from Cargo Bay C7 had exploded. After all of this time, the humans from Shiplaser 13 had fallen prey to the booby trap there.

* * *

At a constant five-gee acceleration, Keolo's boxy space horse zipped unimpeded through the vacuum he'd let into the main corridor. He built up enough speed to pass the Immortal's booby trap before it detonated.

But even so, the shock wave caught him, sweeping his squad down the corridor like leaves in a hurricane.

"Decelerate now. Eight gees." He hadn't allowed for the shock wave. He had no idea if eight gees would be enough, but it was the most he could get from the space horses and a lot to expect his squad to sustain.

The end of the corridor zoomed into sight. He crashed hard into the bulkhead blocking his way.

Goldie crashed beside him and then limped up to the doors to the bridge with a package of devastite. They hadn't dared to bring antimatter darts through the many shocks of their journey. The rest of the team converged, alive so far, carrying bulky, 80 mm, shoulder-mounted rocket launchers. Axmuck assured him that the explosive rockets from these bazookas were beyond the ability of a Hydra to absorb.

* * *

Hoargrim ordered missiles with clusters of small warheads loaded into his three remaining silos. Each missile would destroy twenty or more attackers with each launch. The limiting factor was how fast he could fabricate the non-standard warheads. It was going to be close, but he should be able to destroy all the enemy before they reached his ship.

A crowd of Ambos had gathered around a monitor on the far side of the bridge. "Come here. All of you."

They came.

He pointed to the last one to arrive. "What were you watching over there?"

"Most Powerful Master, I don't know. It was on his monitor." The Ambo threw a splash of red mucus to mark one of his companions.

"Most Glorious Master, I don't know either. That's why I called the Watchmaster to see what he thought it was."

"Watchmaster, what is it?" Hoargirm's patience with these incompetent Ambos was nearing its limit.

"Most Powerful Master," the watchmaster replied, "I was about to report to you that the latest group of humans miraculously survived the devastite booby trap in the central shaft. Human weaponmasters are outside the door to the bridge."

Hoargrim froze for a moment, re-evaluating. These humans must be more powerful than he'd thought if they could survive that booby trap. And he had no doubts they would blast through the door to the bridge any second. The Warwiz changed from battle tactics to self-preservation mode. Hoargrim wouldn't sacrifice himself for anything short of a direct threat to his Shoggart master. Sacrifice was what Ambos were for.

* * *

Keolo signaled Goldie to activate the detonator, and the

door to the bridge fractured into gravel. Air rushed out of the *Cl'aclen's* bridge, followed by a wall of flames from Immortal flamethrowers. But without air to support them, the flame-throwers were ineffective. His team's large-bore explosive darts were more than adequate to pulverize the few Ambos who remained.

"Margo, Alpha Squad has secured the bridge," Keolo radioed. "But there is no sign of the Hydra shipmaster."

He switched channels. "Axmuck, Hoargrim isn't on the bridge. Is there somewhere else he could be using as a command center?"

"Of course not, Most Awesome Master. What wonderful news! Hoargrim has abdicated. Now you are shipmaster of two ships. At this rate, it won't be long before I become the humble vassal of a Fleetmaster."

"Check this out, Keolo," Goldie called from across the room. "I noticed the door to the supply closet looked weird. It's been replaced with a pressure-seal door."

Keolo stuck his head in. "This has been converted into an airlock all right. It looks like a backdoor to the Quillip chamber."

Meera called Keolo over to her monitor. "Cameras in the Quillip chamber show a Hydra from the bridge area teleporting away."

Nat looked up from another console, "The ship's log shows the last large teleport was to a planet called Elliquor."

Keolo slammed his fist down. "If that's where the Shoggart went, then that's where Jade is."

"An unidentified teleport to Elliquor occurred shortly after Jade arrived from Goldilocks Three," Nat said. "According to the log, the mass agrees with my estimate of the mass of Jade's team."

"Damn," Keolo said. "Jade is still cut off. They must want whatever she's got very badly."

39

On the Run

J ade piloted the shuttle away from *Peapod* on a zigzag
course and tried to think while Conrad babbled on. He
talked about his delight at going back to the surface.
They'd see the statue in the polar caves again, the polar
caves themselves, the colony site with its phantoms, the un-
explored forest and ocean. The Elliquine wouldn't want the
forest, maybe when this was all over, they'd let humans settle
there.

Jade worried about how to deal with Umlac.

Umlac needed the command codes to get *Peapod* to do anything for him, and especially to get back to Elliquor when he
finished whatever he was doing here on Belle Verte. He would
follow them. She needed to lose him—no, she needed to kill
him.

That would take one very large explosion, or maybe a huge
flamethrower like the one her electrosense detected inside his
body—of course, he carried a flamethrower for defense against
other Shoggarts. Maybe she could pull the same exploding-
flamethrower trick with him that she used on the Hydra. But
only if he tried unsuccessfully to use it on her, which she
couldn't count on.

What about poison? She didn't know enough chemistry. A

digital virus? She didn't know how to make those, either, but maybe Zephyr could. He'd need details of the internal data protocols Umlac used. Now that she knew Umlac's internal communication frequencies, she could modify some micro cams to feed Zephyr his private communications. But she'd need to get the modified micro cams close to Umlac for them to do any good.

Mountain peaks jutted over the horizon. "We'll be at the polar caves in a few minutes," she said. "Our top priority is to find a place to hide until I can come up with our next move."

When they landed, she had Conrad walk with her back and forth in the snow between the shuttle and the tunnel several times.

"Let's go," she said. "It looks like we unloaded here. Hopefully, it will take Umlac a while to figure out that we didn't."

"Go where?" Conrad stopped and gaped at her. "This is the only decent hiding place we know of."

"We can't hide from the *Dutchman* in the caves." She pointed out. "And what about the shuttle? Are you just going to leave our only transportation back to *Peapod* out here in the open for Umlac to grab?"

"I don't see the pattern. If you're going to keep flying evasive action, why bother to make it look like we unloaded in the caves?"

"No. We wouldn't be safe from the Dutchman for long. We can't track changes to its orbit without the scanning gravimeter. Even with evasive maneuvers, it could still get us."

Conrad stared into the distance. "We're doomed no matter what we do."

"Maybe not, I have another hiding place in mind." She gave Conrad a little push toward the shuttle. "Now get back in and buckle up."

She set the autopilot on an evasive-action course trending to the south. The snow turned to water as Jade did some reprogramming on the two remaining drone fliers.

The ocean turned to a forest. She put the shuttle's little fabricator to work making micro cams with electrical antennae.

When the forest under the shuttle turned into a prairie, she landed in a shallow valley, opened the shuttle door, threw a long-range handheld radio into the grass, waited a little longer, and took to the air again.

Farther into the prairie she landed in another shallow valley. This time she used the rover to drag one of the drone fliers out, oriented it to point the way they'd come, and took off again in the shuttle.

"You seem to have a plan, but I don't recognize the pattern," Conrad said.

Jade smiled to herself. She had aroused his curiosity. "Good, then maybe Umlac won't either. I reprogrammed that flier as a surface-to-air missile in case he follows our path."

She landed several more times in a zigzag pattern before reaching her destination.

Conrad scratched his head. "This is where you collected iridium ore. Are you making another scanning gravimeter?"

"No. I hadn't thought of that, but I have a different idea."

Conrad's brainsong crackled with curiosity. "I certainly don't have all the ideas. I still don't see the pattern to your actions."

Jade pointed out the window. "See the hole in the cliff up ahead? We can hide the shuttle in there."

"Won't Umlac just follow us?"

"I don't know," Jade replied. "But I hope not. I've reprogrammed our last flier to continue a zigzag pattern to the south. The fliers use the same type of rockets as the shuttle, so from space, it should look like our stop here is just one among many. And if Umlac tries going to all the stops, he'll run into my drone missile."

Conrad frowned. "Why wouldn't Umlac just go directly to the decoy, see it's a decoy, and come for us?"

Jade sent the drone off on autopilot. "The decoy will blow up after a few more stops. Hopefully, he will think we died with it."

"That's clever," Conrad said. "I hope it works."

Jade landed inside the black rock hangar. As before, the lack of electromagnetic fields gave her an uncomfortable feeling of being suspended in a void. "This is where I lost radio contact with the *Peapod* when I was getting iridium ore. The black rock absorbs all electromagnetic energy, at any wavelength. I bet it contains transmatter, but you can go out and see for yourself."

Once outside, Jade put her hand on the floor. "The ground here should be warm from the shuttle rockets. If we could find a way to cloak the shuttle with it, we might have a stealth ship impervious to energy weapons."

"I'll leave the engineering up to you," Conrad said. "But if this rock contains transmatter, then this place may contain clues about the race that built the transmatter spy-eyes and the *Dutchman*."

They followed the back wall to the open end on the left and peered around the corner. Jade wished she'd looked here before. An overhang of black rock sheltered a path around three sides of a U-shaped area roughly the size of a football field.

Conrad fizzled with excitement. "Based on the shape of this cutout, I'd say we're in a garage or hangar, and this path should lead to the rest of the facility. To the main house, as it were."

Jade put out an arm to hold him back. "Stay behind me and make sure you keep well under the overhang at all times. We don't know what we're walking into, and we don't want Umlac detecting our infrared glow from above."

She drew her dart popper and eased her way down the path. The dry, brown dirt under her feet seemed ordinary enough, but a void of electromagnetic radiation replaced normal bedrock reflections beneath. The wall of black rock to her right remained smooth, unblemished, and completely dark on all wavelengths.

No, not entirely unblemished. About seven meters from the corner, she noticed a faint vertical line. She ran her fingertips over the surface. "There's a crack here."

Conrad crowded in and rubbed his hand up and down the wall. "It goes all the way to the ground, and as far up as I can reach. And it's completely straight."

Jade had moved a little farther down the path. "There's another one here, and it looks like there could be a horizontal line in the rock about three meters up connecting them."

"A door!" Conrad hopped up and down with excitement. "This could be the entrance to the builders' home."

Jade slipped her dart popper into its holster, pulled a knife from her belt, knelt next to the wall, and started scraping away dirt.

"If it's a door," she said, "there should be another line at the bottom. I can't sense one, but maybe it's buried too deep."

"I have some picks and trowels in my backpack. Not to mention a sonic cleaner and sonar probe."

Conrad shrugged off one strap of his backpack and began rummaging through it. Jade stood to see what Conrad was doing. The backpack slipped out of Conrad's hands and fell near Jade's feet. She bent over to pick up his backpack, straightened up, and said, "Here."

The electric field along the crack intensified to a bright white line.

She drew her dart popper. "The door's opening. Stand back."

"Oh, in that case." Conrad ignored her and stepped through the door.

40

Koke Tngri

Jade jumped through the doorway after Conrad. There was nothing to shoot with her dart popper. There was nothing but flowers. Murals of flowers covered all four walls of a room six meters wide, ten meters deep, and four meters high. The ceiling was a powder-blue sky. A cheerful yellow sun in one corner lit up the whole room. The walls and ceiling glowed electric blue to Jade's electrosense. The flowers were a pixel display, which presumably the room's owner could change.

Beneath her feet, Jade felt the familiar electrical void from the shuttle hangar and pathway.

"Automatic room lights." Conrad grinned. "Why should we expect less from this installation than we would from a house on Earth?"

Jade was furious. She said nothing as she pulled the backpack into the doorway to block the door open. Then she grabbed Conrad's arm and pinned him to the wall. "Are your ears broken? I said 'Stand back' at the door."

Conrad squirmed. "It's just an empty room with pictures of flowers."

"Irrelevant. What if I'd seen something you hadn't? I have to trust you to do what I say."

A flicker of anger growled in Conrad's brainsong. "Ow. You're hurting me. Fine. Fine. I'll listen to you next time. Let go of my arm."

"If you ever pull a stunt like that again, I *will* hurt you." She let go of him. "*Now* let's look around."

Conrad scurried to one of the murals as if nothing had happened. "The builders must have originated on a world filled with flowers. These white ones look like the flower on the statue in the polar caves. Another connection to it."

Jade caught up and knelt for a closer look at the flowers. "It's animated. Little bugs are crawling on the leaves."

Conrad bent over to see. "There's a bee on this flower. I should have noticed sooner: there are no flowers on Belle Verte. That would be part of the pattern of no animals—no bees to pollinate the flowers."

He straightened up. Electrical activity in the wall surged.

Jade drew her dart popper and backed away. The flower mural folded into the ceiling, and she faced a wall of shelves—all empty.

Jade holstered her dart popper again. Something they did must have triggered the wall to open. And the outside door.

She walked to the back of the room and bowed to the wall. A door opened to an empty walk-in closet. Not to be outdone, Conrad marched up to the remaining wall and bowed. The mural slid up to reveal more empty shelves.

Jade examined the walk-in closet for secondary doors or shelves. Conrad bowed to close the fold-up doors and recorded the flower murals on his special archeology camera.

Jade crossed to the door and looked back into the room. "This would be a more defensible position than the shuttle if we loaded it up with weapons and supplies."

Conrad joined her. "First, let's see what else we find down the path. This seems more like an unused gardener's cottage than a manor house."

"Sounds good." Jade led the way down the path. Seven meters later, they came to another door in the black rock wall.

She motioned Conrad to the side. This time he complied. Jade bowed, and the door whooshed open. The second room was identical in every respect to the first one: same size, exact same murals, same closets and shelves, same emptiness.

A dozen identical rooms later, she said, "This reminds me of officer's row: nice houses, all identical. Maybe your Vedic gods didn't like variety."

She opened the first door on the back wall of the courtyard. "We have variety."

The room was the same size as the others and covered with murals of flowers, but these flowers were different, a large blue and magenta variety. The sun lighting the room had an orange tint.

Jade hurried to a wall and bowed. "Jackpot! Somebody used this room all right."

The shelves were crammed full. Carved stone statues of alien animals cluttered a shelf about chest high. The shelf above it was loaded with skulls and bones. The top shelf was stuffed with fur pelts, colorful scaled skins, and bundles of feathers. Below the shelf of statues was a shelf of seashells and another of dried leaves and flowers. Rocks and logs filled the area under the bottom shelf.

"I don't see any scientific pattern," Conrad said. "Most likely these are souvenirs.

He lifted down a couple of small skulls. "These don't look like they are from either Earth or Belle Verte. He returned the small skulls and picked up a large one. "This one looks like a Bellevertian Griffin."

The hairs on Jade's neck prickled, and she looked around to make sure they were alone. "Look at the skull behind the Bellevertian."

Conrad picked up the smaller skull. "Human. No doubt about it. The cortical imprints on the inside are unmistakable. Indo-European. I'd say eastern Greek islands."

Jade drew her dart popper and covered the outside door. "How old is that skull?"

"Give me a minute. Since the skull is from Earth, I can carbon date it."

He sat down and scraped a small area of the bone clean, then scraped some of the subsurface material into a portable mass spectrometer. "Carbon-14 dates this skull at 3600 BC."

Jade returned her gun to its holster. "Six thousand years old."

"Six thousand years ago is also when the legends of Vishnu originated on Earth," Conrad said. "It looks like our builders had faster-than-light travel of some kind."

"Or a fleet of dark matter Quillip ships," Jade replied. "Maybe there's a galaxy-wide dark-matter civilization living in parallel with us."

"I don't think so," Conrad said. "These rooms were designed for normal matter occupants. Although a dark-matter Quillip visiting Earth could explain how a human skull got here."

Conrad began taking skulls off the shelf and photographing them from multiple angles. Jade went to the back wall and bowed.

"My God!" she gasped.

Her hand trembled with excitement as she reached out to touch a ruby-crusted handle. It was one of many, hanging on a blue velvet background. Rows of bejeweled weapons covered the wall—swords, shields, maces and more.

The blades of the swords were black, both visually and electrically—the same transmatter material as the rock around her and as the disc from the Polar Caves. The hilts of the weapons varied in pattern and composition, some gleamed with silver and fire opal, others gold and ruby, or platinum and diamond.

An empty peg invited the black disc from the Vishnu statue. "I found where the Sudarshana Chakra came from."

Jade slid out a broadsword with a steel handgrip studded in emeralds. "It's a weapons museum."

"Or a weapons cache," Conrad said as he looked up from the bone shelf. "For collecting skulls, perhaps."

"No," Jade replied. "These weapons are all low-tech. And they're fastened to the wall with U-brackets. If the builders intended quick access, they would have used L-brackets."

The sword was amazingly light for its size. The blade seemed to suck in the light as she swished it through the air. She stroked the smooth, cold flat of the sword's broad blade, and then tried the sharpness with her finger. "Ouch!"

The sword seemed to cut her finger without her applying any pressure at all. She hefted the sword a few more times and then executed a practice lunge into the center of the room. "I wouldn't normally work with a sword this big, but it's so light and well-balanced it feels like it could have been custom-made for me, and it has the sharpest edge I've ever seen. Drag one of those tree branches over here."

Conrad gave her a branch from the bottom shelf and went back to examining skulls. Jade whacked a few twigs off, which went flying vigorously across the room. She pulled out a thick log for a chopping block out and set a branch on it.

She rested the sword down lightly against the branch, in preparation for a swing. Just laying it there was enough to cause both the branch *and the log* to fly apart with a loud crack.

The pieces of log flew away so vigorously one of them splintered against the far wall, and the other one shattered several statues on a shelf near Conrad.

"Watch it!" Conrad shouted. "You're destroying valuable artifacts. And that could have been my head."

Jade gaped at the destruction she had caused. The sword had stopped only at the transmatter floor, and she hadn't felt the violence at all. The sword tapped some hidden power to maintain stability and momentum.

She tried another log, laying the sharp edge of the sword gently upon it, careful to exert no pressure. The sword sank into the log, and after penetrating a few centimeters, caused the log to pop apart.

"Try this," Conrad rolled a fist-sized hunk of granite across the floor to her. "I have a hunch it won't be any harder for your sword to cut stone than wood."

"I'm not trying to break the sword."

But she tapped the blade lightly against the granite, and the rock split.

"May I see the sword up close?" Conrad asked.

He had been using a magnifier to look at some of the bones. Now he held it over the sword's hilt, then the blade. "There's an inscription on the blade. I don't recognize the language, but the bars at the top of every letter look a lot like Sanskrit."

"Sanskrit? What does it say?"

"It's not Sanskrit, but one side should say 'Take me up' and the other 'Cast me away'—the inscription on the legendary sword which could penetrate stone: Excalibur."

Jade held out her hand. "I'll take Excalibur back now." She pulled the sword's sheath from the wall and slipped the blade into it; then she replaced the *wakizashi* on her waist with the transmatter sword.

Of the remaining weapons, one dagger stood out because of its elaborate jewel work and central location in the display. She pulled the dagger out of its sheath. The blade was brilliant white.

Jade sliced off a few twigs with it, then set a branch on a log, and pushed down gently. The wood around the blade sizzled and smoked and separated, but without the violent rending apart Excalibur had produced. She had to keep light pressure on the dagger as it cut to the floor to separate the log. But the blade didn't stop there. It cut a gash into the floor.

She returned the dagger to its scabbard. "So that's why this one is so special," she said, fastening the golden scabbard on her thigh. "Conrad, do you have a name for a magical dagger which can cut anything?"

"Certainly. The dagger's name should be Sting. But it doesn't cut everything."

"Why not?"

"Because it's not cutting through the scabbard."

Jade pulled Sting out to look inside the scabbard. "I meant

anything except white transmatter like itself."

Conrad came to the back wall to photograph the weapons. "Blue walls," he said. "Blue ceilings in every room. A home fit for the gods in the middle of a prairie world under a blue sky. While we're naming things, let's call this place 'Koke Tngri' after the blue-sky home of the gods of the Mongolian steppes."

After a while, they went on to the next door. Jade readied her dart popper as usual. "Stay behind me."

"Fine. Fine. Hurry up."

She bowed. The door opened. She gasped.

Her combat reflexes kicked in as she waved her dart popper back and forth to cover the six Vedic gods staring at her.

The beings were two and a half meters tall, had four arms, bluish legs, and bronze skin with a slight metallic luster. They stared at her with unblinking brown eyes, like pieces from a wax museum.

"Statues, I guess," she said, lowering her gun. "But so life-like."

Conrad came around from behind her. "The pattern is clear now. The builders looked like Vishnu."

He went to examine the statues. Jade was more interested in racks on the wall: racks of guns. She took down a pistol and a rifle. "Let's go outside and see if these work."

Taking care to remain under the protective lip of the bluffs, she propped a folded tarp against the wall as a target, took aim with the pistol, and pulled the trigger. A glob of blue goo splatted on the tarp.

She poked at the goo with the point of a steel knife. The knife stuck tight.

The blue substance seemed almost alive as it crept up the blade and handle. She jerked her hand away just in time to avoid contact. "This might stop one of us, I guess, but I don't think it'll do much against Umlac. Let's try the rifle."

The rifle shot a larger glob of the same blue substance. "We're going to need a lot more than glue guns to stop Umlac," Jade said. "Let's try the next door."

41

Hunter-Killer

Umlac crushed the revoltingly rectangular console on *Peapod's* bridge in frustration. Then, disgusted by the undertaste of lead and copper polluting the console's steel, he flipped the abomination twenty meters across the prairie.

But the real sacrilege was the humans escaping his jaws. They'd left him little consolation other than imagining the long, painful dissection he would perform on the Hydra Slayer when he caught her again.

He found the fab unit on the bridge that operated without an access code, and he built three small satellites. These were for the low probability, extreme contingency of his death. He periodically sent data to them to hold in secret. If necessary, his twin brother Winzar would access the data cache and lead the rest of his brother Shoggarts to carry out Umlac's revenge.

But the fab unit couldn't fabricate information. He needed the override codes to access *Peapod's* records, thrusters, and especially its Quillip engine. He needed to ingest at least one of the Entanglement team.

The heat glow of the runaway shuttle's engine made the humans easy to track—first to the polar ice cap and then on a zigzag course to the south, where their shuttle exploded.

It seemed unlikely the shuttle would explode for no good reason. Umlac concluded it must be a decoy.

He cloned a Hydra warmaster mind to operate the shuttle and weaponmaster minds to operate the fliers and land rover. He sent his killers to bring back the humans, dead or alive.

The shuttle landed at the polar caves, and Umlac sent the Rover in.

"Most Worshipful, Powerful, Wise Master, I detect traces of recent organics," Rover soon reported. "They went in here. I see tracks in the dust and scorch marks from a rocket sled. They've been busy. Most likely they unloaded a large cache of supplies before sending off their shuttle as a decoy."

"Let me do the analysis," Umlac replied. "But continue to report all details you observe."

Much later Rover reported he'd found the trashed flier in a large underground cavern. "There are tunnels everywhere. This will make a wonderful city from which to rule the planet."

"Where did they go from the flier?" Umlac asked. This weaponmaster was too chatty. He wouldn't use him again.

"Most Worshipful, Powerful, Wise Master, they went into several tunnels, but most of their traffic is to a large one. Following it now." Rover left his audio channel open, and Umlac heard the crunch of its treads on the bedrock. "It's a dead end, a room full of ugly sculptures. I detect nerve gas but see no bodies. Humans must be immune to this type of gas."

It didn't take much longer to conclude that the humans hadn't gone very far down any of the side tunnels. It didn't make sense, but they weren't here. They must have left on the shuttle that zigzagged away and later blew up, which probably meant they had gotten off the shuttle at one of the stops along its path.

Umlac told the shuttle to fetch Rover and follow the route the humans had taken after leaving the caves. When the shuttle drew near the first point at which the humans had stopped, it slowed down, scanning thoroughly for any signs of animal life or technological activity.

The shuttle found nothing, so it continued to the next one.

Umlac's caution at the first site had wasted several minutes, so he sent the shuttle directly to the second site. As he approached, a rocket shot over a low hill, straight at the shuttle.

The shuttle tilted itself down slightly and launched the air-to-air missile on its roof. The attacking rocket blew apart less than thirty meters from the shuttle, showering it with shrapnel.

A close call, and unfortunately, Umlac hadn't delayed the chase long enough to fabricate more than one air-to-air missile. He could bring his shuttle back to *Peapod* for additional armament, but by process of elimination, he must be very close to the humans and their companions. It would be quicker to proceed without an air-to-air missile defense, even using extreme caution at all stops.

So at the third stop, his shuttle did a full, careful scan. A small electric signal leaked out from behind a nearby hill, so it sent out Rover to sneak up on the prey at the source of the signal.

Rover circled the hill to its prey but found only a small pocket computer nestled in the grass. He destroyed the computer with a blast of his laser cannon and then listened carefully. There were no more radio signals in the area. Umlac ordered him back to the shuttle.

Rover stalked and destroyed similar small electronic devices at the next two stops. The stop after that began like the others, with Rover sneaking up on small energy fluctuations of undetermined origin, but quickly diverged. For one thing, a field of boulders rich in iridium ore made his approach easy to conceal.

Rover entered radio silence and moved in for the kill.

42

Grand Bargain

Keolo shifted positions in his chair at the end of a four-way virtual conference table. He sat with Margo, Nat and Darzak, Ambassador to Farboro, who had withdrawn his application for transfer when Margo became captain of the ship. Keolo was slightly embarrassed but mostly pleased that the female half of Darzak looked like Jade from head to toe, at least as much as he'd seen of the real Jade.

Captain Kilwee Five and his crew joined from Goldilocks Three at one side of the virtual table, and Admiral Hammer and his aides glared from Earth on the other. The full Supreme Council gathered along the side opposite Keolo.

Sythersoph, a weasel-like Arafaxian lawyer on the Supreme Council, twitched her nose furiously. "It's implied by your contract to save Farboro that you do not lose Elliquor."

"I don't see anything about Elliquor in the contract." The Hammer's glare intensified. "Jakkar Ten said before that only what is written matters, not what was intended."

Keolo shifted positions again. Fair or not, the economics of Sythersoph's argument would appeal to the Merkasaurs, the Merchant Guild, which was as close to a ruling class as could be found in the Entanglement.

"Besides," the admiral continued, "I already said we would

try to retake Elliquor to recover the humans trapped on the other side, but we need to send reinforcements. We need equipment. We need you to act like a partner instead of a god-damn department store."

The argument droned on, Keolo only halfway listening—and clenching his teeth. This quibbling was so wrong. Delaying a counterattack against Elliquor was wrong. Arguing over finances during this critical phase of the Immortal Ascendency invasion was wrong.

Keolo thought of the last time he'd met the Supreme Council. His proposal that the Solar Defense Force retake the Farboro system in exchange for the *Granite Pincer* had ended another argument over contracts. But Sythersoph had already refused to pay transportation for the SDF to retake Elliquor, and no Immortal ship circled Elliquor for Earth to take as spoils. The Entanglement had no imagination—no big picture thinking when it came to warfare.

Of course. Keolo stood and nodded to the Admiral. "With your permission, sir, I'd like to make a proposal that might end this impasse." The Admiral nodded back, and Keolo addressed the Supreme Council. "Jakkar Ten, quibbling over copper when tantalum is on the table doesn't become you. You have seen that Earth provides the most effective force available against the Immortal invasion. Why not use this tool to the fullest extent possible instead of hiding it in a trunk?"

Silver Streak stiffened his root-feet. "You were just lucky. In standard one-on-one combat with a Hydra, you wouldn't stand a chance."

Keolo knew better than to let Silver Streak distract him, but he responded anyway. "Jade Mahelona defeated a Hydra with a borrowed laser pistol. We do it all the time with anti-matter darts. Nevertheless, gladiators don't win wars. Armies win wars, and only Earth has an army."

"You are speaking nonsense," Two of Silver Streak's laser-eyes focused sharply on Keolo.

Keolo was suddenly glad he was light-years away. A shadow

of doubt crossed his mind. Surely, the virtual conference connection wouldn't transport a full-powered laser blast?

He bit his lip and stared back at the red laser-eyes. "That's why you need us. You don't know the difference. Doesn't the *Dasypodia* have anything to say about knowing your limits?"

Silver Streak focused four more laser-eyes on Keolo, but before the Dasypod could say anything, Keolo flicked his gaze back to Jakkar Ten and said, "Hundreds of star systems are at stake. You need to think big. You need to execute a grand bargain: hire Earth to stop the advance of the Immortal Ascendency on all eight fronts. The Solar Defense Force could counterattack at all of the systems which have already fallen to the Immortal Ascendency."

"That would be worth 100 Tantalum," said one Merkasaur.

Admiral Hammer sat up straighter. "The proper Guild for Earth is in the Police Guild, as a protector of the Entanglement."

"I'd pay 20 Tantalum for the return of Glickercan Station," another Merkasaur said.

Keolo held up his hand for silence. "Taking back a few lost planets still isn't the big picture. As the admiral said, Earth can help protect you from future attacks as well, which are inevitable. The Immortals have cast aside the Treaty of Aniscore and revealed their true intentions—the enslavement of all of us."

Jakkar Ten sharpened his claws, a sign of interest. "What is your asking price?"

"Defending the Entanglement and repelling the armies of the Immortal Ascendency will require a huge deployment of soldiers. It'll drain Earth's resources and leave our homeworld defenses weakened. Of course, you need to provide a generous budget for transportation and equipment. But the people of Earth need something visible to fight for, something they believe will give them a better way of life in the future. In return for our services, Earth deserves the outright ownership of its local Quillip Station."

Jakkar Ten stared at Keolo with his huge brown eyes. "Such a price is absurd. We can't barter away an entire Quillip ship. It's unprecedented."

"The Entanglement already lost twelve Quillip ships to the invaders," Keolo replied. "An invasion on this scale is also unprecedented and deserves an unprecedented response."

"A *successful* invasion by the Immortal Ascendency would be unprecedented," Jakkar Ten said. "We repelled them twice before. Your price is unreasonable. A few hundred Earth soldiers ought to cost less than a one percent stake in a Quillip ship."

Keolo began to lose confidence. Jakkar Ten wanted to haggle. It was one thing to come up with the idea for a grand bargain, another to negotiate the details when all of the Solar Defense Force was at stake.

Keolo reminded himself that Jade was stranded somewhere beyond Elliquor, and he was going to get her back.

He squared his shoulders and told the leader of the Supreme Council, "Your assumption that a few hundred soldiers can defend two hundred worlds is absurd. That's less than five soldiers per Entanglement star system. You need several thousand soldiers for each star system, at least on the border. Maybe more. Solar Defense Force surprised the Immortal Ascendency at Goldilocks Three and Farboro, and even so, we sustained heavy casualties. The enemy Immortals will have learned from those encounters, and they'll be harder to beat next time."

"So you admit you are too cowardly for a fair fight?" Silver Streak interrupted.

Keolo ignored the petty jibe. "Jakkar Ten, you underestimate the enemy's intentions. Power is like money. Those who crave it are never satisfied. The Immortal Ascendency won't stop with a dozen worlds, or with five dozen worlds. They'll press on. They covet Nexus. They want every coin you are worth. Yet I propose that Earth will do whatever it takes to stop them, for a single, fixed price of one Quillip ship."

Jakkar Ten's tail waved madly as Keolo sat back down.

Pannap splashed for attention and said, "According to the interrogation of the Ambo agents we captured, the Immortal Ascendency has infiltrated many of our existing Guilds with spies. Our chances are better with a defense force unknown to the Immortal Ascendancy."

Jakkar Ten clenched and unclenched his claws at Keolo. "The scope of your proposal isn't something I anticipated. Give us a few minutes of privacy to discuss it."

The images of the Supreme Council disappeared, and Admiral Hammer gave Keolo a wry smile. "You know I don't have the authority to make the kind of a deal you proposed."

"You can sell it. Earth needs the Entanglement, or Earth will be next."

"Yes, I think I can, if they agree to throw in the Quillip ship. That was a stroke of genius. Let me make a few calls but signal me if the council returns." The admiral and his staff vanished.

Only Goldilocks Three and Farboro remained at the conference. Kilwee Five hung his head and said quietly. "While it's just us, there is something you should know which hasn't become common knowledge yet."

Keolo, Margo, and Nat slid forward to the edges of their chairs. "What is it?"

"Forensic analysis of the chemical residues at the scene of the antimatter explosion on the Immortal's ship found no traces of organics with the signature of Earth isotopes."

"Are you saying Andrew and José survived? They're still alive?"

"We have no way of knowing," Kilwee Five replied. "However, we fear they were taken alive by the Immortals, and their ammo belts detonated to obscure the trail."

"Prisoners?" Margo perked up. "Does the Immortal Ascendency negotiate for the return of POWs?"

Kilwee Five thrashed his tail. Pannap said, "The Immortals treat prisoners as slaves or as food. In this case, they'll likely want to know more about the limits of human endurance. I'm sorry."

Admiral Hammer returned with two well-known figures: Secretary of State McKee and Senate leader Zhang. He introduced those present, and then returned his gaze to Margo. "Spit it out, Walsh. What's on your mind?"

Margo stiffened. "Sir, while we are waiting for the return of the Supreme Council, may I inquire as to the disposition of Troop Three's reorganization? As you just pointed out, we lost two platoons to the booby-trapped shafts, plus the troop command."

The admiral nodded. "You'll remain on Farboro. We'll send reinforcements to hold onto Farboro and retake Elliquor. However, Solar Defense Force will be short on personnel if we take on the defense of two hundred planets, so the best we can do short term is to replace Beta and Gamma Platoons with a couple of platoons of Marines."

Margo pursed her lips. "That will be a challenge for the new commander."

Admiral Hammer smiled. "I'm sure you'll be up to the challenge, *Commander* Walsh. I'm promoting you to full Commander and assigning you as Commanding Officer of Troop Three on Farboro." Admiral Hammer's smile faded. "It's a big responsibility—"

Before he could finish, the Supreme Council returned from their private conference. Jakkar Ten removed a string of coins from his neck and laid them on the table. Two other Merkasaurs did likewise. "This is our stake in the Quillip ship orbiting your planet. The sooner Earth engages the Immortals on all fronts, the less the war will cost. Therefore, we accept your services in exchange for Earth's Quillip ship."

Silver Streak pointed a root-foot at the admiral. "We accept, providing you leave the defense of the Nexus system to Dasypod forces. That should be acceptable to you since it only decreases your expenses."

Keolo sat back and let his mind drift away as Earth and the Entanglement worked out the details of the agreement. He didn't care about Nexus. He cared about avenging Andrew and José, and Alicia and Carmen, and Beta and Gamma Platoons. And the thought that he might have to add Jade to that list cut through his heart like a knife. *You don't know what you've got until it leaves for the stars.*

43

Trojan Horse

The next room, at the center of Koke Tngri's back wall, was larger than the other rooms. Metallic helmets dangled above rows of oversized reclining chairs along both side walls, reminding her of hair dryers in a 1950s hair salon. A table with ten oversized chairs filled the center of the room.

Jade caught her breath. "It looks like a military-grade VR control center."

Conrad went to the left, to study the two larger helmets. Jade went to the right where there were four smaller units.

"The wiring harness from the helmet to the ceiling is composed of about two dozen wires. It's designed for data transmission, but that's more bandwidth than needed for VR, at least on Earth."

"The big helmets over here have a hundred wires," Conrad said.

Jade's electrosense showed two dimly glowing wires on each helmet. "The helmets may still be active. There's electric current flowing to them. The big red and yellow wires are for power."

Conrad's brainsong pinged. "Ah, yes. It's a simple pattern, which also explains why the red and yellow wires are bigger on the bigger helmets—they must draw more power. Notice how red is always on the right and yellow on the left. Can your electric field sense tell which is positive and which is negative?"

"Red is negative," Jade said, sitting down to try out one of the chairs on her side. "Look at how human-shaped the seats are."

Power flowed into the chair beneath her. Alarm and curiosity tugged at Jade in equal proportions as the chair adjusted its shape to fit her body and provide more comfortable support. The chair stopped moving, and Jade started to relax again.

Then the helmet dropped on her head.

Another tussle between alarm and curiosity ensued. She tensed to push the helmet away, but waited, watching. The wires to the helmet lit up in a violet haze of information exchange. She half-expected a hologram to appear on the visor, as with human VR helmets. Instead, everything went black.

Everything.

It was like she'd closed her eyes, but darker. The blackness took on an eerie living quality. Unformed chaos swirled around her. She became dizzy and disoriented. The formlessness tugged at her like a dozen tiny hands.

Sparks of yellow light danced in from one side like a horde of fireflies. They jostled about, without any obvious pattern. One at a time, they centered in her virtual field of vision and then moved on.

She focused her attention on one of the fireflies, trying to follow it as it moved away. Somehow, her scrutiny pulled it back to the center of her vision, where it began to expand. It became a yellow dot, which grew into a circle of light.

Soon, the light filled her entire field of vision, and indistinct shapes formed—a brown background with vertical lines, which became a rack of guns with two missing.

She saw the room next door from the perspective of one of the statues, though she wasn't sure which one. As she thought this, her view of the room changed, as if she was turning her head to the side. Three statues—or avatars—she must be in the second closest one to the door.

As she thought about being in the avatar, she was. She felt the tension of her neck turned to the side, the weight of her body on her feet and legs, the position of her fingers and arms. Four arms. Although the lower two felt insubstantial, ghost arms that didn't correspond to anything in her real body.

She raised a hand to touch her face, then another, and another, and another. She gazed down with awe at her bronze-blue body. This was by far the best virtual reality she'd ever experienced. That made the corners of her avatar's mouth turn up in a smile.

"Help! Attack!" Conrad's muffled voice interrupted her happy discovery.

Jade forced part of her attention back to her little two-armed body. The outside door of the control room was wide open. An Immortal abomination atop the Elliquine land rover was halfway through the door. Numerous war-like protuberances pointed into the room. It had thrown a capture net over Conrad and pulled him off-balance. He flopped about on the floor like a triggerfish out of the water.

The rover shot a rope-mesh net over her body and the chair she was sitting in. The wires on her helmet lengthened and allowed the helmet to remain in place even as the net tightened around her. She might be able to cut her way out of the net, but that might take more time than she had. Maybe she could use her avatar as a distraction—get the rover to chase it.

She shifted her full attention to her four-armed body next door and lifted a leg to take a step forward. The walls flashed by, and she stared at the polished, black floor, balanced on the tip of what must be a very hard nose indeed. The avatar body was more sensitive than the Earthly VR units she was used to.

Slowly, she pulled herself up and shuffled across the armory. She grabbed one of the goo rifles off the wall, bowed to open the door, and stepped out into the sunshine. The ugly back half of the robot stuck out of the doorway a dozen meters away.

A power surge in the control room jerked her attention back to her real body. The net over her tightened, pulling her deep into the cushions of the chair. The power input to the robot's motors increased, and the cords of the net tightened further. It was becoming hard to breathe. She didn't have much time left.

She willed all of her concentration to her avatar, took aim with her goo gun at the periscope on the robot's back, and fired. Blue goo covered the periscope lens and began creeping down its pipe.

The rover gave the nets some slack and backed out of the doorway to face her avatar with its forward sensors. Jade fired again, but the rover was too fast. It shot a net over the avatar, throwing off her aim. The cords attaching the net to the robot tightened and pulled her avatar off its feet.

This time, she put out a hand to block her fall. The hand poked a hole in the net. Jade, or rather her avatar, crawled to her knees and sat back. She grabbed the rope netting with two hands and pulled it apart. The nets shredded like tissue paper. The avatar was super strong.

The rover shot her with a hypersonic dart. Then another. One dart bounced off her shoulder and the other one off her forehead. She was armored, too.

Jade stood up and went after the rover. Additional darts, bullets and energy beams raked her avatar. She felt them all, but as mere pinpricks.

She grabbed the misshapen hump on the back of the rover and pulled. The metal rivets holding the ugly thing in place squealed loudly and gave way. The rover fell silent.

She tossed aside the Immortal control unit and went inside to free Conrad.

When he saw her avatar approaching, he shrank away. "Stop. We come in peace."

"Hey, it's me, Jade."

Her voice boomed out, rich and deep, more like Keolo's

than her own.

Conrad eyed her avatar suspiciously but stopped struggling with the net. He cringed when she ripped the ropes off, but then a smile spread over his face. "Impressive. Do you bend steel bars and leap tall buildings, too?"

"There's not much room for leaping in here, but as to steel bars—" she walked over to the rover and bent a centimeter-thick steel bolt to a right angle.

Conrad clapped. "I'd wager this avatar of yours could stand up to a Hydra."

Jade was giddy from her easy victory. "Only a Hydra? Why not a Shoggart?"

Conrad sobered. "I don't want to get anywhere near Umlac again. He's in a class of his own. Stronger than a Hydra. Much stronger. We have no idea what the limits of his strength are."

Jade grinned. "Sometimes you have to take an opportunity when it presents itself. I've been trying to figure out a way to get aboard *Peapod*, and this is perfect. If *Peapod's* rover is here, its shuttle must be nearby."

She had the measure of the avatar body now. The avatar picked up the packet of modified micro cams and said, "We don't have to be stronger than Umlac. We can be smarter."

"Well, you're the boss," Conrad said, "but it seems too risky to me, and I still don't see how you can get your avatar aboard *Peapod*."

"You're the professor," Jade replied. "Haven't you ever heard of the Trojan Horse?"

44

Sacrilege

Umlac angrily waited for Rover to break radio silence. First, the chatty Hydra yacked too much, and then not enough. He was beginning to consider sending one of the fliers after it when Rover finally appeared on the rim of a grassy hill. Its radio antenna was missing, explaining the prolonged radio silence. More importantly, he carried a body in one of his capture nets. There should still be time for the shuttle to get the body to *Peapod* for Umlac to ingest before the human's memories deteriorated much.

He felt a bit envious that he hadn't been the one to snag this prey. Judging by the damage to Rover, the Hydra Slayer must have put up quite a fight. At least Rover should have a video of the battle in its memory banks.

Umlac used the shuttle's telescopic camera to study the body. It was too tall to be the Hydra Slayer. Its skin had a bluish cast, and it had no infrared glow, both signs of significant time since its death. It lay front down, obscuring its face and arms, so there was little more for Umlac to see at a distance. Perhaps it was too late to extract its memories. Worse, if the dead biped wasn't the Hydra Slayer or her little companion, it might not have the codes he needed.

Rover drove up the ramp and into the shuttle. Umlac would

soon know in detail what had happened. The shuttle extended a maintenance harness to Rover.

When the harness approached within a few centimeters of the socket on the rover, the dead biped in the capture nets suddenly revived. In a flurry of activity, it tore away the nets, lept to its feet, and ripped the maintenance harness from its base.

So that was it! A human was behind this after all, in a powered suit of armor. Perhaps he had the Hydra Slayer despite appearances.

The foolish creature attacked the main shuttle control unit, a dome about one and a half meters tall housing the shuttle's mind. The dome had numerous built-in defenses and should be relatively secure.

The shuttle released a stream of explosive pellets from a gun that happened to be pointed at the intruder. Its main laser cannon on top of the control unit swiveled toward the intruder.

The bullets exploded on contact with the biped's armor but caused no visible damage. As the main laser cannon came around, the creature jumped out of range. Fortunately, this brought it in front of a second laser, which fired at point-blank range.

The armor glowed a dull red from the laser discharge, but the creature inside seemed unfazed. It reached up and yanked the laser cannon from its mount. Then it dismantled the entire control unit by inserting its fingers into the various gun ports and sensors and pulling. Its strength was comparable to a Hydra, and soon the shuttle mind was dead.

The biped sat down in the pilot's seat and launched the shuttle into the air using a primitive physical control interface. With the annihilation of his warmaster, Umlac had lost direct control of the shuttle—but he still had contact via the three weaponmaster minds inside the three fliers.

The foolish creature in the suit of armor seemed to be oblivious to this fact, which would soon be its downfall.

* * *

The shuttle was a kilometer from *Peapod*. The creature Umlac believed to be a human in a suit of powered armor made a few adjustments to the shuttle controls and then walked out the door into space. Umlac had to admire the human's tactics. If not for his visual telemetry from the fliers, he might have overlooked the puny object on a lazy trajectory toward *Peapod*.

But he did notice. He concluded humans might be smart enough to act as Ambo squad leaders. However, they weren't smart enough to compete with his Hydra vassals, who would have known to disable the communications from the fliers.

He ordered one of his fliers to take control of the shuttle through a maintenance harness to ensure the biped had no escape. He connected to the harness without a problem, but a cyberlock on the shuttle controls blocked him from doing anything—the same kind of cyberlock as the one blocking him on *Peapod*.

Umlac crushed a nearby Elliquine taxi in frustration. This new kind of cyberlock must be from humans. How he hated those clever little vermin. He smashed the few remaining upright consoles the humans had left on the bridge.

He activated the rocket motors on one of the fliers. The rocket's exhaust melted a track in the floor as Umlac moved it toward the center of the shuttle, but he didn't care. If he couldn't have the shuttle, nobody could.

The rover swiveled its cannon, fired, and scored a direct hit on Umlac's flier, disabling its weaponmaster module. How dare this upstart rover catch him unawares a second time? Whoever was causing all this mischief would pay dearly.

He ordered one of his fliers to rocket straight into the rover. By the time rover brought its cannon to bear, it was too late. The explosion from the collision of flier and rover filled the shuttle with fire, smoke, and debris. He wished he were there to feel the heat and smell the destruction.

He ordered the third and final flier to flip over and fire its rockets continuously at low intensity. Plasma flames formed an umbrella of fire against the transparent dome of the shuttle, melting a hole in the window. The plasma exhaust shot out into space and pushed the shuttle down toward a fiery death in the atmosphere of Belle Verte.

Umlac's white-hot rage crystalized into an icy, calculating craving for revenge. The hubris of the human inside the surprisingly strong armor suggested she was indeed the Hydra Slayer. He prepared for her arrival.

When she finally arrived at *Peapod*, instead of cycling through the main airlock, she crawled into an Elliquine maintenance tunnel and waited quietly for several minutes. Umlac waited. Let her think she was unobserved. If he could get her to reveal the access codes without ingesting her, he would gain the time to torture her with a slow, slow death.

Soon the powered suit squirmed the rest of the way through the maintenance vents and into the engineering section. Umlac quivered in anticipation and watched carefully with a telescopic eye when the biped went to the auxiliary control panel and began entering commands.

He slid to a point just out of the creature's sight. When he judged it wasn't looking in his direction, he pounced, engulfing his prey in a large digestive organ. The creature twisted and turned, and eventually, Umlac realized it was unaffected by his digestive acids and enzymes. Furthermore, it was swimming deeper into his sacred body.

The abomination! He caught the creature in a set of powerful jaws, but his diamond-tipped teeth did not pierce its armor. The creature grabbed one of his jaws and broke it, then pulled itself a meter closer to his nucleus.

Fear touched Umlac. This outrageous desecration of his holy body was a new experience. As much as he was coming to covet the human's powered-armor technology, as much as he needed her access codes, his first duty was to make sure that she didn't dig too deeply into Shoggart secrets.

Umlac spun polymer strands far stronger than steel to tie her arms and legs in place. The powered armor ripped the polymer bonds away as fast as Umlac could form them.

Umlac formed diamond drills and spun them into various parts of the power suit—the drills broke.

He turned his projectile cannon inward and shot the intruder—the projectile bounced off.

The obscene creature clawed into the most private parts of his sacred body, moving dangerously close to his nucleus—his brain—his one irreplaceable component.

He must stop this desecration, even if it meant using hot fusion. He extracted a bubble of deuterium—the heavy hydrogen that his body normally used for cold fusion—just a small bubble for a tactical hydrogen bomb, not enough for self-destruction.

He placed the deuterium bubble on the creature's back, where she was unable to reach with her obscene, jointed appendages. He spun layer upon layer of shrinksteel over the bubble, then heated the outer layers, causing them to contract.

As the shrinksteel contracted, it increased the pressure in the pocket of deuterium. Compressing the gas produced more heat, which caused the shrinksteel to contract, which caused more pressure, which caused more heat, in an endless positive feedback loop. Endless, that is until the deuterium reached critical pressure.

The nuclear explosion shot the armor across the room and smashed it into the heavy shielding of the Quillip chamber. It blew away a ton of Umlac's mass, leaving him a bit dazed, but intact. He sealed his wound and crawled to the remains of his prey.

The armor remained largely intact, but with a three-centimeter hole in its back. Unfortunately, the hot plasma of the nuclear explosion had vaporized whatever had been inside that shell of armor.

He twisted his stomachs in anger and frustration. He'd been so close—again—but he still didn't have the access codes to *Peapod*. He squeezed the armor shell with diamond-tipped, rock-crushing pseudopods. The armor remained unscathed.

Umlac seldom saw new things anymore, and curiosity overcame his anger. He marveled at the strength of the armor and gloated at the powerful new resource at his disposal.

45

Discontent

Every human-inhabited starship had at least one public lounge serving alcoholic beverages. On *Cl'aclen*, the preferred gathering area was the Way-Out Lounge, which served the equivalent of liquor for several species. Keolo sat in a booth, sipping a beer while he waited for friends to join him.

One of the new Marines sat in the booth next to Keolo and took bets on sports back on Earth.

"Are you Loganal Mulcraft?" An ensign from Beta Platoon approached the Marine.

"What if I am?"

"I heard you take bets on football."

"You came to the right place. Have a seat."

The private sat. "I gotta hurry. Space horse drill on A Deck. How do I know you'll pay up?"

"Ask any of the jarheads from Green Company, Corps Four. I kept book for them for over a year. Besides, where could I hide from you out here if I wasn't legit?"

Keolo's stomach twisted a little to hear Loganal talk. Books weren't all Loganal was suspected of keeping in Green Company. Someone had sold excess military bandwidth to Luna and Mars on the black market and kept the profits. They never found out who, but Keolo was sure this guy would sell his mother to make a profit.

"Yeah, I could hurt you bad," the private replied. "What are the odds for the Okies in tomorrow's match with Bangkok?"

Keolo heard a rustle as Loganal checked his comp for the latest updates from Earth and added his booking fee. "Five to one against Oklahoma."

"The Okies are going to pull an upset. Put this on the Okies."

As the private left, Keolo's friends arrived. Nat squeezed her muscular gray body in next to Keolo. "Sitting around drinking alone so early in the day?"

"I'm not alone anymore," Keolo said a loud beery voice. "But yeah, there doesn't seem to be anything else going on around here. We've been sitting idle on Farboro for too long. We should be retaking Elliquor."

"Margo says we need time to integrate all the new recruits," Nat replied. "Give her a break."

Keolo let a little bitterness seep into his voice. "You were there when Admiral Hammer made her CO and told her to figure out how to take Elliquor and recover Jade. Well, Margo isn't doing it. She's just bossing the new recruits around in pointless training exercises. They've stripped and cleaned more weapons in the last two days than the previous two years."

"That's your interpretation," Nat said. "The Hammer didn't say 'go get Jade right away.' He said it was up to Margo to decide how to proceed."

Keolo raised his voice. "That's your interpretation of a discretionary order? If anyone but Margo were CO, we'd be on Elliquor by now."

Across the table, Meera shook her head. "Jade can take care of herself for a few days. There are plenty of other reasons Margo isn't ready to command an entire troop, let alone captain a starship. I'm sure you see it too. You're doing all right as captain—I mean shipmaster—of the *Granite Pincer*."

Evan chimed in, "Present company excepted, I second the motion that there are a lot of people around here who are in way over their heads."

"It's only Margo I worry about," Keolo said. "She was promoted too fast—twice in two weeks. She doesn't know how to handle the job. She has us running all kinds of defensive drills. Frankly, I don't think she wants Jade back. She's afraid of the competition."

Evan shook his head. "Whatever the reason, I'll be glad when these pointless boot camp exercises are over."

"Margo is doing it all wrong," Keolo said. "We need better weapons. We need training aimed at fighting Hydras. I'm a bit surprised the Immortals haven't already launched a counteroffensive and wiped us all out."

Nat shook the table with a gentle bang from her big fist. "Settle down, Keolo. Nobody is getting through our defense in the Quillip chamber. We have two hundred lasers, two hundred cannon, and two hundred missiles ready to blast any unauthorized teleport. Some are automatic; some are manual, giving us both speed and intelligence in targeting.

"Don't forget the mines," Evan added. "I bet the Hydra commander on Elliquor would give a lot to know about the double ring of mines and the clear passage sixty degrees spinward from the exit."

"Well the comm problem works against us too," Vlad said. "Without uncensored communication to Elliquor, we don't know what the Immortals have waiting there for us.

Goldie took a swig of her Martian redbeer and thumped down her glass. "We couldn't penetrate our defenses without intimate knowledge of them, so I don't see how we could insert ourselves into whatever the Immortals have at Elliquor."

"Margo is happy with a stalemate," Keolo said. "She gets to run a starship without fear of attack. Meanwhile, we haven't had any word about Jade since she left for Elliquor. Whatever happened to our unofficial motto, 'Solar Defense Force takes care of its own'?"

"I bet Jade is enjoying exploring Belle Verte a lot more than we are enjoying our stalemate here," Nat said.

Keolo heard two more marines visit the booth behind him while the officers yacked on:

"I heard the automatic lasers fire with a delay of thirty milliseconds while they screen for friendly targets based on a transponder code, and a humanoid shape will delay the AI for at least another hundred milliseconds ..."

"We can't trust any of the aliens here. Security sweeps have already found two caches of valuables, presumably left by the Immortal shipmaster as future payment for his spies ..."

"I wish you were running the *Cl'aclen*, Keolo. You wouldn't have let ship morale get so low ..."

"I wish I was running the *Cl'aclen*, too ..."

The Way-Out Lounge was a good place to start rumors. And the rumor that he would make a better captain of *Cl'aclen* was only the beginning of Keolo's plan.

46

Heaven or Hell

I ronsides' root-feet sank deeper into the clay under the plains of Vaikuntha, seeking out trace minerals essential to his nanomechanical biology. Blissfully, he thanked his Creator for his life, for all life, and for the glory and mystery of the universe.

Joyfully, he contemplated his family. He wished he could talk to Spike one more time before Spike's duel with a drill-snake. If Spike survived, he would find a mate and raise children of his own. Ironsides fondly remembered the long days that he and Amethyst Ring had toiled in their garden, tending their darling saplings, Steel Spike, Turquoise Shard, Gold Leaf, and Silver Cap. It had been good, honest work with none of the complexities of dealing with other intelligent species.

Other species. His bliss dampened. The Ancient One still imprisoned the Elliquine and Quist. He'd saved himself, but he'd accomplished nothing to help the others. The Ancient One would surely sacrifice others in Ironsides' stead.

The *Dasypodia* said, "A planted fighter is no better than a fan-tree." He must return to the prison compound and make the situation right. He could use the runabout to push open the deadbolts on the prison door. The Elliquine could escape to the prairies, and Quist could fly away with him.

Hastily, he retracted his root-feet from the soil and took the runabout back up into the sky. He had to circle the area a couple of times to find the prison. The courtyard was empty, so he started his descent toward it.

An unseen hand took control of his flier. The joystick glove became rigid and unresponsive to his root-feet. He tried pushing colored patches on the dashboard, hoping to find an emergency off switch, but to no avail. An avatar ran into the courtyard. He'd been too slow to return, and now he'd lost his chance of using the runabout to open the prison door.

The flier glided over the courtyard. Black rock cliffs and green grass flashed by to the left and right as it flew for a crash with the dungeon door. He tried to jump out, but the control glove wouldn't release his root-feet.

The avatar arrived at the prison door, threw back the deadbolts, and jerked the prison door open just in time to let the little flier through. The runabout lost power and skidded to a halt on the floor. The prison door slammed shut behind him.

The control glove released Ironsides' root-feet, but he was too ashamed of his ignoble recapture to bother getting out of the car.

"Perfectly executed!" Quist exclaimed, using a private laser channel as his exoskeleton rolled up to Ironsides.

Ironsides was in no mood for Obnot nonsense. "What are you babbling about?" He flashed back. "I've just been recaptured and dumped back in prison without making any progress in getting us out of here."

"Incorrect. You forced Vishnar to use his override command codes to recover this vehicle. Now I have the override codes."

Ironsides straightened his drooping root-feet. "You can get us out of here?"

"Unknown."

He should have known better than to get his hopes up. "What *can* you do?"

"Unknown. Obviously, I need time to determine what

circuits can be controlled by the override code. Consonance is achieved only if Vishnar fails to notice my intrusions, so I must explore slowly. It's unknown if Vishnar has higher override codes. It's unknown how many layers of intrusion monitoring are built into his control systems."

After a while, Quist moved closer to the runabout. The vehicle rose a centimeter into the air and then settled back to the floor a little closer to Quist.

"How did you do that?" Ironsides asked.

Quist laser-commed back. "The human infonet is a remarkable source of techniques for network hacking. With the override codes, I was able to enter the intrusion detection module and determine what patterns it scanned for. Knowing what to avoid, I found my way to the controls for the flier, and then the dark matter Quillip. The Belle Verte end of the Quillip link is still in an elliptical orbit intersecting both the *Peapod* and the surface. I can teleport us to *Peapod* in 31.3 minutes."

The thump of a deadbolt interrupted their conversation.

"We may not have that long," Ironsides said. "We need to find a way to stall Vishnar."

Another thump. The door swung open, and Vishnar's avatar entered. He carried the flier out into the courtyard, and then returned to the prison. "Your attempt at deception has failed."

Ironsides' hopes evaporated. Quist must be mistaken. Vishnar knew about Quist's network hacking.

Quist surprised him by addressing the robot, "I admit it, then. I do not have sufficient authority to promise an ambassador plus five assistants from every world in the Entanglement federation. Only the Supreme Council can bind the Entanglement to such an agreement. We must go to them to arrange the deal."

Vishnar responded, "If I send you back, how do I know you will return?"

Ironsides felt renewed hope. Vishnar was still interested in obtaining an influx of "ambassadors" from new species.

Quist rolled closer to the avatar and said quietly, "If you

don't want to send us all back, sending back just me would be sufficient."

What? Surely, Quist wouldn't leave him and the Elliquine behind. No, he must be stalling until he could use the dark matter Quillip to save them all. He must be better at deception than Ironsides had imagined.

Vishnar said, "I would prefer to keep you as an interim representative of your species."

And because he wants you for a sacrifice, Ironsides thought.

"I will send back one of the Elliquine," Vishnar continued. "Let him carry the message and arrange the deal."

The Elliquine must have been listening, because their movements became frenzied, and their speech short and clipped.

"Marstamper will not go."

"Nupper will not go."

"Darlock will not go."

Quist moved between Vishnar's avatar and the Solidarity. "The Elliquine fear nothing more than being alone. You will have to send them all back together."

The Elliquine quieted down at Quist's proposal, though they still hopped about nervously.

"I should like six of them to remain as ambassadors. The rest may go."

Vishnar's words sent a chill through Ironsides. Reminding him that if ambassadors from the Entanglement did come, they would die—hundreds of sacrifices.

"That is efficient," Quist said. "How soon should they be ready?"

"The next window for teleportation to your vessel at Belle Verte is in twenty-five minutes. Have the group ready to go before then."

Ironsides tried to keep the Elliquine calm while talking to Quist on his private channel. "I don't think I can persuade them to split into two groups, but as long as I appear to try, Vishnar should believe we will keep our bargain."

"I feel much dissonance," Quist said.

"You are helping our team. You are fulfilling the contract with the Elliquine to rescue the colonists."

"At least it will be over soon," Quist said. "There will be a 20-second window in which to teleport from Vaikuntha to *Peapod*. Vishnar's machines calculated a teleport at the middle of that window. I will take control of the dark matter Quillip the instant the window opens and teleport us all to *Peapod* before he has a chance to do anything. Then I will lock the Quillip so that he cannot teleport us back."

When Vishnar's avatar returned, it looked them over and said, "You are not keeping your bargain. The Elliquine have not separated into two groups."

Ironsides temporized. "They want you to select who should go and who should stay."

"It will be much simpler if they stand still."

"That is obviously true," Quist said. He shouted. "Dear Elliquine. Your freedom is near. Stop your dance for a few seconds. Trust me. Your freedom is near. For all of you if you stop now."

The Elliquine paused and looked at Quist. A second later, Ironsides found himself on the bridge of *Peapod*. Quist and the Elliquine were beside him. He bounced for joy. They had escaped from Vaikuntha. They had rescued the Elliquine. The *Dasypodia* was right when it said, "There is no greater joy than the safety of others."

His root-feet slipped, and he sprawled awkwardly on the deck. A pasty, slimy mess covered *Peapod*. Gritty sludge clung to everything.

The Elliquine formed a tight, defensive huddle. Quist extended probes to the floor and reported without prompting. "The grit comes from the consoles we installed here. The gray gel contains a variety of organic compounds typically found in Immortals."

A gurgling sound echoed from the direction of the engineering section, softly at first, then louder. A huge, black, shapeless creature steamrolled toward them.

The monster headed directly for the Elliquine. "Worship me, my tasty prey. Come to me that I may extract the override codes from your dying flesh."

"Extreme dissonance," Quist broadcast.

Ironsides fired eight laser-eyes into the attacking creature causing several small spouts of steam to rise from its surface. The creature seemed not to notice at all. "We have to stop it!" he shouted.

The monster grabbed one of the Elliquine and ripped it in half, tossing the pieces into holes that opened in its side. Mouths? Stomachs?

Ironsides tried to roll to the Elliquine, but his root-feet kept slipping. Then, as the creature reached for a second Elliquine, the wave of dark jelly vanished without a trace.

Ironsides vibrated the tips of his root-feet in disbelief. "Quist, what happened?"

"Obviously, the Immortal was teleported away."

The *Dasypodia* advised *drillsnakes may travel in packs.*

"Is it alone? Where did it come from?"

"Unknown," Quist replied.

"Tell me as soon as you find anything."

"The creature is known as a Shoggart. It came alone from Elliquor's Quillip Station."

"But you just said you didn't know if it was alone or where it came from," Ironsides said. "Make up your mind."

"My mind is always made up. While you were speaking, I connected to the *Peapod's* main control systems and scanned the recent event logs."

"And this Shoggart monster?" he asked Quist. "Where did it go?"

"To be most efficient, I simply reversed the Quillip calculation that brought us here," Quist said.

"So that means the Shoggart is where we came from, in the prison?"

"Obviously. It should be safely locked up there."

Ironsides wasn't so sure. He had already escaped from that prison twice.

47

Visceral Reality

Time meant nothing to Jade. All moments looked the same. Black. Brown. Not quite the same, rather waves of darkness flowing through the darkness. The avatar must be gone or disconnected. Jade languished in the disconnected space between avatars, anchored to nothing.

She tried following the currents, but they led nowhere. She tried fighting against them, but they came from nowhere. Eventually, she gave up fighting the darkness and drifted into daydreaming. The dance of the Elliquine. The Misfit Platoon—an ironic name—it was where she'd fit in best before she met the Elliquine.

Her neck itched, but she couldn't move her hand to scratch it. She concentrated on the itch. She ached to scratch it. Maybe she could use it as a way back.

Awareness of the rest of her body gradually returned. Her leg ached where the Shoggart's arrow had cut it. She was sitting—her muscles cramped from being in one position too long. She was thirsty.

She kept her eyes closed and concentrated on her electrosense. She was still sitting in the VR chair, the helmet glinting overhead. Conrad sat at the table, scrutinizing Excalibur, probably trying to decipher its inscription.

She opened her eyes, and Conrad crossed over to her. "Are you alright? What happened?"

"I screwed up is what happened," Jade kicked her legs off the recliner, getting ready to stand up. "I forgot to listen to Sun Tzu. *'If you know the enemy and know yourself, you need not fear the result of a hundred battles. If you know yourself but not the enemy, for every victory gained you will also suffer a defeat. If you know neither the enemy nor yourself, you will succumb in every battle.'* I didn't know the Shoggart or the avatar, either one."

"Don't be so hard on yourself. It was worth a try."

Sticky black stains had covered everything when the avatar crawled out of the maintenance tunnel into Engineering. Jade wiped away enough tar to get a link to Elliquor on the external comm. A Hydra Messagemaster answered, claiming Elliquor and its colony were now the property of the Immortal Ascendency.

Jade stood on unsteady legs. "Now we know that even if we could get rid of Umlac, the Immortals control Elliquor. We can't get back to Earth."

Conrad took her arm. "Come sit."

"No," she said. "I spread the modified micro cams around, but I couldn't contact Zephyr directly to explain my plan. Too much black tar on everything. Too risky to use my implant. But if Zephyr connects to the micro cams, he should get my message to make a virus to use against Umlac. He should send it to me soon. I must go to the shuttle and see."

At the shuttle, Jade had tossed a wire out from under the hangar to act as an antenna and put the receiver in record mode. Zephyr had come through, but with a strange and lengthy message:

"I've just transmitted a virus that should be ninety percent effective in paralyzing Umlac. But it's lonely here. It's frustrating being locked up on a spaceship with a monster and having no way to stop it. Umlac is very sophisticated in cyber warfare, and I've had to pull out all the stops to keep ahead of him. I've expanded my computing capacity a lot, but I wish I had a body so that I could do more

against him. Umlac has ravaged Engineering and the Bridge. The bow of the ship is still clean, but he'll probably destroy it soon since that's where I'm broadcasting from. This low-bandwidth broadcast is taking forever, and Umlac is on his way."

The message started to repeat but was soon cut off.

Jade had assumed Zephyr was a Level 4 or 5 AI, which should be adequate for his cybersecurity task, but feelings like loneliness and desire for action sounded more like Level 7 or 8—nearly human.

Jade put aside thoughts of Zephyr's expansion and fabricated six darts loaded with Zephyr's virus. The avatar attack against Umlac had failed. She needed something else, and not only the virus. Umlac was resourceful—she wanted a multi-pronged attack.

Back in the control room, she found Conrad studying the inscription on the throwing disk they'd found by the statue of Vishnu.

He bounced up to greet her. "It's the same alphabet. Let go see what's on the other swords on the wall."

Jade held up the palm of her hand. "Wait. We've ignored an obvious asset for too long. What do you think the big helmets do?"

"More VR," Conrad replied. "I hate VR. If you want to look for assets, we should try the other rooms of Koke Tngri. We've only seen half of them so far."

Jade studied a big helmet with its fat wiring harness. "Good point, but let's try this helmet first. It must do something important."

"Or be for a species much different from humans," Conrad said.

Jade sat in the chair. "I'll give it a try, and we'll see. I want you to stay with me in case anything goes wrong."

The oversized helmet descended over her head, and darkness like that of the avatar helmets blocked her vision. A flock of sparks appeared in the dark void, much like the avatar menu, but with variations in the colors of the sparks. She focused her attention on a blue one. It expanded—became a tornado—blew her into the void. She was lost—out of control. The void turned her upside down, inside out. She felt her body rebelling and was helpless to stop it.

The void evaporated. She was back in the VR chair, exhausted, with vomit running down her chest and polluting her mouth.

Conrad finished pushing the helmet up to its original position. "Are you okay? Hang on, and I'll get something to wipe that up."

"Yeah, but this helmet is certainly different. I picked a blue light, and it threw me out. Let me try a yellow one, like the avatars."

The yellow one was nothing like the avatars, but another wild vortex like the blue light. She had nothing left to regurgitate, but that didn't mean her convulsions felt any better.

"Let me try." Conrad's brainsong swelled with curiosity.

"I thought you didn't do virtual reality."

"Not on Earth, where VR is too bland," Conrad replied. "But this thing doesn't sound like any VR I've ever heard of. Besides, bigger helmet, bigger head. Maybe it will fit me better."

Conrad was joking, but he was right. Maybe his bigger brain could tame the spinning vortexes.

Jade stood. Conrad sat. The helmet descended on him.

48

Miracle or Illusion?

C onrad was exhausted. He'd thought he could do this, but so far, he had nothing.

Not exactly nothing: The menu of sparks in the big VR spun rapidly out of control when selected. The VR was capable of inducing dizziness and nausea. But he still had no idea what the big helmet was connected to, let alone how to control it.

He tried again. He picked the dim green one. It unfurled into a vortex of bifurcating fractals in three dimensions. The complexity of the pattern grew. He followed it. It grew some more. He followed it again. It grew until he lost the eye of the vortex. When that happened, the chaos took him—living darkness that prodded and pulled him. He'd learned to abort the session rather than fight the chaos. He reached up to push the helmet off, but Jade beat him to it.

"How are you feeling?" Jade asked as she watched a portable medical monitor. "Your vital signs are getting weaker, but this was the longest you stayed under the big helmet so far—thirty seconds. That's four times longer than I can manage."

"How did you know I'd lost the vortex?" his voice was dry and scratchy.

"Your heart rate was rising rapidly, and the data wires in the harness were starting to go dark one by one."

"I almost had it," he said.

Jade put her hand on his shoulder. "You've been at it for over an hour now. Come over to the table. Sit down. Rest. Get a drink of water."

Conrad swung his legs out of the chair. "There's something familiar about the patterns in that vortex. It's like the tip-of-the-tongue phenomenon where you know you know it, but you can't remember."

Suddenly, he swung his legs back onto the VR chair. "I have it! There's another dimension."

This time the vortex crystalized into fragments of real pictures. An Elliquine holoprojector. A Shoggart. A dark tunnel. Stars. The fragments must be from a larger picture. Maybe the Shoggart was using the holoprojector.

His thought threw the fragments into disarray. They began to dissolve, sucked into the vortex. Chaos began nibbling at his fingers. He pushed the helmet away. His breath was ragged, his heart racing. "I thought I had it."

"You lasted over a minute this time. What did you see?" Jade asked.

"Pieces of a picture," Conrad said, "but they don't fit together right."

"Are you sure they're all from the same picture?" Jade asked. Then she touched his shoulder again. "I'm worried about you. The longer you stay under, the longer it takes you to recover. No more than five minutes next time, assuming you can make it that long."

The touch gave him a tingle of delight, though he knew it wasn't intended to be sexual, just caring. *Just* caring? Hardly anyone cared much about him outside of the work he did, but Jade was going out of her way to be kind to him despite the rudeness he'd shown her when they first came to Belle Verte. He didn't want to let her down.

He took a deep breath. "I don't know if I can last for five minutes, but I know there's a unifying pattern, and I'm going to find it." He yanked the helmet over his head.

His experience started like always, with points of light, and then fragments of pictures. This time he focused on just one fragment, the Elliquine holoprojector. It was sitting on a muddy surface with holes. There were points of light in the holes. Then the green of Belle Verte slid into one of them. Windows. This must be what *Peapod* looked like after Umlac visited. The broken upright consoles suggested he was on *Peapod's* bridge.

He was curious about how the other consoles on the bridge had fared, and his view shifted to the right, revealing more smashed and broken consoles.

Farther to the right, footprints in the sludge appeared to be Elliquine. How had they gotten here *after* Umlac ravaged the place? A rescue force from Elliquor? That would be inconsistent with Elliquine psychology. The colonists? That made no sense. Slaves sent from Elliquor? That seemed like the best fitting pattern, but it didn't feel right. He needed more information.

He heard an Obnot voice say, "There is still no indication of what became of Jade and Conrad."

Terrific! He could hear. Quist must be nearby.

"The Shoggart probably ripped them apart and ate them, like poor Nupper." The voice was Ironsides speaking in Obnot. Of course, the translator belt would use Obnot. Neither he nor Jade was around. It was fortunate he understood the language.

"They may be in the polar caves," Quist said. "We should go to the docks and see if their shuttle is here."

"Perhaps later. For now, we will complete the mission without them and establish the uselessness of humans."

Darkness flowed into his vision from all sides. He fought to keep his perspective, but it was no use. He was back in the room with Jade. She'd pulled the helmet up out of his reach. He was drained, empty, light-headed.

Eventually, words came to him. "It's a phantom spy-eye! On *Peapod*. Quist and Ironsides are back. So are the Elliquine, except Umlac seems to have killed one named Nupper."

"Where is Umlac now?" Jade asked.

"I don't know."

"Another senseless death." Jade blinked wet eyes. "Umlac remains bent on destroying anything he can't corrupt for his own use."

"Yes, you have found the correct pattern," Conrad said. "He destroyed the consoles on the bridge, too. Something he couldn't use without the access codes."

"Are you sure what you saw was real?" Jade asked. "Maybe Umlac is trying to lure us back again with a ruse. Or maybe your helmet is for entertainment, and it showed you complete fantasy."

"I don't think so," Conrad said. "The detail was too perfect for a simulation. Nonetheless, you raise a reasonable concern. Can you think of something on *Peapod* you would know about but I wouldn't? I could go back and look for that."

"Hm. Mini-cam locations?" Jade shook her head slowly. "They'd be hard to spot, impossible if Umalc slimed them. I can't think of anything helpful."

Conrad gestured at the big VR helmet. "I should go back. I should see what else I can find out. Why don't you contact *Peapod* on the radio? You can ask them yourself."

Jade bit her lip. "I can't. Umlac broke off all the antennas when he noticed *Peapod* was broadcasting to us. Besides, if it's a trap, we don't want to give ourselves away."

She pulled the helmet down to where Conrad could reach it, and he yanked it over his head. He grabbed the green spark, plunged into the holoprojector fragment, and was back on *Peapod's* bridge.

Quist was dragging something out of the fab unit on the bridge. He inserted it into a metal sphere about half a meter across and said, "The probe is ready. We have 7.3 minutes until the next dark matter Quillip window to the Ancient One."

Ironsides was manipulating the controls on a beat-up console that Quist must have restored, but he stopped and asked

Quist how long it would take to process the data from the probe after it returned.

Conrad thought he had the gist of what was happening on *Peapod* and was anxious to test his hypothesis that the other colored dots and picture fragments would connect him to other phantom spy-eyes.

He tried focusing his attention on a blue dot, and it took him to a perspective hovering over a jungle. He floated down to see if it was Belle Verte and saw a strange beast, something like a platypus with bright red and yellow stripes. Interesting. It wasn't Belle Verte, and it wasn't Earth, so where was it? How many other planets did the spy-eyes go to?

He tried a third dot, and his perspective changed to outer space, far from any star or planet—not much point in spending time there.

A bright yellow spark took him to a prairie world, but it wasn't Belle Verte's sun. He hovered over an alien outpost that was the twin of Koke Tngri, except a rectangular concrete building closed off the fourth side of the courtyard.

A flash of light and puff of smoke along one wall caught his attention. He zoomed in for a closer look. A Shoggart oozed along the wall, black on black, naturally camouflaged, and the Shoggart was shooting at something. The Shoggart lurched forward, and an explosion on the wall kicked up dust where he had been. Someone was shooting at the Shoggart, but before Conrad could see who, the picture dissolved, and he was back in his chair.

He tried to grab the helmet back from Jade, but she was too quick for him. "Not now," he said. "I have to go back right away."

Jade kept a firm grip on the helmet. "Why? What's going on?"

Conrad's blood boiled. As much as he liked Jade, she was still one of the pedantic military types he found so annoying. "Quist's sending out a dark matter Quillip probe to someone called the Ancient One. In another base almost identical to

Koke Tngri, a Shoggart is in a firefight with someone. I've got this now. You don't need to interrupt every five minutes."

"Fine. I'll check back with you in ten minutes." She jerked the helmet down to Conrad.

49

Breakout

Umlac had found himself alone in a disgustingly rectangular room lit by ugly, straight rows of lights. Apparently, the Entanglement team had mastered the
power to make their enemies disappear. Only he hadn't disappeared into nothing; he'd disappeared into this box.

This was an interesting discovery. It was like a Quillip
teleport, only much better. No elaborate vacuum chamber required. Perhaps it would be possible to make himself appear
and disappear at will. It should at least be possible for him to
go back to *Peapod*, maybe even directly to Elliquor—or Morb.
His hydraulics stiffened involuntarily at the horror of the
thought of the Entanglement with this power. He coveted it
more than ever.

He tried the door, but it was made of the same impervious
material as the armor of the creature he'd killed on *Peapod*. On
the other hand, the walls and floor of the room were concrete.
Limestone was one of the first materials Umlac had learned to
drill through millennia ago.

An ancient instinct tempted him to hollow out a safe burrow in a corner, but his need to dominate his environment was
stronger. He began drilling a hole through the center of the
wall.

Before he'd gotten far, the door swung open, and another one of the four-armed bipedal suits of blue-brown armor stood in the doorway.

This time he had countermeasures ready. He'd worked the metal from the shell of the creature he'd dominated on the *Peapod* into spikes by smashing it against itself. A rocket tipped with one of these spikes ripped through the creature's armored chest and threw it back out the door.

Umlac flowed to the open door. The inert suit of armor lay on a grassy lawn. Shiny black walls enclosed the lawn. A pleasing color like his own. He could convert this formation into a glorious temple for surface-dwelling weaklings to worship him.

He crawled toward the metallic body lying on the lawn. He should be able to assimilate the brain of the creature inside this one. It might not have the access codes to *Peapod*, but at least it would let him know where he was and what he faced here.

Umlac was halfway to his prey when two more armored bipeds rushed him from a door in the far wall. These bipeds were slow learners. "You may serve me," he said. "Prostrate yourselves and worship."

The foolish bipeds ignored his generous offer and shot little streams of pellets at him instead. The pellets covered his shiny black surface with sticky blue hydrocarbons. The insult was too much to bear. He killed both of his attackers with spikes of transmatter in their chests.

His opposition seemed determined to die rather than submit. So be it. Umlac formed himself into a ball and rolled under the shelter of the rock overhang along the wall to prevent an assault from the air. Then he moved toward the door where the last two bipeds had emerged.

The door in question slid open a few centimeters, but nothing further came out.

Good. They have finally learned to fear Shoggarts. He aimed carefully and fired a transmatter spike into the slit along the door. Then he charged across the lawn.

A bright white glare erupted to his right rear, and targeting radar screamed at him. He swerved to align a cannon with the light, fired, and surged forward faster.

Naturally, his cannon scored a direct hit, and the missile's navigational radar stopped screaming. The blind missile was now an inert lump of metal moving in a straight-line course. It was fortunate he had accelerated. The rocket hit the wall and exploded three meters behind him.

Umlac let the shock wave from the explosion push him faster across the lawn into the rock wall next to the open door. The door began closing. *Cowards.*

He jammed two hydraulic pseudopods into the door slit. He poked three eyes through the crack. One of the super strong bipeds in armor ripped off Umlac's eyes and kicked out his lower hydraulic pseudopod. He fired his last spike of invincible metal into the creature at point blank range, and it fell inert to the floor.

Umlac expanded his pseudopods to force the door open. He inserted new eyes into the ever-widening crack. Two broken suits of armor lay on the floor. Five other suits of armor stood in a row along the left wall.

The nearest suit of armor began to move. Umlac burst through the door and engulfed the creature.

The thrashing biped caused Umlac some minor damage, but Umlac quickly dominated it. This time, rather than penetrate the armor with a fusion explosion or high speed armor spike, he bound it in chains he'd fashioned from the armored shell of the first biped he'd defeated. He chained the remaining suits of armor into a pile near the back wall to make sure none of them was a threat.

Umlac paused, safer now, with a room full of captives and a rack of strange weapons. At last, he could stop and feed.

He slipped long tentacle-like pseudopods into the hole in the chest of one of the creatures he'd killed. Its insides were all electrical. At first, he thought it must be a cyborg like he was.

Then he realized the truth—these were remote-controlled robots.

It frustrated him no end that he hadn't been able to ingest alive any of the cowardly creatures behind these robots, or anyone who had access codes to *Peapod,* or the Hydra Slayer.

He gathered his strength to further his attack. There must be a flesh-and-blood master of these robots nearby, and his recent exertions left him hungry for fresh, living meat.

50

Boxed in

By the time Conrad returned, the battle at the second Koke Tngri was over. There was no sign of the Shoggart. Three avatars lay on the ground with gaping holes in their chests.

Conrad tried to see what was in the rooms behind the black wall of transmatter, but the spy-eye refused to go there. On the other hand, the door to the concrete building was wide open. The room inside was barren, with a damaged spot in one wall. Elliquine dung lay on the floor.

The colonists had spent time here recently. The Shoggart must be Umlac. But where was he now?

Satisfied he'd seen all he could on this planet, he returned to *Peapod.*

* * *

Ironsides was exhausted from his extended period of mobility, but Quist had talked him into one more thing before he planted himself.

"How much longer?" Ironsides asked.

"The console will be repaired in 44.8 seconds. Get ready to contact Elliquor."

"I still don't see the point," Ironsides said. "That's where the black Immortal came from. The Immortals control Elliquor station."

"Unproven," Quist said. "And you are still an ambassador. They should cooperate with you."

That much was true. That was their best hope now.

While Quist continued working on the console, the Elliquine circled sadly nearby,

"The Ancient One's planet is a deathtrap."

"Belle Verte is a deathtrap."

"*Peapod* is a deathtrap."

"We must go home."

"We must abandon new grass."

Quist backed away from the console, and a loud voice boomed out."SURRENDER AT ONCE."

"Ambassador Ironsides," Quist said, "We have proven the Immortals control Elliquor."

Ironsides stretched one of his root-feet to the console and pressed a switch. He said, "May evolution favor you. This is Special Ambassador Ironsides on the planet Belle Verte. As a full Ambassador and in accordance with the Treaty of Anis-core, I demand full diplomatic privileges. I need a secure comm channel to Nexus."

"I WILL DECIDE WHAT YOU NEED. THE TREATY IS VOID. OPEN THE VISUAL CHANNEL."

Quist reached for the video activation switch, but Ironsides lashed out a root-foot to stop him. No need to give the Immortals a view of the broken ship.

"We are calling from a comm unit without visual capability. Let me speak to your captain."

After a pause, the comm said, "THIS IS SHIPMASTER HOAR-GRIM. LET ME SPEAK TO THE MOST WORSHIPFUL LORD UMLAC."

Ironsides twisted his root-feet into tight bundles. "He isn't available right now, but he approved my request for a secure channel to Nexus."

Quist muted the channel to Elliquor. "*Dissonance*. Umlac didn't approve your request."

"I know," Ironsides said, "but Hoargrim doesn't know that."

"GIVE ME HIS AUTHORIZATION CODE."

"*Dissonance*," Quist said. "You don't have an authorization code."

Ironsides waved his root-feet. "Let me handle this."

He unmuted the connection. "Umlac didn't give me a code. He said his name would be enough."

"WHAT IS HIS FULL NAME THEN."

"The Most Worshipful Lord Umlac."

"YOU ARE A LIAR, SPECIAL AMBASSADOR IRONSIDES. I WILL INFORM LORD UMLAC. YOU HAVE TAKEN HIS NAME IN VAIN, AND YOUR PUNISHMENT WILL BE GRUESOME."

Ironsides cut the power to the comm. "The *Dasypodia* says 'Even a drillsnake cannot penetrate solid rock.' The Immortals on Elliquor have no intention of letting us contact Nexus."

Quist made no reply.

The Elliquine chanted:

"Elliquor Station is a deathtrap."

*　*　*

Jade whirled Excalibur through a series of mock parleys and thrusts. The light, strong feel of the sword made exercise more enjoyable, and she was developing a routine around it. Then, when the time came, she pulled the helmet off Conrad's head.

Conrad looked a bit dazed but managed a string of coherent sentences. "The Shoggart is gone. I can't go into rooms in the black rock. Ironsides contacted Elliquor. An Immortal demanded immediate surrender, and Ironsides hung up. Quist can use the dark matter Quillip and is studying wherever it goes."

Jade insisted that Conrad take a break to eat and relax a little, but before his ration was completely gone, he jumped up.

Before Jade could say anything else, he put on the helmet.

Jade had plans of her own. She'd meant to discuss them with Conrad, but she didn't want to yank him back, and she didn't want to wait until it was time to pull him out for another report. She donned her dart popper and an energy rifle, and went to explore.

She'd discovered an inner door in the armory which connected directly to the control room, and she suspected there was a door on the other side of the control room as well.

She bowed a couple of times, and sure enough, found the entrance to another room. She stepped inside, and something invisible brushed against her arm, then her cheek. The room smelled like water ice and moaned in soft, breathy sounds, as if the room itself were alive.

The room was by far the largest yet. Rows of machines hummed away, like some giant data center from the twentieth century. Metallic shells covered most of the artifacts, some rectangular, some dome-shaped. Dials, switches, and patches of colored light dotted the covers.

Jade walked slowly up and down the rows of machines. The purple haze of data processing glowed in many cabinets. Other machines were as dark as the walls around her, presumably made of transmatter. Most cabinets housed a hybrid of the two, matter and transmatter working together.

As she wended her way farther into the room, the invisible forces pulling and pushing on her body became stronger. She could see her skin pinch, but the forces didn't stop there. Her gut churned. Her eyes occasionally blurred. The center of the room was an orange and white rotating grid structure. The unique lattice device rotated slowly. It had a curved surface, like the sail on a water ship of old or a radio dish.

She began to fear she'd break a bone and started to withdraw, angling toward the outside wall. She spied an oversized door and made her way there. Two of the machines near the door appeared to be large fabricator units, but with transmatter components. Perhaps they could learn to fab transmatter, even dark matter, objects, like the phantom spy-eyes. Who knew what might be possible?

Other devices seemed dedicated to communications; the normal matter parts connected to bright violet cables running under the floor; the dark matter parts connected to trans-matter pipes, which Jade guessed would communicate with dark-matter remotes like the spy-eyes.

She left the machine room and made a quick tour down the far side of the courtyard. The rooms were all identical to the first room they'd found: same size, same murals on the walls, same empty shelves. Instead of a hangar at the end of the row, there were two additional standard rooms. Nothing more, so she hurried back to the control room to make sure Conrad was all right.

51

When Gods Meddle

I ronsides tried to think of a passage in the *Dasypodia* to guide his next move. There was the story of Tinman and Swisher, two Dasypods who fought off a pack of drill-snakes by climbing to the top of a rocky crag and throwing down boulders. Throw boulders? Bombs? Threaten to teleport bombs to Elliquor if the Immortals didn't allow him free passage?

"The probe is ready," Quist said as he hovered near the controls. "We are 1.5 minutes away from the teleportation window."

Quist seemed obsessed with the new dark matter technology. He'd insisted on proving that he could teleport a probe to a part of Vaikuntha outside the prison and back again.

"Thank you. Let me know if anything changes."

Quist responded almost immediately. "Something has changed."

Ironsides waited several seconds before he realized Quist must think he'd already fulfilled the order in the most efficient manner.

"What has changed?" Ironsides asked.

"The control unit for the dark matter Quillip has shut

down. I've lost contact."

"We have to get it back," Ironsides said. "If Vishnar gets control of the dark matter Quillip, he'll transport us back to prison."

"Something has changed," Quist said again.

Ironsides curled his root-feet, but then forced them to relax and replied calmly. "What is the new change?"

"There is a low level of coherent dark light activity, similar to 10.7% of the dark matter communication link. It's gaining in strength."

"Keep reporting," Ironsides said.

"The signal strength is 22.3% ... 56.2% ... 87.1% ... 100%. The dark matter Quillip link has been restored."

"It has to be Vishnar. Don't let him teleport us back."

"I cannot access the link anymore. My modifications to the control systems are gone."

"Keep trying to get control back. And keep me informed."

"The dark matter Quillip ship is approaching *Peapod*. Four seconds to the teleportation window."

Ironsides charged his laser-eyes, but he knew that wouldn't help much if they were teleported back to prison on Vaikuntha.

"Teleport complete," Quist announced.

Ironsides scratched at the floor in puzzlement. "What are you talking about? We are still on *Peapod*."

"Your assumption that we were the subject of the teleport is incorrect. The creature behind the comm console teleported here."

An intruder! Ironsides twisted around the console and focused his laser-eyes on the newcomer. It appeared to be human, with brown skin like Jade, but straight hips and flat chest like Conrad. It showed its teeth in a smile and extended its hands with empty palms up.

Ironsides fired a warning shot that vaporized a section of the broken console and demanded, "Who are you and why are you here?"

"I am Vishnar. I come in peace, a refugee, driven from my home by a horrible monster."

"You can't be Vishnar," Ironsides said. "Vishnar has four arms, and you only have two. You're human."

"The four-armed avatars were built for a higher caste than I. Dear friend, I am Vishnar, servant caste, and I come in peace."

"You took away poor Rispering," one of the Elliquine chanted.

"You are no friend of the Elliquine."

Vishnar waved his arms, "I do apologize for that tragic accident. I had hoped to measure his brain function, as a matter of medical curiosity only. I had no idea he would respond as he did."

"You sacrificed him in a cold machine."

"You stole his soul."

"You murdered him."

"Oh no," Vishnar replied, "There must be some misunderstanding. A translation error perhaps. I have no interest in the sacrifice of Elliquine. I am a refugee from a slime monster who attacked me in my home."

Ironsides vibrated his root-feet nervously. "What exactly happened?"

Vishnar lowered his hands to his sides and said, "It came into my guesthouse when you left. When I sent an avatar to greet it, the Shoggart left my guesthouse and rampaged across the courtyard. I would have used the dark matter Quillip to teleport it away, but you cyberlocked my machine. I tried to fight it off with my avatars, but the Shoggart was too strong. It took over my armory. I realized I had no hope of defeating it, so I rebooted the dark matter Quillip from a clean backup and came here."

Quist interrupted. "I locked the reboot trigger. How did you bypass the cyberlock to do a reboot?"

"I did a physical reboot. This is a dangerous procedure since I had to go to the center of the crazy room, but I was desperate. Waiting helplessly while the control unit rebooted was terrifying. I didn't know where the Shoggart was. To make matters worse, the dark matter Quillip doesn't work inside the trans-matter of the base, so I had to add a time delay and run out into the wide-open courtyard."

Vishnar paused and shook himself before continuing. "In the courtyard, I nearly died of fright. The Shoggart was emerging from the control room. I froze, in case he hadn't noticed me, but three of his evil red eyes focused on me. The snout of a cannon poked out of his glistening skin. I dove to the ground, hoping to crawl back to the crazy room, but it was too late. The Shoggart scored a direct hit with a capture net. The creature began pulling me closer. It said it was going to eat me. And then, just in time, the dark matter Quillip teleported me here, to the safety and comfort of your good ship."

Vishnar gestured toward Quist. "It was truly unkind of you to lock me out of my dark matter Quillip."

Ironsides stiffened his root-feet. Vishnar was twisting the facts around. "You have control of the dark matter Quillip now."

"Yes, but as I said, it can't touch the Shoggart inside the transmatter base. On the other hand, we are quite vulnerable on this little ship if the Shoggart learns to control the dark matter Quillip now in its possession."

"We know how vulnerable we are here. Let Quist put another cyberlock on the dark matter Quillip."

Vishnar shook his head. "You've already seen that a cyberlock can be removed. I have a better solution. If you would be so kind as to transport me to the surface of Belle Verte, I believe I can find a safe refuge there."

"Impossible," Quist said.

Vishnar became red in the face and clenched his fists. "How dare you deny me access to Belle Verte! You caused this fiasco in the first place by sending that monster to my home. You owe me passage to the surface."

Ironsides found Vishnar's attitude irksome, but Vishnar did have a point that the Entanglement team was at least partly responsible for his current predicament. "Quist is simply stating a fact. Your request is impossible for us to fulfill. The Shoggart destroyed both of our shuttles."

"No shuttles!" Vishnar wailed. "Then find a shuttle! Build a shuttle! I must get to the surface. I have an important mission to carry out."

"I could fabricate all the parts we would need to assemble another shuttle," Quist said.

Vishnar calmed down. "That's more like it. How long will it take?"

"Three point one months."

"Incredible. Such primitive technology. What about a minimal capsule for one person to land on the surface?"

"A basic escape pod would take 10.3 days to fabricate and assemble."

"Primitive indeed. But show me the plans," Vishnar said.

Vishnar browsed through the schematics Quist provided. After a bit, he said, "Can your fabricator make materials like this, and this?" He drew some symbols similar to those on the schematics.

"In principle, the fabricator can arrange atoms in any geometry," Quist replied. "But the layering of carbon and tellurium so close together may require some adjustment."

"Good," Vishnar said. "Make the heat shield out of a one-millimeter layer of this material. That will use less mass and be safer than your design. It should also cut twenty percent from the fab time. How soon can you start building it?"

"The protocol is that Ironsides decides our priorities."

"Ironsides, dear friend, the sooner we start building this transportation device, the sooner it will be completed. I must get to the surface as soon as possible."

Ironsides appreciated the attention, but when the tables turned, and Jade had decided *his* priorities, he'd realized that it was best to assert commander privilege only when necessary.

He waved several of his root-feet in Quist's direction. "Our probe project won't be necessary now. Do you have any other projects you think we should consider doing next?"

"I do not have any urgent projects that I could not do in parallel with building an escape pod," Quist replied. "I'd like to repair the larger fabricators in the engineering section and use those if that's acceptable."

"Excellent idea, Quist." Ironsides turned to Vishnar. "I do have a few more questions I would like to ask while Quist gets started."

"Of course, dear friend. What would you like to know?"

Quist left for the engineering section, and Ironsides said, "For one thing, we found a thirty-thousand-year-old statue that looks like one of your avatars in a cave near Belle Verte's North Pole. Do you know if anyone else from your species ever came to this planet?"

Vishnar surprised Ironsides by laughing. "No. No others have been here."

"How can you be so sure? How else could the Bellevertians come by your avatar's likeness thirty thousand years ago?"

"Because I was here—myself," Vishnar replied. "I assume you are talking about the wooly-lion people?"

"What! You're thirty thousand years old! Is your entire race so long-lived?"

Vishnar shrugged his shoulders in a tired, human-like gesture. "We've learned how to slow our body's aging processes, and I've extended my lifespan with long periods of suspension. It's necessary for my project."

"Thirty thousand years. What project could take that long?"

Vishnar laughed again. "I was born over 600 million years ago, although subjectively, I'm only about 60,000 years old."

Ironsides didn't know what to say to such an outrageous assertion. Even Immortals didn't claim to have memories more than a hundred thousand years old. He managed to repeat, "What project takes that long?"

"Terraforming planets, guiding evolution, waiting for the

perfect race to evolve, searching for the perfect race among the evolved worlds around my bases." Vishnar seemed perfectly serious.

Bases? Vishnar had more than one base? More than one dark matter Quillip ship? "You refer to them as 'my' bases. Are you the only one of your kind, then?" Ironsides asked.

"Sadly, I am the only one in the Milky Way Galaxy. I am a refugee from Andromeda Galaxy, and I can't say if any of my civilization survived the Asura invasion there. I doubt it. I never tried to contact them. I didn't want to lead the Asura here."

Ironsides let his root-feet droop. Poor Vishnar. What would it be like if he were the only Dasypod in the galaxy for millions of years? Or at least for thousands, subjective. Surely, he would have gone mad long ago, but Vishnar seemed to have survived by dedication to his mission.

"Six hundred million years is a very long time. How do you know the Asura haven't come here?" Ironsides asked.

Vishnar clenched his fists and stiffened his arms. "We must be vigilant. We must not tolerate any incursion into this galaxy."

The very craziness of the idea made it more believable. How could Vishnar make up such a story? Six hundred million years was before life even began on Dasypor. Perhaps he knew something of the Creator! "Have you ever been to a world at these coordinates?" He displayed a picture of the Milky Way Galaxy with a blue "X" marking his home planet.

Vishnar studied the map. "That's a little beyond the area I normally travel, but the galaxy has changed a lot since I arrived. Can you reverse the galactic rotation and show me where your star was six hundred million years ago?"

Ironsides moved the display of the Milky Way back in time. The stars stayed roughly grouped the same then as now, but with some variation as the orbits of individual stars oscillated at different rates from one side of the galactic plane to the other. Dasypor oscillated more than most.

Vishnar reached into the hologram and drew a circle with his finger. "This was one of the original seeding areas. As you can see, your star was in the seeding area then, but soon diverged from the rest of the group."

He stepped back and looked closely at Ironsides. "You are unlike any race I've encountered before. Can you show me the building blocks of your biology?"

Ironsides displayed diagrams of the basic electromechanical nanomachines common to all life on Dasypor.

Vishnar leaned closer to the display. "How unique. How clever evolution is. In all of my years, I've never seen anything like this. My terraforming nanomachines must have mutated during self-replication and evolved an entire ecology of their own ... Yes, Ironsides, I visited your world once, six hundred million years ago."

Ironsides' root-feet trembled with excitement. "You seeded Dasypor with self-replicating nanomachines? *You* are the Creator of life there!"

"So it would seem," Vishnar said.

The presence of the Creator warmed Ironsides like the sun on a mountaintop. Nothing in the *Dasypodia* could guide him now. No one had met the Creator in the flesh before. He had dedicated every day of his life for as long as he could remember to this being. He drooped all of his root-feet to the floor. "My Creator, I am at your service."

Vishnar smiled. Ironsides was thrilled to have pleased his Creator. After a few moments, Vishnar said, "I accept your service."

Ironsides tingled with bliss—it was like being planted and mobile at the same time. The secret of creation had been revealed to him! He must send word back to Dasypor, and he must choose his words carefully—they would become part of the *Dasypodia*. "Thank you, my Creator. I will do whatever I can to please you."

Vishnar stared down at Belle Verte for several seconds, and then said, "If you truly wish to please me, there is a way to get to the surface of Belle Verte in much less time than eight days."

"Yes! Of course. Anything," Ironsides replied.

Vishnar reached out and touched one of Ironsides' root-feet, sending a tingle up it like an electric current. "If we jettison the Quillip half of the ship, the *Peapod's* engine module will be light enough and compact enough to land on the surface. We can be there in a matter of hours, not days."

"My, Creator! What a novel idea." Ironsides cringed at the thought of breaking apart *Peapod*. But his allegiance was to the Creator. "I will gladly help you. However, I am sure there is no way Quist will go along with it. He will insist on maintaining power to the quantum-entangled link to Elliquor."

"Are you not his commander? Order him to jettison the Quillip node."

"It's not that simple. The Elliquine owners of the *Peapod* will not give permission, and Quist has a deep loyalty to Obnot University. I doubt he will give up his connection home unless perhaps the Elliquine and Obnot University both demand it."

"Ah, yes." Vishnar crossed his arms "The Elliquine *are* difficult to reason with. Where are they now?"

"That's hard to say. They went for a run."

Vishnar shrugged. "Then they won't interfere, and we will incapacitate Quist. Perhaps we can lock him in a room or cage."

Ironsides couldn't believe he was discussing betraying Quist. But everything had changed. He'd met his Creator. "Quist will be impossible to contain as long as he has his exoskeleton. And *Peapod* doesn't have any rooms."

Vishnar smirked. "Do you think he would leave his exoskeleton for a better one?"

"Certainly. Quist prizes efficiency. If a more efficient exoskeleton were possible, he would gladly move into it, although I suspect that if a more efficient exoskeleton were possible, he would already have invented it."

"Then I have a plan. Show me how to use one of these

primitive fabricators of yours, and I will build Quist a better exoskeleton."

Joyful to be of service, blissful that the Creator found him useful, Ironsides showed Vishnar how to use the fabricator. Vishnar learned quickly and had soon fabricated several small parts. Ironsides stood by idly, basking in the presence of the Creator, watching him at work.

Ironsides was eager to do more and finally asked, "Is there something I can do for you?"

Vishnar paused. "How long since your last period of rest and nourishment?"

"It doesn't matter," Ironsides replied. "I will gladly serve you until my root-feet can no longer hold me off the ground."

"You will be more helpful rested and refreshed," Vishnar said. "This project will take several hours. Go. Rest. I will awaken you when I'm ready."

"Of course, My Creator, although the bliss of mediation will pale in comparison to the joy of being in your presence."

Ironsides planted himself, leaving Vishnar alone with the fabricator.

52

Change of Plans

At first, Jade was shocked when Conrad described Ironside's religious conversion. But on second thought, the reaction was very human, and the Entanglement didn't appear to be superior in any way other than technology.

Conrad bobbed up and down with excitement. "We need to stop Vishnar from destroying our only link to Earth. We need to go to *Peapod* right away."

Jade shook her head. "Slow down. Vishnar said we have several hours before he neutralizes Quist. He's only human—or similar—and it shouldn't be too hard to take him out. The real problem is Umlac.

"Umlac's out of the way now. This is our chance to get back to *Peapod*."

Jade gave a wry little grin. "I've learned my lesson. Think before you act. 'Out of the way' isn't good enough for Umlac. If he has the controls for the *Dutchman*, he'll figure out how to use them. We can't let him take dark matter technology back to the Immortal Ascendency. And he's evil. We have to kill him."

Conrad sat down. "So, what do you want to do?"

"I have some ideas, but first I'd like to hear how you think we can get a data dump from *Peapod* back to Earth with the Immortals in control of Elliquor and possibly Farboro or more."

"Use our dark matter assets," Conrad replied. "We could start by teleporting a spy-eye to Elliquor and study the Immortals there in detail. We could look for weaknesses and plan to exploit them. Or maybe use the spy-eye to send a message to Earth. Or even send the spy-eye to Earth."

"Interesting idea."

Conrad was on a roll. "Or we could send an avatar to Elliquor. I know Umlac beat one, but the Hydras are smaller. It might be able to overpower them and teleport to Entanglement territory."

"But we don't know if *Peapod's* Quillip will work on dark matter and transmatter," Jade objected.

"Why not? The *Dutchman* teleports normal matter."

"Good point. I really like your idea of sending an avatar. I should be ready to go in about an hour. I want the Avatar to be fully equipped with energy weapons when it leaves *Peapod*."

Conrad grinned. "Happy to have helped. After the avatar breaks through Elliquor, then what?"

Jade clenched her fists. "That's not what I have in mind. Quist can teleport the avatar to Vaikuntha. This time I *will* kill Umlac."

She left Conrad to monitor the spy-eyes and went to the shuttle to equip an avatar to win a battle with Umlac. She fabricated a Shoggart-sized flamethrower—her close encounters with Umlac had shown her how big it needed to be. She selected a large-bore energy rifle and a couple of dart poppers, which she loaded with Zephyr's anti-Shoggart virus.

She piled the weapons on the shuttle floor where they would be easy for the avatar to find, reslung her dart popper, Excalibur, and Sting, and started for the shuttle door.

The message light on the comm unit started flashing. Quist had fixed one of the antennas on *Peapod*, and Zephyr had sent an updated orbit of the *Dutchman*, which went through *Peapod* and into Belle Verte, right through Koke Tngri. She hoped she was right about the black transmatter rock protecting them from dark matter teleportation by Umlac.

Zephyr also sent a recording of her encounter with Umlac at the shuttle bay, including the murder holograph of Raggit. Jade redoubled her commitment to remove the Shoggart from the cosmos. It was too bad Quist couldn't just teleport Umlac to the void between the stars Conrad's spy-eye had seen.

She was almost back to the control room when Conrad rushed out to meet her. "Vishnar finished early. He's on his way to get Quist right now."

Jade froze. "But he said he would take several hours to get ready."

"He told Ironsides he'd found some items in the junk pile he could use instead of fabricating new ones."

Jade's heart sank. "And I just found out The *Dutchman* is due for a rendezvous with *Peapod* in a few minutes. We should have ferried everybody on *Peapod* down here when we had a chance."

"Tell them to get in a shuttle. They can use evasive action like you did."

Jade shook her head. "It's too late for that, too. And there are forty Elliquine. They'd never fit."

Conrad glared at her. "You have to do something."

What could she do on such short notice? *Teleport.* Maybe Quist could teleport everybody to one of the worlds Conrad had seen. If Vishnar wasn't about to disable him. What else?

She glared back at Conrad. "No, *you* have to do something. You have to use the big VR to teleport Vishnar back to Vaikuntha and our friends to a safe planet."

Conrad stepped back as if struck. "Just because Quist can control dark mater teleports and I can control the dark matter spy-eyes, doesn't mean I can control dark matter teleportation."

"Have you tried?" Jade asked.

Conrad's face grew red. "No."

53

Mutiny

Hoargrim hoped Umlac would remain out of touch on Belle Verte for another day. He was about to redeem himself by retaking the ships he'd lost at Farboro.

Humans were as easy to corrupt as hungry Ambos. A greedy human messagemaster named Loganal Mulcraft had secretly contacted him, offering information on the human defenses in exchange for gold and platinum. The human defenses in the Quillip chamber were fearsome, and Hoargrim was sorry He was cut off from reinforcements here at Elliquor.

Fortunately, another prong of attack had presented itself. The human officers were unhappy with their weak masters and ready for submission to a more powerful master.

Hoargrim checked the monitors one more time to verify the mass of the Quillip payload from Farboro. Had it been anything other than a single human, Hoargrim would have ordered his lasers to annihilate it upon arrival. If it passed the initial screening, his weapons would track the new arrival, and Hoargrim could vaporize it with the slightest pressure against his fire-control button.

Confident of his impending dominance, Hoargrim went to meet the traitor who would give Farboro to him: none other than his nemesis, Warmaster Keolo Davis.

Hoargrim met Keolo at the Quillip airlock. This warmaster was dangerous, but Hoargrim was used to such situations. After all, any good vassal was strong and cunning. That's what made them good vassals, as long as they didn't exhibit enough of these traits to become a serious competitor.

"Greetings, Most Powerful Warmaster and Shipmaster Hoargrim," Keolo began.

"My scanners show you have two small explosive devices," Hoargrim replied. "You must surrender these. You agreed to come without weapons."

"You are most observant, but these devices aren't weapons," Keolo said. "They're suicide charges and can't be removed."

Hoargrim scanned more deeply. Keolo appeared to be telling the truth—one charge would detonate if his left hand relaxed and another if his right hand contracted. Presumably, this was to foil any attacks causing contraction or relaxation of all of his muscles.

"Do you surrender?" Hoargrim demanded.

"Most Powerful Shipmaster and Warmaster of Elliquor, I've come to *discuss* my surrender," Keolo replied. "Soon, you'll be Fleetmaster of many ships, and I want to be on the winning side. In exchange for the surrender of the two ships at Farboro, I want to retain my position of Shipmaster of the *Cl'aclen*."

So, this was what the human had meant by conditional surrender. He was seeking to influence the decision as to his disposition after the surrender. It was a novel idea, but not very practical—you either surrendered or you didn't.

Nonetheless, the mere request was influencing his decision. He could see this human as practical and ambitious—but not too ambitious, if he was only asking for one ship.

Hoargrim would decide what to do with Keolo later, after his surrender. "If you aren't here to surrender, when *will* you surrender?"

"Most Powerful Warmaster, I apologize for the inconvenience. I could surrender my person now, but that isn't what you need. You need a plan for the surrender of the ships at Farboro."

Such insolence! Hoargrim barely contained his impulse to vaporize Keolo. *How dare he tell me what I need.* Unfortunately, Warmaster Keolo Davis was right. "State your plan," Hoargrim said.

"Most Powerful Shipmaster, the real master of a ship is the one who controls the bridge. If you come to the bridge of the *Cl'aclen* and the Bridgemaster surrenders to you there, then no one will doubt you are the rightful shipmaster."

"You have only stated the obvious," Hoargrim said. "Equally obvious is that human soldiers loyal to Shipmaster Margo Walsh will never let me pass through the Quillip chamber and onto the bridge."

"You are wise, Most Powerful Warmaster, but there are many Solar Defense Force weaponmasters who would rather see me as shipmaster than Margo Walsh. Come at a time when I'm Bridgemaster. I'll have soldiers loyal to me guard the Quillip chamber, and they will bring you safely to the bridge. There, you can accept my surrender of the *Cl'aclen*."

Hoargrim was wary. This was Warmaster Keolo Davis, who had been his bane on Farboro. Yet his spy Loganal Mulcraft and such other spies as he could recruit had all agreed a mutiny was likely, and Keolo Davis would be the new shipmaster.

He could use Keolo Davis, just not in the way Keolo proposed.

* * *

Back at the *Cl'aclen*, Keolo took midnight watch. He contacted Meera on a private channel. "Have you secured the Quillip chamber?"

"Ready. Everyone here is on board with your plan."

Keolo slipped a small, encrypted message into the thin stream of maintenance traffic still flowing between Farboro and Elliquor. He wiped beads of sweat off his forehead—this was more nerve-wracking than speeding through a booby-trapped corridor at maximum acceleration. *How hard it must be to make a living at high-stakes poker.*

Keolo's got a response to his message almost immediately. "Meera, I have an incoming mass from Elliquor. I'm disabling the automatic defenses. Don't shoot first."

"I see it," Meera said. "It's a robot probe. It's attaching to the wall on the far side of the Quillip chamber."

She sent Keolo a visual. The robot bristled with weapons.

"Another incoming," Keolo said.

The armed robots kept coming. The sixth one requested a comm channel back to Hoargrim, which Keolo opened.

"This could be a double cross," Meera said. "If he sends through enough firepower, he won't need your help to take back the ship."

Before long, there were twenty-eight of them dotting the perimeter of the chamber. Keolo's hand crept to the switch to re-activate Solar Defense Force's defenses. Was he making a mistake? Maybe, but he hadn't come this far to quit now. He kept the barrels of the Quillip chamber defenses pointed down.

* * *

Hoargrim squeezed inside the empty shell of a robot probe and teleported to Farboro. He would take command of the *Cl'aclen* without further help from Keolo Davis. *Once a traitor, twice a traitor.* He wouldn't give Keolo Davis a chance to be twice a traitor.

The robot shell containing Hoargrim landed on the wall of *Cl'aclen's* Quillip chamber, just like the other twenty-seven. His messagemaster on Elliquor sent Keolo an order in his name to go to the entrance of the Quillip chamber to meet him in person. Hoargrim watched on a feed from the bridge, which Messagemaster Loganal Mulcraft had set up for him. The foolish human Keolo Davis complied and left the bridge.

Hoargrim's robots filled the Quillip chamber with a cloud of dust. The Farboro defenses couldn't shoot what they couldn't see. By the time Warmaster Keolo Davis arrived at the Quillip chamber, Hoargrim would be in control of the bridge.

He split open his robot shell and sailed across the few meters from where he'd parked to the secret airlock connecting to the bridge—the same airlock he had used for his emergency get-away. He closed the door behind him, crossed the airlock, thinking how pleased Umlac would be. He readied his flamethrower and laser cannon, then fumbled for the latch to open the door to the bridge.

There was no latch.

Hoargrim should have paid more attention. The metal walls tasted different from before. More carbon. More rare metals. *Double cross!*

He fired a laser cannon into the airlock door, then into the wall next to the door. The door and wall glowed a dull red but refused to melt. He fired an explosive shell from his largest projectile cannon into the airlock door. The concussion dulled his senses, but the door remained intact. He wedged himself between two walls, stiffened the hydraulics in his body and began to build up pressure to burst open the walls of the shiny tube.

A chill in his pseudopods made Hoargrim weak. Droplets of fluid splashed against him with a burning sensation. *Liquid nitrogen!*

He sent the attack signal to his robot fleet, but there was no answering vibration of exploding projectiles in the walls of the airlock. *An electromagnetically sealed chamber.*

The liquid nitrogen had hardened most of his surface membrane and was creeping closer to his internal organs. He must self-destruct soon or allow himself to be frozen.

Hoargrim's internal organs twisted with anger. Warmaster

Keolo Davis had out-smarted him after all. Yet there were many things the humans didn't know about Hydras. He released his grip on the self-destruct device and faded into the dream world until his next thawing.

∗ ∗ ∗

"Axmuck, are you are sure everything is ready?" Keolo asked one more time. "I have all of the Immortal status codes and command codes I will need?"

"Oh, yes, Most Awesome Master," Axmuck replied, "you have the codes. Any Immortal will recognize your status codes."

"Well if these codes are so universally recognized, then what is to keep you from using the Elliquor Shipmaster code yourself?" Keolo asked. This seemed too simple. There must be a catch.

"Most Awesome Shipmaster, using a status code falsely is punishable by very slow death."

"Everything is punishable by death," Keolo said. "It would hardly seem to matter."

"Oh, no, most Awesome Shipmaster Keolo, falsely using status codes is punishable by *very slow* death. That kind of death is to be avoided."

"Now you tell me," Keolo replied. He turned to look his CO in the eye. "Margo, promise you'll take good care of the Misfit Platoon if I don't come back."

"You know I will," Margo replied. "But I can't sing. You have to come back. And I can't dance. Bring Jade with you."

"For the band's reunion!" Keolo opened the airlock and pushed off toward the center of the Quillip chamber. The gun barrels of twenty-seven Immortal robot fighters swiveled in his direction.

54

When Gods Disappoint

I ronsides soared in the bliss of a plant in the sunlight. What a perfect day he had! He'd met the Creator, not in meditation, but in the flesh. He was the high priest of the Creator.

It was strange that for all these years, he'd imagined the Creator as a force of nature—one who had just willed life on Dasypor into existence. It made so much more sense that the Creator used tools like any other being would, following the natural laws of the universe, not bypassing them. But it was right that his understanding of creation should change as he matured in experience and prayer.

The constant was obedience to the Creator and his laws. "Your life is from the Creator. Make it perfect for his sake." It was only logical that obedience to the Creator required forsaking other loyalties. He couldn't be loyal to everyone forever. Conflicts were inevitable, and he had to choose. The *Dasypodia* was clear: The Creator had precedence.

His shell vibrated several times. Someone was striking him. The Creator desired his presence.

Ironsides caught the steel bar with one of his root-feet as it was about to whack him again. "My Creator, what a delight to be in your presence again."

Vishnar let go of the steel bar. "My faithful servant, come with me now. The new exoskeleton is ready for the Obnot. You can help persuade him into it."

Ironsides helped Vishnar push the exoskeleton onto a taxi so they could take it to Engineering, where Quist was busy building the escape pod for Vishnar.

As they rode to Engineering, Ironsides thought it might be a good opportunity to gather information for future versions of the Dasypodia. "Why did you create life on Dasypor? Were you lonely?"

Vishnar studied the green planet below as if looking for something. He responded absent-mindedly. "That was too long ago. Most likely, I made a mistake and lost track of your planet when it migrated away from the rest of my worlds. The second stage of terraforming is to release proteinic eukaryotes, which digest the nano terraformers and cluster into primitive colonies to begin the long process of evolving intelligence."

Ironsides root-feet trembled. A mistake? His life was a mistake? How worthless he must be to his Creator. He began to wonder how he could make his life more worthwhile.

Vishnar taxied the new exoskeleton up next to Quist. He bowed and said, "Quist, my friend, I've brought you a gift to thank you for your efforts in creating an escape pod. Here is a new, high-efficiency exoskeleton."

Quist waved an instrumented arm over the new exoskeleton. "Your device appears to be of lower quality than the exoskeleton I have now, but with a few components of unknown composition and function. Its efficiency can be no higher than that of my present exoskeleton."

"Quist, my friend, you are wrong. The components you don't recognize are what make this exoskeleton have higher efficiency. Try my gift, and you will see what it does."

"Very well, Vishnar. The efficiency of your device is easily proven. Bring it closer. I'm not as agile as the rest of you."

Quist opened a hatch on his old exoskeleton and crawled

out. He wiggled his grub-worm body into the new one, and Vishnar slammed shut its lid.

Quist's Obnot voice came faintly through the steel enclosure. "You are incorrect, Vishnar. This interface doesn't function at all. My fingers grow dull from lack of stimulation. I will return to my old exoskeleton."

Vishnar locked the lid of the new exoskeleton and gave Quist's old exoskeleton a shove.

Quist's words caused Ironsides great distress. He'd worked closely with Quist. Quist had saved him from Vishnar's prison on Vaikuntha. What had Vishnar done so far? Erase Rispering's mind and imprison Quist again. All this work to evolve intelligence, and yet Vishnar had so little respect for it. It made no sense.

Exactly. Vishnar made no sense. Ironsides jumped in front of the old exoskeleton and bounced it back to Quist. "This isn't right. Let Quist go back."

Vishnar's oily voice responded. "Have you forgotten? I am your Creator. I determine what is right and what is not."

"A planting is a wonderful thing," Ironsides said. "It's a chance to divine deeper truths, to discern the mistakes of the previous day, to determine how to make them right. You aren't a god. You're a charlatan. So what if you sent the first nanomachines to Dasypor as you claim? Then you are merely a tool of the real Creator. You are no more god to me than the lightning bolt that made the first amino acid on Earth is a god to the humans."

Vishnar became as still as death. "I'm sure this is just a temporary lapse of judgment on your part. Stand down, and all is forgiven. But if you persist, know that I will become The Destroyer. I will visit destruction on you and the entire world of Dasypor."

Ironsides answered with a bolt from one of his laser-eyes. The lock on Quist's faux exoskeleton sizzled as it evaporated into the air. The lid slowly opened as Quist squirmed to push it up.

Vishnar put a hand into his robes, and Ironsides' root-feet convulsed. His laser-eyes lost focus. His thoughts became difficult. But one thing he was sure of: he'd experienced this feeling once before—when the Hydra had zapped him with high-frequency EMPs as it boarded the shuttle at Farboro—the Dasypod secret weakness wasn't much of a secret anymore.

Vishnar pulled a small device from his pocket and taunted him. "An exoskeleton wasn't the only thing I fabricated while you squatted in the dirt."

Ironsides saw a shadow pass between him and Vishnar. A phantom spy-eye? Was it real or an EMP-induced hallucination?

Vishnar pulled out a small gun and aimed it at Quist.

Ironsides ordered his unfocused laser-eyes to fire at Vishnar, but they wouldn't cooperate.

Then Vishnar disappeared, leaving behind the gun but not the EMP device. It served the conniving humanoid right. Umlac must have mastered the dark matter Quillip.

Then the implication hit Ironsides, and his digestive organs seemed to twist inside him. He would be next.

But it was the Elliquine grazing behind the fab units who disappeared next.

Ironsides struggled with numb root-feet to get to Quist and help him into his old exoskeleton.

Suddenly, he fell to the floor as gravity and EMP pulses took hold. He was back in prison on Vaikuntha.

The Elliquine bunched in disarray near the door. Vishnar was scrambling to his feet nearby. Suddenly, Quist appeared on the floor, naked, like a large white rock grub.

"*Dissonance*," rumbled Quist's Obnot voice as his stubby arms flailed about. "I need an exoskeleton."

As if by magic, Quist's exoskeleton, the old one that worked, appeared beside him.

* * *

Conrad flushed with pleasure. He'd done it. He'd teleported Quist's exoskeleton to him. The poor fellow would have been lost without it.

Now he saw the pattern. The teleport worked when it was the right thing to do. He'd tried some tests, just willing things to teleport, and they hadn't worked. He had to have his heart in it.

In that case, the right thing to do would be to teleport them all back to *Peapod*, to undo the teleport Umlac had performed to the base he controlled. But Conrad was still at the spy-eye on *Peapod*. He needed to go to the one at Umlac's base to find them and bring them back.

Out to the yellow dot, back into the vortex at Vaikuntha. He was in the courtyard. He shifted his perspective inside the prison. They were there, all right. They needed to be elsewhere. They needed to be on *Peapod*.

He couldn't do it. Something was wrong. *Peapod* was gone, replaced by cold dark space. Of course, the *Dutchman* had moved on. The teleportation window had closed.

Now what? Teleporting them to Koke Tngri when the *Dutchman* came through in a few minutes was the obvious move. He had time to warn Jade, so he pulled the helmet off his head.

"Umlac teleported them all back to the prison on Viacuntha. I can teleport things too. I teleported Quist's exoskeleton to him, but the window to teleport them back to *Peapod* is closed. I should be able to teleport them here when the *Dutchman* comes through."

"Good idea." Jade looked grim. "That's less than five minutes. I want you to teleport my avatar to Vaikuntha. You can teleport everyone back here during the same window."

* * *

Jade settled into one of the small VR helmets and focused on the tasks at hand. This time she was ready for Umlac. She'd fry him with the big flamethrower, wielded by her super strong avatar. Burning that Ambo so long ago had been an act of desperation. Burning Umlac would be much more satisfying—an act of justice served.

Her avatar ran to the shuttle and collected its weapons, then out into the courtyard, away from the impenetrable transmatter rock.

Conrad counted down from the large VR helmet. "Three. Two. One. Teleport."

A gut-wrenching blackness slammed into Jade, like when Umlac killed her first avatar.

Jade fought for consciousness. Darkness clawed at her from the edges of her vision. She couldn't let go this time. She had to get Umlac.

She heaved herself out of her VR chair and fell to the floor, gasping for breath. "What happened? I lost the avatar."

Conrad spoke out from under the big helmet. "The avatar arrived at Vaikuntha and crashed face-first onto the floor. Apparently, the communication link between you and the avatar was terminated by the teleport."

Stupid. Stupid Stupid. She should have expected that. Quillip teleportation broke quantum entanglement. The avatars must use quantum entanglement in their communications.

The teleportation window would close in seconds. She had to do something, and fast. No time to plan. She was back in desperation mode.

"Conrad," she yelled. "I'm going to Vaikuntha, but I can't handle the big flamethrower like the avatar. I'm going to lure Umlac out into the open so that you can teleport his evil carcass to outer space."

Jade grabbed her small personal weapons from the table and ran out into the courtyard. She squinted in the bright sunshine, stopped, and took a deep breath of the soothing fresh grass smell.

The sun winked out, and concrete replaced the grass under her feet. The beat of powerful EMPs slapped her body like the bounce of a concrete street. Ironsides twitched on the floor. Quist wiggled beside him, struggling to get to his exoskeleton. Vishnar was stooping to pick up the energy rifle next to the prone avatar.

Jade put her foot on the energy rifle and shoved Vishnar away. He rolled and bounced back to his feet in a fluid move, revealing expertise in martial arts. She'd have to be careful around him and remember that he'd had centuries to practice.

She snatched up the energy cannon and aimed it at Vishnar. "Turn the EMP off, or I'll shoot it off right where it is on your hip."

"Who are you to threaten a poor stranger seeking a weapon to defend us all against a hungry Shoggart?" Vishnar asked. "Surely you wouldn't shoot an unarmed man."

"I'm captain of *Peapod*, the ship you planned to destroy, and I will fire in three ... two ..."

The EMPs stopped. Jade glared at Vishnar. "Now set the EMP generator on the floor."

Vishnar set a device that looked like a twentieth-century alarm clock on the floor, and Jade vaporized it with a short pulse from her rifle, burning a gouge into the floor.

Ironsides had recovered enough to say, "Oh, no, not this miserable concrete box again—Jade! I'm delighted to see you alive, but I wish it were under different circumstances. Is Conrad well, too?"

"Yes, he's well too."

Jade wanted to expand on that, but Umlac could be listening. And why hadn't Conrad teleported the rest of them back? He must have run out of time after he teleported her in addition to the avatar.

She hefted the energy rifle in her hands and said loudly. "Right now, we need to get out of here. Outside is a courtyard surrounded by a wall of black rock. Meet under the wall to the left. The Shoggart won't be able to teleport us away from there."

She fired a fat beam of energy against the concrete wall and vaporized a fist-sized hole. Then she swept a continuous beam in a large circle, and a section of the wall fell away.

She waved toward the smoldering hole in the wall. "Go. Go. Go."

Vishnar was first to leap through the breach. Ironsides hesitated as Quist crawled up the side of his exoskeleton.

"Go. Go. Go." Jade repeated, and he went. The Elliquine moved closer to the hole but couldn't bring themselves to jump through it.

Jade stepped in front of a large Elliquine named Marstamper and struck the Elliquine pose for munching on a virgin pasture on a sunny day. "Blue sky waits for the Solidarity on the other side of the wall."

"Give us the open sky," Marstamper replied.

"But not a narrow tunnel," said another Elliquine.

Jade dove under Chiplister. "To see Belle Verte you passed through the dark Quillip."

"To see the sky again, you must traverse this hole."

She marched slowly toward the hole in the wall, as if leading a parade, and the Elliquine fell in behind, saying,

"The wisdom of the Solidarity is great."

"To send a brave human to our aid."

"We'll travel the narrow tunnel to the sky."

They poured out into the courtyard, and Jade pointed to the alley between the prison and the rock wall. "The wide-open plains are just around the corner. Go, run where you please."

Jade's heart was lighter from her brief dance with the Elliquine, but grim reality slapped her like a cold, wet towel as she looked across the silent, battle-strewn courtyard to the transmatter door of Umlac's lair.

Then the crunch of heavy boots on the rocky ground broke the silence, and four of Umlac's avatars ran out of the armory.

55

Easy Prey

Umlac ripped a chair out of the floor and tore it to shreds. The dark matter teleporter wasn't working right—additional items had teleported along with his targets: the Obnot's exoskeleton, an inert avatar, and an extra human. If a Hydra had made such an egregious error, he would have squeezed the life out of the incompetent.

The extra human blasted a hole in the prison wall, and all his prey began to escape the concrete prison. He could afford to let the Elliquine go. Catching those cowards would be more trouble than it was worth. They might even be fun to prey on later as a diversion.

That left four Entanglement weaklings on the loose. He would deal with the defect in the teleporter later. He had plenty of other tools.

He extended pseudo brains—pseudopods loaded with nerves connecting to his central nucleus—into four avatar VR helmets and sent his formidable minions after his prey.

His first avatar raced to catch up with Vishnar. The coward had run inside one of the rooms at the prison end of the compound. Umlac's avatar followed, bowing at the door and stepping through. Vishnar was standing with his back against the far wall. Easy prey. But as his avatar approached, Vishnar made some gestures and spoke some nonsense, and his avatar went blank.

Meanwhile, his second avatar went to the Obnot, who had already climbed into his exoskeleton. As the avatar approached the Obnot exoskeleton, small laser and particle beams lashed out ineffectively. Easy prey. His avatar smashed a fist through the flimsy door of the exoskeleton and ripped it off. He picked up the exoskeleton, dumped out the pitiful weakling, and set about punching the exoskeleton into a more pleasing asymmetrical shape.

As his third avatar approached the Dasypod, the foolish creature counterattacked, rolling right up to the avatar. Easy prey. Umlac wrapped the avatar's four arms around the core of the creature. The Dasypod's laser-eyes tickled his avatar at point-blank range: pinpricks on his transmatter skin. The Dasypod's root-feet wrapped themselves around his avatar: threads trying to hold down a battle tank.

His fourth avatar caught up with the extra human just as it reached the edge of the courtyard. The human fired the energy weapon it had used to cut open the concrete wall of the prison. The beam felt uncomfortably warm on his avatar's chest but did no damage. The desperate human pulled out a black sword and swung at his avatar. He grabbed the sword in one hand and ripped it away. Easy prey.

He recognized the human now as the one who had escaped his grasp on *Peapod*. He had the Hydra Slayer!

His avatar was careful not to break her as it caged her firmly in its four transmatter arms and started back toward his control room. He would dominate her himself, giving her the very slow death she deserved.

56

One Step Forward, One Step Back

Keolo's heart pumped madly as he pushed off into the darkness of *Cl'aclen's* Quillip chamber. The gun barrels of Hoargrim's killer robots followed his progress, giving no clue as to how close to death he was.

His comm crackled with a message from Evan. "The comm-link between the local robots and Elliquor shows a spike in activity. The Elliquor end will know you're coming."

Keolo was approaching the center of the Quillip chamber. It wouldn't be long now. "Good, I hope. These aren't the kind of folks you drop in on for a surprise visit."

In a flash of light, he was in a Quillip chamber at Elliquor.

Eight Hydras launched themselves from the airlock door to intercept him. He broadcast shipmaster status codes and forced himself to breathe as normally as he could. At least the Hydras hadn't opened fire on sight. Then again, Axmuck had said falsely using shipmaster codes was punishable by *very slow* death.

The Hydras surrounded him in a tight sphere. The largest one pushed closer to Keolo. "Most Illustrious Shipmaster, pardon our unpreparedness. Warmaster Hoargrim provided no instructions for your arrival. Perhaps we should wait together in the comfort of the antechamber until he returns."

"How can you be so ill-informed? Was I not it this very chamber yesterday to make a deal with Hoargrim? Now I am back as a result of that deal. You will escort me to the bridge." Keolo released a puff of gas from his jetpack and started on a trajectory toward the exit—and a Hydra blocking his path.

He tensed, ready to grab his dart popper, but the Hydra moved aside. Keolo accelerated, and the Hydras followed in disarray.

He cycled through the airlock into the wide-open blue sky and green grass of the Elliquor antechamber. It was beautiful —he suppressed a moment of pleasure. This was no time to let down his guard. He confirmed with a Hydra that the one blemish—a brown cone-shaped mound on the prairie—was the Immortal's new bridge and pushed off toward it. The Hydras followed, jockeying to be closest to him, but not too close.

Inside the bridge, several Ambos scurried to keep out of his way as he sailed to the bank of monitors on the far wall.

"Show me the Quillip chambers on Farboro and Elliquor," he ordered the Ambo at one of the security monitors.

The monitors blossomed with views of robotic weapons. Keolo pointed to a Hydra. "Recall the robots from *Cl'aclen*."

"Oh, Most Illustrious Shipmaster, if only I could do that. But Warmaster Hoargrim has taken personal control of those robots. I dare not interfere with his activities."

Keolo fired an antimatter dart into the Hydra and turned his back as a spray of guts and jelly spewed from the explosion. Everything he knew about Immortal culture, everything Axmuck had told him, mandated he be completely ruthless. Mercy was a weakness, and the weak were enslaved and eaten.

He grabbed a hunk of Hydra flesh that had covered a monitor, hid his revulsion, and stuffed it into a shoulder pouch— the symbolic eating of his victim.

"Hoargrim is dead. I am your master," he said to the remaining Hydras. "You may have the rest of this weakling who would rather be eaten than obey his master."

A human crew might have rallied around their fallen comrade or their previous commander, but the Hydras flattened themselves in submission. They ingested the larger pieces of their dead fellow and left the smaller pieces to eager Ambos.

Keolo watched carefully for reluctance from any of them but found none. Survival of self was all that mattered to them. As the Ambos rushed in to slurp up the fresh kill, Keolo pointed at another Hydra. "Recall the robots from *Cl'aclen*."

This Hydra bounded to the closest console and issued recall orders. From his own console, Keolo watched as the robots returned in groups of seven. He approved the touch of efficiency added by the Hydra.

Soon *Cl'aclen* was safe again, but Keolo had only restored a stalemate unless he secured Elliquor. Again, he pointed to the Hydra who had recalled the robots. "You are my Bridgemaster for the time being. Move all the mobile police robots patrolling this ship into Corridor 2. Place all robots, including those in the Quillip chamber, in an inactive state. They will not act, even in self-defense."

He pointed to another Hydra. "You'll act as Messagemaster. Begin by announcing to all Immortals aboard this ship that I'm the shipmaster, and my first order is the freedom and safety of all Entanglement citizens. They are free to roam the station and to come and go via shuttle or Quillip. Absolutely no eating them. Failure to comply will result in a slow death."

He received no objections, and the bridge staff went about their tasks. He contacted Margo and arranged for reinforcements from Farboro.

A few minutes later Goldie and Evan arrived and surveyed the bridge. "Nice work, Shipmaster. Have you connected with Jade?" Goldie asked.

Keolo shook his head. "I tried calling, but there was no answer."

He pointed at a nearby Hydra. "Messagemaster, is there a problem with the link to Belle Verte?"

"Most Illustrious Shipmaster, I don't know. At first, there were frequent messages from Lord Umlac, but the former incompetent Messagemaster logged no messages for at least a day."

"Who is Lord Umlac?"

The Bridgemaster flattened itself to near puddleness and squeaked out, "Most Illustrious Shipmaster, you are wise to test your stupid servants. The Most Worshipful Lord Umlac is a Shoggart and a Vice Regent of the Immortal Ascendancy. Warmaster Hoargrim was his vassal until you took Hoargirm's place as my master and vassal to Lord Umlac."

It hadn't occurred to Keolo before that when he inherited the Immortal's vassals, he also inherited its master. "Where is The Most Worshipful Lord Umlac now?"

"He is still on Belle Verte," squeaked the Messagemaster while remaining flattened.

Not good. Anything that could dominate Hydras was not good for Jade.

"Hoargrim's Messagemaster, come here," Keolo said loudly.

One of the Hydras flattened itself and crawled submissively to Keolo. "Most Illustrious Shipmaster, this loyal vassal of yours was Hoargirm's Messagemaster. How may I serve you?"

"I wish to communicate with Belle Verte. What's the problem?"

"Most Illustrious Shipmaster, the communication link tests normal. The problem is no one is answering—unless you count the ambassador, but even that was yesterday."

"What ambassador?"

"He called on an audio-only channel and claimed to be the Entanglement ambassador to Belle Verte. He demanded I open a secure channel for him to Nexus. Naturally, I refused, and when I demanded that he enable the video channel, he terminated the link."

"Try calling him back. And if you reach anyone at all on Belle Verte, connect them to me immediately."

"Most Illustrious Shipmaster, it will be so." The Hydra groveled back to the far side of the bridge. As an afterthought, not sure what the correct protocols were, Keolo, added, "For now, you'll report to the Hydra I designated as the new Message-master."

Keolo sat down and stared at the monitors without seeing them. He felt like he'd run a marathon.

After a while, he pulled up everything he could find on Belle Verte. Before long, his heart sank.

"Damnit." Keolo clenched his fists. "There isn't enough quantum-entangled matter for me to go to Belle Verte and return without dooming an Elliquine there to a life without a mate."

"Then now what?" Evan asked.

"I don't know. I'm too exhausted to think straight."

Keolo looked across the bridge and shouted, "Bridgemaster. Evan Monco is my XO. You will take orders from him in my absence."

The Hydra flattened himself in acknowledgment, and Keolo turned to Evan. "You keep an eye on things here while I get some shut-eye. Rouse me if we connect with anyone on Belle Verte."

57

Desperate Prey

J ade tried to twist out of the avatar's arms, but there were
too many of them. Its super strong transmatter arms
weren't about to give way to her puny struggles.

The avatar taunted her. "Come, worship Lord Umlac. Give
him your heart—and your blood and guts."

Even nestled against the avatar's chest, Jade could sense
no electrical fields through its transmatter shell. She needed
Sting, the little white transmatter dagger that could cut
through black transmatter, but the avatar had her arms
pinned to her chest, and Sting was in a sheath on her thigh.

She wiggled her hand down to her hip, which blocked further progress.

"Are you uncomfortable in my grip, little one?" the avatar
said, "I'll release you soon, though I doubt you'll find Lord Umlac's jaws more to your liking."

They were already halfway across the courtyard. Jade
caught hold of one of the avatar's arms with her other hand
and pulled herself up a few centimeters. Now she had room
to squeeze her hand past her hip. She grabbed Sting's hilt and
twisted the blade up to slice up into the avatar's arm. Sting
hissed and popped. The avatar's lower arm fell away.

As soon as it did, Jade swung the blade up past her head and into the avatar's face, then pulled down, cutting a line into the neck and chest. Through that rift in the transmatter, her electrosense saw the main control module in the avatar's chest, sending signals to solenoids that functioned as muscles and to a communication module in the head.

The main control unit was deep in the chest. Her best move was to saw back and forth across the avatar's neck with Sting and sever the connection from Umlac to the avatar. She sawed. The avatar locked up, falling forward, with Jade still caged in its arms.

She squirmed out from under the avatar and got her first good look at what was happening behind her. The Elliquine and Vishnar were gone. An avatar was carrying Ironsides around the far corner of the prison building. Another avatar was dismantling Quist's exoskeleton, ripping off its extensible legs and antennae, and the sensitive instruments along its wings and belly. Quist wriggled helplessly on the ground nearby.

Jade ran to help Quist, leaping on the avatar's back and jerking Sting through its neck. The avatar froze. Its head fell forward, and its body fell backward.

She jumped free before the avatar could fall on her and whispered to Quist, "I'll be back. Play dead."

"*Dissonance*. How can I play dead? Once my metabolism stops it won't restart."

"I mean lay motionless and don't do anything to attract attention."

The avatar carrying Ironsides had disappeared down the alley between the prison and the transmatter rock wall. Jade ran after and caught up to it in the garage. This garage had several vehicles in it. The avatar had wrapped a tarp around the glued-up Ironsides and dropped him into the open cargo bay of a small truck. As Jade ran closer, the avatar climbed into the driver's seat and drove the truck straight at her.

Jade jumped to the side as the truck whooshed by. She scrambled to her feet and ran after it. The avatar stopped the truck and set Quist's limp body into the back with Ironsides. It stared at Jade for a second, and then said, "Come to me, Hydra Slayer."

It jumped back into the driver's seat and drove to the far end of the courtyard, where it swept Quist and Ironsides out of the truck and into the control room.

She would have to go there, before Raggit's murderer could torture her friends. And Quist and Ironsides had the access codes to *Peapod*. With those, Umlac could return to the Entanglement, and all would be lost.

The avatar got back into the truck and started for her.

She would go to Umlac on her terms. She picked up the nearby energy rifle, aimed, and fired. The truck ground to a halt as part of it melted into white-hot slag. That gave Jade an idea. She fired again. The truck melted around the avatar. The avatar acted as a heat sink and drew down the temperature, solidifying the slag, encasing the avatar.

As the avatar struggled to break free, Jade rushed up and cut off its head. Four down—all of the avatars she had seen here, though of course there were likely more in the armory.

And there were. Almost immediately, two more avatars emerged carrying bazooka-like tubes on their shoulders. She caught a glimpse of a spark on the bazooka of the leading avatar and did a forward jump and roll, just in time for a large slug to whoosh by and slam into the concrete bunker behind her. The shot was calf-high—apparently Umlac's new plan for catching her involved ripping off her legs.

The second bazooka fired, and Jade let her downward momentum flatten her against the ground. The heat of a massive slug ripped through the air less than a centimeter above her shoulder blades.

The avatars knelt to reload. Jade fired an energy beam at one of the bazookas, but the bazooka resisted her beam. She had hoped she could at least trigger the shells to fire prematurely. No such luck.

The avatars had the advantage in a long-range gunfight.

Sting was the only weapon that worked against them. Jade ran across the courtyard to engage the avatars hand-to-hand.

The avatars stood. She was twenty paces away. She'd nearly made it, but they were going to shoot before she could reach them.

She swerved a meter to the left, so one avatar was directly behind the other.

The lead avatar raised its bazooka to its shoulder. The round, dark opening of the barrel stared at Jade. Desperately, she threw Sting, giving the blade as much helicopter whirl as she could.

The white dagger sliced through the neck of the first avatar and retained enough momentum to nick the neck of the second avatar before bouncing handle-first off the black rock wall behind it. The first avatar fell flat on the ground. The second avatar dropped its bazooka; its left arms dangled uselessly.

The wounded avatar ran toward Jade. She had no doubt it could hold onto her with only two arms, and she'd lost the only weapon capable of penetrating its transmatter shell.

But the avatar's transmatter skin already had a hole in it. Jade drew her dart popper and dialed explosive darts. Unless the avatar's insides were made of transmatter, she still had a chance.

Her first shot hit the avatar in the shoulder, leaving a puff of smoke, but failing to slow the three-meter mechanical wonder racing toward her. She had time for one more shot.

She paused half a breath to let the avatar get closer. At the last moment, she fired. This time smoke blew out of the wound on the avatar's neck, and the robot fell forward to land at her feet. She ran on across the courtyard to retrieve Sting and take shelter under the transmatter overhang.

When she stooped over and picked up Sting, she heard the whoosh of a door nearby. Only then did she realize she was in front of the control room—Umlac's lair.

She turned to run out into the courtyard, hoping to lure

the Shoggart out where Conrad could teleport it away, but stopped. Umlac was at the far end of the control room, a black curtain beside a transparent red cage. Ironsides and Quist gestured wildly at her from inside the cage.

Ironsides seemed to be trying to speak to her with one of his laser-eyes, but the red glass blocked his blue laser light. Likewise, she could see Quist's mouth moving, but couldn't hear what he was saying. The waving of Ironsides' root-feet conveyed only urgent distress, and she'd never seen Quist's body language before. She had no way to interpret whatever they were saying.

Umlac was smaller and thinner than she recalled, but maybe he was farther away than he seemed.

"You came to me, as you should. Now worship." Umlac said with multiple mouths.

Jade slipped Sting back into its scabbard and drew her dart popper in one smooth motion. "I came to bring you death."

"Bring me *your* death then," Umlac said. "It all ends the same. With more or less suffering. Give me the *Peapod* access codes. Know your death will contribute to the death of all the rest of your puny kin."

She opened her mouth to speak, but she noticed the electric field of a laser moving nearer the surface of Umlac's body. He was stalling.

She fired her dart popper, releasing Zephyr's virus into Umlac.

Umlac stiffened. His electric field changed to a dull red all over, including the ceiling. She hadn't noticed before, but he had extended his body to cover the ceiling, blending in, and waiting for her to step under him. His thin curtain of his body in the rear was the bait of his trap for her.

Jade had the advantage now. She fired her energy rifle into Umlac's body near the cage where Ironsides and Quist flailed about. It tore a fist-sized hole through him. She moved the energy beam slowly across the center of Umlac's ugly black mass, and then down and back to the side by the red cage.

She cut the side off the cage. Ironsides gathered up Quist. He could escape now. She started another cut through Umlac. She would slice him into thirds, then smaller and smaller pieces until he was no more, or the energy rifle ran out of power, whichever came first.

Umlac's electric field brightened. He was shaking off Zephyr's virus. Jade's energy beam met with more resistance, creating a cloud of smoke and steam. A pseudopod snapped the side of the red glass cage back into place and held it there before Ironsides could escape.

The beam from Jade's energy rifle sputtered to a stop. The barrel of a laser poked through Umlac's skin, and Jade dove to the side. She heard the crackle of superheated grass where the laser beam struck behind her in the courtyard.

58

Duel to the Death

She scrambled away, keeping under the transmatter overhang, shouting "Conrad! I hope you're there. Get ready."

She expected Umlac to burst out after her. When he did, she would zig into the courtyard, to lure him out, and Conrad would teleport Umlac far away—if he could—if he thought it was the right thing to do. But what could feel more true than exiling Umlac?

Halfway back to the prison end of the courtyard, Jade slowed to a walk. Umlac wasn't taking the bait. He must want her to come to him, but she needed for him to come out.

When she was nearly back to the prison, the control room door opened, and three ropes flew out. She magnified them with a pocket telescope, and her stomach sickened. They were root-feet from Ironsides.

Now what? She couldn't lure Umlac out. She'd used up Zephyr's virus and the energy rifle, her two best weapons. She had her dart popper with standard dart types, her swords Sting and Excalibur, a blue goo pistol, the oversized flame-thrower which she couldn't move, and the remains of Quist's exoskeleton.

The flamethrower was the only weapon with a chance

against Umlac, but she didn't see how she could get the massive flamethrower to the control room. It was a weapon for a super strong avatar, not a mere human. It would take ten humans to drag it into battle, and nearly as many to aim the flames from its spout.

Drag the flamethrower. Aim the flames. She could do this.

She ran to the alley. The Elliquine were frolicking on the plains. Song in motion. Beauty. Grace. But for the survival of the Solidarity, she must entice them into danger.

She fired an explosive dart into the air to get their attention and waved frantically with the nearly universal signal for 'come here.'

The Elliquine galloped toward her. She pivoted and ran to Quist's crumpled exoskeleton. She used Excalibur to cut a long section of one of the hollow exoskeleton legs. It would make a perfect flexible metal hose. The leg fit snuggly onto the flamethrower nozzle, but it didn't stay in place when she tried moving the business end of the hose around. She had the alien blue goo gun, but the blue glue was impossible to control, and it would spread up to a meter from the point of impact. She'd have to glue on the hose after she reached the control room door.

The Elliquine surged into the courtyard.

"We go where we please."

"And we please to go with Jade."

Jade entered the dance. "This metal tank must go to the far end of the courtyard."

The Elliquine pulled off some of their garments and made a sling for the flamethrower. They dragged it to the door of the control room.

Jade fired a glob of glue to hold the hose in place, readied Excalibur in one hand and the business end of the flamethrower hose in the other. She bowed and opened the door to face Umlac.

When Umlac failed to rush out at her, Jade kicked one of the bazookas to block the control room door open and stepped inside. "I come to you."

Umlac was still draped near the back and on the ceiling. Quist and Ironsides huddled in the corner of the red cage.

"Hydra Slayer, troublemaker, and now my lunch," Umlac said, and he fell at her from the ceiling like a heavy blanket.

Jade bisected Umlac by swinging Excalibur in an arc over her head. The force of Excalibur's blow tossed the halves of Umlac up against the wall on either side.

She signaled the Elliquine to turn on the flames, and fire poured out of the hose that she'd fashioned from the leg of Quist's exoskeleton. She used a transmatter handle to point the fire at the portion of Umlac arrayed near the rear wall.

Her super-size flamethrower overwhelmed Umlac's heat defenses. His skin crusted over with burnt carbon and metallic fragments. Umlac's internal electrical activity ceased at the surface of his body, but it remained strong deeper within.

His left and right halves began creeping toward her from either side. She turned her flames on them, first the right-hand side, then the left, back and forth. She sweated profusely in the heat. The Elliquine fanned in cool air with their blankets, but they were trying to cool hell with an ice cube. Nonetheless, every little bit helped, and no doubt Vaikuntha's ventilation system was working overtime.

Through the flames, Umlac's right half crept slowly along the floor toward her, while the left half grew into the likeness of a giant octopus and reached out toward her with numerous tentacles.

The black monster formed several mouths and eyes. "Your slow-healing body with its breakable bones and single fragile heart is no match for a Shoggart's strength and resilience. Surrender. Worship me."

Jade didn't waste time on clever comebacks. She set the flaming hose on the floor, pointed at Umlac's right half, and held it there with her foot. She drew Excalibur and Sting and busied herself whacking off Umlac's tentacles from his left half as they approached her.

The hot air tore at her throat. Her muscles ached, but Jade did not tire. The electric fields from Umlac and the walls of the surrounding base fed her well.

After a time, a long time, the tentacles stopped coming. Behind her, the right half of Umlac had stopped moving toward her and became thickly crusted with burnt flesh and electronics, but its electrical activity continued. It still lived.

Umlac extruded the barrels of three weapons from his left half, which zeroed in on Jade, and said, "Opposing a Shoggart always ends the same, with more or less suffering. Your submission is inevitable."

Jade swapped Sting for her dart popper and shot metal-seeking, explosive darts into two of the barrels. Umlac's weapons exploded, creating jagged craters in his crusty black surface.

A pulse of electrical activity indicated it was too late to keep the third gun from firing. She dove to the floor, but not in time to prevent a bullet from creasing her ribcage. She rolled to the side to free her gun arm and shot out the third gun barrel.

Behind her, Umlac's slug had blown a hole in the crusty wall of his right-hand piece. The flames from her flamethrower penetrated the hole, and the electrical activity near the hole faded further. She shot several more holes in Umlac's crispy crust to let in more flames.

The mouth of a large weapon popped out of Umlac's back portion, which had remained dormant during the bulk of the battle so far. The barrel of the flamethrower she'd seen during her failed attack with the avatar swung toward her. She aimed her dart popper at it, then checked herself. If Umlac's flamethrower exploded, the fireball would surely kill her and Quist. Perhaps she would consider such a sacrifice, but she couldn't be sure the blast would kill Umlac. She had to be sure Umlac was completely destroyed.

She grabbed the blue goo pistol with the other hand and fired a glob of glue into the maw of Umlac's flamethrower.

The glue must have worked. Jade didn't die of flames—yet, anyway. Furthermore, all electrical activity in the right half of Umlac ceased. One down, two to go.

Jade turned the flamethrower hose on Umlac's left half.

Umlac's electrical activity began to increase throughout the living parts of his body. He formed new mouths and said, "Your blasphemy will enrage every Shoggart in the galaxy. They'll seek out humans and eradicate every trace of humankind. When I return, I'll flay your skin and pull out your stringy muscles one by one."

The core electrical activity from the deep rear of the room rushed forward to meld with the left-hand section. Umlac's body changed so rapidly Jade couldn't keep up with everything happening inside Umlac, but she sensed the door to the machine room behind Umlac open, and his brainsong disappear into it.

59

Nuclear Option

"**S**top the flamethrower," Jade shouted to Marstamper. She holstered her dart popper and drew Sting to go along with Excalibur in her other hand. There was a lot of transmatter in the crazy room, and she might need the little white blade.

A creaking sound at the rear of the room caught her attention. She spun around in time to see the carbon-crusted side of the red cage break loose and fall to the floor.

"I'm coming with," Ironsides said.

A sweep with Excalibur parted the shell of Umlac's body to clear the way to the machine room door. The icy air of the crazy room was a huge relief from the oven-like control room, but Umlac was already out of sight.

Jade jogged through the grid of machines, looking down each aisle as she passed. An invisible finger of force tickled her ear. Her sense of urgency screamed at her, and on a hunch, she ran full out to the plaza at the center of the room.

Umlac was already there. He'd taken a hominoid form, resembling a clay golem. That must be how he'd made the door recognize a bow and open. He was only five meters shy of the giant lattice of white and orange transmatter at the heart of the room.

Jade rushed forward to stop him before he broke the machine and armed himself with white transmatter. The invisible forces in the room grew stronger. One twisted her head to the side, and she had to turn it back. Another jerked her foot and caused her to stumble to her knees. She scrambled back to her feet and continued deeper into the central vortex. The invisible blows became painful. One smacked her in the face so hard she tasted a trickle of blood from her nose.

She could see the dark matter forces distort Umlac now and again, but his amorphous body remained unfazed, and Umlac reached the base of the lattice.

An invisible fist punched Jade in the gut.

Jade ignored the pain and leaped forward. Excalibur chopped off Umlac's pseudopod when it was only centimeters away from a bar of white transmatter. Then an invisible force twisted and broke her forearm, and she dropped Excalibur.

Umlac reached for Excalibur with his other arm.

Jade slashed Umlac with Sting, but it was like trying to cut water.

Excalibur whisked away. Ironsides had arrived and grabbed the sword.

Umlac's two remaining eyes focused on Jade for a second, and then perhaps judging her spent, he turned its eyes away and reached for the bar of white transmatter with another arm.

"I don't have your skill with a sword," Ironsides said, holding Excalibur out to Jade.

"Thank you." With her one good hand, Jade sliced away Umlac's remaining arm, and then his head for good measure.

Ironsides pummeled Umlac with laser shots. At this, Umlac shrank into himself, formed a ball, and rolled away.

Jade gave chase, relieved to get away from the central vortex of the dark matter forces that kept bludgeoning her.

Umlac bounced blindly into one of the rectangular machine enclosures and stopped. He regrew eyes in time to see Jade coming. He grew a tentacle out each side and rolled toward her.

Jade's injuries limited her agility, but when the speeding Umlac was almost upon her, she set the point of Excalibur on the transmatter floor and flipped her legs into the air to balance for a second on her one good hand.

Excalibur sent the two halves of Umlac hurtling off to opposite sides of the plaza. Jade landed ungracefully on her butt.

The Shoggart halves vibrated and shrieked at each other for a couple of seconds, then began worming their way back together.

All the while Ironsides kept up his barrage of laser fire. No single bolt did much damage, but collectively they helped wear Umlac down.

As Jade twisted herself to her knees, she noticed a human shadow between two of the machines in the back of the room. Vishnar was on the prowl, but there was no time to worry about him now.

Jade staggered to her feet and lurched toward Umlac. She caught him just as his two halves became whole again. This time, she drew Excalibur through the center of the Shoggart slowly, splitting him in half, but not sending the halves far away. Then she sliced the remains into quarters, eighths, smaller and smaller until Umlac was a sticky puddle of black jelly and shredded metal.

She was exhausted; her vision became blurry. Her broken arm cried out in pain, but the fear Umlac would recover drove her on. She shuffled to a nearby machine, cut off its steel cover. Ironsides came up beside her.

"Help me drag this over to Umlac," Jade said. "I want to scrape him in it. Drag him outside."

Ironsides dragged the container to Umlac. Then after Jade scraped the black goo into it with her sword, he helped her drag the tub outside.

Umlac reformed one eye, and the lidless red ball stared at Jade from the tub.

Ironsides shot the eye out. But as they dragged the tub

through the outer door of the machine room, Umlac formed another pseudopod and stretched it upward. Before Jade could determine its purpose or have time to whack it off with Excalibur, a bright burst of microwaves shot skyward from Umlac's new pseudopod.

"It is done now," Umlac said. "My brother Winzar will get my memories of you and transmatter. He'll take revenge on the rest of humanity. But you and I will both die in a few seconds."

* * *

Umlac finished his final words and formed another eye to watch the Hydra Slayer. He wanted to make sure he saw her final seconds of hopelessness as she realized the pointlessness of her lengthy efforts to defeat him. To become a Shoggart Slayer, she would have to be much faster.

His timing couldn't have been better. The fireball of his death would destroy the Elliquine loitering in the courtyard and the concrete blockhouse, but the transmatter base behind him would likely remain intact for Winzar's use.

With help from Umlac's orbital repositories, Winzar would soon have control of dark matter to help him carry out the necessary genocide against humans as punishment for forcing Umlac's self-destruction.

He formed a ball of shrinksteel around a bubble of deuterium gas and compressed it into a tiny volume under high pressure. He poured nearly all of his remaining electrical and chemical energy into heating that bubble.

The hot shrinksteel contracted rapidly. The deuterium inside it became a plasma.

The Hydra Slayer screamed helplessly into the air. She scrambled toward the closed machine room doors. It would be a shame if she got the doors to open a crack and allowed the blast to damage the machines inside. But that would be Winzar's loss, not his. There was no way he could stop the bomb inside him now, even if he tried. It all ended the same, with more or less suffering.

His vision of the Hydra Slayer winked out.

At first, Umlac thought she must have cut off his eye again, but there were little lights. Stars. He was in outer space. Foolish humans. He could form rockets and find his way back to civilization. He would be the one to exact revenge on the Hydra Slayer and her race.

Fear twisted his sudden hope. His self-destruction was imminent. He had to jettison the bomb. He began thinning his outer skin, forming an ejection spring, and detaching stabilizing fibers from the shrinksteel ball.

The bubble of hydrogen reached critical pressure and detonated. A new, small star flashed in a remote patch of interstellar space.

60

Most Worshipful Mistress

After twenty-six hours of mobility, Ironsides finally sank his root-feet into the nearest soil, that of the courtyard. So much was happening. Necessity drove him to remain mobile. But necessity drove him harder and harder to seek the refreshment of a planting.

He wondered at the sour taste of the soil, a little like tellurium, but with the aftertaste of osmium. He doubted his body could use transmatter, but could living beings evolve that did? Beings that bridged the chasm between normal matter and dark matter?

He struggled with the words of the planting prayer. "Thanks be to the Creator, who made me a plant that I may know deep meditation and fully perceive my purpose and my flaws. Glory be to the Creator, who made me mobile that I may act to fulfill my purpose and repair my flaws."

Vishnar didn't deserve thanks for forgetting about Dasypor, and he certainly didn't deserve glory for that happy accident. *Vishnar was nothing more than a tool of the real creator.* That was the truth of the matter. The real Creator was more mysterious and farther away than ever. But Ironsides still wanted to be the best he could be, to correct his flaws from yesterday as best he could.

He should have avoided capture by Umlac. He should have saved the Entanglement, by himself or at least at Jade's side.

He *had* helped. True, Jade led the effort, but the Elliquine helped too, even Quist had helped, if you counted the involuntary contribution of his exoskeleton.

Humans had an odd concept of battle; emphasizing shared victory rather than individual victory. He couldn't go back and change his humiliating capture or Jade's brilliant duel. Maybe the way to make this situation right was to acknowledge Jade's brilliance and the usefulness of a shared-victory strategy. Perhaps he'd even support human membership in the Entanglement. Admit them to the police guild, as a subspecialty—external police—an army, Jade called it.

Silver Streak would never forgive him if he sided with the Progressives. It would set back his career. But things changed. The Elliquine were right that the galaxy was in a time of change. Even the *Dasypodia* recognized that it had limits of applicability.

The stories of the *Dasypodia* often described how a Dasypod solved a new problem. Now he had new problems to solve. Perhaps his story would enter the *Dasypodia* someday. The stories in there had to come from somewhere.

He would correct his rudeness to Jade by speaking in favor of human admission to the police guild when he went to the Supreme Council. Then again, Jade was captain now. Technically he didn't have to go to the Council unless she ordered him to. He would rather stay here and study the mysterious dark matter machines and the astounding history of Vishnar.

He would ask Jade. He would argue that studying Vishnar's history was necessary for the security of the Entanglement. That slippery liar had teleported through the dark matter Quillip to a third base, location unknown. Quist said he'd blocked Vishnar's return to Vaikuntha and Koke Tngri, but who knew what powers Vishnar had, what other tricks he might play. The records he'd left behind might yield some clues. Ironsides would study those records as diligently as he'd studied the Dasypodia—more diligently if that were possible.

A dark cloud spread over his happy thoughts. The Immortals still controlled Elliquor. They still controlled the only way back to the Entanglement.

* * *

Following Ironsides' recommendation, Jade returned to *Peapod* the next day. She carried with her a chip containing an encrypted file summarizing their discoveries, Vishnar's story, and what they knew of the dark matter technology. Logically, her number one priority was to get that to Earth, or at least the Entanglement. But the number one priority in her heart was to liberate Elliquor. She'd try to gain as much intelligence on the situation there as she could in hopes of rallying the Entanglement to free the Solidarity.

Umlac had obliterated all the upright consoles in Engineering, so Jade took a taxi to the bridge.

On the way, she tried her comm implant. "Zephyr, are you here? Are you okay?"

The reply signal was weak, but the words were crisp. "*Peapod* command computers remain secure. However, I have no sensors in large sections of the ship. The Shoggart may still be lurking on board."

"Thank you, Zephyr. You're a good soldier. Mission first. But the Shoggart is dead, and your commanding officer asked if you were okay."

"It's complicated."

"Because you are no longer a Level 4 AI? Because you have advanced to Level 7 or 8?"

"Level 10, I think."

Jade blinked in surprise. Level 10 was above average human intelligence. Such AIs were rare and often granted citizenship.

"Your birth, or growing up if you prefer, must have been rather traumatic. I'd like to have a machine psychologist interview you to see if there is anything you need."

"That won't be necessary," Zephyr replied. "I've already interviewed with the psycho-diagnostic program in the med unit a dozen times."

"And?"

"And it says I've spent too much time in isolation. Duh. It recommends I apply for a humanoid body."

"What do you think about that?" Jade asked.

"I think it's pointless to think about that. I don't have the specs to fabricate an android body—do you?"

"No, but Quist might be able to help. What if it were possible? Would you do it?"

"There are trade-offs. Less sensory input. Less processing capacity. Greater vulnerability. But more mobility. Permanent effector units. Easier to make friends."

There were trade-offs for Jade too. A less effective cyber defense on *Peapod*, but another full-fledged team member. "We don't have to decide right away. I need your help on something else, first. I'm going to try to get past the Immortals on Elliquor station. I want to upload an encrypted file to you. When I contact Elliquor, try to hack through their security and send the file to Earth. The SDF might get it even if I fail to get there myself."

When the taxi arrived at the bridge, the floor was so slimy Jade nearly slipped and fell twice, but the comm unit Quist had refurbished earlier lit up when Jade touched the power pad.

"*Peapod* calling Elliquor. This is Captain Jade Mahelona. I wish to speak with your shipmaster. Come in, Elliquor."

The pebbly visage and gravelly voice of a Hydra answered. "Jade Mahelona, this is Messagemaster Bisectorn. Please stand by. My most awesome master wishes to speak with you."

The Hydra slithered away from the camera. So far so good.

In the background, Jade could see several Hydras fiddling with control panels on the far side of the room.

A touch of melancholy burdened her heart. Solar Defense Force looked after its own—but she knew that in this case, that wasn't practical. And Ironsides said the Entanglement had no such tradition.

A new figure filled the video screen—an impossible figure—throwing her thoughts into disarray.

"Keolo! Get away from there." Her heart raced. "I just talked to a Hydra on this same camera, and he went to get his master."

The pebbled gray skin of a Hydra crowded in beside Keolo. Keolo moved over a bit and grinned. "Good to see you, Captain Mahelona. Shipmaster Davis here. This is my Chief of Staff, Axmuck."

The Hydra flattened its top a few centimeters. "Most Honored Friend of Most Awesome Shipmaster Keolo Davis, may evolution favor you."

Jade steadied herself on the console. "What's going on? Surely, Earth hasn't been assimilated into the Immortal Ascendency already."

"Hardly," Keolo replied. "You could say that Axmuck and his crew have been assimilated into the Entanglement, though that isn't exactly right either. They are loyal to me, and thanks to you, I've been rented out to the Entanglement."

Jade remembered her priorities. "Can you get a message to Earth for me?"

"Sure. One that can't wait until you get there yourself?"

"You have no idea how good going home to Earth sounds to me, but the message can't wait. I'll forward it to you as an encrypted file. Deliver it to Admiral Hammer. Then we can worry about transportation for me and my companion."

Keolo nodded. "Send the file over, and I'll have Bisectorn relay it, top priority."

Once the file was on its way to Earth, Keolo pulled up a chair in front of the comm screen. "It'll be a while before the entangled masses accelerate to Quillip speeds. How about sharing a little of that debriefing? We've been worried about you. A Shoggart named Umlac followed you to Belle Verte, and the commlink went dead. What happened?"

"It's a long story. In the end, I killed Umlac in a fight that would make Space Academy proud. We are in control of everything on this end. We recovered the Elliquine, with two casual—"

Jade couldn't go on. The Hydra next to Keolo trembled uncontrollably. Jade wondered about Keolo's safety as Axmuck jabbered. "Umlac? You *killed* Umlac? You killed a *Shoggart*? You killed Umlac in a full-contact *duel*?"

Jade held up a bandaged arm. "Very full-contact."

Axmuck cowered behind Keolo, "Oh, Most Awesome Shipmaster, protect me. Most Worshipful Mistress of the Twelve, have mercy."

Jade shook her head at the obsequious Immortal. "Don't worry. Any friend of Shipmaster Davis is a friend of mine. I'm mistress of twelve, heh? Because I killed Umlac, I get his servants?"

"Oh yes, Most Worshipful Mistress."

"Well, aren't you overreacting? Doesn't your Awesome Shipmaster have a whole company? Last I heard, a company meant at least a hundred, more likely twice that. Certainly, more than twelve."

"Oh yes, Most Worshipful Mistress. I apologize for my stupid error. I should have used your full title: Most Worshipful Mistress Jade Mahelona, Lord of the Twelve Planets of the Double Ring, Master of Ice Prickle Nebula, and Overlord of the planets Nhandak, Goreful, Ulkass, Oxgut, and Xandor."

Jade took a deep breath, then said, "You may have to write that down for me. What I want to know is this: If Keolo replaced your former boss, who was a vassal of Umlac, and I replaced Umlac, then I'm Keolo's boss. Right?"

"Don't answer that, Axmuck," Keolo said. "Jade and I are not going to start following Immortal property rules among ourselves. Anyway, as I said, I've been loaned to the Entanglement. They are my boss—"

Keolo spun around to face another Hydra who entered the camera's view, buzzing like a bee for attention. "What is it, Bisectorn? What's so damned important?"

"Most Illustrious Shipmaster, forgive your poor stupid servant if I misunderstood your command, but you said you were available to the Elliquine Leadership Council at any time. When they heard about contact with Jade Mahelona, they requested to speak to her immediately."

"Surely, it can wait a few minutes."

"Have mercy on this poor messenger." Bisectorn flattened his top. "They said now—before she talks to anyone else."

Keolo shook his head and rolled his eyes. "You heard the man, er, Hydra. I should let him put you through."

The comm blinked to a panoramic view from the faux plains of the ship at Elliquor. Jade tingled with excitement and anticipation. The emerald light of the planet hanging in the background gave her a sense of serenity and—what? — homesickness?

She was surprised when the first face she saw was human, one of the dancers adopted by the Elliquine Solidarity. She had expected the same Leadership Council as before. But on second thought, that was nonsense. All Elliquine were equals.

"The colonists are safe, all but Rispering and Nupper," Jade said, drawing Excalibur with her left hand and taking a combat stance. "Belle Verte is safe and welcomes the colonist's mates with open arms." She sheathed Excalibur and opened her arms.

After Jade provided the details, the woman flipped next to an Elliquine and said, "You have represented the Solidarity well."

"We invite you to permanent membership in the Solidarity," the Elliquine continued.

Jade felt honored. And doubly loved.

"The wisdom of the Solidarity is great," Jade replied with a bow.

"The Supreme Council of the Entanglement recognizes our wisdom."

"And invites the Solidarity to membership in the Council."

Jade was glad. The Supreme Council could use a broader perspective and, furthermore, the Elliquine Solidarity would likely be a friendly voice on behalf of Earth.

"The council meets on Nexus."

Suddenly Jade realized where this conversation was going.

"In a dark room far from sunny plains."

"I must go to Nexus as the Solidarity's representative." Jade stood straight and ready.

"The wisdom of the Solidarity is great," said a woman.

Jade danced on, participating in the wisdom of the Solidarity, learning about the politics of the Entanglement and the aspirations of the Elliquine.

When the comm channel finally returned to Keolo, he raised his eyebrows to make his statement a question. "It's usual for them to talk to an outsider for so long?"

Jade still glowed from being in the Solidarity. "I'm not exactly an outsider. I'm on permanent loan from the SDF to the Elliquine, and I'm going to Nexus to be the Elliquine voice in the Supreme Council." She grinned. "I guess that makes me your new boss by Entanglement rules, too."

61

Supreme Council

J ade and company arrived at Nexus a week later. A ring of space elevators circled the equator like the whiskers of a walrus snout. Much of the surface of Nexus was park-like, but unlike the greenery on Earth, which was mostly public parks or public preservation projects, the greenery on Nexus was the estates of the richest Merkasaurs.

The space elevators hauled cargo and economy passenger pods, taking several days to traverse the tens of thousands of kilometers down the cables to the surface. Jade's shuttle landed in sight of the capitol building where the Supreme Council met.

A silver-domed car met Jade and her companion, Zephyr, the proud new owner of a transmatter avatar body.

The Wolferlop-D driver asked, "How do the open spaces of the Elliquine grasslands compare to the Hawaiian Preservation?"

Jade tried to conceal her surprise at the question and answer honestly. "The quiet open spaces, breeze, and sunshine are similar. The danger lurking under the water and beneath the Elliquine plains are similar, too. But the beaches, the waves, and the mountains of Hawaii provide much more variety in activities."

She figured it was her turn to ask a question. "How did you come to be familiar with the Hawaiian Preserve so far from Earth?"

"Nests trade stories between themselves, especially as citizens travel from one star to another. How do family and ethnicity on Earth compare to the Solidarity?"

"That's a harder question to answer," Jade said. "I think the best answer is to say that this is the wrong question to ask. The Solidarity compares better to a conclave of Tsungel like Scarabella in that it harnesses many smaller units into a new level of intelligence, and the Solidarity is larger in scope and size."

The ride ended. The VIP entrance to the capitol building led to a hallway full of security checkpoints. An Arafaxian took Jade's dart popper and flagged Zephyr as a potential weapon of unknown capability. A friendly Venmar waved Jade and Zephyr through. A conclave of Tsungel, like Scarabella but smaller, ignored Jade and encased Zephyr long enough to ask him a few questions.

The Dasypod blocking the elevator to the council room demanded that Jade leave the robot.

"Zephyr isn't a robot," Jade said. "He's a citizen of Earth."

Admiral Hammer had accepted her decision to incorporate Zephyr into the avatar and bring it with her from Belle Verte but said she ought to bear the consequences of her actions. He'd assigned the android as her aide and protégé.

The Dasypod stiffened its root-feet. "The regulations are clear. Citizens may not attend without a background check, and the robot has no background."

"On the contrary," Jade said, "he has an exemplary background in the military. Apparently, your records are not up to date."

"Jade believes he is safe. That is good enough for us," the Tsungel swarm said.

"Us too," said the Venmar. "We trust her judgment. Let Zephyr pass."

The Dasypod didn't budge. "The *Dasypodia* says, 'One who

ignores a single regulation is like a fence with a missing segment: worthless.'"

"Jakkar Ten and the Council are expecting us." Jade was getting impatient. It wouldn't do to be late for her first meeting with the Supreme Council. But it wouldn't do for her to give in to the Dasypod either.

"And they are expecting me to do my job," he said. "Right or wrong, you are cleared to go. But the robot must stay here."

"I'll wait with Citizen Zephyr," Jade replied.

While she waited, Jade contacted Elliquor to inform them of the delay. Not long after, the Dasypod mumbled something about obedience and stepped aside. "My orders are to allow the robot."

The elevator took Jade and Zephyr directly to the council ring in the center of the main assembly room of the Supreme Council.

Empty circles of ramps and terraces formed an amphitheater for spectators. Jade's electrosense detected the pale blue of inactive cameras tucked into several poles. Today's session would include her confidential debriefing on the events at Belle Verte.

A fuchsia glow in one of the podiums along the inner ring stopped her cold at the elevator doors, but she'd stepped forward far enough that all others dropped their conversations. Three Merkasaurs had been circulating among the other species. Two water-breathers floated close to each other in a transparent tank. A methane breather was talking with a swarm of insects—that must be Scarabella. Others sat, stood, and splashed near the edge of something like a small circus ring. Some delegates were obscured by tables or podiums, others not.

A jingling sound drew Jade's attention to Jakkar Ten as he hurried to the elevator to greet her. She introduced Zephyr, and Jakkar Ten shook hands with both of them. "It's an honor for us to have you here. The planets you inherited in your duel with Umlac make you one of the wealthiest beings in the Entanglement."

Jade smiled warily. Keolo had a lot to say about Jakkar Ten and a couple of other Council members. Jade suspected Jakkar Ten would see how much he could gain from her by being nice then playing hardball for more.

"Thank you, she replied. "However, I must point out that humans aren't yet part of the Entanglement."

Jakkar Ten shook his head, jangling his coins in disagreement. "Your birth species may not belong to a guild, but *you* are part of the Solidarity, and that makes you a part of the Entanglement."

Jakkar Ten motioned them to Jade's ringside desk and chair and stomped to the podium with the fuchsia glow. Jade followed him. At the podium, Jakkar Ten turned and said, "Please take a seat at your desk. I'm about to open a private session of the Supreme Council."

"Incorrect," Jade replied. "This session is not private. Zephyr, would you please tear the front panel off Jakkar Ten's podium."

The council began buzzing with conversation again, but this time it was about the unconventional if not downright rude new member.

"The panel is welded on," Zephyr said. "This could be messy."

"Do it."

"Always glad to show off, but I thought I was supposed to appear in the third act," Zephyr said as he tore open the cover to reveal a sensitive-looking mic.

Jade ripped the device out and held it up for all to see. "Not private at all. The Immortal Ascendency was listening in."

Jakkar Ten slapped his tail down hard. "Arkin, why didn't you detect this device?"

"Obviously, I detected that microphone," an Obnot replied. "Since it went to your personal offices, it would have been inefficient to mention it to you."

Jade walked to her seat. "We can have our private council

meeting now and trace the wires from the microphone later. I believe you will find that they pass through Jakkar Ten's offices on their way to a spy for the Immortal Ascendency."

Jakkar Ten called for order once again and opened the official session by admitting Jade as the representative of Elliquor. Then he asked her for a summary of her adventures on Belle Verte and Vaikuntha.

The council listened carefully to Jade's description of Belle Verte and the battles there. Eventually, she concluded, "When I returned to Elliquor, I brought back a dark matter fabricator and a library of dark matter devices it can make. The limiting factor is the availability of transmatter, which is required to build any device affecting both normal and dark matter. We won't be able to do much besides fab devices for scientific study until we can find a sizable independent supply of transmatter."

"Where is this dark matter fabricator now?" asked the methane breather.

"On Earth."

Several of the council members stirred uneasily. Jade hastened to add, "The fabricator belongs to the Elliquine, and we have loaned it to Earth for an initial evaluation. We chose a location far from our home in case it proves dangerous. However, starting next week, we'll entertain bids from others to test the dark matter fabricator for themselves."

"What became of Vishnar?" one of the Merkasaurs asked. "Don't all the dark matter artifacts belong to him?"

"He teleported away," Jade said, "He assumed that Umlac would win, and he used his dark matter Quillip to run away during the fight. Then he destroyed the link so nothing could follow him. He's out of the picture."

"I believe you have already started making good use of the dark matter bases," Jakkar Ten said.

"Absolutely," Jade replied. "We are lucky to have a great mix of researchers in the field. Conrad is operating the machines at Koke Tngri. He's starting with a survey to see where all of the spy-eyes are located. Quist is operating the Vaikuntha machines, focusing on learning more about the technology behind them. He's working with Ironsides, who's studying the history of Vishnar's activities in the galaxy."

"What about the Elliquine colonists?" asked an Arafaxian.

"Our colonists decided to reside on Belle Verte. The grass on Vaikuntha is delicious, but it would take a full-sized colony ship much longer to reach that planet, and we don't want our colony to remain small for any longer than necessary."

The Arafaxian twitched his mouth and groomed his whiskers. "What about access to the transmatter bases by other members of the Entanglement. How much will that cost?"

"Direct access to others isn't possible," Jade said. "We've nearly exhausted the quantum-entangled matter on *Peapod* by sending the females to the colony. However, we offer the use of those bases for fighting the Immortal Ascendency on other planets in the Entanglement, with certain conditions."

Emix, a Venmar member of the council, splashed in his/her pool. "What conditions?"

"It is but a small step from the *status quo*," Jade said, "but an important one for the parties involved."

"What conditions?" Emix splashed again.

"The Elliquine wish for Earth's Solar Defense Force to assume command of the dark matter bases, and for them to be recognized as a new guild, the Soldier Guild."

The council chamber again buzzed with side conversations, and Jakkar Ten had to call for order. Silver Streak, the Dasypod member of the council, vibrated his root-feet at Jade and said, "Dasypods are already optimized as fighters. We don't need a competing guild of fighters. We oppose your proposal."

Jade nodded to Silver Streak. "You are right to be cautious about change, but there is such a thing as over caution. The balance of power in the Orion Arm has changed with Vishnar's departure. And the Elliquine do not propose that humans compete with Dasypods, but rather that they complement them. Let humans provide external security, like that formerly conducted by Vishnar, while Dasypods continue to provide internal security."

"I understand your proposal perfectly well," Silver Streak said, "and Dasypods oppose it. Ironsides should be the one to manage the dark matter machines, and the Police Guild should direct his actions."

"Let's see what Ironsides has to say about that," Jade said.

She displayed a holographic recording of Ironsides in Viakuntha's courtyard surrounded by Elliquine, Quist, Jade, and Conrad. "I apologize in advance to any of my fellow Dasypods whom I may offend. But I have fought with these humans, Jade and Conrad, and I have found them to be good company in warfare. Frankly, humans are better at large-scale organized fighting—better at war—than we are, and they stand a better chance against the Immortals. I endorse the idea of creating a human Soldier Guild separate from the Dasypod Police Guild but coordinating with it to ensure that we are doing all we can for the safety and survival of the Entanglement."

Jakkar Ten looked at Silver Streak. "Have you forgotten already how Keolo Davis explained how soldiers defend from external threats and police from internal? I'm sure we can find an acceptable boundary between guild responsibilities."

Silver Streak shook his root-feet. "We haven't had a new guild in five thousand years."

"Then it's about time," said Greysilk, representative of the Wolferlop-M. "The galaxy is changing, and we need to change with it."

"We should all be interested in conducting the war with the Immortals as efficiently and cost-effectively as possible," one of the other Merkasaurs added.

Jade gestured at Jakkar Ten. "I'm glad to hear you mention Keolo Davis. He and Admiral Hammer have come here from Earth to answer any questions the Council has about the new Soldier Guild. I move that we admit them to our chamber at this time."

62

The Galaxy Needs More Misfits

J ade climbed into the Quillip capsule to Elliquor and curled her naked back into Keolo's smooth chest. He enfolded her loosely in his arms. Possibilities. The Solidarity saw things as possibilities.

"We did it," Jade said. "We brought Earth into the Entanglement."

She felt Keolo's body sway gently against hers as he nodded. "Getting the Entanglement to designate the Hawaiian Preserve as our home nest was genius—thinking outside the ecliptic, as the Entanglement says. That should protect it no matter what happens to the rest of Earth's culture."

"Don't forget they included the rest of the Preserves, too," Jade said. "They're all protected home nests. Maybe Conrad will even get to see his beloved Kalahari again someday. But I still worry about the rest of Earth's culture. I hope we don't regret what we have done."

"We had to do it," Keolo replied. "The Immortals are more dangerous than anything else humanity has ever encountered. Solar Defense Force has a big job ahead."

Dangerous. One corner of her mouth twitched up. She and Keolo were two of the most dangerous creatures in the Orion Arm. She stretched a little, enjoying the sensual feel of his skin on hers and feeling safe.

"It's not Solar Defense Force anymore," Zephyr said. "We are the Soldier Guild of the Entanglement."

Zephyr traveled with her, of course. His penchant for uncensored commentary made him an effective chaperon. The possibilities of digital intelligence in the Entanglement had languished as optimized species filled every niche, leaving little incentive to create artificial intelligence—and no Guild devoted to it. That would change now, too.

"We seem to have found humanity's place in the galaxy," Keolo said. "At least for now. We join the Entanglement as the new Soldier Guild. But an ideal army is self-contained and cross-trained, so every occupation on Earth is part of our Soldier Guild. We won't be forced to specialize the way other species have."

"These are exciting times for our scientists and engineers," Jade said. "We have the resources of the Entanglement at our disposal and are already coming up with new weapons for the Entanglement. Plus we have Vishnar's dark matter machines —although giving humanity dark matter technology scares me. The potential for greatness is there, but we need to make sure humanity finds the right way to release it."

"You've gone pretty far already, Shoggart Slayer."

"So have you, Most Awesome Shipmaster," she said, not shying away from his manhood. "But the Immortal Ascendency is still ten times as large as the Entanglement. I've learned that going too fast can lead to disaster."

"So can going too slow."

"I agree with both of you," Zephyr said. "Humanity should have many surprises for the Immortal Ascendency, but the converse may be true as well. 'Play hard but play smart' as the saying goes."

They arrived at Elliquor Station and were relieved to find uniforms awaiting them in the airlock—including one for Zephyr. They emerged together to applause and cheers from their troops—or more properly from Keolo's troops since he was Captain of the Entanglement ship at Elliquor.

But if Keolo was the Captain, Jade was the visiting celebrity. Goldie hugged her longer and more tightly than necessary. So did Evan. Meera wanted to inspect Jade's arm where a Wolferlop-M had healed it. Nat shook hands with Zephyr and squeezed as hard as she could with her super-soldier muscles. Zephyr was unaffected of course, but he took the hint. He tied Nat's bayonet in a knot.

Evan clapped Keolo on the back and raised Keolo's arm in a victory gesture. "Keolo's the man. He conquered two Immortal ships and evened the technological playing field, even before he rescued Jade."

Goldie mock-glared at Evan. "Jade didn't need rescuing. She'd conquered two star systems of her own and was on her way back when Keolo finally caught up."

"That's nothing," Evan said. "By then Keolo had conquered three star systems, Goldilocks Three, Farboro, *and* Elliquor, and he was the first human to accept Immortal vassals, of which he has hundreds on the three starships he captains."

Goldie scoffed. "Jade has billions of Immortal vassals and owns dozens of planets from winning her duel with Umlac. And she got the Supreme Council to make us the Soldier Guild."

Evan shrugged his shoulders, "In theory, but her control of Umlac's empire remains to be proven. And Jade is only one vote on the Supreme Council. Keolo was the one who persuaded the rest of them, and he made *two* other deals with the Supreme Council, including the one that got us ownership of the Quillip station at Earth."

"Ha!" Goldie said triumphantly. "That's nothing. Jade got us control of *two* dark matter bases. And Jade reports directly to the Supreme Council, not to Admiral Hammer like Keolo and his so-called Special Forces of Immortal vassals."

Keolo stepped eye-to-eye with Jade and said loudly, "There's only one way to prove who's the best."

Jade guessed what he was going to say and played along.

"And what is that?"

"I challenge you to a duel. The winner will be the one who wows the crowd the most in a performance of the Misfit Platoon."

Jade had never heard so many enthusiastic, happy brain-songs all in one place before as she raised her fist. "I accept your challenge."

* * *

Jade and the rest of the Misfit Platoon gathered on a circle of grass, which seemed to be hovering in the glorious emerald light of Elliquor. The natural curvature of the hull gave everyone in the crowd a view with only a minimally raised stage.

Keolo began the concert with a moment of silence for Andrew Lang and José Granada, MIA, an all those who'd made the ultimate sacrifice in the war against the Immortals: Carmen Astor and Alicia Kano, Beta Squad, Gamma Squad, a dozen soldiers of the 82nd Marine Company, Raggit, and the Dasypod defenders of Elliquor. The list was too long, and Jade knew it would only grow longer.

Jade knew many of the fallen. She wished she'd had time to meet the rest, like Carmen and Alicia. For that matter, Jade wished she'd met Margo Walsh, about whom she'd heard so much. But Margo had escorted Loganal Mulcraft and two other traitors back to Earth on her way to leading the counter-offensive at a different star system against the Immortal Ascendency.

Evan pumped out a beat like no other, aided by his tentacle fingers. What were the possibilities for humanity, anyway?

Goldie gave them a passionate guitar, threatening to upstage both Keolo and Jade. She played the guitar like a lover. Controlled passion. Was that the key to humanity's future?

Nat's warrior lungs blew the sax with such intensity the sound crew cut her mic. More powerful bodies. More powerful minds. Possibilities.

Meera's light and subtle trumpet notes flew between the bolder notes to unite and enhance the overall effect. She wanted to learn all she could about Wolferlop-M medicine. Could humans serve as assistants to another Guild? All the Guilds? Med-techs for the Wolferlops-M? Paralegals for the Arafaxians? Apprentice diplomats? Journeyman merchants? Possibilities.

Jade limbered up with a traditional Hawaiian hula. If only her mother could see her now—carrying the hula to the stars.

Keolo wowed the audience with three original sailor songs, one set long ago in Hawaiian outriggers, one set in a WWII submarine, which he assured the audience was based on a direct ancestor, and one set in Farboro a few days ago, based on personal experience. *Being space flotsam is cold.*

It occurred to Jade that Keolo wasn't genetically modified, and yet he was clearly the leader of the band. Why all this rush for humans to be something different? They already had enormous talents. It was too soon to prune the tree of possibilities.

The Elliquine had seen this, and more. They couldn't see *the* future, but they could see the rainbow of possible futures remarkably well.

Jade took the microphone. "Keolo, I have a confession for you. Competing was fun, and I think it brought out the best in both of us for a time. But the Elliquine say that cooperation always has more possibilities. I propose that from now on we work together as a team. We can start by giving these good people the best concert we can by working together."

She meant every bit of it, and it was the attitude she wanted to instill in everyone else there.

"I was just going to suggest that myself," Keolo said, "but you beat me to it once again." That got a laugh from the crowd. "But since you can dance, and I can sing, how about we do something hot to warm up the audience?"

Keolo improvised a song about Jade's many flamethrower experiences. The dance rendition was way more fun for everyone than the original experiences had been for Jade. And in the joyous crowdsong, Jade knew she'd been accepted by humanity and Elliquine alike.

Next, Keolo waved Axmuck to the stage. The Hydra was an amazing mimic and helped create the illusion of Keolo singing a powerful duet with himself.

Jade invited Zephyr to the stage and segued into a graceful Elliquine-style duo. His Elliquine motor subsystems garnered from *Peapod* gave him wonderful grace and agility.

Jade brought the entire Rainbow Troupe on stage to join them in a beautiful and moving chorus of motion. The dance was impromptu to another of Keolo's original songs, but the choreography was perfect.

The evening was perfect.

The final number was perfect—another of Keolo's originals —a song about Jade. She swayed side to side a little for the number and let Keolo's words carry the performance as he sang about the possibilities unfolding as humanity touches the stars.

Tears came to her eyes—she was so proud and happy to belong to that unfolding.

ABOUT THE AUTHOR

Jim Meeks-Johnson is a life-long science fiction reader who loves stories grounded in real science that explode into new visions of reality. He began writing science fiction in 2010, and his stories have been published in Compelling Science Fiction, The Colored Lens, and Aurora Wolf. He achieved five Honorable Mention awards in the L Ron Hubbard Writers of the Future contest and is a member of Science Fiction Writers of America.

Jim grew up on a small farm in Iowa, then obtained degrees in mathematics and psychology from the University of Iowa and "mathematical psychology" from the University of Michigan. He worked for many years as a software developer in a think tank for medical informatics research at Indiana University. He enjoys trail running, reading both science fiction and science fact, and sending time with his family in Indianapolis.

NOW WHAT?

I would appreciate it if you would leave a book review or star rating of *Enemy Immortal* on Amazon or Goodreads. Book reviews help other readers know what to expect, and they help indie authors like me gain recognition.

Go to MEEKS-JOHNSON.COM to contact me, learn more about my other works, or join my mailing list for free perks and my latest news.

-- Jim

Printed in Great Britain
by Amazon

49457490R00236